The Christmas Swap

Sandy Barker

One More Chapter
a division of HarperCollins*Publishers*
The News Building
1 London Bridge Street
London SE1 9GF

www.harpercollins.co.uk

This paperback edition 2020

First published in Great Britain by
HarperCollins*Publishers* 2020

Cover design by HarperCollins*Publishers* Ltd 2020
Cover images © Shutterstock.com

A catalogue copy of this book
is available from the British Library.

ISBN: 9780008390044

Set in Birka by Palimpsest Book Production Ltd, Falkirk Stirlingshire

Printed and bound in Great Britain by
CPI Group (UK) Ltd, Croydon CR0 4YY

For my parents, Lee, Gail, and Ray
Thank you for always believing in me, even when I didn't.

Prologue

Twenty-two years ago

"Well, we're all eleven, so it could be something about that," said Jules.

"True, but we won't always be eleven," retorted Chloe.

Jules wasn't easily intimidated, especially by someone like Chloe, who was at least six inches shorter than her. "What about The Maui Babes, then? You know, 'cause we're on *Maui*." Chloe made a face and Jules rolled her eyes. "Well, what do *you* think, Lucy?" she asked.

Lucy had been silently watching the other two girls, an air of awe wafting about her. She'd been reluctant to join the kids' club at the resort—she didn't really like large groups—but by happenstance, she'd met two girls her own age, an American and an Australian, and both of them just brilliant. "Um, I don't mind."

Chloe put her hands on her hips. "See? She doesn't care. Sooo ... what about ..." She tapped a fingertip on her bottom lip like her mum did when she was thinking. "Hang on, when's your birthday?" she asked, pointing at Jules.

"In May."

"Oh, wow, me too," replied Chloe. Lucy was about to say that she was also born in May, but Chloe talked over her. "Hang on, what *day?*" Chloe narrowed her eyes at Jules, hoping she was older.

"May third," Jules replied. Where was the Aussie girl going with this?

Chloe deflated. "Hmm, mine's the tenth," she mumbled.

Jules clocked Chloe's pout, not really understanding it. "So, I'm a week older than you," she stated matter-of-factly. "What about you, Lucy?" she asked. "When's your birthday?"

"Mine's in May too. May seventeen."

"Hey, that's cool, we're all born in May," said Jules, right as Chloe interrupted.

"So, *I'm* a week older than *you.*" Chloe perked up as Lucy nodded at her. "Well, if we're all born in May, how 'bout we call ourselves the May Babies? Oh, and our initials in order of our ages are J-C-L, so how about the JCL May Babies?" She raised her eyebrows and looked expectantly at her new friends.

Jules shrugged in agreement. She really didn't care what they were called; she just wanted to wrap it up. They were supposed to be going to the beach that day and she'd finally convinced her mom to let her wear a two-piece.

"Lucy?" asked Chloe.

"Yes, that's good. I like it. Definitely the JCL May Babies." She pressed her inhaler into her mouth and took a slug. Lucy wasn't used to this much excitement first thing in the morning. It was much more interesting than when her parents chitchatted about what was in the newspaper.

"Actually," added Chloe. "Maybe 'babies' is a bit ... *babyish*." Lucy nodded, agreeing—definitely babyish. "How about the JCL May *Ladies*?"

Lucy grinned. "I think that's even better. The JCL May Ladies." She beamed at the others.

"It's settled." Chloe's authoritative voice rang out over her parents' balcony. "The JCL May Ladies are officially BFFs forever." Jules couldn't help but laugh. The Aussie girl was a little over the top, but she was also sorta fun.

Chloe stuck her pinkie finger in the air and, unsure what to do, Lucy pressed the tip of her pinkie to Chloe's. Chloe tutted and Lucy turned a fantastic shade of crimson, right as Chloe hooked Lucy's finger into her own and turned expectantly to Jules.

Jules, joining in with good nature, hooked her pinkie with the others' and recited, "BFFs forever," with Chloe. Lucy chimed in a beat too late, more excited than she could ever remember being. She was someone's BFF.

"Now, JCL May Ladies ..." began Chloe.

"Uh, shouldn't we have a nickname?" suggested Jules.

"Why, what do you mean?"

"It's just ... don't you think it's a lot to say *every* time?"

Chloe, in a rare moment of introspection, was quiet. Lucy would normally have been quick to fill the silence, as it made her uncomfortable, but she waited patiently for her BFF to say something, feeling very grown up.

Finally, Chloe nodded decisively. "You're right, let's just go with the May Ladies."

Lucy let out her breath, her mouth stretching to its widest girth. "Great," said Jules, glad they'd settled on a name. "We're the May Ladies. Now, can we *please* go to the beach?"

Chapter 1

Lucy

London

"Good lord, what is that smell?" Lucy bundled through the front door of her flat, dropped the keys in the catchall by the door, and dumped her handbag and laptop bag on the floor. She stepped out of her heels and, feeling the relief at once, scrunched her toes into the fluffy runner that led down the hallway to the main room, a combined kitchen-dining-lounge.

She followed the smell to discover her flatmate, Val, elbows-deep in a giant bowl. "Hiya," chirruped Val.

"Hiya," replied Lucy, far less enthusiastically. "What are you making?" She wasn't sure she wanted to know, but whatever it was, the flat would undoubtedly smell like rancid feet for days to come.

"Cheese."

Well that explained it—somewhat. Weren't there a thousand different kinds of cheese?

5

"Right, well, I've had quite the day and I'm opening some wine. Would you like a glass?" she offered.

"Always," grinned Val.

"Hmm." Val was always up for drinking a glass of wine, just never actually *purchasing* said wine. Lucy pulled a bottle of chenin blanc from the mini fridge under the counter and retrieved two glasses from the shelf above the sink. She poured two equal, but generous glasses and took hers to the sofa, while Val bustled about the kitchen.

The smell seemed less intense now than when Lucy first got home. She sighed involuntarily as she sank into the seat and propped her feet up on the pouffe. She sipped her wine, starting to feel the tension release from her shoulder muscles, and surveyed the flat. Every now and then, she liked to take stock of her lovely home and after a day like today, it was a calming ritual—a bit like the wine.

The garden flat was south facing with high ceilings and lots of windows, and it was filled with natural light on days when the sun dared to show its face. The main room was spacious enough for a modular sofa, a square coffee table— thank you, Mum and Dad, for the flat-warming gift—and a long, low TV cabinet along the wall. A four-chair dining suite sat in the corner near the glass-paned door to the small conservatory.

The kitchen was compact but most of the fixtures were new, including the hob, the oven, and the backsplash of white subway tiles. Lucy had sprung for an updated kitchen and bathroom when she'd bought the flat, unwilling to put up with the Victorian plumbing, which had been patched up so many times over the years, it had been on its last leg. In Lucy's mind, a decent bath and shower were not luxuries, contrary to how she'd been raised.

That said, the updates had cost a bit and though she was exceptionally good with money, she'd stretched herself as thin financially as she was willing to go—which was far more comfortable than most people—and had got herself a flatmate to offset the mortgage.

Val was a friend of a friend of a friend and she'd been living with Lucy almost a year now. She was a nice person, Lucy's primary criterion, but she was also a bit of a homebody, which meant that Lucy was rarely alone in her own home.

And now it smelled like feet.

"So, what was particularly difficult about your day?" asked Val. A cream-coloured blob wrapped in muslin hung from the wooden spoon she was now balancing over the bowl. Val looked well-pleased with herself and Lucy supposed it was fair when she'd made *cheese*—from *scratch*.

Lucy sighed and took a hefty swig of wine. Did she want to go through the ins and outs of her shockingly bad day? And with *Val*? This was probably better nutted out with Chloe, or even Jules. But Val was there, and she was a good listener— as she'd evidenced many times. And, really, it would probably feel good to tell *someone*.

"It's my manager ..." she began. Val set the bowl to the side, washed her hands, and came and joined Lucy on the sofa, bringing her wine with her.

"Is this the woman you said you're unsure about? The one that just started?"

7

"Yes, that's right, *her*."

"So, what's happened, then?" Val peered at her intently.

"Well, I thought we were just finding our way with each other, you know, testing the waters? But after today, it's clear that she thinks I'm an incompetent nitwit."

As Lucy spoke, Val leapt up for top-ups from time to time until she'd shaken the last drops from the bottle and dropped it into the recycling bin. She listened without interruption to Lucy's litany of workplace crimes—all perpetrated by a woman called Angela, who tended towards micro-management, belittling Lucy in senior meetings and, today, undermining Lucy in front of her team.

"Hmm," Val said, when Lucy had exhausted her tales of woe. She tapped her chin and seemed to mull over her response thoughtfully before settling on, "She sounds like a proper cow."

It was said with such earnestness that Lucy found it incredibly funny—or perhaps it was the wine that caused the eruption of giggles. Either way, both women succumbed to fits of laugher and soon Lucy was wiping away tears—the good kind.

"Ooh," she said, expelling a long breath. "I needed that. Thanks, Val. It did help to talk it through."

"No need to thank me, Lucy. I feel awful for you. You *love* your job—well, you did. I hope it all gets sorted soon." It was a nice sentiment, but Lucy doubted it.

While Lucy had worked in the finance department of the legal firm for eleven years, Angela had only just been hired and, apparently, she was there to "shake things up". Lucy was starting to wonder if that was just corporate speak for "make everybody miserable".

"Shall I order a curry?" asked Val. "Or something else? It's on me."

Well, this was a first. "That sounds great, Val. I don't even have the energy to heat up a Marks & Sparks ready meal."

"How about you run a bath while I get it sorted."

Val's so lovely, she thought, as she leapt off the sofa to run a bath.

Chapter 2

Jules

Boulder, Colorado

"Well, damned if I know," she muttered to herself. Jules let her face fall into her hands, then rubbed her temples with her thumbs. She'd been reviewing and running the code for hours now and knew there was a bug *somewhere*, but where?

"Still no luck?" Her colleague, Wes, propped himself against her desk and she lifted her head.

"Kill me now."

"Nah, too much paperwork. Hey, we're going over to Pepper's. Wanna come?"

Jules glanced at the clock at the bottom of her screen—6:22pm. And it was Friday. Go or stay? It could be hours before she found the bug and with the size of her headache, it was unlikely she was in optimal coding mode. But if she went to Pepper's, she'd drink too much beer and probably end up sleeping with Wes—*again*.

Or she could just go home.

Her condo hardly called to her. It was on the outskirts of Boulder and she'd rented it fully furnished. It was a little, "Hey, IKEA called—they want their showroom back," but she didn't care. She'd settled into a "just fine" routine of work-home-gym, which she broke up with visits to see her family and occasional colleagues-with-benefits hook-ups with Wes ... or Rob ... or Arjun.

"I'm good," she said, flashing a smile she didn't feel. "Thanks," she added as an afterthought. He shrugged and left. Even though they worked for a tech start-up, Wes wasn't one of those guys who rolled out of bed and stumbled into work wearing pyjamas, a three-day growth, and the stench of the unwashed. He *cared* about his appearance and, not for the first time, Jules acknowledged that Wes was hot. He was also particularly good in bed.

Bed. The thought of curling up in her bed and sleeping off the headache was the most appealing one she'd had all day. Her phone buzzed on her desk.

Decided last minute to head to dads. Wanna come?

It was the lifeline she needed, time with two people from her extremely short list of favourites. She tapped out an affirmative response before saving her work and shutting down her computer. Will's next text popped onto the screen.

Pizza or sushi?

As much as she loved sushi, Colorado was hardly the place for fresh seafood, and she'd yet to find a local sushi place that didn't disappoint. Good takeout pizza, however, was plentiful.

Duh.

She watched the dots flicker on her screen, then stop, then start again, before her brother sent her a triple emoji reply that got her laughing for the first time that day—actually, it had been days since she'd laughed.

Forty minutes later, she was reclined on her dad's couch, a craft beer in one hand—a new brew from one of her brother's clients—and a slice of prosciutto and feta pizza in the other—both a nod to the "Hipsterville" status of her hometown.

"So, how's the app?" asked her dad. She knew he didn't *really* know what she and Will did, other than that they were both software developers working on their respective apps, but he knew enough to ask the question.

"It was being a shit today, actually," she replied. She wiped some grease from the side of her mouth with her thumb knuckle. "I'm going to have to do some work this weekend."

"Not tomorrow, though, right?" asked Will. "We're still going biking?"

"Biking is *on*." She wouldn't miss it. It was supposed to be eighty-two degrees tomorrow—perfect weather—and Boulder Canyon Trail was a favourite of hers. Besides, busting out the mountain bikes with her baby brother was just the panacea she needed after the week she'd had.

"Awesome. I can take a look at that code, too, if it'll help?" Will offered.

"Maybe, but I don't wanna think about that right now." She popped the last of the crust into her mouth and washed it down with some beer before reaching for another slice of pizza.

"Anything else new with you, sweetheart?"

"Not really, Dad. I still hate everyone but you two." Will barked a laugh at her retort and she joined in with a soft chuckle.

"Hey, we could watch a movie," her dad suggested. He needn't have said anything. It was what they always did—choose some movie that she and Will had seen, but somehow her dad hadn't, then she and Will would talk through it, driving her dad crazy. "How about the new *Star Wars* movie? *Rising Skywalker*, or something?"

"Do you mean *The Rise of Skywalker*, the one that came out forever ago?" asked Will. He threw Jules an our-dad-is-so-adorable look.

"I think so, yeah."

"Sure, Dad, sounds good." Jules and Will had seen the movie opening weekend—*and* they'd already watched it again at his place—but it had been too long since the three of them had had a night in like this, too long since Jules had felt surrounded by love and the ease of "just being" that came along with it.

She vowed not to let so much time pass before the next time.

Chapter 3

Chloe

Melbourne

"It couldn't have held off for five more minutes?" Chloe frowned out the window at the pelting rain as the Uber neared the drop-off point.

"We should have brought umbrellas," said her bestie, flatmate, and colleague, Ash.

"If we did, it wouldn't have rained."

"Exactly. Hashtag Melbourne."

Chloe shook her head at Ash. She wasn't sure when Ash had picked up the habit of *saying* "hashtag" but maybe she was doing it ironically.

The car pulled up next to the rear entrance of their building. "Here you go, misses," said the driver. Ash and Chloe shared a look across the back seat. "Ready?" asked Ash.

"Nope, but let's go." They opened their doors in sync and, heads down, stepped out into the deluge, the door slams barely making a dent in the soundscape of the mid-winter storm.

Ash ran around the back of the car and met up with Chloe, who was fumbling with her electronic fob at the door.

"Damn it! Of all the times to play up."

Ash reached across her and waved her own fob in front of the panel and the glass door slid open. They burst into the foyer and straightened up, eyeing each other before dissolving into laughter. "I am *so* wet," said Ash, shaking her hands.

"Title of your sex tape," retorted Chloe. She wiped rain from her face and pressed the button to call the elevator.

"Good one. So, who gets the first shower?" They each had their own bathroom, but the hot water pressure in their flat was so low, only one of them could shower at a time.

The elevator announced its arrival with a "ding", and they got in for their short ride to the fourth floor. "You go, but be *fast*," said Chloe. "I'll make some eggs or something."

"Breakfast for dinner? Will you marry me?"

"Yeah, well, consider it a reward for being so awesome today. That event, Ash, you killed it." Her bestie beamed at her, just as the elevator said, "Fourth floor," in a sexy voice that had never made any sense to Chloe. Why would *anyone* hire a voice-over artist who made arriving at the fourth floor sound like she was announcing an orgasm or something?

*

"Delish. Thank you," said Ash, as she stood and took Chloe's plate from her.

"It was just eggs, Ash."

"Yeah, but I didn't have to make them." Ash loaded the

dirty plates into the dishwasher and started cleaning up the rest of the kitchen. "Hey, so I was going say something before, but I've been going back and forth, and I wasn't really sure until today, but ..."

"Say it ..." Chloe's words turned into a yawn.

"What do you think of Carl?"

Chloe cut her yawn short and peered at Ash. "Well, he's fantastic at social media, but I'm guessing you don't mean *that*." What *did* Ash mean exactly? She'd only just come out of a long-term relationship and this was the first time she'd mentioned another guy.

Ash continued her clean-up. "He's kinda sexy, don't you think?"

Chloe decided to keep her reply light. "Uh, no, not really. And if *you* think so, then you don't want *me* to think so."

"Hah! You're right. It's just ... I caught him watching me a couple of times tonight, and did you see how weird he was acting when we said goodbye?"

"Sorry, Ash, I must have been too shattered to notice Carl's unobvious flirting."

"He's incredibly smart, like *incredibly*." Ash draped the wet tea towel over the handle of the oven door, flicked off the kitchen light, and re-joined Chloe on the couch.

"*You're* incredibly smart too, Ash." Ash shrugged her shoulders, her usual way of deflecting a compliment. "Anyway, I haven't worked that closely with him," continued Chloe, "but props to him for that Insta campaign for tonight. It was pretty impressive." The campaign had been *unreal*, but Chloe was tempering her enthusiasm for all things "Carl". If she'd been a betting person, her money would be on Ash getting back together with her ex.

Still, maybe a distraction was something Ash needed. She clocked the wistful look on Ash's face. "So, you're into him?"

"Maybe. But what are you *not* saying?"

Ash knew her tells too well, but there was no way Chloe was going to spill about what she was actually thinking. "Uh, nothing, it's just ... maybe it's the name—*Carl,*" she said, going with something that was partly true; she *didn't* like the name.

"Oh, come on. What's wrong with 'Carl'?"

Good, she bought it, Chloe thought. "Eh, it's like Kevin, or Bruce—just ..." She mimed shivers running up her spine.

"Carl in *Love, Actually* is the hottest guy in the movie," countered Ash.

Chloe chuckled to herself. "Yeah, true. Oh, wait, there was Andrew Lincoln too—"

"But he played the shitty best friend who was all stalkery with Keira Knightley."

"Also true. Anyway, I'll concede that sometimes 'Carl' is the hot guy."

"So, *do* you think he was acting weird?" asked Ash.

"I really don't know ... maybe?" Ash looked crestfallen. "Look, I promise to pay more attention to the 'Carl' situation and, if needed, I'll be your wingman."

"Wing*woman*."

"Yes, that," she said, succumbing to another yawn. "Sorry, Ash, I've got to go to bed." Chloe stood and stretched her hands above her head. A full day of work, then an evening event—even though Ash had been on point and she'd only played a supporting role—had left her exhausted. Ash must have been shattered too, only she had picked up the remote and was scrolling through Netflix, so maybe not.

"Night, Ash."

"Night. And thanks again for all your help tonight."

"For sure. It was a great event."

Just as Chloe loaded up her toothbrush with toothpaste, she heard her phone ring from her room. Toothbrush in hand, she raced in, grabbed the phone and tapped the green button just before it went to voicemail. "Hello?" she said.

"Chloe, it's Mum and Dad."

"Oh, hi, what's up?" It was a little unusual for her to get a call from her parents at 10:30pm on a weeknight.

"We have some news, love," said her dad. *Well, that sounds ominous*, she thought as she plonked down on the end of her bed.

"O-*kay*," she said, her stomach tightening.

"It's about Christmas ..."

Chapter 4

The May Ladies

"Chloe, your camera is turned off." Lucy frowned at the screen.

"It isn't. It's just the middle of the night."

"It's 6:00am there. It's hardly the middle of the night," said Jules.

"Is it too early? Should we call back in an hour?" asked Lucy.

"*She* called us, Lucy. Chloe, turn on a light."

Chloe was abruptly illuminated and blinked into the camera. "Happy?"

"Ecstatic. So, bad morning?" Jules knew her tone was borderline snippy, but she'd had a particularly shitty day.

"Yes. It's a sucky morning, actually," Chloe whined.

"What's wrong?" Lucy's confused frown morphed into her concerned one.

Chloe sighed dramatically for effect. "It's my parents ..." She wiped sleep from her eyes, oblivious to the horror on her friends' faces.

21

"What's happened?" whispered Jules, suddenly brimming with sympathy. She would get on a plane that day if she needed to.

Chloe looked at the screen. "Oh, no, sorry, they're fine. I, just—"

Two sighs expelled simultaneously, one from Colorado, the other from London, and Lucy's hand patted her chest to self-soothe.

"You scared the crap out of us, Chloe." Jules *was* going to get on a plane, if only to smack her friend in the head.

"Sorry."

Lucy blew out another long breath. "It's all right, but what *is* going on?"

"They're going on a cruise."

Jules was starting to get really pissed off. "There's more to it, though, *right?*"

"They're going on a cruise for *Christmas*."

A pair of simultaneous "Ohhhs" echoed about Chloe's lounge room. She took it as solidarity and an open invitation to rant. "I know! Christmas! And they didn't even invite me and my brother, so he's going off skiing in Canada and I'm going to be all alone. On *Christmas*."

A muffled voice said something to Chloe and another light turned on, illuminating the kitchen behind her.

"Hi, Ash!" called Lucy through the screen.

Ash walked up behind Chloe and leant over the back of the couch. "Hi, girls. How's life in the northern hemisphere?"

"Quite lovely, actually," said Lucy. "It's that time of year when you forget how cold and grey London can get—you know, daylight 'til ten-ish and warm weather. It was *twenty-two* today!"

Ash grinned into the screen. "Yeah, that sounds way better than Melbs at the moment. I frigging hate winter. How 'bout you Jules?"

"Yeah, pretty good," she said, glossing over the reality. "I *really* need to get out to the coast soon, though. I'm thinking I'll go see my girlfriend in San Diego—just for a weekend. She's into sailing, so that would be cool."

"Uh, *hello*! We were talking about Christmas. About how I'm going to be *alone* on Christmas."

"Are you two sick of Chloe's whining yet, because I am?" teased Ash.

Ash was one of the three people on the planet who could get away with saying something like that to Chloe's face. The other two people were on the screen, both stifling laughs.

"Very funny, all of you, but you know what Christmas means to me."

"Yes!" This time it was three voices in sync.

"Look, I told you last night, you *won't* be alone"—Ash gave Chloe a pointed look—"*if* you just stay here." Ash looked back at the screen. "Orphans' Christmas is at our place this year."

"And what's that?" asked Lucy.

"I'm going to let Chloe explain. Gotta jump in the shower. See ya, girls."

"So, an orphans' Christmas is with your friends, right, the ones whose families aren't around?" asked Jules.

"Yes."

23

"That sounds fun!" Jules replied. If it was possible, Chloe moped even harder.

"So, you won't be alone then? You'll be with the other Christmas orphans?" asked Lucy, helpfully.

"It's not the same. I don't want to be a Christmas orphan. I just want a normal, traditional Christmas. That's not too much to ask, is it?"

"What do you mean by 'normal'?" Jules knew what a normal Christmas was to her, but the three of them had never shared the holiday before.

"Well, you know?" From the blank looks on their faces, they did not. "Well, *family*. Family is a big part of Christmas. And presents. And a *tree*. And Christmas lunch and wine—you know, a *normal* Christmas."

"But won't you have all that with Ash and your friends?" Jules asked.

"Not the family part." Chloe seemed to have an answer for everything.

"But they're your close friends, right? Like us. Aren't *we* like family?" Surely Jules could make her see reason.

Chloe shrugged. "I suppose."

Jules blew out a frustrated laugh. "Way to make us feel special, Chlo."

Great, now she'd insulted her best friends. "Sorry, you're right. You girls *are* like family. And Ash."

"I know!" Jules could almost see the little lightbulb illuminate above Lucy's head. "Why don't you come here for Christmas?" Lucy's russet brown eyes peered up at Chloe from the screen.

"To London?"

"Yes! Why not? Oh, actually, it wouldn't be London, because I go home at Christmas, to Oxfordshire, but you'd be most welcome. You could share my old room; we could get a cot for you." Chloe blinked at the word "cot" but Lucy didn't notice and kept prattling. "And there's the village Christmas Fair, and carol singing at the church, and Mum makes the *best* Christmas cake, absolutely drowning in sherry. All *very* traditional. Not *your* kind of traditional, of course, but still, just lovely.

"And I suppose I *should* say it probably won't be a white Christmas or anything. In fact, I can't remember the last time we had one of those. It's usually more of a slushy, wet, grey day. It can get a little depressing sometimes, if I'm completely honest, because you just end up longing for snow, especially because there's always snow in the Christmas films, isn't there?" Lucy was whipping herself into quite the festive season frenzy.

"I mean, *Bridget Jones's Diary*—snow. *While You Were Sleeping*—snow. *The Holiday*—snow. God, I love that film. Jude Law—*mmm*. But anyway, it so rarely *happens* at home. I'd love a white Christmas, now that I think of it." Her frown returned.

"Well, you should come here, then Luce," joked Jules. We've got snow, that's for sure. So. Much. Damned. Snow."

Lucy's eyes brightened, completely missing Jules's tone. "Do you mean it? Could I really come?"

Jules barked a wry laugh. "I don't see why not—if you want a big, loud, crazy Christmas. It'll be up at our cabin in Breckenridge—and my aunt and her whole family come, so

25

we'd have to share a room. I mean, Christmas with my family *can* get a little intense, Luce ..." She saw Lucy's face fall just a fraction; she'd have to dial it down. "But I can one hundred percent guarantee you a snowy one."

A grin split Lucy's face. "But wait, Chloe, what should we do about you?"

"Sorry?" Chloe, only half-listening to the chat about Christmas in Colorado, was pulled from her thoughts. She'd been imagining herself in a tiny English village having a proper traditional Christmas. Plum pudding, Christmas carols, sitting by the fire drinking mulled wine—even the Christmas Fair sounded fun. And with Lucy off in America, she wouldn't have to sleep on a *cot*.

"Actually, even if you do go to America, I think I *would* like an old-fashioned English Christmas. Do you think your parents would let me come?"

Lucy answered immediately. "Oh, they absolutely would. You're my best friend!"

"Ahem!" Jules teased.

"Well, you both are. And I'll miss you, of course, Chloe, but you'll get the Christmas you want, and I'll get my snowy one." She grinned into the screen.

Chloe scrutinised her American friend's face. "Wait, Jules, what's going on with you?"

Jules tilted her head to the side and sighed. "I think it's just ... you know, it's the middle of summer and all this talk about Christmas and winter ... to be honest, it exhausts me."

For Lucy, the penny finally dropped, and she uttered a guilty, "Oh." She'd been so wrapped up in what *she* wanted.

"I mean, I love the holiday itself—well, no, *that's* not even true anymore. And that time of year ... it's ... well, I *hate* it! I hate being cold, I hate being snowed in, which seems to happen more and more. And yes, I *love* my family, but sometimes"—she threw up her hands—"they're too much. I leave Christmas feeling like I need a vacation."

Lucy couldn't stand it any longer. "Jules, I'm so sorry. Here I am just going on and on about it."

"Hey, no, it's okay. I love that you love Christmas so much—both of you. It's just not like that for me, not anymore. Honestly, Chlo, your orphans' Christmas sounds amazing, especially the summer part. I'm actually jealous."

Chloe's large green eyes got even larger. "Oh, my god. That's it. We should do like they did *The Holiday* and swap Christmases!" She let the thought hang in the air, watching her friends' faces closely.

Jules's sigh turned into a contemplative smile and Lucy's mouth formed an O, then settled into a pout. "But wait, that means I'd be in America by myself."

"But you'd get your white Christmas, Lucy," prompted Chloe gently. "Just imagine ..."

Jules, completely on board, picked up where Chloe left off. "And my mom would love it, Lucy. So would my dad. They'll spoil you rotten, I promise."

Lucy chewed her bottom lip and twisted a long red curl between her fingers. "Be brave, Lucy," Chloe whispered. If Chloe had a soft spot, it was for Lucy.

Jules imagined herself on a *beach* in *Australia* at *Christmas* and willed Lucy to agree to their plan.

"You know what?" Lucy lifted her head and declared, "I want a white Christmas! Let's do it. Let's swap." She grinned at her best friends.

"Yes!" Jules gave the air a little victory punch.

Chloe did a chair dance. "Ash!" she called over her shoulder, "we're swapping Christmases—you get Jules." She looked back at the screen. "Guys, this is going to be amazing!"

Chapter 5

Lucy

Lucy unfurled from the back seat of the Uber awkwardly, still seemingly unused to her long limbs, even though she'd stretched to five-foot-eleven at the precocious age of thirteen. Her eyes fixed on her handbag until she reminded herself that she didn't need to pay for the ride.

The driver got out to retrieve her case from the boot. It was exactly twenty-three kilos—she'd weighed it on her digital scales in her bathroom—so he struggled with it a bit as he set it on the pavement.

A harried man brushed past her as she extended the handle and she offered an unnecessary apology, then turned to thank the driver, who waved a hand over his shoulder and grunted in reply.

All of a sudden, Lucy was rooted to the spot, a slow terror creeping up from her toes and burrowing in her stomach. *What the sodding bollocks, Lucy?* she asked herself. It was just a holiday to America. She'd been there several times on their ML holidays.

A family of four, each of them at least thrice her girth, bundled past. The girl, about eleven, rolled her eyes self-consciously at Lucy, a small act of solidarity as the girl silently apologised for her *utterly embarrassing* family.

Lucy found herself smiling. She was once that awkward tubby girl, horridly embarrassed by her parents, and mortified just to be seen in public. Eleven was such a terrible age.

To her delight, the girl grinned back. And it was just the fuel Lucy needed to quell her unfounded fears, grab the handle of her case and stride into the terminal to catch her plane.

*

Lucy emerged from the double glass doors and scanned the crowd. She'd never seen so many people waiting for passengers before, and she'd just left *Heathrow*.

The sharp twang of American accents permeated the air and the final scene from *Love, Actually* played out around her. Hugs, tears, grins, slaps on the back. It was impossible not to feel moved by it all—*and* just a touch of melancholy.

Her first Christmas abroad and being an only child, it was easy to feel the sting of remorse for leaving her parents at this time of year. It had always been just the three of them, with their own family rituals and traditional ways of doing things. As she scanned hundreds of faces searching for Will, Jules's baby brother, she wondered if she'd done the right thing.

There.

He stood a head above the people around him with a shock

of dark blond hair, exactly the same shade as Jules's until she'd started highlighting it.

And he was unbelievably handsome.

Lucy wasn't friends with Will on Facebook, but she'd had a quick look at his profile before getting on the plane so she'd recognise him. In his photo, he was cute, boyish, a male version of Jules, but *this* Will! This Will was a *man*. A very hot, very tall man.

Lucy gulped, then raised her hand above her head to catch his eye. When she eventually did, after some rigorous waving and yoo-hooing, her knees nearly buckled. His eyes locked on hers and a grin spread across his face. He raised one hand in a greeting, then started making his way through the crowd to her. Lucy remained where she was and in moments, he was there looking down at her, the grin still intact. "Lucy?" he asked.

She nodded, gulped again, then finally found the ability to say, "Uh, yes. Hello," which she followed up with, "Very nice to see you again." Even when dumbstruck, which was more often than she liked, she tended to use her manners. Still, she wished she had something more eloquent to say.

"Yeah. For sure. So, you want me to take that?" he pointed to her case.

"Oh, yes please. Sorry, just a little discombobulated." He seemed to like her choice of word and a smile danced in his eyes—his gorgeous, cobalt blue eyes.

"Oh, no problem. I'm always a little out of it when I fly too. Come on, let's get outta here. This place is insane." Lucy followed the blond hair and the man attached to it out of the terminal.

There was *nothing* that could have prepared her for the blast of cold that hit as soon as they walked through the automatic doors—not the boots or woollen coat or leather gloves she was wearing—not even a lifetime of living in the UK.

"Oh, my god," she gasped.

Will looked over his shoulder and stopped. "You okay?" She stood, stock still, her hands flying to her face as the pain in her lungs intensified. "It's the cold," he stated, matter-of-factly. She nodded vaguely. "Let's get you to the car. Come on." He took her hand and stepped up the pace to the car park. She didn't even have the presence of mind to notice the hand-holding.

A few minutes later, they were ensconced in a four-wheel-drive and Will was blasting the heater. "There are seat warmers too," he said, flipping a switch on the dash.

As the warm air spewed from the vents in front of her, she started feeling her muscles uncoiling. Her cheeks stopped stinging and she could breathe without it hurting. "It's really cold here," she said eventually, her voice barely above a whisper.

"I'm guessing London doesn't get like this, huh?" She shot a look across the car. He was watching her, one hand resting on the steering wheel and one on his thigh. His hands were large, strong-looking, and unblemished. Her mind flew to all the things he could do with those hands. *Stop it, Lucy*, she admonished. He'd asked her a question; manners dictated that she should answer it.

"I suppose. Maybe it does, but just a different kind of cold."

"It's fifteen below, right now." She didn't even bother doing the conversion from Fahrenheit to Celsius; it was ridiculously cold on either scale.

"Well, bollocks," she replied, her manners eclipsed by the frigid weather.

Will bellowed out a laugh and started the car. "So, hey," he said, as he pulled out of the parking space, "I know Jules told you we were going to my mom's place overnight, but if it's okay with you, I think we should head up the mountain today. There's a blizzard coming and it could close the pass."

"Oh." A blizzard that closed mountain passes sounded worrying, but for all Lucy knew they were a common occurrence in this part of the world. "So, we're going straight to your family's cabin?"

"If that's okay with you."

"Of course. How far is it?"

"It's about a hundred miles from here. It usually only takes a couple of hours, but it might take a bit longer today."

"Oh, right."

"My mom, my stepdad, and my dad are already up there. My aunt and her family aren't flying in from Seattle 'til tomorrow, so hopefully they'll be able to make the drive in the morning. Depends on the pass."

"Sorry, did you say your mum and your stepdad *and* your *dad* are all there together?" For some reason, Lucy thought Jules's dad wouldn't be there at Christmas. Had Jules mentioned it and she'd forgotten?

"Yeah, it's a little unconventional, but they're all good friends."

"Huh." Her parents, Max and Susan, popped into her head

and she struggled to imagine a third person with them, a stranger who was married to one of them, and all three of them being the best of friends.

It was going to be an interesting Christmas, that was for sure.

*

"Hey, I'm sorry about this." It was the third time Will had apologised in less than an hour.

"Honestly, it's not your fault. It's the weather."

They were stopped on the mountain pass, surrounded on both sides by snowdrifts, which were growing incrementally with the light snowfall. They'd been creeping along for the past two hours, often stopping for five, ten, or even fifteen minutes at a time. With the blizzard imminent, it seemed the entire population of Denver was trying to get up the mountain before the pass closed.

Lucy hadn't minded the delay. She and Will had been talking nonstop since they'd left the airport. She'd learnt all about the tech company he'd built from practically nothing. He had started it only a year ago, working from home at night and on weekends. In six months, he'd been able to quit his job as a software consultant, and he now had an office and four employees.

It was a vastly different career path than her own, having worked in the same department at the same law firm since leaving university. Sure, she'd been promoted several times and now managed a team of three, but it was the certainty of the work that she enjoyed most. The laws and regulations she had to adhere to provided her with a sense of stability and she loved knowing that if she did everything exactly right, the numbers would always add up.

And even though Will's company supported micro-breweries and boutique distilleries, something she knew precisely *nothing* about other than her love of a good G&T, there were quite a few similarities between their jobs—namely, finances and laws. It was all very impressive what he'd accomplished, especially for someone who was only just coming up on thirty.

"I really didn't think traffic would be *this* awful." Will's words permeated her thoughts. "It's just bad timing, I guess. I mean, we could have waited out the storm in Boulder, but then we were risking missing Christmas."

Lucy indulged the fantasy of being snowed in with Will—just the two of them. There was a roaring fire in the fantasy *and* those big strong hands. Her cheeks flushed and she chided herself again. She chanced a glance across the car; he was looking at her and scratching his chin.

"Uh, Lucy, this is sort of awkward, but ... oh hell, look, I really have to pee." He punctuated his admission with a frustrated sigh.

"Oh." Her eyes widened and she felt the flush in her cheeks spread to the rest of her face. She was, at once, both embarrassed and relieved. She'd needed a wee since just after they'd left the airport. Only, how was this going to work?

"Yeah. So, look, we haven't moved in a while. I'm thinking I'll head over that way." He pointed to a stand of trees about thirty feet away. Well, that sorted Will, but what about her?

Realisation seemed to dawn across his face. "Oh, you need to go too, right?"

"Yes." She pressed her palm to her chest, like she always did when she was nervous or embarrassed.

"Okay, how about this? I'll go over there, and you open your door and the back door, and you go, uh, there—in between. That will give you some privacy." He looked out of the windscreen and laughed. "*Or* you could just do what she's doing."

Lucy followed his gaze and saw a woman, trousers and pants down, squatting in the snow on the side of the road. A bark of a laugh escaped her, breaking the nervous tension in the car.

She glanced at Will. "Your plan seems better."

*

Ensconced back in the warmth of the car, rubbing her chilled hands together and blowing on them, Lucy waited for Will. She didn't want to look towards the trees in case she saw a flash of his bum, or worse yet, a yellow stream arcing into the snow. She needn't have worried, though, because moments later the driver's door opened, and Will climbed back into the car.

He fiddled with a dial on the dash and the air from the vents got warmer. "Well, I have to say," he said, "that was a first for me."

"What, weeing outside?" Lucy teased.

Will laughed and Lucy was delighted that she'd elicited

such a wonderful sound. "Uh, no. Definitely not. I meant peeing outside in daylight in view of dozens of strangers and my sister's hot friend."

Lucy felt the sting of another flush. *Hot friend*. She ignored the scoffing inner voice, the one that still thought of her as an awkward, podgy eleven-year-old, and instead picked up her end of the banter.

"Oh, I didn't peek." He flashed her a grin, one eyebrow raised; she'd always wished she could do that. She was fairly certain it was a flirtatious move and emboldened by her own adventure in outdoor weeing, she continued.

"I've always thought it was better to wait until Christmas morning to unwrap presents, rather than to peek beforehand."

Oh, Lucy, that was utterly cringeworthy.

There was a moment before Will answered and Lucy seriously contemplated getting out of the car and walking the rest of the way to the cabin.

"You know," he began eventually, "this doesn't happen very often, but I am actually speechless."

Oh god. He thinks I'm a total slapper. Well, in for a penny, in for a pound.

"Horrified speechless or intrigued speechless?"

The car in front of them started moving, but before he put his in drive, Will pinned her with a look. "Oh, definitely the latter." Then he turned his eyes to the road, a smile tugging at the corner of his mouth.

Lucy, relieved not to have made a *total* fool of herself, looked out her side window. It was so beautiful there, everything blanketed in white, snow hanging heavily on the boughs of the pine trees like nature's fondant. The thought made her think of her mum's Christmas cake, which she loved as much for the generous layer of marzipan and fondant, as for the brandy-soaked cake itself.

"Oh!" Lucy exclaimed, startling Will. "Sorry, but I've just been thinking about Mum's Christmas cake, and remembered I've got one with me."

Lucy's mum had sent her across the pond with her very own Christmas cake—something to share with Jules's family. It had arrived at her flat in the post the week before, wrapped in foil and tucked snugly into a box surrounded by scrunched up newspaper. It was now packed in her carry-on bag. "We could have some—if you're hungry, that is."

"I hope this doesn't sound rude, but I don't really like Christmas cake."

"Sorry, what?" Who didn't like Christmas cake?

"It's just too dry and crumbly and it always tastes like it's been out of date for, like, I dunno, a *millennium*."

"Mum's cake isn't like that. It's homemade and it's wonderful." Lucy caught the slight edge in her voice and lightened her tone. "Not to worry, more for me." She just knew he'd think differently if he tried some. She turned in her seat and unzipped her carry-on, rummaging about for the cake.

"I've insulted you."

"No. Honestly, you haven't." She pulled out the dense bounty and even though it was tightly wrapped, the smell of spices and sherry started filling the car.

"Well, then I've insulted your mom ... Hold on, is that it, that smell?"

She sat the cake on her lap and carefully started peeling back the layers of foil. "Uh, yes," she said nonchalantly. "Look." The cake sat in its bed of foil, the snowy white fondant perfectly smooth.

Will glanced at the cake, then his gaze went back to the road. They were still crawling along, but at least they were moving. "Well, that does *smell* amazing. I've got a pocketknife in the glove compartment—unless you think we should just tear off chunks with our hands." The smile was back and Lucy succumbed to one herself.

Minutes later, she placed a generous slab of Christmas cake sitting on top of a Burger King napkin—also from the glove box—onto Will's thigh. The wedge sat tawny brown and glistening with delicious moistness. "See? Definitely not dry and crumbly."

She watched him take a bite, then heard his guttural groan. *Maybe I'll get to hear more of that groan later*, she thought before rolling her eyes at herself.

"It's good, isn't it?" she said, taking a bite of her own piece. "It's even nicer with a thick slice of Wensleydale cheese," she added, her hand covering her mouth.

"It's amazing. I'm not sure about the cheese though. Is that an English thing?"

Lucy thought about it and realised she didn't know. She'd just always had it that way *and*, ever since she was an adult, with a glass or two of sherry. "Hmm, not sure."

"And, just asking, but is there alcohol in this?"

"Oh, loads. Mum practically empties an entire bottle of sherry into it in the month leading up to Christmas." She had a realisation and her head spun towards Will just as he glanced at her, then down to the cake. "Oh, bollocks. You're driving."

"I was just thinking that."

"Sorry, I should have realised. No cake for you, I'm afraid." She took the cake off his leg, noting how taut his thigh was beneath his jeans, and wrapped it up in the napkin. "At least not until we get there."

"It's really good, though. You've definitely changed my mind."

She smiled to herself as she took another bite. Looking out the window, she went back to her "snowed-in alone with Will" fantasy, which now included a boozy Christmas cake.

Chapter 6

Jules

"Here you go, sweetheart," said her dad as he manoeuvred his SUV between two others. Denver airport was mayhem this time of year.

"Thanks again for driving me. You didn't have to. I could have Ubered."

"Jules, this may come as a huge surprise, but I'm going to miss you, sweetheart, and this way I got to spend a little more time with you."

Jules wondered if she was imagining the sheen of tears in her dad's eyes. He made a gruff man-sound and climbed out to retrieve her luggage from the trunk. Jules took a deep breath as a wave of melancholy washed over her. Yes, she was a grown woman with a job and her own place and a *life*, but this was the first time she'd be spending Christmas away from her family, from her dad.

The sound of the trunk slamming shut brought her back to the present. She gathered her carry-on bag and her satchel from the footwell and braced herself for the blast of cold.

Her dad was waiting on the pavement for her, stamping the way he did when it was close to freezing outside. She felt a pang of guilt—not just that her dad was standing outside in a snowstorm guarding her luggage, but that she was abandoning him—*and* her mother, her brother, her stepdad, and her aunt's whole family—at *Christmas*. A gust of wind whipped her honey-blonde hair into her face, and it felt like a slap.

This is why I'm going to Australia where it's hot.

"Bye, Dad," she said, throwing her arms around her dad's broad shoulders.

"Bye, sweetheart." He enveloped her in a tight hug. "Text when you land, so I know you're safe."

"I will."

Her dad's hugs were the stuff of dreams, but there was no putting it off any longer or they'd both get frostbite. It was time to go. Jules stepped out of the hug and grinned at her dad. "See you next year!" She grabbed the handle of her luggage and jogged off towards the terminal door, the sound of her dad's laughter catching on another gust of wind.

*

Denver-LA-Melbourne—as flights went, it was an easy journey. Even the two-hour layover at LAX wasn't as bad as she had expected. Maybe the tacky piped holiday music and even tackier tinsel, Christmas lights, and gaudy Santas had worked their magic. People were actually smiling.

Or maybe, five days before Christmas, everyone was just in the holiday spirit. Everyone but her. On the short flight between Denver and LA, she had convinced herself she was doing the wrong thing.

She should have stayed and had the loud, chaotic Christmas that her screwed-up, but lovable family had every year. Or, at the very least, she should have waited and welcomed Lucy. She loved Lucy. Lucy was the sort of person who, just by being around her, made Jules's spirit soar.

She should have stayed for her dad.

She knew, on the surface at least, that everything was amicable and her parents still shared some weird kind of love—just that it was platonic now. She knew he got along with her stepdad, Joe, and that he could handle himself among the brash familial love that Aunt Jackie and her family would bring to the holidays.

And yet ...

Jules also knew she was her dad's biggest ally, that when the family dinners and games of Cards Against Humanity or Trivial Pursuit got too rowdy, she could catch his eye across the table and they'd share a moment of calm, just with a look. Those moments were a sort of "time out" from their maelstrom of family life, shared by two introverts who loved everyone there, but longed for a breath of quiet and stillness.

She knew her brother, Will, would do his best. He was under strict instructions to look out for their dad—and for Lucy—but he didn't see the world quite the way Jules did, and she was worried he would neglect his duties.

Why, oh why, am I going all the way to Australia for the holidays? she'd asked herself, just as the plane touched the tarmac in LA.

But she knew why. Sometimes, getting on a plane was the only way to shake yourself out of a rut—a rut that you had created and that was slowly eating you up.

*

While she waited for her luggage to pop out of the shoot in Melbourne, Jules peeled off as many layers as she could—coat, sweater, and long-sleeved T-shirt—and stuffed them into her carry-on, still wearing a tank and her jeans. She was also still in her boots, but her flip-flops were packed, and there was no way she was going through the rigmarole of swapping them out at baggage claim.

Her luggage arrived and she cleared customs, then followed signs through the terminal to the Sky Bus. Ash had offered to pick her up, but Jules was fine with finding her own way into the city. She didn't want to be a burden.

The heat felt glorious when she stepped into the bright sunshine. Her feet prickled with it inside her boots, but the rest of her body was relieved. Her entire life she'd lived in Colorado and every year she dreaded the icy winters. *Summers* in Boulder were gorgeous—eighty-five degrees, bright blue skies that stretched on forever, light breezes—but the winters were something to be endured.

With her luggage stowed on a rack, she chose an elevated seat in the middle of the bus so she could see out the large window. The first half of the journey was unremarkable, except when the driver pointed out a field next to the highway that was brimming with kangaroos.

Dozens of pointy furry faces with big ears watched as the bus flew by and Jules grinned. *Australia*, she thought. *I'm in Australia!* A young couple in front of her spoke rapid Japanese to each other and tried to take photos, but the bus was going too fast.

The second half of the journey revealed glimpses of the skyline and then, after one bend in the highway, the city of Melbourne was revealed, taking up her window and the ones either side. It was nothing like Boulder, or Denver for that matter. Melbourne was dense and tall, with dozens of skyscrapers earning their name. And she'd never seen so many cranes in her life.

There was also a Ferris wheel like the one in London, although it looked out over an industrial area and a giant yard of shipping containers. Somewhere from the back of her mind, she retrieved a memory of Chloe saying that no one went on it because the view was terrible—oh, and one year, the frame had started to crack. She'd avoid it.

Twenty minutes later, Jules regretted turning down Ash's offer to pick her up from the airport. It was a much longer walk from the bus station to the Docklands apartment than she'd anticipated. She'd looked it up a few days ago, thinking it would be an easy walk, but now she was hot, tired, and cursing herself—*and* her damned boots.

"I should have caught a cab," she grumbled.

Just then, as she crested the rise of a bridge, the marina came into view, with dozens of moored boats and a large bridge spanning the water in the distance. It was just what Jules needed to give her a boost of energy and she picked up her pace.

At the marina, she turned right and walked briskly as her

eyes locked on the high-rise apartment buildings in every shape and design, then scanned the array of boats—everything from small runabouts to luxury yachts tied up and still in the calm, but murky water.

She'd thought the marina was on a freshwater river, but as she breathed in the tangy brine of the air, she wondered if she'd been wrong. Or maybe the marina was close to the beach. "Oh, please let that be true," she uttered to herself. She was *hankering* to get to the beach. That was the other disadvantage of living in Colorado, being landlocked. Sometimes it felt like a form of claustrophobia.

Jules stopped one last time to consult her phone, then turned onto the promenade. Chloe had said that the entrance to their building was opposite a gelato shop, adding that the gelato was excellent and that she and Ash practically kept them in business. *There!* Jules laughed to herself because the shop was shaped like a giant ice cream cone, and opposite—just as Chloe had said—she spied the building's entrance.

Standing outside was a tall man with jet-black curly hair and a stubbled chin, wearing faded jeans, work boots, and a tight black T-shirt. He was carrying a box and speaking into the intercom—probably making a delivery. As she approached, he glanced back at her and a smile, the kind strangers exchange, flickered across his face.

Maybe it was jet lag, or sleep deprivation, or even heat exhaustion, but that smile roused something in her. She waited her turn at the intercom so she could buzz Ash, taking the moment to appreciate the tight fit of his jeans.

He's sorta scruffy, but seriously hot.

She reproached herself as a muffled voice replied to him and the glass door slid open. She was in Melbourne for Christmas and to spend time with Chloe's friends. She was not there to get her groove on.

The man disappeared into the lobby and Jules pressed the apartment number on the intercom.

"Hey, Jules!" The voice startled her, then she realised she was on camera.

"Hi, Ash." She was relieved to hear a welcoming voice, even if it sounded like the intercom at a McDonald's drive-thru.

"Come on in and take the lift up to the fourth floor."

The glass door slid open again and Jules heaved her satchel back onto her shoulder for the final leg of an extremely long journey. When she got to the elevator, she was surprised to see that the man with the box was still waiting.

He turned towards her. "Hey, what floor are you going to?" *Those eyes—deep brown, almost black. Holy crap.*

"Four."

"Hmm, me too, but it looks like the lift's out. I think we'll have to go up the stairs."

"What?" She'd heard him; she just hoped he was kidding. Jules looked up at the display above the elevator and where she expected numbers, there was just a bunch of red dots rolling across the screen. He wasn't kidding. The thought of dragging her luggage up all those flights of stairs to the fourth floor hit hard.

"Yeah, apparently it happens quite a bit. My friends are

always complaining about it." He shifted the weight of the box in his arms. It seemed heavy.

"Oh, your friends live here?" So, he wasn't a delivery guy. Maybe she'd get to see some more of him then.

"Yeah, just dropping this wine off. We're doing the Chrissie orphan thing."

"Hang on, then you know Chloe and Ash?"

"Yeah! Oh, you're the friend from America."

So, I'm spending Christmas with the hot guy, she thought as she imagined him standing nude under a sprig of mistletoe. She flashed her excellent example of American orthodontia and said, "I'm Jules."

"Matt." He smiled back, then seemed to remember they were both standing there with heavy things. "Oh, sorry, I was going to offer to take your bag upstairs for you."

She looked down at her luggage. "Oh, no, you don't have to do that. It weighs, like, fifty pounds."

He grinned again. "Yeah, that's okay. I'll manage. So, how 'bout I head up with your bag, then come back down for you and the wine?"

There was no sense in arguing. He had offered and she had no desire to lug her luggage up all those stairs. "Sure," she said, surrendering it.

Matt placed the box of wine on the floor, retrieved his phone from the front pocket of his jeans, swiped a couple of times, then pressed it to his ear. "Hey Ash, the lift's out. Can you meet me at the top of the stairs? Yeah, she's here. I'm bringing up her bag. Cool, ta."

Then he pocketed the phone, took the handle of her luggage

and disappeared through the door to the stairwell. "Be right back," he called as the door swung shut.

As she waited, Jules settled on one thought. Christmas far from home and far from her dad, was definitely looking up.

Chapter 7

Chloe

"Stop right here, thanks."

The taxi driver pulled to the kerb, cutting off another car. Chloe ignored the long horn that sounded and handed over her credit card. She was running uncharacteristically late and waited impatiently for the driver to tap it.

"Receipt?"

"No thanks." She took her card and opened the car door, throwing a look over her shoulder. "Can you get my bag out of the boot?" The driver huffed out a sigh, but she ignored that too. Surely, he didn't expect *her* to lift that massive thing.

It was too hot to be wearing ankle boots, jeans and a jumper, and a thin sheen of sweat prickled her brow. She'd be fine once she got in the terminal—*if* the driver would hurry up.

She double-checked the backseat to make sure she hadn't left anything behind before closing the door. The driver heaved her bag onto the footpath and grunted, "There you go."

He was rewarded with a million-watt Chloe Sims smile,

which seemed to disarm him instantly. "Have a good flight," he chirruped.

She pulled the handle up with a snap and strode towards the terminal, mentally rehearsing her get-an-upgrade strategy. One in three times it worked, mostly because of her frequent-flier status. She hoped this would be one of those times, because the thought of all those hours in economy did nothing to lift her mood. An upgrade would, though.

*

Twenty-nine hours she'd been in transit, counting the layover in Dubai, immigration at Heathrow, and the bus ride to Oxford—*and* she'd been unlucky with the upgrade. But the worst part of the journey was waiting at the open-air bus station in the freezing cold hoping she'd recognise Lucy's dad from a photo on Facebook.

According to the glary orange digits of the overhead clock, the bus had only dropped her off fifteen minutes ago, but fifteen minutes standing in the cold felt like *years*. Where was Mr Browning?

She shoved her hands deeper into the pockets of her Kathmandu puffer jacket. Her top half was warm, but the damp icy wind was biting through her jeans and her toes were so cold, they'd gone numb. She may not have packed appropriately for winter in the English countryside.

And she realised that her face hurt. *Surely, that's not normal?* People can't go about their everyday lives with their faces hurting every time they step outside.

"Chloe?" she heard behind her.

She spun on her heels, so relieved to see the friendly face of her friend's dad that she uncharacteristically blurted, "You're here," before throwing herself into the poor man's arms.

He patted her stiffly on the back and cleared his throat. "Right then, shall we go?" Chloe stepped back and nodded like a four-year-old who'd been asked if she wanted a pony ride. "Shall I get your case for you?" He indicated her bag and before waiting for an answer, took the handle and with a smile that drew his lips taut across his face, said, "This way."

Chloe followed, more excited to get into a car than she could ever remember being.

*

"Here you are, love," said Mrs Browning as she opened the door to a tiny upstairs bedroom. "This was our Lucy's room before she moved away." She needn't have added the last part, because the room had Lucy stamped all over it.

The single bed, which was pushed against the wall, had a bright pink doona cover and about a thousand throw pillows in various shades of pink—Lucy's signature colour until Chloe and Jules had finally talked her out of it, at age twenty. Not in time, it seemed, to talk her out of pink curtains, a fluffy pink rug, and a hot-pink light fitting.

On the wall opposite the bed was a massive array of framed photographs of Lucy, ranging from infancy to early adulthood. Chloe scanned her eyes over the many faces of Lucy, seeing the dramatic transformation she'd had in her early teens.

She also spotted several photos of her, Jules, and Lucy from some of their May Ladies holidays—Venice, New York, Vietnam, and Santorini. Mrs Browning must have put those up, because they'd all been taken after Lucy moved to London.

The tall white dressing table was covered in trinkets and catchalls, as though a teenaged Lucy was about to walk through the door and scrounge for a hair tie or some pale-pink nail polish. The room was rounded out with a bedside table, a small desk and a wooden chair—also white—and on the shelves above the desk was an impressive collection of *Sweet Valley High* novels. *Oh, Luce, you total dag.*

"I've cleared out the bottom two drawers of the dressing table for you," said Mrs Browning.

"Oh, thank you. It's lovely." *Like Barbara Cartland had decorated it for her granddaughter.*

Mrs Browning beamed at her and Chloe found herself smiling back. She realised that she hadn't remembered the Brownings very well. The last time she'd seen them, she was deeply ensconced in her new friendship with the other two MLs and adults were "boring". Yet, there they were, opening their home to a virtual stranger—at *Christmas*.

She felt a surge of affection for them both.

There was also a tiny but loud part of her that was dying to give Mrs Browning a makeover. Chloe couldn't remember exactly how old she was—she rarely noted such details about other people's parents, even those of her closest friends—but the kind, broad face of the woman now fussing with the throw pillows couldn't have been any older than sixty. Yet she dressed like she had one foot in the grave.

"Now," said Mrs Browning, turning back to Chloe. "I expect you will want a bath, a hot meal, and bed, in that order. Have I got that right?"

Chloe glanced at the clock on the bedside table. 6:03pm. It didn't matter what time it was in Melbourne. She needed to acclimate as soon as possible to UK time, so Mrs Browning's suggestions seemed perfect. Except the bit about the bath.

"That sounds divine, thank you. But ..." A pair of eyebrows shot up to a hairline inquisitively. "Can I just have a shower instead?"

"Oh, of course, love."

The weight of the journey hit her with full force and all Chloe wanted was that shower. "We have a handheld nozzle for that business." *A handheld what?* "We tend to take baths here, but last time she visited, Max bought the nozzle for Lucy."

"Er, right."

Chloe got undressed in the frigid bathroom and stepped tentatively into the massive bathtub, her flesh covered in tiny bumps. After fiddling with the taps and waiting for what felt like *forever*, she discovered that tepid was as warm as the water got and that the handheld nozzle put out little more than a trickle. She rinsed as quickly as she could, bracing herself against the cold water and even colder air, then got out and wrapped the towel tightly around her, attempting to get warm.

"Maybe I'll just use a wet washcloth 'til I go home," she muttered to herself as she dried off. The thought made her giggle. What on earth had she signed up for? Maybe this was part of the traditional English Christmas.

Dinner was a plate piled high with sausages, mashed potatoes, and peas—all of which, Mrs Browning mentioned, came from a local farm. Chloe cleaned her plate and enjoyed every mouthful—the fresh bursts of the peas, the creamy, buttery potatoes that were an indulgence she would never allow herself back home, and the spiciness of the pork sausages.

Regardless of whether it was Mrs Browning's cooking or the farm-fresh produce that made everything so delicious, Chloe was going to have to watch herself. If she ate like this the entire time, she'd go up a dress size.

Seated in the front room, as the Brownings called it, Chloe sipped a tiny glass of after-dinner sherry while admiring the traditional charm of their Christmas decorations. They'd strung a piece of red wool from one end of the longest wall to the other, with Christmas cards of all sizes and colours hanging from their spines. Placed along the mantle above the fireplace was a faux fir-tree garland and six small brass candlesticks, each holding a red candle. None were lit. Perhaps that only happened on Christmas.

There were four stockings hanging from the mantle, three of them much-loved and one new one with her name embroidered across it in gold thread. Chloe was surprised to feel the sting of tears in her eyes. Would her parents have done the same for Lucy? They would have, she decided—not stockings, because her family didn't do those—but had they not been cruising around the South Pacific, she was sure they'd be spoiling Lucy, or Jules, or whomever she'd swapped Christmases with.

Actually, if her parents weren't on a cruise, she wouldn't be here.

The Christmas tree was only as tall as she was, but it was real, and the heady scent of pine filled the room. Chloe stood to admire it, taking her sherry with her. She was not particularly into sherry—it was far too sweet for her—but apparently it was Mrs Browning's after-dinner ritual. *When in a tiny village in Oxfordshire, right?*

"Oh, Mr and Mrs Browning, your collection of ornaments is beautiful." Amongst the dense assortment of nutcrackers and angels, all very traditional in design and colour, were the handmade ornaments of a child. Chloe carefully held the bottom of an angel made from cardboard and painted gold.

She sensed Mrs Browning next to her. "Oh, thank you, love. You see that we've kept all our Lucy's ornaments from school days. And many of the others are from her travels with you girls. She's always finding the loveliest things. I think this one is my favourite." She pointed to a Murano glass angel that Chloe recognised immediately, as she'd been there when Lucy had bought it.

"Beautiful," said Chloe softly. She hoped they would like the ornaments she'd brought them from Australia. Nestled back in her chair, she went to take a sip of her sherry only to find the glass empty. "Oh." She looked at it in shock, a little embarrassed that she'd drunk it all already.

"Oh, never mind about that, love. Happens to me all the time." Mrs Browning laughed and got up to refill Chloe's glass. "They're tiny glasses, aren't they? Quite silly really." She threw in a wink and Chloe grinned up at her.

"Thank you, Mrs Browning."

"Love, you really must stop calling us 'Mr' and 'Mrs'. Please, it's Max and Susan."

"Right, Max and Susan." For some reason, it didn't seem right to her to call them by their first names, which was ridiculous, because she called the CEO of the company she worked for by *her* first name and she was even older than Mr and Mrs—than *Max* and *Susan*.

"So, Lucy says that you're a party planner?" Susan asked.

"Uh, an event manager, yes."

"Oh, that sounds like an interesting job. What sort of parties are they?" asked Max.

"Well, they're not really *parties* as such, more like corporate events. You know? Like, when a company is launching a product and they throw an event with giveaways and drinks and music. Like that."

"Like a party." Chloe was certain that Max wasn't being obstreperous on purpose and when she thought about how she'd explained her job, she realised he was right. She was, of sorts, a party planner.

She smiled, "Actually, yes, you're absolutely right. I plan parties for companies *and* do all the PR," she added.

"And is it fun?" asked Susan.

"Sometimes, sure, but it's also hard work. There are a lot of moving parts, and just one thing going wrong can affect the whole event. Mostly, I love it, even if it does get a little 'samey' sometimes. I mean, it's project-based, which is good, and I get to do two of my favourite things—organising and communicating—but I can see myself doing something else in the future, maybe in a related field. I've never been like

Lucy, happy working for the same company for years and years.

"Mmm, well, I'm not sure how happy Lucy is of late. At her work, I mean. She's been having a hard time with her new manager."

This was news to Chloe. "I didn't know that."

"Susan." Max threw his wife a look. From where Chloe sat, it said, "Let's not bring that up now, not while we have company." Chloe watched them both closely as Susan's lips pressed together. There was clearly more to the story, and Chloe planned to ask Lucy about it the next time they talked.

The tension in the room was interrupted by the phone ringing—a proper, sitting on the table, landline phone.

Susan leapt up and answered in the middle of the third ring. "Hello? Oh, Cecily, hello, dear." Chloe noticed how her tone of voice flattened a little as soon as she discovered the caller's identity. "She what? Oh, *no*, the poor thing. That's terrible. No, quite right, she's got to do as doctor says. There's no two ways about it. No, dear, she can't help. She's in America. Yes, for Christmas. Well, no, she's been planning it for months now, with her friends, you see. They've all swapped Christmases. We've got one of her best friends, Chloe, staying ... Hang on a moment, Cecily. I've just had a thought."

Chloe had been listening intently, wondering what had happened to whom. She didn't have to wonder for long, however, because Susan put a hand over the handset and addressed her in a loud whisper.

"Chloe, it's Cecily on the phone," she said, as though Chloe should know who the heck Cecily was. Her face must have betrayed her, because Susan went on to explain, "She's the Co-chair of the committee for the Christmas Fair with Deirdre, and apparently Deirdre's gone and turned her ankle stepping into a rabbit hole while she was out walking her dog." This was a lot of seemingly unnecessary detail and Chloe wished she would get to the point.

"In any case, Deirdre can't run the fair with Cecily anymore. Strict doctor's orders for bed rest, I'm afraid. So, you see what I'm getting at, don't you?"

Chloe stared at her blankly, her mind fuzzy from hearty food, jet lag, exhaustion and, well yes, the sherry.

"Chloe love, would you step in and help run the village Christmas Fair?"

Chapter 8

Lucy

Lucy had never been anywhere as beautiful as Breckenridge. Her mind flew to Oxford, Cambridge, even Stratford-upon-Avon—all picturesque and perhaps all the more beautiful for their rich histories. She thought of Paris—*stunning* Paris, which she had been fortunate enough to see under a fresh fall of snow.

She thought of her home hamlet of Penham, which was quaint and charming, especially when fondant-like snow iced the brown thatched roofs, evoking her mum's much-loved Christmas cake.

But none of those places were anything like this.

Shopfronts like gingerbread houses were trimmed neatly in coloured lights, their windows spilling warm light onto the footpath in cone-shaped beams. The streetlamps wore bright red velvet bows, and were wrapped like candy canes in green garlands, as if they were on their way to a posh party.

And there were thousands—maybe millions—of pinpoints of white light. Every tree was brimming with them, aglow like the flames of giant birthday cake candles. Couples, families, friends—all wrapped in brightly-coloured quilted coats and donning pompom hats and broad grins—wove in and out along the footpaths. Some parents pulled delighted children along on sledges.

As the traffic streamed slowly through the heart of the town, Lucy emitted exclamations in a constant stream of awe.

Then they passed what she assumed was the town square. "Oh, look at that Christmas tree!" It came out as a near-whisper. The enormous tree was so densely adorned, it looked like it was *made* from light. More people milled about the square, the crowd seeming to be in high spirits as many sipped from takeaway cups. She even saw a couple of people dressed up as Father Christmas.

She looked across at Will and saw that he was watching her. "Pretty incredible, huh?" he asked. She realised she had tears in her eyes and blinked them back. "Yeah, it can have that effect on you, for sure," he added. They shared a smile and her gaze returned to the town. Lucy could have stayed in that car forever, watching out the window.

And being with Will.

She indulged the thought, trying it on for size.

It wasn't just that he was handsome—*very* handsome—he was clever and accomplished, and he was unbelievably easy to talk to. She'd never known a man like that; she had even told him about her problems with Angela, her manager.

And in the quiet moments over the past few hours—none of them awkward, she realised—her fantasy of the fireside lovemaking had really taken shape. Had she been asked, she could have described it in as much detail as a love scene from a romance novel. In fact, she could probably *pen* a romance novel now. *The Awakening of Lucy Browning.*

The car felt very warm all of a sudden and she tugged at the prickly neck of her jumper as they started to move again.

"Not long now," Will said. Lucy hoped that in the dim light of the car, he couldn't see how flushed she was. "The cabin's just a couple of miles out of town. Once we get to the outskirts, the traffic should free up. We may actually be able to do more than *twenty*!"

She expelled a breathy laugh at the irony of being so close to their destination but wanting to stay in the car longer.

*

"You're here!" Jules's mum burst out of the cabin and jogged down to the car just as Lucy climbed out. Even in the dim light coming from the cabin windows, Lucy could see right away that she and Jules could have easily passed for sisters, rather than mother and daughter.

Steph—she'd always been "Steph" to Lucy, right from when Lucy met her aged eleven—hugged her tightly and Lucy felt wrapped up in the welcome. Steph stepped back and looked at her. "It's so good to have you here. Jules loves you just like a sister and that means you're family to us too."

The tears from earlier made another appearance. Lucy knew her parents loved her—of course they did—but she had never received such an effusive welcome from her mum. She beamed back at Steph and finally found her voice. "Thank you. I'm very happy to be here. And Breckenridge is just ..." She had no adequate words.

"I know. I feel the same way, even after all these years." Steph squeezed her shoulders.

"Hi, Mom." They turned at Will's voice and Lucy saw that he was laden with her case and his, with the strap of her carry-on over one shoulder.

"Oh, I can—" she started, reaching for the handle of her case.

"It's all good. I got it."

"Hi, honey." Steph reached up to kiss her son on the cheek. "I'm glad you got here safely," she added, then turned towards the cabin. "Come on! It's freezing out here and your dad's made hot chocolate," she called as she jogged up the steps.

"After you," said Lucy, "as you're the one carrying every-thing." He lifted the cases easily up the front steps and Lucy followed him inside, taking in the enormity of the home as she went. To call it a "cabin" was a gross understatement; it was a mansion by any measure of the word.

Standing in the double-storey foyer, Lucy couldn't help but compare the grandeur of the Reinhardt's holiday home to her family's three-up-two-down terraced house with its postcard-sized back garden and a front door that opened practically onto the road.

She hoped Chloe wasn't too disappointed.

Steph called forth her husbands. "Joe! Nate! They're here." The men appeared from different doorways and Lucy recog-nised Nate right away. Without hesitating, he enveloped her in a huge hug, lifting her off the ground.

"Welcome, sweetheart." Lucy knew how much Jules loved her dad's hugs and thought of her friend who was on the other side of the world.

"Thank you," Lucy replied, her voice muffled against Nate's shoulder.

"And this is my husband, Joe," said Steph as Nate put her down.

The contrast between Steph's two husbands was glaring. Nate—six-foot-one, burly with a broad open face, his blond hair tinged with grey—and Joe—only just taller than Steph, with a wiry build, black hair, and olive skin. While both were handsome in their own ways, Steph couldn't have chosen two more distinct men—physically, at least.

Lucy stuck out her hand and Joe shook it warmly. "Welcome, Lucy. I've heard wonderful things about you."

"You too," she lied politely. She'd heard bits and pieces, and she knew that Jules got along with her stepdad, but that was about all.

"You must want to freshen up," Steph offered.

The long flight followed by the long drive had taken its toll, and the thought of getting clean jumped to the forefront of Lucy's mind. "Oh, yes please."

"Will, can you take Lucy up, hon? I've put her in the room next to yours." *What? He'll be sleeping next door?*

"Sure thing." She watched as Will carried her case and his up the stairs as though they weighed nothing, then picked up her carry-on and followed.

"Hot chocolate downstairs when you're ready," Steph called after them.

Hot chocolate sounded divine and so did some thick white toast slathered in butter and Marmite. Lucy was ravenous, and she really wished she'd brought some Marmite with her. She wondered what the Americans would have—peanut butter, she supposed.

"Here you go," said Will, leaving his case on the landing and pulling hers into the second door on the left. She followed him. "Every room has its own bathroom; yours is in there." He pointed to a closed door. "That's the closet." He pointed to an identical door on the opposite side of the room. "This place is sorta set up for short stays, so it's not very big," he added apologetically. Lucy didn't know if he meant the bathroom or the closet, but either way, she didn't care.

This was already a huge step up from her parents' house with its one bathroom and second loo downstairs, and her own much-loved two-bedroom-one-bathroom flat, especially as she currently shared the flat with Val.

"No, this is lovely, really. Thank you. And for carrying my case." She gestured to where Will had left it next to the door.

"Sure. So, why don't you get situated and I'll see you downstairs when you're ready."

"Thank you."

"Oh, and Lucy?" Lucy stared up into his handsome face. "Take your time. It's been a long drive."

She found herself nodding as he pulled the door closed behind him.

She looked around the room. It was bigger than any bedroom she'd ever had and was dominated by a king-sized bed replete with fluffy duvet and six (!) pillows. The dressing tables and bedside tables—two of each—were made of varnished pine and seemed brand new. She opened the door to the bathroom to discover a set of fluffy towels in forest green and a selection of toiletries that would make any grown woman cry. Crabtree and Evelyn? This was like staying at a resort!

There wasn't a bath, but as well as a huge mirror, a modern basin and toilet, there was a rainwater shower. It called to her in a way that no shower ever had before. "Take your time," Will had said.

She stripped off and turned on the taps.

Only twenty minutes later—she skipped some of her usual ablution steps—she was dressed in a pair of casual trousers and a cashmere jumper, as well as her trusty Ugg boots, a present Chloe had sent for Christmas a few years ago. She pulled up her long, curly hair into a messy bun and didn't bother with makeup, not wanting to keep Jules's family waiting too long. Downstairs, she followed the sound of voices to the front room.

When she entered, the first thing she noticed was that Will wasn't there. The second was the fireplace. She'd only seen one like that in films. It was nearly as tall as her, with stones across the hearth and up the wall either side, and a thick, rustic mantle made from a single cut of pine.

On the mantle were a dozen or so framed family photos and her eyes went straight to one of Will as a boy, not much older than when she'd first met him at age seven.

He'd been so sweet then, if a little rambunctious—all big blue eyes, white-blond hair, and a giant gap-toothed grin—an energetic cherub. Lucy had always wanted a baby brother, so she'd been keen to let him play with them, but Jules hadn't wanted him tagging along. She had shooed him off, one time making him cry, Lucy remembered.

Now he was a grown man—a *handsome* one. *Stop it,* she rebuked. *His mum is right there!*

Steph and Joe were sitting on one of the two leather sofas, her feet in his lap. "Feel better?" asked Steph.

She grinned. "So much better. That shower is amazing."

Steph smiled at her. "Will hasn't come down yet, but Nate's in the kitchen, just through there. I'm sure he'd be happy to rustle you up something to eat. You must be starving."

"Actually, I was just thinking how much I could murder a slice of toast." Bemusement flickered across Steph's face before she replied.

"Right, and we've got wine open, too, if you'd like?" Steph indicated to the open bottle on the low glass coffee table.

"Oh, no thanks. Ever since you mentioned the hot chocolate ..."

"Oh, Nate's famous for it."

Lucy smiled shyly and left for the kitchen.

"Hi, sweetheart. Feel good to freshen up?" Nate's warm smile made Lucy feel right at ease as she climbed onto one of the stools at the breakfast bar.

"Brilliant actually. The flight was all right—I mean, it's only nine hours—but the drive was a little, uh ..."

"Unexpected?"

She laughed. "Well, yes, that, but at least on an airplane, you can get up and walk about *and* use the loo. That's an experience I will never forget."

Nate's eyebrows rose in question just as Will made his appearance.

"You telling Dad about our *adventure*?"

"Do I want to know?" asked Nate.

"For sure," said Will.

"No!" said Lucy at the same time. Will shot her an amused look.

"Maybe another time, *Will*," Lucy countered. His cheeky grin was annoying, but she also found it charming, which made her annoyed with herself.

"So!" Nate clapped his hands like dads do when they want to change the subject, "you two must be starving."

"Well, apparently, someone's famous for their hot chocolate."

"Oh, he's famous for it all right. What Mom didn't mention is that it's full of rum."

Lucy's eyes widened.

"Are you game?" Will teased.

The worst that could happen was it would make her sleepy, and considering it was sometime near morning in the UK, feeling sleepy was probably a good thing. Otherwise, she'd be up all night in a post-flight, wide-awake-but-completely-shattered state. And in the absence of mulled wine, spiked hot chocolate sounded divine.

"I'm definitely game."

Nate retrieved two mugs from a tall cupboard and went to the stove where a copper saucepan was steaming. He turned off the heat and ladled the hot chocolate into the mugs. Then he topped each one with a sprinkling of cocoa powder.

Turning to her and Will, he carefully placed a brimming mug in front of each of them.

Lucy took a tiny sip, her eyes lighting up. "That's delicious." Nate beamed. She took a bigger sip. "That is going down a treat," she said before she took another.

"I mean *full* of rum," teased Will. "And, believe me, the heat only burns off *some* of the alcohol." He took a decent slug of his and Lucy could see his smiling eyes above the rim.

"Would you like anything to eat?" asked Nate.

"You're spoiling me, you know."

"Dad doesn't mind. He spends half his time in the kitchen when we're here."

"It's true." She watched as Nate looked about the kitchen lovingly. "She's my baby; I designed her." Lucy retrieved the fact that Nate was an architect from her memory.

"Did you design this house?"

"Guilty."

"It's ..." She struggled to find the right word and settled on, "beautiful."

Nate dipped his head, a bittersweet smile on his face. Lucy didn't want to dwell on why there was sadness in the smile.

"Well, if you're offering, I'd love some toast."

Nate clutched at his chest as though she'd wounded him. "Toast." It came out as a ragged whisper and Lucy giggled. "How about an omelette instead?" he suggested.

"I don't want to be a bother."

He waved off her weak protestation and started assembling his omelette making tools on the counter. "Two, Dad," said Will.

"Two omelettes coming right up."

Lucy watched Nate in quiet awe, enjoying the sense of family togetherness *and* the hot chocolate. As two omelettes cooked in side-by-side frying pans, Nate topped her up with a wink. Will held his mug out too and when it was full again, offered it to Lucy in a toast.

"Here's to peeing in the snow."

Lucy let out an exasperated sigh. Nate laughed, his back to them, then took both pans off the hob and slid each omelette onto its plate in perfect sync—a little breakfast-for-dinner theatrics.

He chatted with them while they ate, doing most of the talking while Lucy and Will replied with nods and "Mmm-hmms". When he was finished, Will leant back. "Great omelette, Dad, thanks."

"My pleasure."

Will raised his arms above his head and stretched his neck from side to side, his T-shirt lifting to show a strip of bare stomach—bare, *muscular* stomach. Lucy gulped down her bite and took a sip of her hot chocolate.

When she glanced at Nate, it was clear that he'd seen the little episode. If she'd been embarrassed by Will sharing the outdoor weeing episode—and she was—this was several notches higher on the mortification scale.

Stop perving on Jules's brother, Lucy—especially in front of their dad!

Chapter 9

Chloe

Chloe woke with a head that felt like it was stuffed with cotton wool. She wasn't sure what to blame, the sherry or the jet lag, but as she lay there looking up at Lucy's garish light fitting, she knew one thing for certain. She was now Acting Co-chair of the town's Christmas Fair and it was only two days away.

Why on earth had she said yes?

She threw an arm over her bleary eyes, blocking out the weak light seeping through the curtains, and indulged a long groan. Then she peeked at the clock on the bedside table. She had precisely thirty-five minutes to get up, get dressed, and head to the planning meeting. Good thing it was being held across the road.

Chloe prided herself on being good with names, but as Susan went around the circle and introduced everyone on the committee, she struggled to remember all of them.

"And this is Cecily," said Susan, pointing to a stout woman with a particularly sour expression. She'd remember Cecily, though, with that "cat's bum" face. Chloe nodded in greeting and Cecily's lips pursed even tighter. Then, along with the other five committee members—Susan included—she stared expectantly at Chloe.

She was only supposed to be *Co*-chair, right? *With* Cecily? She scanned the group—five women and one man. She'd expected a grateful reception and to be looped in on the plans to date, but no, the stares continued. She wasn't even sure if Susan was actually *on* the committee, or if she was just there to spectate.

Tough crowd, but Lucy had handled far worse than this.

She straightened to her full one hundred and fifty-two centimetres and pulled her shoulders back, adopting the power stance that always gave her a little boost of confidence when she needed it. She donned a bright smile. "Good morning." It wasn't. "I am very pleased to be here." She wasn't. "I am sure that you hardly need me at all, but I am happy to be of any assistance I can to make sure your Christmas Fair goes off without a hitch." Another lie—she wasn't happy about any of this.

Five stony faces didn't flinch, and she glanced at Susan, who was watching her with an encouraging smile. "Right, so how about we go around the circle again, and you can tell me what each of you is responsible for."

"We usually start with tea and biscuits," said the man—Simon, Chloe remembered.

"Oh, right." She looked around the group, wondering who was in charge of making tea.

"Cecily, aren't you going to put the kettle on, dear?" Susan prompted. Cecily seemed to remember herself, tearing her scrutinising eyes from Chloe and standing.

"Yes, of course. My apologies everyone." She disappeared through a doorway, presumably to the kitchen. Right, so they were in Cecily's home.

Chloe knew she had to crack the toughest nut and get Cecily onside, so she followed her into the kitchen, hearing a cacophony of loud whispers erupt behind her. Cecily was fussing about with a tea tray and the kettle was already on to boil.

"Cecily, I meant to say before what a beautiful home you have. I was admiring your thatched roof as we crossed the road." Flattery, flattery, flattery—in her experience, the three best ways to earn someone's trust quickly.

Cecily started and looked at Chloe, her lips parted in surprise. "Oh. Why, thank you." Chloe could tell that it was difficult for Cecily to take a compliment.

"What year was it built?" Chloe took in the low ceiling with its exposed beams of dark wood, which contrasted with the whitewashed, uneven plaster. It really was a beautiful building; she hadn't been lying about that.

Cecily started placing biscuits from a tin onto a large floral plate. "Well, the original structure dates back to the sixteenth century." Chloe's eyes widened. She was standing in a building that pre-dated European settlement in Australia. It was one of the things she adored about visiting England.

"Actually, and you can see this better from the outside, this was once four separate structures—stables for the estate—and at some point, in the 1800s, it was converted into houses—four of them. It was only last century, before the war, that it became one house. That's when my grandparents bought it."

Wow, once you got Cecily onto something she wanted to talk about, she opened right up. Still, she'd yet to crack a smile. "Well, it certainly is impressive, and it has a fascinating history." Cecily nodded, her mouth remaining in a taut line. "Can I help?" Chloe asked as the kettle boiled and switched itself off.

"Oh, well, yes, I suppose. You could take these out to the sitting room." She indicated the plate of biscuits and a stack of matching smaller plates. "Oh, and take the napkins too, dear," she added. She'd got a "dear" out of Cecily. Progress.

Cecily continued to flit about her kitchen with skilful efficiency, and Chloe did as she was told. Thankfully, being the bearer of biscuits seemed to win her some much-needed brownie points.

She served the committee members in turn, and as they helped themselves to one or two biscuits, each rewarded her with a smile—except Simon, but Chloe was doubtful he'd ever smiled in his entire life. As he took a handful of biscuits, which Chloe thought was extremely rude, he gave her a bit of a grunt. Perhaps it was his way of saying "thank you".

Just then, there was a loud knock at the door. "Get that will you, Chloe," Cecily called from the kitchen. So far, co-chairing the Christmas Fair was a lot like being a dogsbody for a bunch of pensioners.

Chloe, still holding the plate of biscuits, took herself off to the front door and opened it. In five hundred million years she would never ever, *ever*, have guessed who would be standing on the front step, duffel bag over one shoulder and looking even more handsome than he did on the big screen.

She nearly dropped the plate.

"Hello," said the world's biggest film star as he wiped raindrops from his shoulders.

"Hello," she said, unwittingly blocking the doorway.

"Do you mind if I come in?"

She shook her head, dumbly, then realised she was in the way. "Oh, sorry." *What is happening?*

"Thanks," he shuffled past her and raised a hand at the room of people. "Hello everyone, is my mum home?"

"In the kitchen, darling!" Cecily sang out.

Holy frigging hell. Cecily was Archer Tate's mother.

Once Chloe recovered from the shock of opening the door to the world's biggest film star, the Christmas Fair meeting had gone quite well. After warm greetings from everyone, including Simon, and a kiss from his mother, Archer had left them to it, settling into the guest room while Chloe asked everyone to explain their roles and update the group on their progress.

It turned out that all Chloe would have to do was help Cecily manage the logistics on the day, so that everything from deliveries to set-up to packing up went smoothly.

The committee members departed, including Susan, all with promises to complete last-minute checks and to call if there were any problems, and Chloe had stayed to help Cecily clean up. At least, that's what she'd told Cecily, who was putting the furniture back into its proper places while Chloe was up to her elbows in sudsy water.

Chloe eyed the dishwasher with annoyance as she washed another teacup. Why had she been tasked with handwashing everything if there was a dishwasher? And when was Archer going to come and talk to her? As far as she could tell, she was the only person in the entire village who was even close to his age. Maybe they'd hook up. That would certainly make it a Christmas to remember.

"Hello again." The voice startled her, pulling from her daydream of hooking up with Archer Tate the film star, right back into his mother's kitchen where he was standing beside her, a huge grin on his face.

In a millisecond, she took in the high cheekbones, chiselled jawline, cleft chin, full lips stretched tautly over perfectly straight teeth, and the strong dark brows and thick lashes that framed two of the most famous blue eyes on the planet.

"Hello," she said, wishing she'd opted out of the orange and yellow floral rubber gloves.

"Chloe, right?"

"Yep." *Play it cool, as if you meet super-famous people every day.* She *had* met famous people before. Well, people who were famous in *Australia*. Hardly the same thing. Although, she'd met Hugh Jackman once. He'd been just as lovely as everyone said he was.

"I'm Archer."

She stopped herself from saying, "I know," and instead replied with a casual, "Nice to meet you, Archer. I'd shake your hand but ..." She held up her sheathed hands, then went back to the dishes. He picked up a tea towel and started drying. It was one of the sexiest things she'd ever seen.

"So, I'm a little fuzzy on why a gorgeous Australian woman is in my mum's kitchen doing the washing up." *Gorgeous.* He'd called her "gorgeous". Point one for the "hooking up" daydream.

"Oh, it's just this thing I like to do. Travel to a different country, go village to village, then door to door, and offer to wash people's dishes. It's becoming a bit of a craze, actually. You may have heard of it? Hashtag dirty-dish-tourism?" She handed him the next clean cup.

"Oh, right! Yes, I think I saw that trending on Instagram not so long ago. I wasn't quite sure what it was all about, and here I am meeting one of you in the flesh."

She giggled and looked up at him. God, he was tall. He must have been well over six-foot. She'd need to stand on a stool if she ever got the chance to kiss him. *Please let me kiss him*, she thought. He smelled good too. Spicy, like Christmas. When he smiled down at her, the surrealness of the moment was overwhelming. She looked back at the soapy sink.

"Really, though, I've been roped into helping out with the Christmas Fair. Someone named Deirdre stepped in a rabbit hole and turned her ankle, so now I'm in charge. Well, *co*-in charge, anyway—with your mum."

"Lucky you." He took the next cup and dried it with the tea towel. *Yummy forearms*, she thought. She was a sucker for those.

"Well, to be fair, no pun intended," she said, "there's not much to do until tomorrow. Everyone seems to have their bits in hand. Oh—"

"Bits in hand?" Yep. He'd heard it and his mind had gone exactly where hers had—a shared adolescent response to her

79

gaff. Her hand flew to her mouth as a reflex *just* as she started to laugh, filling her mouth with soap bubbles, which she *then* tried to wipe out of her mouth with the same sudsy glove, making it all worse.

By this stage, she was in a fit of giggles, spluttering out soap bubbles and helplessly flailing her arms about. "Hold still." He was laughing too as he captured her chin with his hand and wiped her face with the tea towel. "Tongue," he commanded. It was the only time she'd been told to stick out her tongue outside of a doctor's office and she obeyed through the laughter. He wiped off her tongue and they both dissolved into a fit of laughter so intense, neither of them was making any noise.

That was when Cecily made her appearance.

"What on earth has got into you two?" Chloe glanced up at Cecily through her fringe from her doubled-over position. She and Archer straightened in unison, their laughter instantly subsiding. Maybe Archer was slightly afraid of Cecily too.

Cecily tutted and shooed them away from the sink. "Thank you for your help, Chloe. I'll finish up." Chloe was being dismissed, but she didn't want to leave. This was the most fun she'd had in ages. And besides, *Archer Frigging Tate!* Just wait 'til she spoke to Lucy, who for *some* reason, the entire time she'd known her, had never once mentioned that she lived across the street from Archer Tate.

"Oh, sure, no problem." Chloe removed the still-sudsy rubber gloves and placed them on the kitchen counter.

"You sure, Mum? We don't mind helping out."

Chloe was beyond surprised at what Cecily said next. "I'm

fine with it, love. Why don't you take Chloe on a walk around the village? She only arrived yesterday, and I'm sure she'd love to see more of it than the inside of this house."

Was Cecily playing matchmaker?

Archer met Chloe's eyes. "How does that sound?" he asked.

Hmm, let me have a think? What to do, what to do? What human being on the planet would say no?

"Sure, that sounds great," Chloe replied, casually. *No biggie—just going to mosey about the village with Archer Tate.*

"Archer, I've that large umbrella in my wardrobe. You can take that," Cecily said to him.

"Oh, right, perfect. Thanks, Mum."

He disappeared, leaving Chloe alone with his mother. "You know," said Cecily as she pulled the plug from the sink. "Archer just broke up with that horrid girl ..."

Horrid girl? Oh, she means the aptly named Madison Strumpet. Chloe had seen the headlines splashed all over *Women's Monthly*—a terrible name for a women's magazine, she thought. "Oh?" *Play it cool, play it cool.*

Cecily turned to face her, wiping her hands on a fresh tea towel. "That Madison. She never deserved him, and she broke his heart running off with that *actor*." She said the word "actor" as though it was akin to "devil", clearly ignoring that her son was one too. "In any case, he's single now—still nursing a bruised heart, but single. Just so you know."

Chloe nodded. "Uh-huh."

Yep, she'd definitely won over Cecily.

Chapter 10

Jules

"Hey," Matt said, bursting back through the door from the stairwell, "thanks for keeping an eye on the wine." He lifted the box from the floor and added, "I'm guessing you're okay with your other bag?" Something clicked in Jules's mind.

"Other" bag ... as in *one* bag?

The horror of her mistake hit her like a punch in the gut. "Oh, shit," she said breathlessly.

Concern crossed Matt's face. "Are you okay?"

Her hand flew to her mouth as her eyes locked onto his. "Oh, shit, shit, shit, shit, shit," she half-whispered, half-whined.

"Jules?"

"I left my carry-on ..." She could barely get the words out.

"You left it somewhere?"

She nodded, mouth agape. "On the bus. From the airport." Tears welled up, stinging her eyes.

"Okay, hey, it'll be okay. Let's get you upstairs and we'll call them, okay?"

She felt a tear escape down her cheek, and she brushed it away like she was swatting a mosquito. Crying wasn't going to solve anything. "I'm so stupid," she spat out. How could she have forgotten her carry-on?

"Hey, don't say that. We've all done stuff like this, okay? Come on, just follow me. We'll sort it out."

Jules was unconvinced. There was no way in hell that someone didn't take off with her bag, the bag with all the presents she'd brought for Chloe's friends, the bag with her—

Oh, SHIT!

With her passport.

There was never a good time to call a call centre, but this was possibly the worst—calling an airport shuttle bus company three days before Christmas. Jules had been in the queue on speakerphone for forty-two minutes. At this rate, she wouldn't have any nails left.

Ash and Matt had been great, though, reassuring her. They'd each left something important somewhere. Ash had left her work laptop at Friday night drinks, only realising the next Monday morning. She got it back. And Matt had left his phone in the back of a cab. He got it back.

Perhaps there *was* hope. Jules hoped there was hope, because how was she supposed to fly back to the States next week without a passport?

"Hello, thank you for calling Sky Bus. This is Alicia. How can I help you?" Jules's eyes flew to the phone. All the tension of the past hour threatened to overwhelm her, and she took a deep breath before she spoke, so she didn't lose it.

She explained what had happened and gave a detailed

description of the carry-on, as well as her best recollection of what time she'd boarded the bus. She was put on hold. Her stomach churned again, and this time it had nothing to do with jet lag or being overtired or the good-looking guy who stood watching her, his chocolate brown eyes intensely focused on her.

"Are you there?" said Alicia.

"Yes, I'm here."

"We're pretty sure we've got your bag." Relief coursed through Jules and she blew out a long breath.

"Brilliant! I told ya," Ash shouted from the kitchen. Matt patted her shoulder and Jules staved off the hysterical laughter bubbling up in her throat.

"That's great. Thank you, Alicia. Where do I go to collect it?'

"You came into the Southern Cross station, yeah?" Jules looked at Ash for confirmation and she nodded.

"Yes, that's right."

"So, there's a little office there. They'll have your bag. Just bring two pieces of photo ID and you're good."

Matt leant over and whispered, "I'll take you."

She whispered, "Thanks," and wrapped up the call. She sat back in the dining chair and let out a sigh.

"Come on. I'll drive you over."

"Are you sure? I can just walk over. It's not that far." It *was* that far, and she was wrung out, but she didn't want to be a nuisance.

"Nah, I'll take you. It's all good."

A niggling thought leapt to the forefront of Jules's mind.

"Hold on, she said I needed to bring two pieces of photo ID, right? I've got my Colorado driver's licence, but my passport is in my carry-on." She looked between Ash and Matt.

Ash waved her off. "I'm sure it will be fine." Ash seemed far more optimistic than *she* was.

"Yeah, that's just common sense, right?" added Matt.

Jules nodded, not wholly convinced.

"Did you want to shower first, though?" asked Ash.

Jules looked down at her wrinkled tank and her dull, grey, post-flight skin. She must have looked terrible—she *felt* terrible.

"You look fine," added Ash. "I just know that whenever I travel, the first thing I want to do when I arrive is shower."

Jules would have killed to stay in the apartment and shower—and *rest*—but she also knew she wouldn't be able to rest properly until she had her carry-on safely in hand.

"Let's go," she sighed.

"Back in a bit," said Matt, leading the way out of the apartment.

It turned out that the errand took a quite a lot longer than "a bit".

*

Several hours later, Jules was back at the apartment, showered and fed—four pieces of toast with peanut butter—and semi-reclined on Ash and Chloe's couch, trying to keep her eyes open. Her fatigue probably wasn't helped by the wine Ash had insisted on opening. It *was* delicious, though.

"I still can't believe I left my bag on that bus," she moaned. "What an idiot."

"You're being too hard on yourself. You'd just flown long-haul. No one is in their right mind after getting off a plane from across the world. *I* never am."

"Seriously, though, when I realised it was a catch-22, I nearly lost it. They can only open a bag with the permission of the owner, but they couldn't confirm my identity as the owner to their satisfaction without opening the bag." She knew she was labouring the point. She'd given Ash the digest version as soon as Matt had dropped her back at the apartment, but she couldn't help dwelling on the "what if" of losing her passport.

She needed sleep.

"I seriously can't believe they didn't just give it to you. I mean, were there *dozens* of hysterical women calling up about a lost bag with that exact description?"

Jules's eyebrows shot up on the word "hysterical" and she looked pointedly at Ash, a smile tugging at her mouth. Ash caught the look. "Well, not *hysterical* exactly. Um, concerned, upset, *worried*."

"Anyway, common sense *finally* prevailed after the supervisor called *his* supervisor at home, and she gave him permission. The passport was bad enough, but that's the bag with all the presents in it."

"You brought presents?" The smile broke across Jules's face.

"Of course. It's Christmas."

Ash grinned. "I love presents."

"Chloe mentioned that," she teased. "Actually, I should put them under the tree," she added. It was a nice thought, but her body refused to budge. Instead, she glanced at the Christmas tree.

She'd only noticed it after she'd returned with her carry-on. It was beautiful, but it would be Jules's first Christmas with a fake tree. And it wasn't even fake, as in, "I'm pretending to be a fir tree." It was made from silver and white tinsel and decorated with blue ornaments—*only* blue. Even the Christmas lights were blue.

"So, what did you bring for Matt?" Jules couldn't decide if Ash had emphasised "Matt" on purpose. Was she getting at something?

"You'll see," she deflected. "I don't want to spoil the surprise."

"But how did you know?"

"What gifts to get?"

"Yeah."

"Chloe told me who was coming on Christmas Day and I ran some ideas past her and, of course, I know *you*, so ..."

"Seriously, no hints?"

"No!" She laughed. "Chloe said you would ask."

"Oh, really?"

"Uh-huh. She also told me where she hid *her* present to you, so you wouldn't find it before Christmas and peek."

Ash's mouth popped open, hung there for a moment, then snapped shut. She lifted her chin and, saying nothing, topped up their wine glasses.

"Well, it's very nice of you to bring presents for all of us. You didn't need to."

Jules shrugged. "You'd have done the same."

"Matt's a good guy, by the way." It was an extremely unsubtle change of topic—so Ash *had* been hinting at something earlier.

Jules pretended she didn't get it. "He is. He did *not* need to do all that for me today. I mean, at that point when the supervisor said no to me retrieving my *own bag* ... let's just say, I was not my best self. I nearly gave up. But Matt was great—awesome, actually. It was his idea to escalate the whole thing."

Matt was a good guy and an extremely *good-looking* guy. She wondered if he and Chloe had ever ... She let the thought trail off as she sipped her wine.

"He had a rough time a little while back but, you know, he's probably ready ..." Ash left the rest of the thought unsaid.

Regardless of Ash's intentions, Jules wasn't up for contemplating Matt's readiness for a romantic entanglement. "Ash, this wine is great, but I am beyond exhausted. I think I'm going to have to call it a night."

"No worries. You did well. Look, it's nearly eight o'clock."

Jules glanced at the large clock on the wall in the kitchen. "They say it's the best way, right? Staying up as long as you can to get on the right time?"

"Yeah. I always try to do that when I fly back to Melbs from overseas." Jules took her unfinished wine to the kitchen. "I'm glad you like the wine, by the way. We're having it at Christmas. Matt made it."

"He *made* it?"

"Yeah. He didn't tell you he was a winemaker?"

"Nuh-uh."

"Yeah, he's kind of a big deal in the wine world. He won

a 'winemaker of the year' award last year—the first Indigenous person to win it. Anyway, he can tell you about it himself."

Adding "talented" to the growing list of adjectives to describe Matt, Jules sleepily brushed her teeth in Chloe's bathroom, quickly slathered on some night cream and fell into Chloe's bed.

A hot Aussie winemaker, who saved the day ... was her last thought as she drifted off into an exhausted sleep.

*

"This way!" Jules followed Ash closely through the market, amazed at how well Ash manoeuvred through the crowd. "Just the prawns and the ham left to pick up," Ash called over her shoulder. They came to a stop at a deli counter that was three people deep, all of them raising their hands and shouting over the hullabaloo of everyone else shouting.

"This place is for the prawns. I pre-ordered so it shouldn't take too long," shouted Ash. "Then we go over there for the ham." She pointed at a shopfront two counters down.

"Is it always like this?" Jules was comparing the South Melbourne market—it was the size of a city block, packed to the rafters, and all under one roof—to farmers' markets back home, with their relaxed atmosphere, outdoorsiness, and *space*. Of course, none of them were open at this time of year. The thought of all that produce snap-frozen from the cold air made her chuckle to herself.

"What, the market? It's a *little* crazier than usual 'cause of Christmas, but it's always busy. It's 'cause *everything's* high quality here—the meat, the seafood, the fruit and veg." They shuffled forward as more people ahead of them turned away from the counter and pushed through the crowd with half-hearted "excuse mes".

"And this is where you and Chloe normally shop?" Jules was trying to get a picture of what everyday life was like for Chloe and Ash.

"Um, sometimes. We'll make the effort if we're having a dinner party or for special occasions. It's expensive, though, so we usually go to Woolies."

Jules assumed that Woolies was just a regular a grocery store. And hearing Ash say that the market was expensive reminded her—she wanted to pay her fair share for what was going to be a spectacular Christmas feast.

"By the way," she started, just as the couple in front of them moved aside and they took their place at the front of the line. "I want to contribute to all of this."

Ash flicked her a look. "You don't need to do that. It's all good."

The man behind the counter pointed at Ash and she rattled off her pre-order to him. He left the counter to get it.

"I want to. If Chloe were here, she'd be contributing, right?"

"Yeah, but you're a guest."

"Yeah, sorta, but Chloe's one of my best friends—like a sister really—and you're one of her best friends, so by proxy, this is like having Christmas with my extended family. I'd be contributing back home." Ash looked unconvinced. "Please just let me?"

Ash pursed her lips. "Sure, okay, but no money changes

hands. We *are* down a dessert with Chloe gone. She usually makes a pav."

"A pav?" Where did Aussies come up with these words?

"A pav*lova*. Like a meringue." And why did they shorten everything? *Does Chloe always talk in Aussie-isms?* Jules asked herself. Maybe she did and Jules just didn't notice. Ash peered up her expectantly.

"Right. Well, I'm not sure my baking skills extend to making a pavlova, but I am awesome at Christmas cookies. That's one of the ways I earn my keep back home. Actually, my cookies are kind of legendary." She shrugged in mock modesty.

The man behind the counter handed over a large package of prawns wrapped tightly in butcher's paper. "You're talking about proper *American* cookies, right?"

Jules laughed. "Yeah, sure, I guess they're American."

Ash took off her backpack and squeezed in the package of prawns, then zipped it up. "But you mean those shortbready ones with all the fancy icing and stuff? Those, right?"

"Yes, they are fancy, *very* fancy," Jules replied with mock seriousness.

"Well, if you're sure—and *please* be sure because I've always wanted proper American cookies at Christmas—then we'll stop at Woolies on the way home for baking stuff. That can be your contribution. How's that?"

"Sounds good to me."

"And *then*, we're going out for coffee. I am *dying* for a proper coffee." Ash forged ahead to the next counter where they would collect the ham, shoving her way through the dense, but amiable crowd. Jules stayed right on her tail, not wanting to get lost. She had no idea from which direction they'd come in.

Ash continued, "I mean, there are some great places for it *here*. Like that one." She pointed to a tiny hole-in-the-wall— more of a counter than a coffee shop—with a long line of people who all looked like they were Jonesing for their coffee hit. "But look at that frigging line!"

She turned to Jules, "Okay, so we get the ham, we bike over to Woolies, get the baking stuff, then drop all this at home, and grab coffee? Sound good?" Jules could see why Ash and Chloe were such good friends. They were both super organised and, just like Chloe, Ash seemed to enjoy being in charge. Jules wondered if that made them the most formidable team ever, or if sometimes it was "the clash of the titans".

"Sounds good," Jules replied. Ash smiled, just like Chloe did whenever her plan was accepted. Two little planners living together. No wonder the apartment was immaculate. As soon as she got up that morning, Jules had made Chloe's bed, almost as though Chloe was hovering over her, "Tuck that corner in! No, tighter!"

Jules *never* made her bed back home. What was the point? She was just going to mess it up again that night. But she'd seen Chloe make her bed in a five-star hotel. The thought tugged at Jules's heart a little. Gosh, she adored that funny little Aussie.

She hadn't realised how far they'd progressed in the line until Ash declared that they were done. "Let's get the flock outta here," Ash declared, elbowing her way to the exit. *Another weird Australian saying*, Jules thought as she followed obediently.

The outside of the market was almost as chaotic as the inside, but the sun was shining. Jules retrieved her sunglasses from the neck of her tank top and put them on. *It's summer. It's hot. This is heaven.*

Not for the first time, she wondered at the odd luck that had made her a Colorado native. She much preferred this warmer weather and she knew the winters were mild here. *Maybe I was an Australian in a previous life*, she thought, unlocking Chloe's bike from the bike rack. *I wonder what it would be like to actually* live *here*, she mused.

Chapter 11

Lucy

Lucy woke abruptly and for a moment, she couldn't remember where she was. Then the scent of Crabtree and Evelyn's Noel brought her back to Colorado and she stretched luxuriously under the fluffy duvet. The only source of light was the glowing blue of the clock on the bedside table, the numbers reading 5:14am. Could she fall back asleep?

A quick calculation and she realised it was unlikely. It was after noon in London and her body was wide awake. Still, she'd managed seven hours of sleep, which was enough. Time to get up. She flicked on the bedside lamp and, bracing herself for the cold, flung back the duvet. Only, it wasn't cold—it was toasty warm. She smiled.

Even in her London flat, she and her flatmate, Val, wouldn't turn on the heat until they got up. And back home in Penham, her parents tended to treat heat as a luxury—the front room always stiflingly hot and everywhere else in the house, icy. She'd grown up thinking that chilblains were normal.

She wondered if having a shower would wake anyone,

especially with Will sleeping right next door. Will. What in the world was she doing fantasising about Will? The last time she'd seen him, he was a little boy. "Definitely not a little boy anymore," she whispered to herself, stifling a giggle.

Regardless, she didn't want to wake him, especially as he'd had to do that long drive yesterday. She would shower later. She slid her feet into her Uggs and pulled on her fluffy dressing gown.

As she tugged the tie tight around her waist, she decided it would be extremely bad manners to have it off with the young man of the house, *especially* at Christmas. She'd just have to ignore how much she fancied him. But what if he flirted with her?

"Gah!" she chided herself, then went off in search of tea.

Fifteen minutes later, she was no closer to drinking tea and more than a little annoyed. She'd looked in every cupboard and in every drawer. Surely there was a kettle here somewhere? She eyed the obviously expensive coffee machine—a proper one like a barista would use—with derision. Useless thing. She hated coffee.

She'd just have to use the microwave to boil water, which everyone knew was a terrible way to make tea. As a frown settled onto her face, she paused. Was it jet lag? She hoped so, because getting cross over something as simple as tea wasn't like her, and she wasn't enjoying it one bit.

"Good morning." The voice from behind made her start and her hand flew to her chest. "Sorry, honey, I didn't mean to scare you." Steph.

"Oh, you didn't. Well, you did, but it's not your fault. I think I'm just a little disorientated."

"Oh, no problem." Steph waved it off. "Coffee?"

"Actually, I was hoping for some tea."

"Tea. Oh, of course. Hold on. I think Nate said something about that. He's always good with that kind of thing." Lucy watched Steph open several drawers. From one in the corner, a drawer Lucy was sure she had checked, Steph pulled out a shiny new powder-blue kettle. "Ah-hah! See?"

Lucy beamed, instantly forgetting her earlier annoyance. "He bought this for you. So thoughtful, that man." *Then why did you divorce him?* Lucy clapped her hand over her mouth as though she'd said her thought aloud, but Steph didn't appear to notice.

"And I imagine there are teabags ..." Steph talked to herself as she moved boxes about in the drawer. "Black tea, right?" She threw a look over her shoulder and Lucy nodded. No potpourri tea for Lucy. She had no idea how people drank something that tasted like toilet freshener. She didn't even like Earl Grey.

"Success!" Steph held aloft an unopened box of Tazo "Awake" tea, and Lucy felt her body relax. "I'm going to let you make it, though, Lucy. I am way out of my depth here."

Not long after, they were seated on opposite ends of a sofa, each with a mug of something steaming and staring into the fireplace. It was one of those fires that turned on with a switch, which Lucy thought was very practical. Steph had been so welcoming the night before, but Lucy felt a little awkward sitting there in silence and scoured her mind for something to say.

"I think Will wanted to take you up the mountain today."

Lucy spluttered a little and wiped tea from the side of her mouth. "Oh?"

"Uh-huh. You ski right?"

"Oh, uh, no, actually."

"Snowboard?"

"It's neither, I'm afraid."

"Well, then he will *absolutely* want to get his hands on you."

"Sorry, what?" This conversation certainly had her on the back foot. What in the *world*?

"Will. He's a fantastic teacher." *Oh, right.* "Skiing, snowboarding—he basically grew up on the snow. He was only three when we first put him on skis." She laughed. "He was so fast. He took off right down the mountain and Nate had to go after him. From then on, he was hooked! Never wanted to come off the slopes, even when his lips turned blue. I think he's mostly snowboarding now, but he'll teach you how to ski if you prefer."

Lucy's stomach twisted at the thought of either.

"Um, I'm not really very athletic." It was the polite way to say, "No thank you very much, please sod off."

Steph waved off her refusal. "Oh, there's nothing to it. You'll be fine."

"But I didn't bring any gear."

"Jules is about your size, and you're only a little taller than her. She's got a few snow outfits here. We'll get you situated. And you can rent the boots and skis up there. You'll love it."

Lucy was sure she would *not* love it, but found herself saying a weak, "All right."

Steph grinned and drank some more coffee.

*

"I look like a Teletubby," Lucy moaned quietly at herself in the mirror.

There was a knock at her bedroom door and she jerked it open, daring whoever was standing on the other side to say *one thing* about the way she looked. Will. *Just brilliant.*

"So, you ready?" he seemed particularly casual about the fact that she was wearing head-to-toe aubergine and resembled either a bloated undercooked sausage or the afore-mentioned Teletubby. Tinky Winky was the purple one, wasn't he?

"I think so. I mean, what should I bring?" Lucy preferred to have everything planned out and this outing was far too ad hoc for her liking.

Will scratched the back of his head. *He* wasn't wearing a daft outfit. He was wearing a T-shirt which had—again—ridden up and shown his extremely taut stomach. Was there such a thing as a twelve-pack?

"Okay, you've got the goggles, the mittens, and the ski socks ..." Those items, all borrowed from Jules, were in a small backpack—also aubergine—on the bed. "And we'll get you a helmet and boots up there. Oh, yeah, you'll need lip balm."

"Really?"

"Yeah, for the cold." He laughed. "You're looking at me like

I said lipstick or something. Just, you know, regular old Chapstick."

She did not like how amused he seemed. How was she supposed to know what to take with her for a day of skiing? She gave him a firm stare and he stopped laughing.

"Okay, um, bring your phone—in case anything *happens*, you know …?" No, she did *not* know, and she didn't want to think about it. "And tissues. There should be those little packets in your bathroom. Bring a few. Your nose runs like *crazy* up there." *Well, that's just brilliant.* So far, nothing he'd said made her any happier about their impending outing. "And that should be it. Oh, and there's these." He retrieved two foils packs from his pocket and held them out.

Lucy had seen them before. They were those little heat packs you put in your boots for when it's *really* cold. She didn't know they made them for hands too, but he'd given her one set of each. "Jules gets numb fingers and toes sometimes, so she uses those. Okay, so meet you downstairs in a few minutes? And you can just wear your Uggs."

"Only Americans wear Ugg boots outside," she muttered to herself. She really did hope it was jet lag making her so ill-tempered. Or perhaps it was abject fear. Was she really doing this?

*

"You're doing awesome!"

They were on a green run—the easiest kind, Lucy soon found out—and Will was skiing backwards in front of her, making it look as simple as walking, which for him, it probably was.

He was watching her form and explaining how to make little corrections and, surprisingly, she was doing very well. At first, she'd been self-conscious about him watching every nuance of how she moved—and she'd felt like a giraffe on roller skates when she'd first stood up on skis—but as the morning progressed and as *she* progressed, she found that she really liked skiing.

Lucy beamed at Will. "Do you think maybe you can start skiing forward now?"

He laughed. "Sometimes I forget." He gracefully changed directions and was soon skiing alongside her. She snuck a surreptitious glance at him, still amazed by how effortless he made it look, and she recalled her conversation with Steph from that morning. Of course, he was good. He'd been on the snow for twenty-six years!

They were coming up on a skiing class of small children and Lucy's stomach twisted into a tight knot. "You've got this," said a reassuring voice to her right. "Just lean ever so slightly to the left and take that path there." She followed the line of Will's arm and gave a sharp nod.

The children seemed to be intent on scattering across the width of the ski run, and Lucy held her breath as she narrowly missed a little boy wearing a Cookie Monster helmet. They passed the skiing class without incident, though, and she sighed, a grin spreading across her face.

"You're a natural," Will called to her.

"I can't believe I'm going to say this, but it's brilliant!"

"We were lucky. It's usually much more crowded than this, but the storm must have deterred some people from making the trek."

"And it's sunny!" she exclaimed. She heard his laugh and when she glanced his way, there was a broad grin under his goggles.

"Yeah, it's kind of perfect. Fresh dump of powder last night, sunshine today. But it's not always like this. That's how you know you're a hardcore skier or snowboarder—you go out even when it's freezing and there's zero visibility. If there's fresh powder, you just want to get out in it."

Lucy had a realisation—she'd been so absorbed in what Will was saying, she was no longer nervous about skiing around other people. She was just doing it. And those two hours of snowploughing on the bunny hill getting her confidence up were definitely paying off. Will hadn't let her try a green run until she could ski with parallel skis, and she'd never worked so hard to follow instructions in her life.

It was the ski lift that had terrified her most, however. What if she fell off and plummeted to the ground below? What if, when it was time to ski off it, she slipped, and the ski lift smacked her in the head and she had to go off to hospital—on *Christmas Eve*!

Just as she was settling into this wonderful feeling of gliding down the mountain, Will skied closer. "Okay, so this *is* a green run, but the end is actually the steepest part." Her stomach twisted again. Skiing was certainly keeping her on her toes, so to speak. "So, just do what we talked about, really bend those knees and lean into the front of the boots, okay?" She nodded.

"And we'll traverse the slope to take some of the heat off the gradient." The twisting intensified.

"I don't—" He lifted a hand and snaked it slowly from left to right, like a shark fin sluicing through the water. She thought she understood; she hoped she did.

"Just follow me, okay?"

"All right."

Lucy could see the run widening up ahead and that it got a *lot* steeper. *Why would they put the steepest part at the end where you're supposed to stop?*

Will carved left in a gentle arc and she followed. So far, so good. But as he made a rather sharp turn to carve right, Lucy got confused about what to do. Her left ski clipped her right and, in a heartbeat, she was tumbling down the slope. She landed with a thud on her back, leaving her slightly winded. Her left ski—the offending one—was still attached. Who knew where the right one was?

She lay still, arms out like a T, her pole straps limp around her wrists, and took stock of her body. Everything seemed to be intact. Will's face appeared above her, his goggles pushed up onto his helmet.

She waved, sort of—more of a limp-wristed fling of her hand into the air. "Hello," she said, as though it was perfectly normal to lie about on the snow with people skiing around her.

"You okay?" Concern etched his face and he reached out a hand.

She lifted one hand to push her goggles up then let it flop back onto the snow. "Are we talking about my body or my pride?"

"Definitely your body. Your pride slunk off that way." He pointed off towards the ski lift.

"Ha ha, hilariously funny."

"Am I helping you up, or would you prefer to stay there?"

"Up please." She thrust a hand in his direction, and he signalled for the other one. When he had both her hands in his, he lifted her from the snow with ease, but as he was downhill from her, she fell into him. He captured her in his arms.

"Oops, hey, are you okay?" They were face to face, barely apart, their breaths mingling in the air between them, and their eyes locked onto each other's. Lucy nodded slowly, not dropping his gaze. He bit his lower lip, and Lucy had to fight the urge to reach up and touch it. He didn't seem to want to let her go, and she didn't want him to.

"Will ..." she whispered, not knowing what words would come after that.

He shook his head slightly and the moment was gone. He leant back and made sure she was stable, before skiing off to collect her other ski, which was at the bottom of the run. He put it under his arm, then skied up to her, cross-country style, propelling himself up the slope by planting his poles and pushing.

Lucy watched all of this without moving. They'd nearly kissed, she was sure of it. And the way he had looked at her, he felt something too. This wasn't just her having a lusty perv at her friend's brother.

He made it back to her and helped her into her ski. "All good?" he asked as he scrutinised her boot bindings.

Lucy put her weight on the ski. "Uh, yes, thank you."

Will straightened and looked down at her, his face set in a neutral expression. "So, another run, or we could get some hot chocolate?" he asked.

Right, she thought, *so we're going to pretend that nothing happened between us. Just brilliant.*

"Let's have a break, shall we?" she replied, feigning a smile.

As she sipped her hot chocolate, the feeling returning to her fingers and toes, she watched the activity outside the café and thought back over the morning. Will had been so patient with her, so generous with his time, encouraging her without a trace of condescension.

He's a good one.

The realisation both thrilled and terrified her, because maybe she *had* imagined there was something between them and it was all one-sided—*her* side. And what was the point of falling for a man who lived in America when her life was in London? The swarm of thoughts buzzed about her mind as the hot chocolate warmed her body.

"You look like you're a million miles away."

She smiled, snapping back to the present and taking in his tousled hair and pink cheeks. She wondered if hers looked like that. "I was, actually. Sorry."

"No need to apologise." Then he reached across the table and took her hand.

Chapter 12

Chloe

"It's a very pretty village," Chloe said, stifling a yawn.

She and Archer were walking down the road away from his mother's house. It was drizzling, but they were sharing Cecily's giant umbrella and despite her toes burning with cold inside her now-soggy boots, she was otherwise impervious to the grey weather. *Archer Frigging Tate!* she mused to herself.

"So much so, it's boring you silly?"

The stifled yawn turned into a laugh. "Nooo, that's just jet lag. Like your mum said, I only arrived last night."

"Well, in that case, I agree with you. It is a pretty village. Very small, mind you. It doesn't even have a school."

"Were you and Lucy the only children when you were growing up?"

"No, there were a few of us. We all went to school in the next town, Watlington."

"And you were both in the same class?" Chloe was fishing. According to the world's tabloids, Archer Tate's age was somewhere between thirty and forty, but he'd always been tight-lipped about it, saying that it shouldn't matter what age he was, as long as he was the right person for the role. It was his act of solidarity with female actors to protest how ageist and sexist the acting profession was. Chloe had always admired that about him—and his acting ability. *And* his ridiculous good looks.

"Well, we both went to the same primary school, but I'm a couple of years older."

Bingo! She'd just mined one of Hollywood's best kept secrets, but she would keep it to herself. It didn't really matter anyway, as long as he was age appropriate. It wasn't like he was *twenty* or, god forbid, *fifty*!

"So, where in Australia are you from?"

"Melbourne. Have you been?"

"Sydney only, I'm afraid, and even that was a fly-in-fly-out visit for some ghastly press junket."

"Did you really just complain about life as an international film star?" She raised her eyebrows and he chuckled at himself.

"I did. You see, this is the real me—a pompous arse who complains incessantly about being, as you put it, an international film star."

"That seems unlikely—the pompous arse part."

"You might be surprised. In any case, would you allow the arse to buy you a drink?" They had stopped outside a small pub called The Ha'penny and Sixpence. Its Kelly-green window boxes were empty, but its whitewashed walls glistened in the drizzle and it had the ubiquitous thatched roof that so many of the village buildings had. This one looked like a giant fur hat.

A car zoomed by so close and so fast that Chloe felt it before she saw it. "Shit." She leapt onto the front step of the pub and Archer followed, his reflexes kicking in just after hers.

"That's my fault, sorry," he said, looking down at her, a crease between his brows. "I wasn't paying attention and it can get a little dangerous on this curve of the road. No footpath, see, and people tend to drive like mad idiots through the village—even in weather like this."

Chloe's breath started to slow, and she blew out a noisy sigh. "It's definitely time for a drink."

He pushed on the white wooden door and stepped aside so she could enter ahead of him. *A gentleman*, she thought. He closed the umbrella and brushed errant rain drops from his shoulder, just like he had when he'd arrived at his mum's house hours before. Chloe watched the simple gesture with wonder. The way he moved, even something as simple as that, was a lesson in elegance. He smiled down at her and Chloe knew exactly why she'd had a crush on him for all these years.

He was an absolute hottie.

The pub, which must have been at least a few hundred years old, had extremely low ceilings and as she followed Archer into a small room off the main one, she watched him duck beneath the beam that spanned the doorway. They found a table for two in the corner next to the window where the milky light from the grey day seeped in, then peeled off their coats before getting settled.

A woman, who looked to be in her mid-sixties, appeared out of nowhere and stood next to the table, peering down at them. "Alan! So good to see you, love," she said. *Alan?*

Archer stood and warmly kissed the woman on her offered cheek. "Mrs D, good to see you too. You haven't aged a day."

She tutted and waved off his compliment the way women do when they are not-so-secretly pleased. "Oh, rubbish, you cheeky boy. I look a right fright." She patted her bright red fluffy curls. "I forgot my umbrella and had to walk all the way from the bus stop in this wet muck." She tilted her head to the side and regarded him, smiling with obvious pride.

As though she suddenly remembered her manners, she turned towards Chloe. "Hello. You must be Alan's girlfriend. Madison, isn't it?" *Oh, god!* Chloe wasn't sure whether to be horrified or flattered that Mrs D had assumed she was Archer's girlfriend—*and* a famous film star.

To his credit, Archer handled the faux pas just as graciously as he seemed to do everything else. How he avoided embarrassing all three of them was a minor miracle, but he did. He took Mrs D's hand in his and feigning conspiracy, whispered loudly, "Actually, Mrs D, this is my *new* friend, if you get my meaning. Chloe."

"Ooohhh," she said, as though Archer and Chloe were engaged in some sort of illicit affair. "I shall keep it under wraps," she added, glancing about to see who else was listening; it was no one. "Chloe," she said in hushed tones, "your boyfriend was one of my favourite students."

Oh, so that's where Mrs D fits in. Archer shook his head and sat down.

Chloe rested her chin on her hand, "Oh, do tell, Mrs D. Maybe you would like to join us?"

"Oh, no, I can't, love. I'm working, see?" She laughed loudly. "I'm supposed to be taking your order. Our John will give me a stern talking-to if I stay any longer chit-chatting. What can I get you?"

Archer ordered a pint and Chloe ordered red wine. On Mrs D's recommendation, she'd gone for the tempranillo over the pinot. When Mrs D retreated, Chloe fixed Archer with a look. "So, *Alan* ..." She let the name hang in the air, a slight smile tugging at her lips.

He raised both hands in surrender. "Now you know *two* of my secrets."

"Two?" She was playing dumb and she knew that he knew that.

"Uh-huh. My age isn't common knowledge, as you know." This time she raised *her* hands in surrender. "And I was born plain old Alan David Tate."

"What's wrong with Alan?"

"Nothing. It is a perfectly serviceable name. But, you see, when I went off to drama school, I had it in my head that I needed something more ... well, impactful. Actually, my mum came up with Archer."

"*Your* mum?" An image of the slight frown that seemed permanently etched on Cecily's face popped into Chloe's head. Archer nodded, chuckling softly.

"Yes."

"Hang on. Seriously, *your* mother, Cecily—the woman who could terrify a grown man at fifty paces just by looking at him—*your* mother came up with your stage name?"

The chuckle turned into a full-blown laugh. "I don't think

I've ever heard my mum described quite like that, but now that I think about it, you're absolutely dead on. And, yes, she did."

Chloe shook her head, still wrapping her brain around Archer's big reveal. "But how did she come up with it?"

"It's her maiden name."

"Ooohhh. Well, that make sense then."

"And, apparently, she'd wanted to call me Archer when I was born, but my dad thought it was a terrible name for a baby, so I was named Alan after his dad."

"Hmm, he does have a point. Archer's a heavy moniker to give an infant. It sits rather perfectly on you, though." She met his eyes and didn't flinch as he stared back into hers.

I am going to have my way with you, you beautiful man, she thought. Just then, Mrs D, retired schoolteacher, arrived with the drinks then bustled away to greet a family of four who'd just arrived, wet and harried looking.

"It's awfully good of you, stepping in like this—with the fair, I mean," said Archer. "It's your holiday after all."

Chloe shrugged. "Honestly and, I promise I am not playing the martyr here, it's fine. Your mother seems to have everything organised, so I'll just be like a conductor of a symphony, you know, keeping everything to time. They probably don't even need me, but I'm happy to help. Besides, I'm a total Christmas freak."

"Oh, really?" He seemed amused.

"I am. I am a bona fide, diehard fan of Christmas. And as a bona fide diehard fan of Christmas ..." She affected a melodramatic voice and a terrible British accent and, with one hand on her chest, one held aloft, asked, "How could I leave the fate of the fete in anyone else's hands? *How*, I ask you?"

She dropped her hands and gave Archer a self-satisfied smile.

"Impressive."

"Yes."

"Have you had training?"

"Self-taught." She sipped her wine.

"Hmm. I would never have known if you hadn't said."

"It's a talent too powerful to share, you see. The world is not ready for Chloe Sims, *act-tor*."

"No, I imagine not. So, Chloe Sims, *act-tor*, tell me, as a diehard fan of Christmas, do you think *Die Hard* is a Christmas movie?"

She nodded as though in deep contemplation. "Yes, yes, that *is* a question for the ages."

He nodded along, stroking his chin, stifling a grin which seemed to break free of its own volition. "You're quite funny," he said, his voice tinged with admiration.

"Me? Oh, I'm frigging hilarious." She flashed him a huge grin. "And yes, of *course Die Hard* is a Christmas movie."

It was about halfway through her glass of wine—a typical British pub pour of about a third of a bottle—that Chloe forgot that Archer was one of the most famous people on the planet.

He was just a very funny, sweet, charming guy who she had an enormous crush on. He was also staying with his parents, so if she *was* going to have her way with him, she'd have to figure out some logistics. Fortunately, logistics were just her thing.

*

The Christmas Fair was in full swing and it was incredible.

Admittedly, when Lucy had first mentioned it back in July, Chloe hadn't imagined *this*. She'd thought of twenty people showing up at the church hall for tepid tea and carols around an out-of-tune piano, like something out of *The Vicar of Dibley*.

This was entirely different.

The committee had appropriated the empty field across from the church and it was brimming with small marquees, all in neat rows and each decorated to the hilt by the vendors. And although they had put their own flair into the decorations, they'd all adhered to the instructions—traditional Christmas decorations only.

No tacky tinsel, no plastic Santas or Rudolphs. Instead, burgundy velvet bows and forest green garlands prevailed, and thousands of fairy lights brightened the grey, but dry, day. Chloe wondered if there were any Christmas decorations left in all of England.

She had been onsite, as requested, at 4:30am, impervious to the hour because her body clock had no idea what time it was. Cecily had nodded at her curtly, then handed over a travel cup brimming with strong, milky tea, a small torch, and a clipboard.

As Chloe had learnt in the meeting the day before, her

main task was to help supervise the set-up. First, there was the installation of proper event lighting, which made the rest of the set-up possible in the dead of night, and then the assembly of the stalls.

She'd sipped her tea with gratitude. It was cold outside and with the jet lag, she had been feeling more than a little out of it. The tea had helped. While she sipped, she'd squinted at the plan on the clipboard, impressed with how detailed it was, then lifted her head to survey the field.

Even in the dim light, which emitted from some of the surrounding houses, it had been easy to envision what was planned and the fair had started to unfold in her mind's eye. She'd experienced this kind of vision dozens of times before, and it was one of the traits that had had her rising through the event management ranks faster than most. That and her freakish organisation skills and excellent comms.

As the lighting technicians had arrived and got to work and as the marquees were delivered and assembled, she'd switched seamlessly into work mode, directing the team of workers just as she'd described to Archer in the pub, like the conductor of a symphony.

Hours after her early morning start, Chloe surveyed the cheerful crowd milling about—some, she'd been told, had come from as far away as Oxford.

They sipped mulled wine as they listened to the choir sing carols, jumping from foot to foot to keep warm. They pored over unique gifts at the artisan stalls and munched on roasted chestnuts and chocolate truffles. There was even a stall selling Christmas pudding cupcakes. Chloe had indulged in one for a late breakfast and it was *so frigging good*. Not surprisingly, the children seemed to be having the most fun, running between the stalls laughing, hopped up on sugar and their faces painted like Christmas elves or reindeer.

And despite the jet lag and being outside in the biting cold—ill-equipped in her Melbourne winter attire—*and* despite being deprived of a decent shower that morning, Chloe was in her element and feeling the satisfaction of a job done well. She was also basking in the Christmassy goodness of it all, glad that she'd come all this way.

She felt a presence beside her. Archer—another reason to be glad.

"You've done a wonderful job."

"Honestly, it's run like clockwork. That's kudos to your mum."

"You've impressed her, and she likes you, I can tell."

"Well, I think she's amazing. She must have done this as her career, right?"

"Running events?"

"Yeah."

"No, not as a career, but she's always been the organiser for village events, ever since I can remember."

"That makes sense. She clearly knows her stuff and she's very well respected. I've learnt so much from her today. I've loved it; it's been reinvigorating."

"How so?"

"Just that a lot of the events I run back home can be kind of tick-a-box, you know? I'm starting to contemplate a move to something else career-wise. Maybe dirty-dish-tourism will take off."

That sparked a loud laugh. "But seriously, well done you for today."

She dipped in a tiny curtsey and shrugged one shoulder in mock modesty.

"Chloe?" Cecily. Chloe dropped the little performance and subconsciously stood to attention.

"Hi, yes, Cecily. It's all going so well. I was just saying to Archer."

"Quite." Still no smile. Chloe doubted Archer was right about Cecily *liking* her—respecting her, maybe. "You've been very helpful, but I do need one more thing, dear."

"Sure, yeah, no problem."

"Actually, I need you, too, Archer. It seems that Mrs Capel has wandered off and got herself all the way to The Lord Nelson. They've just telephoned. Can you go and collect her? I've got to find Mr Capel. He's somewhere in this crowd and he must be frantic."

Chloe and Archer shared a quick look before they both responded in the affirmative. "Best to take the Range Rover. Your car won't really do, will it?" Archer's car, as Chloe had discovered the day before, was a vintage MG—beautiful, but hardly suitable for collecting a wayward pensioner.

Cecily held out a set of keys and Archer took them from her. "I'll take that, dear. No need of it now." She indicated the clipboard and Chloe handed it over.

"This way." Archer weaved through the crowd and Chloe

struggled to keep up. At least she could see his head above most others, carving a path. They cleared the field and he strode around the back of his mother's house to the garage. "It's a tight fit, so I'll back out before you climb in."

"Has she done this before?" Chloe asked as they zoomed down the narrow lane. She remembered the day before when she'd nearly been hit by a car and how Archer said that everyone sped around here. *Including you*, she thought.

"Mrs Capel? Yes. More and more these days, I'm told."

"But why?"

"Why does she go off like this?"

"Yeah."

"There hasn't been an official diagnosis, as far as Mum knows, but she says it's most likely dementia."

"Oh, that's so sad."

"It is, especially considering that before she started to forget where she is, or even *who* she is, Eloise Capel was something of a legend. Quite the character, really."

"In what way?"

"Well, for many years—decades—she would go off travelling by herself—safaris in Africa, sailing down the Mekong, that sort of thing. She even walked the Camino de Santiago when she was sixty-something. By *herself*."

"Wow. And what, her husband just stayed here?"

"Yes."

"And that worked for them?"

"Apparently. He said his job was to keep the home fires burning."

"What an extraordinary marriage."

"It is."

"And how do you know so much about all of this? I suppose it must be local lore."

"Definitely, but also, when I was old enough to start caring about people other than myself"—he gave her a quick self-deprecating smile—"that was just before drama school, I became a little obsessed with them, especially Mrs Capel.

"I started doing some research, you know, back issues of the local paper, that sort of thing. She was well lauded in this part of Oxfordshire, a local celebrity of sorts. Actually, I've always thought her story—their love story, especially—would make an exceptional film."

Chloe nodded to herself as they pulled off the road and into the car park of a pub called The Lord Nelson. "I'll be right back," he said.

He exited the pub minutes later escorting Mrs Capel, her hand tucked into the crook of his elbow. She was tall and slim and wore a soft pink woollen coat tied tightly around her waist. Unlike many women her age, she walked tall, shoulders back and her strong chin lifted proudly. Her silver hair was pulled into a high, loose bun and her high cheekbones had a hint of colour.

"She's beautiful," Chloe whispered to herself.

Archer opened the back door for Mrs Capel and when she was buckled into the seat, Chloe turned around and smiled. "Hello, Mrs Capel, I'm Chloe."

The older woman's eyes met hers and Chloe could see her straining to pull her focus back to the present. The moment wrenched Chloe's heart, but she didn't flinch, instead letting her gaze be a tether to the here and now. A blink and a smile, then, "Hello, Chloe. You remind me of my Daphne."

Chloe beamed and turning back to face the front, she caught Archer's eye. In his look, she could see the compassion and affection he felt for the elderly woman. It turned out that the world's biggest film star was also a spectacularly nice human being.

I'm a goner.

Back in Penham, as they turned off the main road, Chloe saw Cecily standing at the entrance of the fair with a tall man, who Chloe assumed was Mr Capel. He was wringing his hands and he nodded at something Cecily was saying to him. *The poor man,* Chloe thought.

"That's my Richard," said the voice behind her. "Stop. Stop the car."

Archer did as he was told, pulling the car to the side of the road. There were safer places to stop, but perhaps he'd also heard the urgency in Mrs Capel's voice.

Mrs Capel was charging across the road even before Chloe and Archer got out of the car. "Good thing no one was coming," said Archer, looking both ways before they crossed.

On the other side of the road, Chloe and Archer pulled up short at the sight of two octogenarians locked in a passionate embrace. Cecily was tactfully looking at the ground, but Chloe couldn't stop staring at the love scene playing out in front of her.

"Where did you go, my love?" said Mr Capel peppering his wife's face with kisses.

"I got lost."

He pulled her to him, his chin resting on her head. "Oh, darling, you mustn't wander off like that. I was beside myself."

"I'm so sorry, Richard." He pulled back and tipped her chin so she was looking into his eyes.

"Now, now, no tears. You're safe with me, now." He leant down and kissed her. Chloe had to look away at that point; it was too much of an intrusion not to.

When they finally pulled apart, Mr Capel stepped forward and shook Archer's hand. "Thank you, Alan. And you, love." Chloe smiled shyly, unwilling to take any credit for Mrs Capel's return, but also not wanting to downplay his concern.

"Honestly," said Archer, "it was no trouble at all. We were happy to help. She was quite safe at The Lord Nelson."

"Indeed, but it is her journey there that troubles me ... the way people drive on these roads." There was a sombre pause and Chloe assumed they were all thinking the worst, just like she was.

"Right," said Cecily, her tone brightening the moment. "Would anyone care for some mulled wine?"

Everyone seemed to welcome the distraction and as the couple followed Cecily back into the fair, Mrs Capel clung to her husband's hand and rested her cheek against his shoulder.

"Wow," said Chloe, almost to herself. *I want a love like that.* The thought arrived with a jolt. Chloe was essentially a card-carrying pragmatist when it came to love, never once longing for it and always assuming that it would come along, or it wouldn't.

"Now you know what I was talking about," said a quiet voice in her ear. She nodded slowly, only able to tear her gaze away from their retreating backs when they were absorbed by the crowd. When she turned to look up at Archer, he was watching her intently. "You caught me," he whispered.

"You were watching me."

"I was." In the moment of stillness that followed, Chloe's breath caught. Then Archer blinked, seeming to remember himself, and the moment dissipated. "I should move the Range Rover."

"Oh, right." Another moment. "I'll come with you." If she'd thought logically, even for a second, she would have realised how ridiculous and—worse—*obvious* her offer was. Cecily's garage was literally around the corner but for some reason, Chloe felt compelled to stay with Archer.

The situation was made all the more ridiculous because almost as soon as she got into the car, she had to get back out again while Archer tucked it into the tight space of the carport. She waited on the gravel, her heart and her mind racing.

It was one thing to have a crush on a gorgeous celebrity, but in the short time she'd known him, Archer had revealed himself as so much more.

"Shall we get back to the fair?" she heard herself say as he climbed out of the car. He didn't answer, instead striding towards her and stopping only a foot away. His eyes searched hers, almost as if he were asking if she felt it too. She had no idea who moved first, but as his head dipped towards hers, her arms reached up around his neck and she felt the firmness of his hands on the small of her back. Then his mouth was on hers in a kiss so fervent, so all consuming, that her mind started shouting, *This is the best kiss of your life!*

Chapter 13

Jules

"**O**h, my god. Seriously, that is *good*."

"I told ya. They do the best coffee here. Chloe and I joke about getting a drone so we can call in our order, then fly the drone down to pick up our coffees."

Jules laughed. "It's not even a two-minute walk."

"Yeah, but sometimes you want to have your coffee *and* lounge about in your PJs."

"That's fair."

They were at Cargo, a restaurant shaped like a boat that jutted out over the water, with both port and starboard made up of wide floor-to-ceiling windows. Ash had taken the seat that looked back at the kitchen so Jules could have the view.

Jules took another sip—a flat white, it was called. Who knew such a thing even existed? In Boulder it was all "caramel mocha lattes with whipped and a pump of vanilla". You couldn't even *taste* the coffee. This was a whole new level—the best coffee she'd ever had. "You do realise that you've ruined me for life, right? With the coffee *and* the view."

"The view yes—it's Docklands. I love it. But the coffee? Come on. You've *travelled*. Didn't you go to Italy a few years back with Chloe and Lucy?"

"Yeah, and the coffee was good. I mean, hello, *Italy*. But I stuck to espressos and they're crazy strong—like, stand-your-spoon-up-in-it strong. Anyway, I've always thought of coffee as just a caffeine-delivery device. I've never thought of it as ... as *this*."

"Yeah, well, if I'm spending a thousand dollars a year on something, it's gonna be good."

"A thousand ...? Oh, yeah, I guess that's right. Four bucks a day."

"Yep."

Jules savoured the coffee and took in the view. In the middle of the harbour was a long pier with what looked like converted warehouses—bars and function venues, by the look of them. Across the water on the other side of the harbour were more buildings—a mix of businesses and residences, and each distinct. Some were mostly glass tinted in blue or brown, and one building had brightly coloured accents as though a child had decorated it. On their left was the marina, and Jules spied a family of ducks paddling among the boats in the murky water. It reminded her of Vancouver, and she *adored* Vancouver.

Could I live here?

She'd been dipping in and out of the thought for most of the day. Melbourne was certainly a beautiful city and *huge* when compared to Boulder, or even Denver, but would she want that? She'd spent most of her life living in what was essentially a large town. What would it be like to live among five million other people from all over the world? That was the other thing she'd noticed. Melbourne was a truly cosmopolitan city; she could hear several different languages being spoken at that very moment.

Ash looked over Jules's shoulder and waved. Jules, putting on hold her ruminations about a life in Australia, turned to see who the recipient was. A grinning Matt walked across the restaurant. Jules shot a look at Ash, who seemed particularly interested in the contents of her coffee cup. What was she up to?

"Hey," Matt said as he leant down to plant a kiss on Ash's cheek. He did the same with Jules, as though they'd known each other for more than a day, then pulled up a chair. He signalled to a passing waiter and asked for a flat white.

"It's my new favourite thing," Jules said to him.

"Oh, yeah, this place is great. I always try to get here when I'm up."

"Up?"

"Yeah, in Melbourne."

Jules cocked her head in confusion and Ash added, "Matt lives down on the peninsula." The furrow between her brows deepened.

"Sorry, just some Aussie shorthand," said Matt. "I live on the Mornington Peninsula; that's where the vineyard is."

"Oh, that's right, Ash said you made the wine you brought over."

"I did."

"We had some last night. It's really good."

"You cracked open the Christmas dozen?" Matt raised his eyebrows at Ash who threw her hands up in surrender.

"I would *never*. It was one of the pinots you brought last time."

"You're off the hook then. But you'll want to get the whites into the fridge by tomorrow night."

"I'm on it."

Matt's coffee arrived and he thanked the waiter with a smile. It was a small thing, but something that Jules noticed. If she was on a date and the guy was rude to the waitstaff—or ignored them entirely, which she considered just as bad—she'd make an excuse and leave early. She'd left a lot of dinners early.

"So, help me get oriented. Right now, I'm facing south?" Two nods. "And where is the vineyard from here?"

"South east." Matt drew a nearly complete circle on the table with his forefinger. "So, this is Port Philip Bay—it's not really round, but for argument's sake, 'kay?" She nodded. "Melbourne's here, and if you follow the east coast of the bay down here, this area is Mornington."

"It's beautiful down there," injected Ash, "and not too far. You should go check it out while you're here." Yep, Ash was definitely up to something.

Jules would have ignored her, but Matt seemed to pick up on Ash's suggestion. "Hey, yeah, that's a good idea. I'll be heading back down on Friday. You two should come for the weekend." She met his eyes and she could have sworn she saw a hint of flirtation. She *hoped* she did, in any case. God, he was hot. How was she going to subtly find out if he and Chloe ever dated? That was one line she definitely didn't want to cross.

The offer to see another part of the state hung in the air and if she was honest with herself, it was just as appealing as the hot winemaker who'd made it. "You know what? That would be amazing, thank you. I also want to do some sight-seeing in the city before I go home. Chloe put together a list—" She was cut off by a laugh from Ash.

"Sorry, sorry, just Chloe and her lists. She even has a master list of all her lists."

"She is very organised." Jules had travelled enough with Chloe to know what a powerhouse of preparation she was.

"*I'm* organised. You have to be in event management, but even in the industry, Chloe is kind of a freak. I love her, I do, but before she left, she wrote a list for *our* Christmas."

"No way," said Matt.

"She did!"

Jules could tell Ash's remarks were said with love and she had a quiet giggle at her friend's expense. "So, what exactly goes on the list for a Christmas you're not even having?"

"Actually, it's mostly about you."

"Me?" She shared a look with Matt. He seemed intrigued too.

"It's just all the things we have to do so you'll have a proper Aussie Christmas, including the menu."

"Sooo, we're making fun of her for being a total sweetheart?"

"Yes. Sorry. Sometimes I can be a bit of a bitch." She waved a self-deprecating hand in the air.

"Don't say that. You're not a bitch." Matt's voice was firm and Ash met his gaze, then looked into her now-empty coffee cup. Jules sensed there was some sort of story there.

"So," Jules said brightly to Matt, "when you're 'up', where do you stay?"

"Usually at our friends' place—Callie and Thea's. They live in Port Melbourne. Pretty much a straight shot south, right on the coast."

"Oh, they're the couple coming for Christmas, right?"

"Yep. They're awesome." Ash seemed to pep up at the mention of her friends. "They had the *best* wedding. *So* much fun. It was up at Daylesford. Sorry, I keep forgetting that you have no idea what that even means. Anyway, it's this fab little town about ... what do you reckon, Matt, three hours away?"

"Maybe less, but yeah, it's a bit of a drive."

"Anyway, we all went up for the weekend—a few of us rented a house and the wedding was at The Boathouse—god that place is divine—the *food*. That was the Saturday and the girls took off on their honeymoon on the Sunday, but we stayed another night, just hanging out, pretty caz."

"When was this?"

"Only last month."

"Oh, so this is their first Christmas as a married couple! That's awesome." Chloe hadn't mentioned that, but an idea started percolating in Jules's mind and she wondered if she could pull it off.

"Oh, that's right, I didn't think of that. Christmas is even *more* special now. Too bad you don't make bubbles, Matt."

"*Now* I believe you didn't crack open the Christmas case." Ash's mouth dropped open. "You didn't."

"I did. Of course, I did. Special occasion." He sat back in his chair casually, as though what he'd done was no big deal.

But apparently to Ash, it was. She "squeed", then leant over the table and gave Matt a smack of a kiss on his cheek. Jules looked between them, waiting for the explanation, Ash's delight making it impossible for her not to smile too.

"You are the best!" Ash added, beaming at Matt.

"I aim to please."

"Matt went to Red Rock," Ash finally explained. "It's my favourite winery—except yours ..."

"Uh-huh." A wry smile appeared.

"And he bought my fave bubbles, lovely, lovely bubbles." Ash was sing-songing, and Jules's grin grew.

"Only four, so pace yourself."

"Well, we can start with those and move onto the ones I got from Naked Wines." She pressed her lips together until they disappeared, as though she'd said something bad.

Matt laughed. "I *know* you buy from Naked Wines. It's not like I think you only drink my wine. For a start, I couldn't afford it. I have to sell some to actual customers, you know."

"Ha, ha. Hilarious."

"Seriously, though," he turned to Jules, "you've met Chloe. This one's exactly the same."

"Are you calling me a lush? On Christmas Eve Eve? I change my mind, you suck."

Jules watched the banter play out across the table. *They're like siblings.* She smiled to herself, letting her thoughts turn to Will. She had totally lucked out with her brother; she knew so many people who weren't close to their siblings. She couldn't even fathom that. Will was one of her best friends, and she didn't have many of those. Three to be precise.

Maybe she was stuck in a time warp, only getting close to people she'd known since childhood. She'd had this conversation with herself before and she knew that if she dwelled on the thoughts too long, she'd end up in a labyrinth, going around and around, trying to self-psychoanalyse why she'd never been in love.

Now was not the time. Besides, she had a lengthy "to do" list to start on.

"So, I know I'm supposed to be making cookies, but do you think we could go to the beach first? You said Port Melbourne wasn't far."

Matt scoffed good-naturedly. "Don't be like that," Ash scolded.

"What? What did I miss now?" Keeping up with the short-hand between them was beginning to hurt her brain.

"Matt's from Torquay."

"And?" Jules pressed.

"*And* he's a beach snob."

"I'm not a snob."

"What would you call it?"

"Well, it's like this," he faced Jules, "Port Melbourne is on the coast, but it's a *bay* and really, if you want to go to a proper beach, like a *real* beach," Ash rolled her eyes and Jules sniggered, "then Port Melbourne is *not it*." From Ash's exasperated sigh, it was obviously not the first time he'd made the same point.

"I see," said Jules, attempting diplomacy. "Well, I'm from a landlocked state *and* I'm one of those unfortunate Coloradans who loves saltwater, so you see where I'm going with this, right?"

"She doesn't *care*, Matthew. Take her to the frigging beach."

"O-*kay*, Ashley," retorted Matt playfully.

Jules grinned. "She is right, though. I don't care. But what about you?" she asked Ash. "Do you want to come?"

"Meh, I'm from Melbourne. I've been. Plus, I've got a million things to do." Jules doubted that but didn't press. Besides, she would get to spend some time with the hot winemaker and maybe even see him in less than jeans and a T-shirt.

*

"I've taken the long way." They had just turned onto an esplanade and the bay stretched out in both directions on the left side of the car. The bay was a lot larger than Jules had imagined and she could only just make out where the coast curved around on the far side.

She'd been watching the street signs and from what she could tell, they'd just left St Kilda and were heading towards Port Melbourne. Throughout the whole journey to the coast, she'd been mesmerised by the streets of Melbourne, especially the main streets, which were lined with stores and dozens of coffee shops. She wondered how people ever chose a favourite when there were so many.

"In case you were wondering," Matt added.

"I was actually. You said it was close."

"I wanted to show off Melbourne a little."

"Well, you've done a good job. It's a gorgeous city. I adored that suburb with the narrow houses."

"Oh, the terraces? Yeah, most of them go back quite a ways. Some are even heritage listed, and you would have seen some

131

with two storeys?" She nodded. "A mate of mine has one and he and his wife have done it up beautifully. It's a lot bigger than it seems from the street."

"Very different from Boulder. We like big houses and condos and not much in between. No, that's not true, there are some cool converted warehouses. Anyway, I like the terraced houses. *And* the marinas. Seriously, how many do you have here?"

"Personally, zero."

"Ha, ha."

"I've never even thought about it, but I guess Aussies just love the water. We do have a lot of it, you know." He was teasing her. She liked it. "But we don't have the Grand Canyon or the Rocky Mountains—"

"You've got Uluru and the Great Barrier Reef!"

"We could probably have a really good argument about whose country has the best scenery."

"But don't you think it's like what you said about the marinas? When you live somewhere, often things just recede into the background." He seemed to contemplate the idea. "I think that's why I like to travel so much—so that when I get home, I see it with fresh eyes, you know? A renewed perspective. Have you been to the States?"

"America? Yeah, actually, I was there a couple of years back. I took a bit of a sabbatical once the winery was in good shape and I could step away for a bit. My mate, Twoey—that's my business partner—he kept an eye on things while I travelled."

"Twoey?"

"Nickname. Long story." He chuckled to himself.

Jules guessed she wasn't going to hear it, so she went with the sabbatical. "So, how long were you away?"

"It was a couple of months—California, Oregon, Washington."

"Oh, I love that part of the country. What time of year were you there?"

"Your autumn."

"So, picking season, then." He smiled. "Couldn't stay away from the grapes?" she teased.

"Something like that—a working holiday." They had slowed down, and Matt was searching for a parking spot, which was looking less and less likely. It seemed that everyone in Melbourne had left the markets and was now at the beach.

She kept an eye out as Matt continued. "Twoey and I had worked our asses off, see, and there's so much more to it than the wine—the finances, the tax laws, marketing. All that started to get in the way of why I'd gone into it in the first place."

Jules found herself nodding in agreement. She was due for a bit of a shakeup in *her* career.

"So, as I said, I took myself off to America, teed up stints at some wineries, and got mucky." The word didn't translate, and he must have seen that on her face.

"I got my hands dirty. I picked grapes, I sorted the berries from the stems, I worked beside the vintners, doing whatever they asked. A lot of it was menial to start with but once they realised I knew my stuff, we'd get stuck in, you know? Figuring out how to make the best wine from those grapes."

"That sounds awesome."

"It was. It reenergised me to come home and throw myself

133

back into it. A bit like what you were saying before—a renewed perspective." They shared a smile across the car. "Here we are." She'd been so caught up in his story, she hadn't even realised they'd pulled over.

Matt performed a perfect parallel park and as soon as they got out, Jules headed straight for the water, slipping off her sandals and stepping onto the sand. She took in a huge lungful of the briny air as she approached the gently lapping waves, and Matt came and stood beside her.

"What do you think?"

She grinned at him. "I can see what you mean about the beach thing," she conceded, "but otherwise, I love it. Doesn't it smell amazing?" She took another deep breath. "Hey, yesterday when I was walking along the marina in Docklands, I noticed it smelled really briny there too, but that's a river, yeah?"

"It is, but it's tidal. There's backwash from the bay, so there's usually a layer of saltwater on the top. That's why it's kinda murky too. It's constantly churning up the silt on the bottom. Not the prettiest river, the Yarra."

"I don't know. I love the way the city is built around it. I mean all those bridges. I think it's really pretty." Matt looked at her in a way that made her wonder what he was thinking.

"So, are you coming in?" She unbuttoned her shorts and slid them down her legs, then pulled her T-shirt over her head. She stood in her yellow bikini, hitting Matt with a look that said, "come on."

He seemed dumbstruck—and as though he was making a concerted effort not to look at her body. She grinned at him. She knew she had a terrific body—she worked out nearly every day, even in the dead of winter.

"Well?"

He put his hand on the back of his neck and dropped his head, grinning. "Didn't bring my swimmers. *And* it's kinda cold."

"Lame!"

"After you, then." His arm swept in a wide arc of mock chivalry.

Jules strode into the water up to her mid-thigh, paused for a beat and swore loudly. Matt threw his head back and laughed as she spun around and jogged out of the water.

"How? It's like ninety degrees today," she laughed, her skin prickling with goose bumps.

Matt raised his eyebrows at her and grinned with an "I told you so" look. It was the first time she'd noticed he had dimples. She was still staring at them when he added, "Wait here. I have a beach towel in my truck." He was gone less than a minute, but it was long enough for her to start shivering.

"Here." He wrapped the striped towel around her. "You have to be a masochist to swim in the bay. The footy clubs send their teams down here to do laps when they lose."

"Really?" She pulled the towel tightly around her.

"Nah."

She laughed at her own expense but stopped as her teeth started to chatter. Concern etched his face. "Geez, you really are cold. Come 'ere." He stepped forward and wrapped Jules up in his arms, rubbing her back through the towel.

It was completely unexpected, but it felt … what? It felt *right*.

After a moment, Matt stood back, the furrow of concern still between his brows. His hand lifted, as though he was going to tuck a stray lock of her hair behind her ear, but he hesitated. Then she watched as his eyes dropped from hers and settled on her mouth. For a moment she wondered if he was going to kiss her. She *wanted* him to kiss her.

"Well, your lips aren't turning blue, so I think you'll survive."

Oh, so not a kiss then. Matt stood back and Jules felt the absence of him—something else that was unexpected. "Come on, pop your clothes back on. I want you to meet Callie and Thea."

She composed herself, consciously slipping back into I'm-just-a-friend-of-a-friend mode. "Oh, sure," she said, dropping the towel and stepping into her shorts. "Can we walk, or do we need to take the truck?" She slid the T-shirt over her head and picked up her sandals.

Matt retrieved the towel from the sand, then stood and pointed to a block of condos across the wide esplanade. "See the building with the dark blue tinted windows?"

"Seriously?"

"Yep."

"Well, then, let's go meet the girls."

136

Chapter 14

Lucy

The ride back to the cabin was quiet and Lucy wasn't sure if she was grateful or disappointed. Were they going to talk about it? At *all?*

Her hand in his, they'd looked at each other across the table for much longer than would ordinarily be comfortable. But then they finished their drinks and went back to the slopes as though it had never happened.

After skiing two more green runs, Will had tried to convince her to try a blue, but she'd hesitated. "I've possibly had the most perfect first day of skiing ever." She had even mastered the steep part where she'd fallen the first time and had made it all the way to the bottom without falling—twice. "I don't want it to go all pear-shaped because I got ahead of myself."

"You're doing great, though. You could totally handle a blue run. Come on, it'll be fun."

Lucy doubted that very much. As far as she was concerned, she had got lucky—perfect conditions and an excellent teacher.

It was unlikely the day would be enhanced by snowploughing her way down a terrifying blue run, just to say she'd done it. She'd already overcome a massive fear just by letting Will teach her.

They had "compromised" by doing exactly what Lucy wanted to do—once more down the mountain on a green slope that they hadn't yet skied, one that wove in and out of the forest. It had been brilliant and her favourite run of the day. There were only a few other skiers about, and it was so peaceful amongst the trees, the sluicing of their skis through the snow the only sound.

She looked across the car, knowing she had to say something. The silence was becoming a *thing*. "Will?"

"Mmm?" he said, glancing at her.

"Thank you for today."

"Oh, no problem. I had fun."

During which part? Lucy wondered. "I did too, actually."

He chuckled. "You sound surprised."

"Well, you must have realised I wasn't particularly keen on going in the first place?" Understatement of the century.

"I thought you were just a little nervous, that's all."

"Quite frankly, I was terrified."

His chuckle turned into a chortle. "Why didn't you say anything?"

"I was being *polite!*" The chortle morphed into a full-blown bellow of a laugh and Lucy joined in at her own expense.

Many moments later, she gasped, "I can't breathe." How was Will managing to keep the car on the road? He was laughing so hard he was barely making any noise.

They each regained their composure with a series of audible sighs, Lucy with her hand clutched to her chest, and Will saying, "Oh, my god," on repeat.

By the time they pulled up at the cabin, they were both breathing normally again. They shared a smile across the car and before she knew what was happening, Will leant across and kissed her on the mouth—hard and fast, a smack of a kiss, almost like he was staking a claim.

His eyes danced with playfulness as he retreated, and Lucy didn't even mind that he seemed a little cocky. She couldn't remember ever being kissed like that before. She didn't go out with men much and if she did, they were usually far less sure of themselves than Will. All that, "May I kiss you?" nonsense. "Just kiss me!" she would scream inside her head.

This, with Will ... this was different. But what in the world was going on?

There was no time to ponder this question because right after Will kissed her, the front door of the cabin flew open and a very pretty young blonde woman ran out, her long hair streaming behind her. She reminded Lucy of Jules except she was squealing so loudly—something Jules would *never* do— that Lucy could hear her from inside the car.

"Oh, hey, they made it!" Will opened the car door. "Come on. You're about to meet the rowdy side of the family."

*

"Rowdy" did not even begin to describe Aunt Jackie, Uncle Bob, and their three children—all (nearly) grown—Briony,

Bridget, and Bradley. Someone clearly had a thing for Celtic "B" names.

Within moments of being inside, Lucy had been embraced so many times, the names and faces had blurred into one and the loud voices echoing in the cavernous foyer were hurting her ears. After a day of skiing, all she wanted was to stand under the shower, have something to eat, then go to bed. *With Will.* The last thought popped into her mind unbidden and she felt herself flush.

She watched how he was with his family. His charm seemed to come easily, and she could tell that all three of his younger cousins were somewhat starstruck by him. Bradley was the youngest at sixteen. He looked a lot like Will, only he had yet to grow into his height; he was all limbs and a little awkward. *Like me*, Lucy thought.

The cousin who had squealed her way out to the car was the eldest, Briony. She was a senior in college and couldn't stop remarking on how beautiful Lucy's hair was—Lucy's long mass of curls that drove her mental on a semi-regular basis.

Uncle Bob was a bear of a man with a smiley face and cheeks so rosy, Lucy couldn't help but think he looked like a middle-aged Father Christmas. He'd retreated to the kitchen after greeting her with a hug, right as Will was introducing the middle sibling, Bridget.

She was eighteen and about to start her final semester of high school. Unlike her mother, her aunt, her sister, and her cousin, Jules, Bridget was not tall, willowy, and blonde. She was of average height and solid build with brown hair pulled into a simple plait down her back. She seemed quieter than the rest, shy even, and Lucy liked her immediately.

Aunt Jackie looked almost exactly like her twin, Steph, but Lucy could tell right away that they were chalk and cheese. She was brash and effusive and said the sorts of things other people would retain as thoughts. When she turned her attention on Lucy, it was to say something so inappropriate, Lucy wished the floor would swallow her whole.

"Oh, aren't you absolutely stunning?" Jackie took Lucy's hands in hers and regarded her appraisingly, like a prize mare. "And look at the two of you together ..." *What? No.* "You were obviously *made* for each other." *Please, please shut up.* "Oh, you absolutely *must* have babies together." *Oh god.* "Steph, my goodness!" she shouted. "Can you imagine the grandbabies these two would give you?"

"Mom!" Bridget's rebuke was muffled by the rushing of blood in Lucy's ears. She couldn't remember ever being so horrifyingly embarrassed.

"Aunt Jackie, you have seriously got your wires crossed." The sound of Will's voice broke the spell and Lucy took a calming breath. "Lucy is Jules's best friend. You know, from *England*?"

There was a beat of silence—welcomed silence—and Lucy waited for the penny to drop, which it finally did.

"Ooohhh, right. I forgot. That's my mistake. I'm so sorry." Briony seemed to take this as her cue, shaking her head at her mother as she left the foyer. Jackie gave Lucy an apologetic smile, which Lucy returned, even though she was furious with this ... this ... *woman*. She was clearly one of those people who went about saying whatever she wanted without any thought of how it would affect others.

"You must think I'm a total idiot. I am so, so sorry," Jackie added. Lucy could see she'd begun a serious bout of self-flagellation. It was somewhat disarming and Lucy found herself in the odd position of reassuring her.

"It was an honest mistake." *If you don't count the part about having grandbabies, which you should never, ever say to anyone unless they are about to give birth to said grandbaby.* Bridget caught Lucy's eye and mouthed, "I'm sorry." Lucy flattened her mouth into a not-quite smile. It wasn't Bridget's fault.

Steph entered the already brimming foyer. "Jackie! What on *earth*? You've been here, what, five minutes and you've already stuck your foot in it? Did you say something about *grandbabies*? To *Lucy*?"

"I might have." The sisters shared a look. Steph's said, "What the hell?" and Jackie's was accompanied by a guilty shrug. A bubble of a snigger formed in Lucy's stomach.

Steph shook her head at her sister. "Hon, Lucy's our guest and you keep this up, she's gonna get on a plane right back to England."

"I know, I know. I just got excited. I thought Will had *finally* brought home a girl for Christmas." Lucy heard Will groan behind her, and the snigger escaped. She covered her mouth with her hand, trying to contain the breathy laugh.

The two sisters were still bantering when Will leant in to ask, "Is that at my expense?" She shook her head, then it changed directions into a nod. She laughed harder. The whole thing was just so absurd. She felt the shake of Will's laugh against her back before she heard it.

Steph and Jackie stopped talking and looked at them, Steph's eyes narrowing, before a smile spread across her face. "Okay you two, go get cleaned up for dinner."

Without another word, Lucy and Will ran up the stairs like naughty school children. When they reached Lucy's door, she had to lean against the frame because she was laughing so hard. Will made the "shush" sign with his hand, failing to stifle his own laugh. He pulled her into the room and closed the door. She straightened and sighed repeatedly to try and catch her breath, one hand fanning her face, the other planted on her chest.

She hadn't laughed this hard in ages—first in the car and then at the Aunt Jackie debacle. Her stomach muscles were going to hurt in the morning.

Will blew out a long breath. "So, now you've met Aunt Jackie."

She grinned and the laugh threatened to reappear. She quashed it with another breath. "Yes, yes, I have. I *do* think you downplayed what that experience was going to be like."

"I'm sorry you were embarrassed." He stepped forward and snaked his arms around her waist as though he'd done it a hundred times before. Lucy settled into the embrace, her hands resting on his forearms, a tiny part of her mind realising how wonderfully normal it felt to be there.

"She embarrassed you as well. Have you really never brought a girl home for Christmas?"

He shook his head. "There's never been anyone I wanted to bring."

143

"Actually," a frown settled on her face, "come to think of it, I haven't either."

"You've never brought a girl home to meet the parents," he teased.

She tutted. "You know what I mean."

He nodded, his eyes roaming over her face. "She was right about something, you know, Aunt Jackie. You are stunning."

Lucy gulped. Coming from Will, she could almost believe it. The corners of his mouth flickered into a slight smile and he licked his lips, just like he had on the snow. Lucy wasn't letting the moment slip away this time. She stood on her tiptoes and kissed him. When she pulled back, there was what she could only describe as delight on his face, and he leant down and kissed her again, pulling her closer as her hands reached for the back of his neck, her fingers entwining in that glorious blond hair.

They were late to dinner.

*

"Popcorn or paper chains?" Will asked.

"Um, popcorn, I think," Lucy replied.

The whole family was assembled in the living room to decorate the tree, a rather scraggly specimen that Bob and Nate had chopped down and dragged inside earlier that day. It was at least twelve feet tall and Lucy wondered how in the world they were going to reach the top to put the angel on— if there even was an angel. It seemed like the only decorations would be those they were going to make.

Bing Crosby was singing, the fireplace was on, and there were six giant bowls of popcorn scattered about the room, with people eating as much as they were stringing—maybe more. The family sat in twos and threes, chatting while they strung the popcorn and glued strips of red and green paper together, as though they were in some kind of holiday nursery class.

Before she sat down, Lucy helped herself to a handful of green and red M&Ms from the ceramic dish in the centre of the coffee table, eating them one at a time, sucking on each until it dissolved in her mouth. Nate was doing the rounds with mugs of his boozy hot chocolate, and Lucy's was on the table in front of her while she waited for it to cool.

And even though this wasn't her family and she'd never actually had Christmas with so many people before, Lucy felt like she belonged. She was sure Will had something to do with that.

She popped the last M&M into her mouth as Will handed her a large sewing needle threaded with a long piece of thick cotton. She tied a knot in the end and speared the piece of popcorn she'd taken from the bowl next to her. It broke and she frowned at it.

Will, now armed with his own needle and thread, sat on her other side, close enough for his thigh to press against hers. As though she were fifteen and not a grown woman, she found herself wondering if people could tell that they'd kissed. Steph probably knew, she realised. She seemed like the type of person who would notice the tell-tale signs, like two thighs pressing together.

145

Still, nothing could be as embarrassing as what had happened with Jackie.

"The secret is to hold the needle perpendicular to the surface of the popcorn and press slowly." Will demonstrated. "Then you gently pull the popcorn down to the end of the thread." He held his up. "See?"

"Right." Lucy was not going to be beaten by a piece of popcorn. She tried again and the second one broke. "Third time lucky," she said gearing up to spear another piece. Broken.

"I don't think I've ever seen anyone so bad at this."

Her giggle came easily, which surprised her. Maybe the ordeal with Jackie had inoculated her against any further embarrassment. She hoped so. Sometimes it was exhausting worrying about what other people thought all the time.

"Paper chains," she declared, as though she was answering his question for the first time. In the end, she was happy just to sip her hot chocolate and watch the bustle around her, humming along to the music. When the first chains and strings of popcorn were finished, Bridget and Briony took charge of draping them on the tree. An hour or so later, the bottom half of the tree looked quite festive.

"Um, everyone," Lucy called out above Bing and the hubbub of conversation. Everyone stopped talking and listened, their fingers still stringing and gluing. "Two things. One, I've just remembered that I've got my mum's Christmas cake upstairs. I'd completely forgotten, but it's lovely and I'm going up to get it now so you can all have some. And two. I think we need to do something about the tree."

All eyes flew to the tree. "The top half is naked, and I'm

afraid that won't do." This was possibly the longest Lucy had spoken in front of a group of people who didn't report to her and she tried to count exactly how many hot chocolates she'd had. Was it three or four?

In any case, it didn't matter because she was having a lovely time. "Right. I shall go and get the cake." She stood, a little unsteady on her feet.

In an instant, Will was by her side. "I'll help."

"Brilliant."

*

"Will?" Lucy was on her knees rummaging through her carry-on. Had she already taken the cake out?

"Mmm?"

"I am quite drunk."

He kneeled next to her. "I gathered as much."

She stopped looking for the cake. "Are you drunk?"

"No. A little buzzed, but not drunk."

She sighed and dropped her head to the side. "Will?"

He smiled at her and tucked a wayward curl behind her left ear. "Yes?"

"I quite fancy you, you know?"

"I do know, yes."

"A *lot*. Even though you're Jules's baby brother and ... she won't be cross with me, will she?"

"No, of course not. Hey, look, it's late and ..."

"And I'm drunk."

"Right, so maybe, do you want to just go to bed?"

"I definitely want to go to bed with you." Good lord. Had she really just said that? She shook her head to clear it. "Sorry. That was ..." She put her head in her hands. "Oh, Will. I'm very, very drunk."

"Come on, let's get you ready for bed."

It was the last thing Lucy remembered before she was woken by her phone.

Chapter 15

Chloe

When they broke their kiss, there was almost a shyness between them and, as Archer pressed his forehead to hers, they both chuckled softly. Chloe took a long, slow breath, hyper aware of her pounding heart. "You know, I've been wanting to do that since I found you washing up in Mum's kitchen."

She leant back, still encircled in his arms, and looked up at him, her eyes searching his. She could have sworn that behind the playfulness, there was something else, something she guessed was tied to their experience with the Capels, but she would play along. They *had* only just met. "Is that so?" she asked cheekily.

"It is so."

"Was it the rubber gloves or when I accidentally ate soap bubbles that tipped you over the edge?"

"Oh, definitely the soap bubbles," he replied, his eyes creasing at the corners in amusement.

She could have stood like that for the rest of the day, just taking him in and sharing a wistful smile, but they were beckoned back to reality by his mother's voice calling Chloe's name.

Bugger, she thought. Even though Cecily had played matchmaker the day before, Chloe was not looking forward to facing her, not after that passionate clinch with the woman's son, which Chloe felt *certain* was written all over her face. Still, not wanting to get on Cecily's bad side—either as Co-chair *or* as Archer's mother—Chloe smiled at him apologetically, slipped out of his grasp, and hustled around the corner and across the road to retrieve her clipboard and receive her next instruction.

The rest of the afternoon and early evening vanished in a blur of event management business, as it often did when Chloe was in work mode and, before she knew it, it was time to head back to the Browning's for Christmas Eve dinner and a well-deserved sit down.

If she was surprised at Archer's confession about wanting to kiss her, she was even more so to find him waiting for her after the fair, casually perched on a low wall next to the now-empty field and holding a tall narrow gift bag.

"Hello, you," he said, smiling at her.

"Hello to you, too," she replied as she sat next to him.

"This is for you." He handed her the bag and she peeked inside.

"Oooh, bubbles!" she exclaimed.

"Sorry it's, er, a bit, er, ordinary. I didn't actually plan on meeting a gorgeous woman two days before Christmas."

Chloe grinned, both at his thoughtfulness *and* at being

called "gorgeous". "It's lovely, thank you. You really didn't need to get me anything. But to be honest, even though I'm only a few days in, I've drunk my fill of sherry. This will make a nice change for Christmas lunch tomorrow."

He chuckled. "I'm fairly certain it's a village custom for women of a certain age."

"Oh, Cecily too?"

"Yes, that's why I nipped down to the off-licence in Watlington this afternoon to stock up on some wine—*and* to pick that up for you." He seemed shy about the gift, endearing him to her even more.

"Well, thank you again." She absentmindedly twirled the gift tag attached to the bag, only then noticing that he'd written on it.

> *To Chloe*
> *Happy Christmas*
> *From Archer x*

Her breath caught and an unfamiliar, but not unpleasant, warmth wound its way through her as she stared at his words.

"So, Chloe, I never asked. How long are you here for?"

"Uh ..." Chloe shook her head to clear it of her tumbling thoughts. "Oh, I fly home on the twenty-ninth." Archer sucked his breath between his teeth and he grimaced. "What's wrong?"

"Nothing's wrong. It's just that we shall have to make the very most of the next few days."

"Oh." It was all she could think to say.

"Come on, I'll walk you back," he said, standing and reaching for her hand. Yes, it was a two-minute walk, but it was the gesture that counted, and Chloe slipped her hand into his. Archer Tate was turning out to be one surprise after another. One lovely, wonderful, breathtaking, romantic surprise after another.

*

Chloe woke on Christmas Day feeling more refreshed than she could remember being in ages.

Maybe it was sleeping in Lucy's childhood bed, which was so snuggly it was like being enveloped in a giant hug. Or it could have been the long but satisfying day as Co-chair of the Christmas Fair; she usually slept soundly after a large and successful event.

Most likely, though, it was because she'd drifted off to sleep with the thought of Archer's kiss on replay. She stretched dreamily under the doona and luxuriated in the memory once more. Their rescue mission to retrieve Mrs Capel. The Capels's romantic reunion when they returned to the village. How Archer had whispered in her ear and she'd turned to catch him watching her intently.

How they'd practically leapt at each other, without saying a word.

Then the kiss itself.

Oh, my god, that man can kiss.

Should she feel a certain way about the dozens of actresses Archer had kissed on screen? Or about the millions of women and men around the world who could only *dream* of kissing him—like she had until yesterday? Or that, until very recently, those lips were kissing a famous woman who Cecily had referred to as "that horrid girl"?

Chloe brushed aside every thought, deciding that she needn't feel one way or another about Archer's kissing history. The most important fact was that he'd kissed *her* and would very likely do it again.

Merry Christmas to me.

Her thoughts landed on what he'd said while they were sitting on the wall, about wanting to make the most of the next few days. She would have to find a polite way to wangle some time with Archer without upsetting the Brownings. They'd been so lovely to her.

The smell of toast wafted under the bedroom door and Chloe realised she was starving. She threw back the cosy covers and, shivering in the chilly air, stepped into her Uggs and wrapped herself in the fluffy robe she'd brought.

Then she ran down the stairs steeped in anticipation, just like someone thirty years younger.

As Lucy had promised, the Brownings were big on tradition and even though the traditions were different from her own family's, Chloe had one of the best Christmas mornings she could remember.

Breakfast back home in Australia was mimosas, a summer fruit platter—berries, melon, pineapple and mangoes—and more prawns than the average person ate all year. In a tiny village in Oxfordshire, it was the traditional English breakfast, most of which, Susan told her, was sourced from the same local farm as the dinner on her first night in England. No wonder it was the best bacon Chloe had ever had.

After breakfast, *and* after Chloe convinced Susan to let her help clean up the kitchen, the three of them assembled in the front room, still clad in pyjamas and robes—something her own mother would never allow—to open presents.

Max had lit a fire and tuned the radio to Radio Three for classical Christmas music. Chloe carried a tray laden with a teapot, teacups, a milk jug, and a plate teeming with sliced Christmas cake, and as she carefully placed it on the coffee table, she noticed that the red candles on the mantle had been lit. The glow from their flames, along with the crackling fire and the stockings hung from the mantle, formed such a perfect Christmassy tableau, that Chloe's eyes prickled with tears. Even before they'd opened presents, she knew she'd remember this Christmas always.

"I'll pour, shall I?" asked Susan rhetorically, as she poured the steaming tea into three cups. "Now, Chloe love, we usually open our stocking presents first, then the proper presents from under the tree. How does that sound?"

Chloe's eyes settled on the stockings, three of them now plump with gifts and only Lucy's hanging limply from its hook. Was she supposed to have brought stocking presents for the Brownings? Somehow, she hadn't thought of it until then and she felt terrible.

Susan must have picked up on that because she was quick to reassure her. "Oh, the stocking presents are just silly things, trinkets really, bits and bobs."

"Just a bit of fun. Things we find over the year and squirrel away 'til Christmastime. *And* chocolates!" added Max, being uncharacteristically effusive.

"Oh, right," said Chloe as Max pulled himself out of his chair and unhooked each of the stockings, then handed them out before settling back in his chair with an "oof".

The sound made Chloe smile, but she hid it by biting her lip. She didn't want him to think she was laughing at him. Susan and Max had started delving into the depths of their stockings, so she did the same, more intrigued by what the Brownings had got for each other than what was in hers. At each little "oh" or other exclamation, Chloe lifted her head and watched as they shared a smile or a wink across the room.

"Oh, love, how did you know?" Max held up a Terry's chocolate orange, and Susan dissolved into a fit of giggles. It must have been an in-joke, Chloe decided.

"Max! You went back for it, you dear man." She held up a decorative teaspoon, which Chloe knew she'd add to the display board in the kitchen. "Look," she held it up for Chloe, "it's from our holiday to Cardiff, from the castle."

"It's lovely," said Chloe making Susan beam even more.

"Was tricky, that was, with you nosing about the giftshop for so long," teased Max before bestowing his wife with a loving smile.

Chloe continued to open the individually wrapped gifts in her stocking, placing each one in turn on the side table next to her. When her stocking was empty, she'd acquired quite the collection of chocolates and trinkets, including a very cute fluffy sheep with a black face that stood about three inches high.

"That there is an Oxford sheep," said Max. "Been bred around here for nearly two hundred years."

"It's adorable. He shall have pride of place on my desk at work." He seemed to like that and gave her an approving nod. Max had taken some time to warm up to her, but Chloe just adored Lucy's dad, and she could see where Lucy got her quiet demeanour from.

"Right, more tea?" asked Susan as she stood to pour herself a cup.

"I'll have one, love." Max stood again and started foraging under the Christmas tree. "Here, Chloe, this one's from Susan and me, and this one's from Lucy."

"Oh, thank you!" This Christmas was full of surprises. She hadn't expected Lucy to leave something for her but, with only a moment's thought, she realised that of *course* Lucy would have done that. Chloe opened that present first.

It was a photo of the three of them—Chloe, Lucy, and Jules—from their holiday to New York, the last one they'd taken together. They were in Central Park and had asked a stranger to take the shot. It had turned out beautifully with the city skyline in the background. Chloe had a digital copy, but seeing it framed in silver turned a simple photo into a treasured keepsake.

"That's a lovely frame, isn't it?" asked Susan.

"Beautiful." Chloe's eyes roamed over the faces of her two best friends and she missed them intensely. She promised herself that they would plan the next May Ladies holiday as soon as they were all back home in the New Year.

Chloe levered open the stand on the frame so she could set it on the table. The gift from the Brownings was a beautiful tartan scarf that, Susan explained, they'd got in Edinburgh when they'd been there last summer with Lucy.

156

For such a quiet, unassuming couple, the Brownings certainly travel a lot, she thought. She had known this about them—she'd met them when they were half a world away in Hawaii and Lucy had inherited her travel bug from them—but voracious travelling seemed a little incongruous with their life in the sleepy hamlet of Penham.

"Now my gift to you!" exclaimed Chloe as she jumped up from her chair and retrieved it from under the tree. "It's actually two, but I wrapped them together. Who wants to open them?"

"You go ahead, love," offered Max.

Chloe watched excitedly as Susan carefully peeled open the wrapping to reveal a bubble-wrapped blob. Taking even more care, Susan undid the wrap, then held aloft two Christmas ornaments, one made from porcelain—a spray of gum leaves with a delicate red gum blossom—and the other, a blown-glass banksia. "Oh, Max, will you look at these."

Max popped his reading glasses on and crossed the room to inspect the ornaments. He took the banksia in his hand and turned it slowly. "That's magnificent, that is, Chloe. It will have pride of place on the tree, I think. And that one, too. Thank you, love."

He gave Chloe a warm smile and a wave of happiness shot through her.

Just then, there was a loud knock at the door.

The three of them looked at each other, bewildered. "I wonder who that could be," said Max, rising and crossing the room. He opened the door to the entry and Chloe and Susan exchanged a look as they heard the front door open, then the murmur of male voices. Max appeared in the doorway. "Uh, Chloe love, it's for you. It's Alan—from across the road," he added unnecessarily.

Chloe, who hadn't planned on seeing Archer that morning, smoothed her hair, then stood and tightened the belt on her robe. Max crossed the room, throwing a shrug of confusion Chloe's way, as Archer's large frame filled the doorway.

"Good morning, everyone. Uh, Happy Christmas."

"And to you, too, Alan," said Susan. "Would you like a cup of tea, love? Or some Christmas cake?"

"Oh, thank you, no. I just ... might I have a word with you, Chloe?"

She'd been dumbstruck until that moment, then snapped out of her reverie. "Uh, yeah, of course." She gawped at Susan, who threw her a lifeline.

"How about you two talk privately, and Max and I will go and get a start on Christmas lunch?" Susan jerked her head unsubtly at Max, who harrumphed a little as he got out of his chair again. He gave a tight smile in Archer's direction and closed the door to the room quietly behind him.

"Hello," said Archer. He seemed nervous, anxious even.

"Hi." Chloe licked her lips, also a little nervous. She hoped she looked okay. She hadn't given her appearance any thought that morning, and she felt almost naked standing in front of Archer barefaced and in her PJs.

"Sorry, I would have called, but stupidly I didn't get your telephone number yesterday."

"Right." They stared at each other awkwardly, like they were in a Jane Austen novel, or something. Any moment now,

Archer would ask if she wanted to take a turn around the drawing room. The thought made her snigger softly, breaking the tension of the moment—for her, anyway—but Archer's expression remained fixed and Chloe realised he must have come with bad news. She stopped sniggering.

"What is it?" she asked. She barely knew the man, but there was obviously *something* going on. *Oh, god, maybe he got back together with Madison.* She couldn't stand it any longer. "Please, what?"

Archer shook his head quickly, his eyes dropping to the floor. "Chloe, I …" He looked up, meeting her eyes. "I'm so very, *very* sorry, but it appears that we've been papped."

"What?" She'd heard him, but her mind struggled to comprehend the word.

"Papped. You see, there are photographs of us on the internet, um … kissing."

"Ohhh," she breathed out. A thousand thoughts flew about her head in an instant. The one that landed was, *Well, this definitely* is *a Christmas to remember.*

Chapter 16

Jules

"Where's the turnaround point?" asked Jules. She and Ash were running along the Yarra River the morning of Christmas Eve. Ash had set a decent pace, and Jules loved the feeling of the fresh morning air in her lungs, the sunshine on her face, and the rhythmic movement of her muscles. God, she missed running outside, but in her part of the world, she had been relegated to a treadmill for a couple of months now. It was either run inside or risk hypothermia.

"Depends. We can either chuck a uey up at Flinders Bridge"—Ash pointed to the bridge up ahead that was busy with morning traffic—"or keep going and cross over near the tennis centre." Jules knew she was talking about the huge complex where they held the Australian Open. She'd always wanted to go to a Grand Slam tournament, but so far, she'd only seen them on TV.

"And how much further is the tennis centre?"

"Adds a couple of Ks onto the run, I reckon."

Jules thought of all the Christmas indulgences that were coming up. "Let's do the whole thing."

"Okay."

They ran in silence for a moment. "Hey, what's that yellow building with the clock tower?"

"Flinders Station. Come on, we can take a little detour." They approached Flinders Bridge and jogged up a steep set of stairs. At street level, a bustling crowd of people milled about outside the train station. There was a tram stop in the middle of the street—a busy one—with at least a hundred people standing on the platforms waiting for trams into and out of the city.

"I can't believe how busy it is on Christmas Eve," said Jules, jogging on the spot next to Ash as they waited for the light at the pedestrian crossing.

"Yeah, it's not a public holiday or anything, so some of these people will be heading to work. The others are probably doing last-minute Christmas shopping."

There was a mix of people—families, couples, groups of friends, people in business attire and uniforms—but most were casually dressed, so Ash must have been right about the Christmas shopping.

The light finally turned green and Ash took off. Jules followed closely behind, once again in awe of how the petite Aussie negotiated the crowd with ease. She figured that you probably got used to it if you lived here.

Ash shot off to the left, then rounded a corner just past a large building with signs saying, "Taxi Kitchen". They emerged into a large open space and the sight was so unlike anything she'd ever seen before that Jules stopped short. It took a moment before Ash realised she was running alone and came back for her.

"Impressive, huh?" she asked. "It's Fed Square—Federation Square. Don't you love it?"

Jules's eye scanned the open space, which was shaped less like a square and more like a giant amoeba, clocking the mottled brickwork as it undulated up and away from them to the right and formed a set of wide steps to the left. There was a stage with a huge screen above it on their right, and the buildings surrounding the square looked like something out of a science fiction film. Panels, which could have been lifted straight from a space station, met with glass panels at irregular angles. She could have sworn there was a location like this in one of the episodes of *Picard*. Maybe they had filmed it here.

"It's awesome," she said, finally finding her voice.

They were on the move again, this time at a brisk walk, as Ash pointed out the various buildings, the most intriguing of which was named ACMI—the Australian Centre for Moving Images. "Hey, that's on Chloe's list," she said, eliciting a grin from Ash.

"Yeah, it's pretty cool. I'll come with you if you like. Their latest exhibit is supposed to be incredible; it's all about film noir."

"Oh, cool," Jules replied.

"You ready?" Ash motioned towards a set of stairs that led back to the riverside path they'd been running.

"Yeah, let's do it." They jogged down the stairs, then turned left and headed down a mild incline onto an open area of packed, sandy-coloured earth that was surrounded by tall eucalypts. An enormous abstract sculpture that looked like a three-legged dog covered in decoupage dominated the space.

"They hold festivals here," said Ash. "Food festivals, music ... There was a Banksy exhibit here a few years back. It was awesome."

Melbourne is awesome, thought Jules.

At every turn of the river—and the Yarra was quite twisty— the city revealed something new. Jules smiled to herself, her eyes absorbing each little detail—the way the Botanical Gardens on the far shore hugged the river, the varying architectural styles of the city's skyline, the buzz and energy of it all. This city was *alive*.

As they approached the bridge they'd cross to turn around, she watched a team of rowers lifting their oars out of the water in perfect sync while a cox shouted commands from the front of the eight-person scull. Closer to shore, a family of swans paddled about, the cygnets awkward teenagers with fluffy grey down.

She'd only been there a few days, but Jules was already starting to fall in love with Melbourne. No wonder Chloe went on and on about it all the time. There was a lot to brag about.

*

"Oh, my god, it feels good to sit down."

"I'll drink to that." Ash reached along the length of the

164

couch and tapped her glass against Jules's. "Worth it, though. Those cookies look divine."

"And you only stole, like, what? Three, or was it four?" teased Jules.

"It was five. And I'm feeling it now. Sugar crash."

"Hey, thanks for helping with the gift for Thea and Callie."

"No worries. You had all that baking to do."

"True, but you dressed the ham *and* cleaned the apartment." The already spotless apartment was now immaculate.

"Yeah, but still. The present thing was easy—I knew exactly where I was going, and I was in and out in under twenty minutes. It's a really nice idea. I wish I'd thought of it."

"Well, we'll make sure to toast them tomorrow—make it extra special."

"With my favourite bubbles!"

"Exactly. These aren't bad either." Jules had another sip from her glass.

"Haven't you heard? We don't make bad wine in Australia."

"I am sure that's almost true." Ash flashed her a grin. "So, what else did you want to get done tonight?"

Ash jumped up, and Jules wondered at her seemingly boundless energy. "Let me just get the list."

"Ah, yes, the list!" Jules had never really seen the appeal, something that Chloe—and even Lucy—found frustrating about her when they travelled together. Mostly because she'd invariably forget something and they would end up scouring a tiny town in Italy for a phone charger, or flipflops for her size-ten feet, and one time, a DIY bikini-wax kit.

According to Chloe, the waxing kit was only necessary

because Jules hadn't written a pre-departure list, so had forgotten to get her bikini line in order ahead of time. Jules had conceded that one.

"Right!" Ash plopped down on the couch, took her glass off the table for a generous swig, then proceeded to mumble her way through a list of things that were already done. Jules watched, amused.

How had her family got through Christmas all these years without *planning*? She drank more sparkling wine, starting to get a little impatient for Ash to tally up the still-to-do items.

"We should probably iron the tablecloth and the napkins and set the table." Jules scrunched her nose. "Yeah, you're right. To hell with it, we'll do it tomorrow. Or we'll wait 'til the others get here and they can do it." Jules doubted very much that Ash was the kind of hostess who let her guests set the table, and she resigned herself to ironing table linens on Christmas morning. Still, it was better than doing it now.

"Hey, I've been meaning to ask ... your friendship group, the orphans. They're all your college friends, right?" she asked Ash. "I mean, I know you and Chloe met at college, but where do the others fit in?"

"Oh, well, only Callie, Matt, Chloe, and I went to uni together. We did a lot of the same first-year classes—intro to marketing, that sort of thing. And Chloe and I moved in together in second year. We had this dumpy little flat in North Carlton," she explained, as though the suburb name meant anything to Jules.

"But it was cool, you know, to have our own place. Callie crashed on the couch more often than she slept at home."

Ash laughed, the mirth in her eyes revealing the memories playing in her mind. "Anyway, we were a firm foursome that first couple of years, then Matt made other friends—guys—so we didn't see him as much. Well, Chloe did; they always stayed close." Jules wasn't sure how to read that ... *or* what she thought of it.

"And Thea? How long have she and Callie been together?"

"I'd say ... uh, three or four years. Yeah, that's about right. I loved Thea right away. Such a good match for Callie. You met them yesterday, right?"

"Yeah, they're really cool." So was their beachside condo. Jules had been a little envious of their water views.

"And what about David? Where does he fit in?" Jules asked.

"Dav-*o*," Ash corrected.

"Do I really have to call him that?"

"It's his name." Jules rolled her eyes. It was one thing to shorten someone's name to one syllable, like she sometimes did with Luce and Chlo—or like Ashley to Ash—but why add the O? "And anyway," added Ash, "Davo isn't short for David. It's short for Davidson—his last name."

"So, what's his first name?"

"Kenneth." Kind of old fashioned. Jules could see why he preferred a nickname. "And when you meet him, you'll see, he's all Davo and definitely *not* a Kenneth."

"Okay, so tell me about Davo."

Ash dropped the list onto the table and took another sip before answering. "Well—and I'm surprised Chloe didn't mention this—but I guess the big thing is that he's my ex."

Jules must have done a crappy job of hiding her surprise

because Ash laughed. "Yeah, it's probably a little weird that we still hang out together, but mostly it's okay."

"No, no, sorry. It's not as weird as you might think." Jules filled Ash in on her parental situation.

"And everyone's fine with it?"

"For the most part. I mean, sometimes I can tell it's not great for my dad, but he's a good sport."

"Does he have someone?"

"No, not right now. He did bring someone to Christmas a couple of years ago—Paula—but that did not go well."

"Why's that?"

"She was ... I don't know." Jules puffed out a sigh. "Actually, I do. She was okay, nothing special, and definitely not good enough for my dad, who is like the best guy in the world, but all that aside, she was only a few years older than me."

"Ergh ..." Ash made a face that cracked Jules up.

"Yeah. Anyway, it was a little tense all around and they ended up driving back to Boulder on Christmas night. They broke up not long after."

"Well, I hope tomorrow won't be anything like that."

"You hope?"

"There's something wrong with my glass," said Ash brightly, holding her empty glass aloft, obviously deflecting. She jumped up and retrieved the bottle from the fridge. Jules held out her glass for a top-up and Ash poured it carefully, making sure it didn't froth over the rim.

Jules only had one more question and then she'd let it lie. "So, how long ago did you two break up?"

Ash, back in her spot on the couch, frowned. "Um, about

eight months ago?" She posed it as a question and Jules frowned.

Okay, *now* she only had one more question. "And how long were you together?"

"Five years." *Whoa*. Five years might as well have been forever. In the past decade, Jules's longest relationship—if you could even call it that—had lasted about five *weeks*. Jules watched Ash pick at her sweatpants, removing some non-existent lint, and something occurred to her.

"And does the breakup have anything to do with the 'I'm a bitch' comment?" Ash was anything but a bitch, but someone had planted that seed.

Ash's head nodded slightly. "It was a fight ... the one where we broke up. He called me a selfish bitch," she said quietly. "He'd got offered the use of this holiday house up north for a long weekend, but I had this work event... Anyway, things had been kinda stale between us and he *really* wanted us to go away together ... Look, I *know* he didn't mean it; he apol-ogised straight away, but ..."

"It stuck." Jules knew exactly how a word could be hurled at you, even just one time, and embed itself and grow. "Slut" had been that word for her. Apparently, losing your virginity to a boy you thought you loved, a boy with a big mouth and an even bigger ego, was enough to earn that disgusting moniker. She shoved the thought down deep where it lived.

"Ash?" She looked up and Jules saw the glisten of tears in her eyes. "Oh, Ash." She was down the other end of the couch in a flash, one arm wrapped tightly around her new friend's shoulders and her chin resting on Ash's head. She heard quiet sniffles.

"I miss him so much, Jules. It was just a stupid fight and we should never have broken up, but it's been months now and ..." Ash's words were swallowed up with tears.

Jules patted Ash's arm, not knowing what else to do. This was already turning out to be the most dramatic Christmas she could remember—and that included the one with Paula.

*

"Um, hey, don't take this the wrong way, but is that what you're wearing for Christmas lunch?"

Jules, freshly showered and made up, looked down at her crisp white cotton top and pale pink shorts. "Yeah, I was, why?" She thought she looked nice, certainly nicer than if she was at home for Christmas.

Ash was standing in the kitchen, having just cleaned it for the millionth time. The salads were made, all three of them a huge step-up from the salads of shredded iceberg lettuce, cucumber rings, and anaemic tomatoes she'd grown up with. One was a Christmas salad with raspberries, strawberries, dates, and walnuts on a bed of greens; it looked amazing. There was also a giant platter of shrimp—"prawns", as the Aussie called them—and lemon wedges in the fridge, and the ham was glazing in the oven. Jules had happily done Ash's bidding for most of the morning fuelled by sparkling wine and Christmas cookies.

Even the table was set.

It looked *beautiful*—white tablecloth and napkins, ironed to perfection; Ash's good dinnerware—also white; Riedel wine glasses—sparkling, white, *and* red; water glasses; Chloe's good silverware; and as many blue decorations and candles as there probably were in all of Australia, including a centrepiece of a tall glass vase filled with tiny glass ornaments—also blue.

There were these things at every place setting called crackers, long tubes with ribbons on either end, decorated in silver and blue. Ash said they were traditional, but traditional where? As beautiful as everything was, there was nothing traditional about this Christmas.

No ceramic dishes shaped like Santa brimming with red and green M&Ms, no Christmas stockings in all shapes and sizes hanging from the fireplace, no *fireplace*, no bedraggled tree cut down by the menfolk and dragged inside, then decorated as though by a kindergarten class. No *snow*.

No, this Christmas was anything but traditional. It was *perfect*.

"Oh," Jules said, finally realising. Her eyes flew back to the ornate table. "It's formal."

"Yeah, sorry, I don't mean to be a bi— Um ... a cow or anything ..." Ash trailed off.

"No! Oh, my god. That's on me. I totally flaked is all. I mean, at home we just wear jeans and sweaters. I even wear my Uggs." She saw Ash cringe and laughed. "So, you dress up here?"

"Yep."

"Is that, like, everyone?"

"You mean in the whole country?"

171

"Yeah."

Ash shrugged. "Not everyone, but yeah, it's kind of a thing. For us anyway."

"Okay, so what are *you* wearing?"

Ash hung the dishcloth on its hook and grinned. "I'll show you."

*

The guests were due at 12:30pm but Ash, dressed in an elegant silk sheath dress, didn't seem surprised when they heard the buzzer just after twelve. "That will be the girls. They're always early." She picked up the handset and peered into the tiny grey screen. "Happy Christmas!"

A muffled chorus of "Happy Christmas" bleated through the speaker. Ash hung up and surveyed the room as though daring a throw pillow to be out of place. When it occurred to Jules that Matt would be with Callie and Thea, her breath caught.

Something had shifted between them that day at the beach.

She looked down at her strappy silver heels and satin dress in ice blue. She'd brought the outfit in case they went out somewhere, like to a club, and although Ash had reassured her a dozen times, she felt *way* overdressed for daytime.

The front door to the apartment opened and in spilled Callie and Thea followed by Matt, who was laden with gift bags and wrapped presents. Thea held a giant cheese board, wrapped in plastic wrap and she seemed relieved when she put it on the counter.

172

They all exchanged hugs and kisses and Christmas wishes while Jules hung back. Then Callie shone her attention on Jules. "Oh, Jules! You look stunning! Stunn-ing! I love that dress! Happy Christmas!" Callie, who was at least a foot shorter than her in heels, somehow managed to wrap her up in a huge hug and all her shyness at being an interloper in their Christmas dissolved.

Callie stepped back. "We're so glad you're here. Don't you just fucking *love* Christmas?"

Jules grinned back at her, riding the wave of Callie's enthusiasm. "I do! I love it. Merry Christmas, by the way."

Thea gave her a kiss on the cheek, less effusive, but just as warm as Callie, and they exchanged more Christmas greetings. Then there was no avoiding the obvious—she and Matt were next.

Her stomach fluttered as she met his eyes then quickly scanned him from head to toe.

When she'd first seen him a few days ago, she'd thought he was hot, but a little scruffier than the guys she usually went for. But *this* Matt ... he was *gorgeous*. He was wearing a dark blue slim-cut suit, with a pale blue dress shirt—no tie—and his belt and shoes were the same deep brown. He was clean shaven, and his dimples punctuated a very sexy smile.

Jules could have sworn that the others were watching. When she glanced at Ash, she, Callie and Thea suddenly became very busy in the kitchen. "Merry Christmas," he said.

"Merry Christmas." Neither moved.

She saw him take in her outfit appreciatively and she silently thanked Ash. "You look beautiful."

"Thank you. You too."

"People will think we coordinated, though." She cocked her head to the side, not knowing what he meant. He tugged lightly at his collar, and she realised that his shirt and her dress were the same colour.

"Ah, yes. I hate when you go to a party and someone is wearing the same outfit as you," she said, smiling.

"Embarrassing."

"Mmm." She raised her eyebrows. "Even more embarrassing is that we both match the Christmas tree."

She nodded in its direction and Matt threw his head back and laughed. "I didn't even think of that."

Jules held her hands out and shrugged. "What are you gonna do? This is the only formal dress I brought with me. For some reason, I had it in my head that an Aussie Christmas would be, like, super casual."

"Nah, we like to put on a good show, you know?" Another expression to tuck up her sleeve. "It's an incredible dress, by the way."

"Thank you ... again." Flutter, flutter, flutter.

Then he stepped closer, leant down and kissed her cheek, his lips lingering just a little longer than a friendly peck. "We'll have to get some pics together later," he said, his face still close to hers. "For Chlo."

She could only nod in reply and the flutter turned into full-on butterflies. God, he was sexy.

She heard the pop of sparkling wine, then Callie called out, "Hooray," and the moment ended. Matt put himself on bartending duty, as he called it, and Jules went back to feeling a little removed from everything as she watched the friends move with ease around the kitchen.

Within minutes, they were all seated in the living room, each with a glass of bubbles and the impressive cheese platter dominating the coffee table between them. She caught Ash watching the clock. Davo was late—only by seven minutes, but Jules could see the nerves beneath Ash's hostess-with-the-mostest façade.

"So," said Callie as she cut into a rich, oozing brie, "What have you been up to since we saw you the other day?"

"Not much. Just getting ready for Christmas."

"Please don't say that Ash's kept you here captive?" Thea threw Ash a look.

Ash blinked a couple of times, as though snapping out of a daydream. "What? No! She wanted to help."

"I did. It's been great."

"And how else do you think all *this* happens?" Ash waved her arms about to encompass the apartment.

Callie stepped in, "It looks amazing, guys, honestly. That *table!* You've definitely outdone our Christmas from last year."

Within minutes of meeting her, Jules had crowned Callie as the most enthusiastic person she'd ever met—and that said a lot considering her Aunt Jackie and her side of the family. Callie was also the most genuine, her effusiveness anything but a pretension.

She'd made quite the impression on Jules with her obvious love of life and how she found joy in the minutiae. And, as Ash had said, she and Thea were such a good fit. Thea had a gentleness to her, a willingness to let Callie shine, to take the lead, but Jules sensed that Thea was the tether in their relationship.

Did *she* need a tether or a kite?

Jules had felt mired in a sort of middling state for so long, she didn't know what would shake her free from it. And maybe she'd been kidding herself thinking it was all about her job.

She *did* need to find something else—and soon. Something to stretch her abilities, something where she was challenged. But she was starting to realise that her dissatisfaction was also because she'd become complacent in her singlehood.

Sure, she had lovers and she'd go on casual dates from time to time, usually with guys she didn't end up having anything in common with, or guys who behaved like dicks, but maybe she needed to be open to something else, something more meaningful.

She glanced at Matt, who was chatting to Thea. She couldn't remember the last time she'd felt butterflies, actual *butterflies*, just being near a guy. And, yes, he was undeniably good-looking *and* sexy, but he was so much more than that. Just knowing him a few days, Jules could see how caring he was, how fascinating ... and he made her laugh.

Maybe the hot Aussie winemaker was the key to shaking her from the doldrums.

Chapter 17

The May Ladies

"**M**erry Christmas, Lucy!" Jules exclaimed.

Lucy squinted bleary-eyed at her phone, the faces of her best friends grinning up at her.

"Lucy, are you okay?" Jules's grin fell away. "You don't look so good."

"What time is it?" Lucy's tongue felt thick and furry.

"It's Christmastime!" Jules saw on the screen that she was slanting to the left—drinking wine nonstop for twelve hours might have had something to do with it—and righted herself.

"Lucy, seriously, are you okay?" asked Chloe.

Lucy pushed herself up to a seated position and cradled her forehead. "Ow."

"Ohhh," said Chloe. "Had a big night, did you?"

Lucy nodded, instantly regretting it.

"Luce, you lush!" teased Jules. "Although, I can't talk. I've had a buzz on since this morning, trying to keep up with the Aussies."

Lucy ignored the commentary, noticing that someone—

177

most likely Will—had left a large glass of water on the bedside table. She sent him a silent "thank you" and took a swig.

"If you look in the medicine cabinet, there'll be some Tylenol," said Jules. Lucy looked confused. "Pain killers. Headache tablets. Well, go. We'll wait."

Lucy scurried out of bed. "I should have warned her," said Jules. "A hundred to one, my dad's hot chocolate is the culprit. That stuff is lethal."

"I haven't even really started yet. Christmas lunch isn't 'til four. Oh, unless you count three pieces of Susan's Christmas cake. It's basically sherry held together with dried fruit." Jules wrinkled her nose; she hated Christmas cake. "You know, I think I've had more sherry in the past few days than I've had in my entire life." Chloe realised she was probably a little tipsy too. Although, if she lingered too long on Archer's news from that morning, it sobered her right up. Just wait 'til she told the girls. Although, they may already have seen the photos.

Lucy reappeared on their screens. She looked paler than usual, but a little better than before. "Hiya, loves, Happy Christmas." She gave them a weak smile, then shook her head gently at herself. "I can't believe I let myself get totally trollied on Christmas Eve. What must your family think of me, Jules?" *What must* Will *think of me, more like.*

Jules laughed, "Oh they won't care. They were probably all well on their way too—except Bradley and Bridget, 'cause they're underage. Although, I caught Bridget sneaking rum last year. She's not as straight as she seems." Jules felt an overwhelming longing for home. "So, how is everyone. How's my family?" she asked, aiming for nonchalance.

"Brilliant. They've all been so lovely."

"What about the eccentric aunty? What's she like?" asked Chloe. She was stalling, unsure of how to broach her news without killing the Christmas vibe.

"Oh, yeah! How was meeting Aunt Jackie? What mortifying thing did she lay on you? I love her to bits, but I swear that woman's filter gets worse every year."

Lucy felt the burning in her cheeks as she relived the moment in the foyer. "Come on, Lucy, spill," prodded Chloe. "You've turned into a strawberry. She said *something*."

Lucy sighed, knowing her friends would not let her off the hook until she told them. Damn her tell-tale cheeks. "It was just something about Will and me making lovely babies together." Chloe's eyes widened as a bark of a laugh escaped; even *she* wouldn't say something like that.

Jules imagined the scene and a throaty laugh took hold. "Oh, my god! That woman is *hysterical*! You and Will ..." She chuckled some more.

"Um, Lucy?" Chloe scrutinised Lucy's face, which had gone from pink to full-blown red. "Anything *else* you wanna tell us?"

Lucy's hand flew to her cheek, feeling the warmth under her palm. "Well, fuck," she said. Her friends blinked at her in surprise. She didn't drop that word very often.

"Lucy?" Jules's eyes narrowed and her smile started to fade. There was a beat while she scrutinised Lucy's face, then realisation struck. "Oh," she said, her mouth forming a perfect facsimile of the sound. "You and *Will?*"

"Nothing's happened, not really," said Lucy, racing to reassure her friend. "We just kissed, that's all."

179

"You *kissed* him? What the *hell*, Lucy?"

There was no way Jules wanted Lucy, who was completely oblivious to how beautiful she was and what effect she had on men, anywhere *near* her brother—especially after what had happened with his ex-girlfriend.

"It's just silly, really ... just a bit of fun," Lucy lied. It wasn't like that for her, but she would give anything to wipe that look from Jules's face.

Jules scowled at the screen, her mind filled with thoughts of Will falling hard for Lucy, then Lucy disappearing back to England and abandoning him. Poor Will. "Well, if that's the case, Luce, then just stay the hell away from him, okay? The last thing he needs—"

"So, Jules," Chloe cut in, not wanting their Christmas call to devolve into an episode of *The Real Housewives*. Besides, what was the big deal if Lucy and Will got together? Wasn't he, like, twenty-seven or something? "How was the orphans' Christmas?" She was again putting off her news, if only to keep the peace and, thankfully, it seemed to do the trick.

With Chloe's interruption, Jules's mind switched gears, away from thoughts of Colorado and her brother, homing in on the memory of Matt and his goodbye kiss. Yes, it was a cheek kiss, but it had lingered even longer than his Merry Christmas kiss, almost like a promise of something to come. A smile slid slowly across her face as she conjured an image of his dimples.

Lucy, however, felt as though she'd been slapped. She knew that Jules and Will were close, but she'd never seen this side of Jules before—not directed at her, in any case. How in the world was she going to make things right with Jules?

"Jules! Are you off with the fairies or something?" Chloe's voice pulled both Lucy and Jules back into the conversation.

"What? Oh, yeah, the orphans' Christmas was great," replied Jules.

Lucy, no longer in Jules's crosshairs, took another big sip of water. The headache tablets were easing the throbbing into a dull ache, but now her heart was racing. Was Jules *really* angry about her and Will? Of course, she'd been concerned about how Jules might react, but she hadn't anticipated that it would be so *viscerally*.

"Um, hello, perhaps you could elaborate?" asked Chloe.

"Sorry. I'm a little fuzzy. It's late here." Jules concentrated, picking back over the memories of the day to draw out the highlights for Chloe. "Okay, well, it was a super fun day and the food was incredible and everyone loved their gifts ..." She grinned in self-congratulations at her excellent gift selection. "Your friends really made me feel welcome, Chlo."

Chlo was less than impressed. "Really, Jules? *Details*, please."

Jules, fatigue getting the best of her, replied snippily. "Well, okay, here's a detail. How come you didn't tell me that Christmas lunch was *formal*?"

"I told you that."

"No, I don't think you did."

"I told you to pack a nice dress and heels."

"I thought that was for going out!"

Lucy tutted to herself. How did they always end up bickering like siblings? Or, at least, what she guessed was like siblings. Still, the attention was off her for the moment, so she thought better of mediating like she usually did.

"So, let me guess, you rocked up in a T-shirt and shorts and Ash set you straight," Chloe teased.

Jules, not wanting Chloe to know how accurate her guess was, replied, "Something like that. Anyway, it doesn't matter, because I *did* have a dress, 'cause my bestie told me to bring one. *Thank you*, Chloe," she sing-songed.

Chloe grinned, chalking up Jules's pseudo concession as a win.

"Actually, Matt was wearing the same colour as my dress—pale blue—well, his shirt was anyway, so that was ... And, your *tree* is decorated in all pale blue, so there we are, both matching the tree ..." She snorted a tipsy giggle. "Anyway, it was funny." *And he looked incredibly sexy ... That smile ... delish!* The fluttery feeling came back.

A sly smile curled the corners of Chloe's mouth. She'd heard from Ash and knew all about the thing brewing between Matt and Jules. What she hadn't known was Jules's take on it, but that dreamy look on her face said everything.

Lucy watched intently, not sure what was going on. Had something happened between Jules and this Matt person? And if so, why was Jules so stroppy about her and Will? Wasn't it practically the same thing?

"Matt's the best," Chloe wanted to see how Jules would respond to such a generic comment.

"He's a good guy, yeah," Jules replied, not wanting to give too much away. She still didn't know if Chloe and Matt had ever hooked up. The whole "Matt" thing could be a no-go.

"And hot," prodded Chloe.

Well, crap, thought Jules. She might as well come right with it now. "Chlo, did you and Matt ever, you know …?" She let the thought trail off, hoping it was clear what she meant.

Chloe laughed. "Hah! I knew it. Trying to be all cool like that. You're into him."

"I *might* be."

"Well, to answer your question, no. Matt is like my brother. Actually, in some ways I'm closer to him than my brother."

Chloe loved her younger brother, Drew, but he lived interstate and they only really caught up when he was visiting her parents. *And* he was seven years younger than her. His arrival had been a rude awakening, as it had meant she was no longer the only grandchild on both sides. She realised, half-tipsy on Christmas cake, that this *may* have been the reason they'd never really got close. How had she not thought of that before? She vowed right then to make more of an effort with Drew.

While Chloe was ruminating on what a terrible sister she was, Jules rested her head against the bedhead, savouring a moment of relief that Chloe and Matt had never been a thing—until her stomach plummeted. If Matt was single and he and Chloe had never hooked up, then she had a clear path. Did she *want* a clear path?

"So, Jules," Lucy, uncertain what to make of the odd expressions on her friends' faces, bravely leapt back into the conversation. "You said something about everyone liking your presents?"

"Oh, yeah," replied Jules. Presents were a welcome break from thinking about her and Matt. "So, I'd brought this gorgeous snow globe for Callie and Thea, like *beautiful*. And when I got here, I found out this was their first Christmas as a married couple—"

"Hang on a minute," Chloe interrupted, "You definitely knew *that*. You liked my photos of the wedding on Insta." Why had she even bothered prepping Jules for her Aussie Christmas? Seriously, for an engineer, Jules was the most disorganised person.

Jules scoured her brain and realised Chloe was right. "Oh, right, sorry Chlo. Anyway, Ash helped me get it engraved with 'Our first married Christmas'."

"That sounds lovely!" chimed Lucy with far more enthusiasm than she felt.

"That was really sweet, Jules," added Chloe. She could just imagine Callie gushing over that.

"Yeah, they thought it was awesome," Jules humble-bragged. She had a sudden thought. "Hey, Chloe, what's with Ash and Davo, and how come you never said they used to be a couple? Or wait, did you tell me?" Jules added, second-guessing herself.

"Actually, no, I didn't. That was for Ash to tell you if she wanted to." Jules nodded solemnly as she remembered how hard Ash had pretended to be cheerful throughout the day, even though Jules had caught her looking wistful on several occasions. "So, how *are* those two? Have they worked it out yet?" asked Chloe.

"That they still love each other?"

"Yeah," Chloe replied.

"Well, Ash definitely has. And it seems like he's pining for her, too, but they spent the whole day in 'just friends' mode." She raised one finger in half-assed air quotes.

"They'll get there eventually. I hope."

"Yeah." The conversation was getting far too morose for Jules. "Hey, so Matt got me the most awesome present," she said, to brighten the mood. "I mean, *so* thoughtful. He's taking me horseback riding in wine country on the weekend. Ash and I are going to his vineyard for a couple of days."

"Oh, I knew you'd love that."

"So, you've been *conspiring*?"

"Maybe. I just wanted you to have a good Christmas."

"Hey, Chlo, I know. You've done so much. *And* Ash; she's a doll. You've both made my first summertime Christmas amazing." *First*. Jules wondered if there would be more.

Chloe shrugged half-heartedly. It felt good to know that her plans for Jules were working out, despite Jules's best efforts to mess them up.

"Just keep an eye on Matt, though. He's never ridden a horse before. We don't want a repeat of Cabo."

"Yeah, yeah. I will," Jules replied, but Chloe doubted her warning had sunk in.

"It *was* a little weird waking up to hot weather and eating salads and cold shrimp on Christmas Day," continued Jules, "but it was a fun day. We played Celebrity Heads after lunch and, of course, there were all these Australian celebs who I had *no* idea about. Anyway, I can't remember the last time I laughed like that—probably when the three of us were together in New York."

At any other time, it was just the sort of comment that would have sent a warm shot of nostalgia through Lucy, but even though she was glad the playful bickering had died down, she was still stinging from Jules's callous disapproval of her and Will, and she sat in silence.

"And the wine! Matt the winemaker really knows his stuff!" Jules giggled. "His pinot is one of the best I've ever had."

And watching Jules get all gooey eyed over this Matt fellow when she'd just scolded her about Will was making Lucy cross. She wanted to change the subject. "So, what about you, Chloe?" she asked, deliberately redirecting the conversation. "How are Mum and Dad?"

"Honestly, Lucy, your parents are the *best*. They've been *so* nice to me. And your mum is the most amazing cook. I can't even tell you how good it smells in here." She didn't need to; Lucy knew exactly how it would smell in her parents' kitchen. "They even got me a Christmas stocking!" added Chloe.

Lucy couldn't help but laugh at Chloe's childlike delight. "Mum said she would. Was it filled with all sorts of silly nonsense? That's what she usually does."

"Oh, yeah, like, stickers and coloured pens and I even got a rubber duck—you know, like for the bath—and this gorgeous little fluffy sheep. Oh, and *so* much chocolate. I feel like I've been eating nonstop since I got here."

Lucy imagined her mum fussing over Chloe and wished she could switch places—just for a moment, only long enough to hug her and wish her a happy Christmas. Then she'd want to pop straight back to Colorado. To Will. Honestly, how was she going to get Jules onside? Or perhaps it was Jules who needed to make things right between them.

"I'll pass you over when we're done," said Chloe.

"Sorry?" Lucy hadn't quite caught that.

"When we're done talking, I'll pass my phone over to your mum and dad."

"Oh, yes, please." Lucy felt the sting of tears. As lovely a time as she was having, it really did feel odd being away from home at Christmas.

"Right, now I have some news—some good, as in *very* good, and some not so much, but first … Lucy, I have a bone to pick with you." Chloe's change in conversation was abrupt, as it often was, but Lucy wasn't prepared to have both her best friends mad at her. What had she done now? Chloe continued, "When were you going to tell us that Archer Tate grew up across the road from your parents?"

Jules, who was succumbing to the wine and had nearly nodded off, sat up, fully alert. "Hold on, what? Seriously?" How had Chloe kept something this juicy quiet until now?

It took Lucy half a second to catch on. "Ooohhh, right, *Alan* … yes, sorry, but I didn't think of it to be perfectly honest." Lucy knew—of course, she did—that he was incredibly famous now, but to her he was just the boy she knew from the village.

Predictably, when she was old enough to succumb to typical teenaged angst and longing, she'd had a crush on him. She'd been about thirteen, if she remembered correctly.

It was right about the time when she'd stretched to her current height and he to his. There was a sort of solidarity in being extremely tall teenagers amongst their peers, even if she was a fluffy-haired redhead with constantly pink cheeks and he already looked like someone out of a boy band. He was too young for Take That and too old for One Direction, but he'd had that carelessly handsome look, even back then.

What had sealed the crush, however, was how kind he was—just a very nice boy, really. She blinked the memories away. "So," she ventured carefully, not knowing if she was still in trouble, "have you met him yet?"

Chloe nodded. "Yes, actually I *have* met him. And he's an absolute sweetheart." Lucy sighed, hoping she was off the hook. This conversation was almost more than her sore head could bear. "But here's the thing—"

"This is like if there was a Hemsworth living down the hall from you and Ash," interjected Jules. She lingered on the thought, considering which one she'd prefer, Liam, Chris, or Luke? Liam. *Definitely* Liam.

"Sure, Jules, but I—" Chloe made a second attempt to explain her current, confusing situation.

"Hold on," said Lucy, "But *how* did you meet him? And *where?*" Lucy had a sudden image of Chloe peeking through the windows of the Tates's house and stifled a giggle. "You didn't find out and then go skulking about the village to 'accidentally' run into him, did you?" The giggle took hold.

"You will be pleased to know that I did not. It was a complete surprise. It was because of the Christmas Fair ..."

Chloe went on to tell her tale, starting with Dierdre's foot stuck down a rabbit hole and finishing with the Capels's reunion. Lucy wiped tears from under her eyes with her ring finger and Jules blew her nose loudly.

"Wow," said Jules quietly, a pang in her chest. Why was everything suddenly signposting how *single* she was?

"I adore the Capels," said Lucy with a little sniff.

"Right? I mean, you should have seen that kiss. This is

probably going to sound really naïve, but I had no idea older people still, you know ... kissed like that."

Jules nodded sombrely. Even the Capels were madly in love.

"And I think Alan's right," said Lucy. "I mean, *Archer*, sorry, old habits and all that, but right about their story. It would make a *wonderful* film. 'Inspired by true events ...'" Lucy smiled to herself. She *loved* a good romance.

"Oh, for sure, and he's already done a bunch of research," added Chloe.

"He should interview them," suggested Lucy. "Especially as Mrs Capel is not likely to remember things for much longer ..." She trailed off.

"And, if they're both eighty-plus ..." noted Jules.

"Hmm," murmured Chloe, the underlying urgency of the situation tugging at her heart.

"So, are you and Archer, like, a *thing*?" asked Jules. She'd been watching Chloe closely, and was sure there was something going on. She'd never seen Chloe this infatuated before—with a *guy*, anyway. Chloe did have an almost freakish love of closet organisers and stationery.

Lucy was shocked to see the pinkness rise in Chloe's cheeks. "You're blushing," she declared.

Chloe couldn't conceal her grin. "He kissed me."

"Oh, my god!" Jules exclaimed. How awesome was it that her best friend had kissed a Hollywood hottie?

Lucy squealed, ignoring the sharp pain that stabbed her temples. "Chloe, that's wonderful. Alan's—Sorry, *Archer's* so, so lovely."

"Yeah, he is. And look, I know it's only been a couple of

days, and it's definitely surreal at times, but honestly, being kissed like that, Lucy ... I've never ..." She sighed. "Let's just say, it's a first for me." She bit her lip, realising as she said the words, that it was more than just the kiss. The feelings she was having were a first too.

"I'll tell you what's a first—you're practically tongue-tied," said Lucy. She and Chloe exchanged grins.

Jules watched Lucy's face, seeing how genuinely delighted she was for Chloe, and felt like crap. Why had she given Lucy such a hard time about Will? She knew why—sort of—but still, Lucy was one of the people dearest to her and it was *Christmas*. She'd been such a shit, but before she could say anything to make it right, Chloe interjected.

"There's something else, though," said Chloe, her good cheer fading. "So, just trust me on this and do exactly what I say, okay?" Jules sat up a little straighter and Lucy nodded solemnly. "I want you to google Archer, then select 'news'. Go ahead, I'll wait."

Chloe watched as her friends' fingers flew over their respective phone screens. Their twin looks of shock—or was that horror?—landed at almost exactly the same time. "Yep," declared Chloe. "That. That happened."

"Oh, my *god*, Chlo," Jules exclaimed. She seriously wished she were more sober for this conversation; she was barely able to keep up.

"Oh, Chloe, I'm so sorry. Are you all right?" asked Lucy.

"Thanks, Luce. I'm a little shaken up, to be honest. I mean, Archer came and told me as soon as he knew—this morning, actually."

"Well, Merry Fricking Christmas, huh, Chlo?" asked Jules

rhetorically. "I don't know what's worse—your face splashed all over the tabloids or that you don't even have a name. You're just 'mystery woman'."

"Yeah, thanks for stating the obvious, Jules," said Chloe with a laugh.

Lucy, damned if she was going to let this conversation devolve back into another quarrel, stepped into the fray. "So, Chloe, what now? Do you think you will continue ... uh ... things with Al-Archer?"

Chloe sighed. "I've been going back and forth all day. He was *so* lovely this morning, Luce—*devasted* to have dragged me into all this, just by the very nature of being who he is. And he gave me an out. He told me straight up that he completely understood if I never wanted to see him again."

"But do you?" asked Lucy. Even with only a few minutes to get used to the idea, she could just imagine Alan—Archer, rather—with Chloe. They would be wonderful together.

Jules was silent, also invested in her friend's reply.

"I think I want to see him again. I mean, it's a *lot*. I'm not going to lie. But he's so lovely, just a wonderful person. You should see how he is with everyone in the village. He's ..." She sighed. "I think I need to see how things go," she said simply. She saw Lucy nodding as though she was listening to some unheard music.

"Jules, what do you think?" Chloe asked.

Jules chuckled. "Dude, seriously, it's Archer Fricking Tate. You *have* to give this guy a chance. Even if it's just for bragging rights."

Lucy scrunched up her nose, as though she'd smelled

something bad, but Chloe just laughed. "Actually, a tiny part of my brain *has* considered that. And I am not proud of this—and I'll only ever tell you two—but how cool would it be for Gia DeLorenzo to open up a copy of *Women's Monthly* and see photos of me and Archer all dressed up at some premiere?"

"Who the hell is Gia DeLorenzo?" asked Jules.

"High school bully, remember?" replied Chloe. "The one that sat behind me in Maths class and put gum in my hair."

"Oh, that's right, Chloe, how horrible," cried Lucy.

"Eh, I got over it … mostly." Chloe grinned at her besties, and Lucy returned the smile with a slightly sad version. Jules fixated on Lucy's face, again feeling a pang of guilt for being such a shit.

"Hey, Luce, have you looked outside yet?" Jules asked. She decided she'd be extra sweet to Lucy for the rest of the call. It was a start.

Lucy's mouth popped open and she shook her head. How had she forgotten? She pushed aside the duvet and ran to the window, pulling the curtains aside. "Oh," she sighed, clutching both hands to her chest and her phone along with them.

"Luce?" she heard Jules's muffled voice and looked into screen.

"It's beautiful, look." She swivelled the camera so Chloe and Jules could see. The ground was blanketed by snow, fondant covered mounds peppered across the landscape. A range of snow-dusted mountains stood proudly in the distance, and the brilliant blue of a cloudless sky contrasted starkly against the white of the snow and the deep, dusty green of the conifers.

Tears prickled Lucy's eyes, which was silly, really. She'd had this exact view since she'd arrived. *But now it's Christmas and that makes it even more special.*

"I'm going to make a snowman!" she declared, climbing back into the snuggly bed. She swivelled the camera back to catch her friends laughing, possibly *at* her. "Not right at this minute, of course, sillies, but today. In honour of my first proper white Christmas in, well, practically *forever*."

"Well, take lots of pics. As you predicted, it is grey and wet here. It hasn't stopped raining all day. But at least it didn't rain during the fair yesterday. Maybe that was our Christmas miracle," said Chloe.

"I knew you'd love the fair, but I didn't think you'd end up *running* it. Sorry about that, lovely."

Chloe waved off the apology. "I had a ball, to be honest, and I got to know Archer's mother a little. Cecily."

"Oh, she's scary."

"Archer's mom is?" asked Jules.

Lucy nodded slowly, eyes wide, and Chloe laughed. "She's okay. I kind of like her."

"Maybe it's because *you* can be scary, Chlo," teased Jules. "*Moi?*"

"Oh, yes, that will be why. Two peas in a pod," added Lucy, giggling.

"Hey, Lucy, I just remembered, your mum said something about your new boss, that things have been kinda shitty for you at work lately." Lucy's elated expression dissolved, and Chloe knew that with one thoughtless comment, she'd put a dampener on Lucy's day.

"Sorry, Lucy. We'll talk about the work thing another time, okay?"

Lucy nodded numbly, a tiny frown between her brows. Chloe willed Jules to step in and, thankfully, she picked up on it.

"Sure, Luce, don't worry about all that now. You're gonna have a great day with my family. Tell them I'll call them tomorrow, okay? I mean, *my* tomorrow." Lucy's mouth pulled into a tight smile that didn't reach her eyes, and Jules knew that it was her fault. She'd have to fix things with Lucy, but not right now. She could barely stay awake. "Okay, well I'm gonna sign off now, girls." She stifled a yawn. "Have a very merry Christmas. I love you." She waved into the phone and ended the call.

"Lucy?" Chloe was hellbent on making amends. How had she been so insensitive as to bring up the work thing *today* of all days? What was wrong with her?

"I'm fine."

"O-kay." Chloe wasn't convinced.

"You don't have to treat me like I'm this fragile little thing, Chloe." Lucy saw Chloe bite her lip. "Sorry, that was a bit rude." She blew out a short, sharp sigh, and Chloe waited. Clearly, Lucy wanted to say something else. "Why was Jules such a cow about me and Will?"

"Is that what's bothering you? Or is it the work thing?"

"It's, well, it's both, but I don't want to think about my job right now. Besides, the more pressing thing is Will. I have to go downstairs this morning ... and it's Christmas ... and he's so lovely and so *scrummy*. And now I feel like I've totally stepped in it." She knew she was whining, but she didn't care.

"Oh, Luce. Maybe Jules is just being a big sister, you know?" Lucy's eyes narrowed. She wasn't buying it. "Look, do you want me to talk to her?"

"No. I'm a big girl."

"I know that, Lucy."

"I just ... Jules is one of my best friends, and even *she* doesn't think I'm good enough for her brother."

"I'm sure *that's* not true. There's something else going on."

"It doesn't matter, anyway. It really is just a bit of fun." Hearing the lie out loud made Lucy feel even worse.

Chloe wished more than anything she could give Lucy a hug. "Luce?" Lucy blinked back tears—*again*. Why was she so emotional? Maybe it was the hangover. "Lucy, tell me."

It wasn't the hangover.

"I like him, Chloe. A lot. And what if something actually does happen between us? And what if that messes up my friendship with Jules?"

"Look, if something more serious happens, then Jules will just have to get over it. Okay?" Lucy, unconvinced, said nothing. "I love you, Luce. It will be okay."

"I love you, too. And thank you."

"Do you want to talk to your mum and dad now?" she asked brightly. Relieved, she saw Lucy perk up a little. "Hang on, two secs."

A smile broke across Lucy's face as her mum peered up from the phone. "Happy Christmas, Mum, I miss you so much."

"Oh, love, we're missing you too."

Chapter 18

Chloe

"How did Lucy seem to you, love?" Susan had caught Chloe in the kitchen sneaking another sliver of Christmas cake. The question hung in the air as her mouth twitched. "You know, love, we'll be sitting down to Christmas lunch soon. You won't want to spoil it, now."

Chloe put down the slice of cake and apologised sheepishly. "Sorry, it's just *so* good."

"How about I make us some tea instead. It doesn't take up as much room." Susan patted her stomach and put the kettle on, adding what Chloe had come to know as her signature wink. As she bustled about, checking on Christmas lunch, Chloe sat at the small kitchen table noticing again how good everything smelled; it smelled like *Christmas*.

The apple sauce simmering on the stove was definitely a culprit, its heady spices of cinnamon, cardamom, and star anise filling the air. There was also a stuffed goose roasting in the oven, along with Brussels sprouts, parsnips, and potatoes, all bathed in goose fat. Chloe hadn't had goose before, but if the aromas from the oven were anything to go by, it would be another new favourite.

Chloe was humbled by the amount of effort it had taken—was taking—to put this meal on the table, but Susan had approached it all with practised ease. She *did* say she was cheating with the Heston Blumenthal pudding and vanilla-bean custard from the shop, but Chloe had assured her that it was all going to be spectacular and that she'd heard the Blumenthal puddings were something to behold.

She had also helped as much as she was allowed, putting her hand to chopping and peeling, but as soon as she was done with her assigned tasks, Susan had tried to shoo her out of the kitchen. "At least let me help clean up," she'd insisted, being a clean-as-you-go cook herself. She was permitted on the proviso that she'd then go and keep Max company, which meant reading her Kindle while he read the latest Harlan Coben book he'd got for Christmas.

Max did not offer to help in the kitchen, but only because he would, "just get underfoot." He did, however, set the table. Chloe knew that if her dad sat down to read on Christmas Day while her mum was buzzing about the kitchen getting all the food ready, he would have been on the end of some *seriously* passive-aggressive comments until he relented. But her dad would never do that; he wouldn't dare.

Just as Susan was about to heap some loose leaves into the teapot, Chloe had a better idea. "Actually, Susan, what do you think about cracking open the bubbles Archer gave me?"

If a woman of sixty-something can giggle, then that's what she did. "Oooh, bubbly would be lubbly." She giggled again and Chloe joined in. "Oooh, and I have some proper glasses put away somewhere." Susan disappeared, presumably to the front room where they seemed to keep all the "good stuff"— the china and crystal—while Chloe retrieved the bottle from the fridge.

"Dusty," Susan declared before heading straight to the sink to wash the flutes. With her back turned, she again posed her earlier question about how Lucy had seemed, and Chloe felt a twinge of guilt. "I think I stuffed up." Susan turned, a glass in one hand, a tea towel in the other, and looked at her inquisitively. She was an expert listener, Chloe realised. "I mentioned the job thing." Susan nodded and pursed her lips. Chloe doubted it was with derision, but it certainly didn't make her feel any better.

Susan brought the now-clean glasses to the table and picked up the bottle. "She will want to talk to you about it eventually, I imagine, just not on Christmas." So, Chloe *had* stuffed up. "She's had a hard time of it lately, poor Lucy," continued Susan, "and, quite honestly, I'm surprised she hasn't mentioned it to you girls already. That woman—" Susan cut off her own thought, her anger palpable. Chloe felt a little helpless, not having an immediate fix, but she'd just have to wait until Lucy was ready to talk about it.

But Chloe's concern turned into wonder as she watched Susan peel back the foil on the bottle with one pull, untwist the metal cap cleanly, grasp the bottom of the bottle with one hand and the cork with the other, and turn the bottle until a whisper of a pop echoed around the kitchen.

Susan caught Chloe's look. "I wasn't always a librarian who

lived in a tiny village, love. There was once upon a time when I was quite the London party girl." She raised her eyebrows, poured, then handed Chloe, still dumbstruck, a glass. "Should I be insulted that you look so surprised?"

"What? Oh, no, sorry. It's just ... as well as having no filter sometimes—like with Lucy today—I often find myself underestimating people. Sorry."

"I see. Well, not to worry, love. I won't take it personally." She winked again, then raised her own glass which was now brimming. "Happy Christmas, Chloe. It's been lovely having you here." They clinked glasses. "So," said Susan taking the seat next to Chloe, "Now that everything's humming along for our lunch, *and* we've spoken to our Lucy, why don't we dig into your dilemma."

Chloe almost choked on her bubbles, which was a shame, as it was French Champagne and utterly delicious. She composed herself, wiping her bottom lip. "My dilemma?" she squeaked, then cleared her throat. She adored Lucy's mum, but she wasn't sure she wanted to "dig into" the depths of the paparazzi horror show that Archer had shared with her, especially as it was Christmas and she was hoping to immerse herself in the rest of the day without giving it another thought. Still ...

"Look, and please tell me if I'm just being a nosy busybody, but Alan's face when he arrived ..." Susan sighed and shook her head. Chloe waited for her to add a series of tuts, but they didn't come. "And after he left, you seemed ... well, not yourself, Chloe love. I'm just saying that if you want to talk about it, I'm here."

Chloe *never* talked to her mum about this type of thing. She only divulged the ins and outs of her love life—so to speak and such that it was—with Ash, Lucy, and Jules. Susan took another sip of her bubbles, smoothing down her apron with the other hand. It was a masterful interrogation technique, the patient pause, and Chloe found herself succumbing without further resistance.

"Well, you see, Archer and I, we were papped."

If Susan was surprised, she did a brilliant job of hiding it. Maybe she'd been more than a London party girl. Maybe she'd also worked for MI6. "I see," she said, nodding solemnly.

"Kissing," added Chloe.

That did evoke a slight raise of the eyebrows. "Mmm." Susan's eyes dropped to the table and her brow furrowed slightly. After a few moments, Chloe practically on the edge of her seat for each one, Susan lifted her eyes. "Chloe, I have known Alan Tate all his life. He is a truly good person. Talented? Yes. Handsome? Undeniably ..."

Susan raised her brows again, this time her eyes glinting with humour, and Chloe responded with a grin.

"But all of that is superficial. There are dozens, *hundreds* of handsome actors in the world. Alan is ... he's special. He has a big heart, and I know that Cecily has worried about him over the years, with how many times that heart has been broken. She's a tough nut to crack, is our Cecily, but I'll come back to that later. What's important is that Alan showed up here as *soon* as he made that discovery, even though it was on Christmas morning, and *that* tells you everything you need to know about him."

Chloe nodded slowly, her own brows knitting together. "At least that's how I see it," added Susan before taking another sip of her bubbles.

Chloe had been going back and forth on the "Archer-paparazzi" matter for most of the day. Did she really want to get involved with the world's biggest film star? Yes, he seemed to appreciate her warped sense of humour. And yes, that kiss had been something else. But having her life splashed all over the tabloids ... And not just premieres and awards shows, but regular, everyday life ... But, then again, everything Susan had said about him was true. Even though it had only been a few days, Chloe knew that Archer was special. She'd *seen* it.

"And I dare say," said Susan, interrupting her thoughts, "that you are one of the few people to have brought a smile to Cecily Tate's face in *years*."

"Really?" Chloe asked, lifting her gaze to Susan's. If that had happened, Chloe hadn't seen it.

"Oh yes. I caught her raving about you to Simon, you know, from the committee." Chloe did know Simon, yes—he of the impossibly sour expression.

"Well, that's very nice to hear, especially as Cecily really impressed *me*. She's as good as any pro I've worked with in Melbourne. Actually, she's better than many of them."

"Well, I think she's taken a shine to you." She paused. "And *I* was very proud of you, too, you know." Chloe was shocked by how much those words meant to her and, truly humbled, she smiled. "Especially, how you and Alan helped with Mrs Capel. It's worrisome, that she wanders off sometimes."

"Oh, yes, it must be. And I didn't do much …" Susan's look indicated that she thought otherwise. "I was just happy to help. And Archer told me all about the Capels on the way to collect her. Such an extraordinary couple."

"They are. Actually, I don't think I mentioned it, but we're taking them their Christmas lunch before we sit down."

"Oh, that's …" Chloe was speechless and felt the sting of tears.

"We've done it every year for some time now—the whole village. This year just happens to be our turn. Mrs Capel—Eloise—you see, she's not up to the task, and their only son lives in Australia with his wife and daughter, so the village … we're their surrogate family, as you saw yesterday."

Chloe nodded, biting her tongue about the expectation that it would be *Mrs* Capel's responsibility to make Christmas lunch. Things were certainly different in that little English village than they were back home. "In any case, we'll make up some dishes for them—the full lunch and some pudding—and drop them 'round right after the Queen's speech. I was thinking you might like to come with me?"

"I'd love to. That would be amazing." Chloe had a thought—*Archer will want to come with us*—but it gave her pause. Was she ready to see him again so soon? Regardless, this wasn't about her and she knew what she had to do. "Actually, would you mind if I asked Archer to come? I think it would mean a lot to him, especially after yesterday."

"Not at all. How about you telephone the Tates when we finish our drinks."

"Thanks, I will," she said, feeling a twinge of nerves. She

wanted—no, *needed*—to talk about something else. "Susan, I meant to ask you, did Lucy mention anything *else* when you spoke to her?"

"You mean about the young man, Will?" Chloe nodded. "She was somewhat coy, but I know my daughter and there seemed to be more talk of Will than the rest of the family put together. He's Jules's brother, correct?"

"Yes. And that might be another reason she wasn't quite herself." Chloe would *not* mention the third reason, Lucy's hangover. "Jules was kind of a bitch to her about it when it came up."

"About Lucy and Will? But why?"

"It's unclear. But she really shut Lucy down. It's a bit rich, really, because I think something's going on between her and one of my friends in Melbourne."

Susan's look was a mix of perplexity and anger. She pursed her lips. "Well, that would explain it, I suppose, Lucy not being her usual bright self."

"Look, I'll talk to Jules. I think Lucy really likes Will. And I can't *remember* the last time she really liked someone."

"She *was* going out with that Edward for a while, last year, remember?"

"Oh, right. *Him.*" Chloe had never met Edward, but she'd seen photos of him on Facebook—nothing special—*and* she'd heard the stories from Lucy—again, nothing special. Just a normal boring guy, who for some reason thought he was too good for her—for beautiful, brilliant, lovely Lucy—and had dumped her during her work party. The dick. Chloe had hated him from across the globe.

"Exactly. It does strike me, sometimes, that Lucy has absolutely no idea."

Chloe laughed, glad she'd just swallowed her mouthful of bubbles. "Do you mean about men in general, or that she's an absolute goddess?"

"Both, really. It doesn't seem to matter how many times we tell her how proud of her we are, or how clever she is, even how beautiful, it never seems to sink in. Is she the same with you girls?"

"Yeah. And there's nothing put on about it, you know? She's not, like, pretending to be humble; she just *is*. I think that's part of her appeal. There are a lot of good-looking people out there who think they're all that and a bag of chips and treat people like crap. I see a lot of that in my job."

"Well, do let me know about this Will fellow ... if she lets on any more than you already know."

"For sure."

"Shall we toast her, our Lucy? I miss her terribly today."

Chloe held her glass aloft. "To our Lucy, the goddess who hasn't got a clue."

Susan smiled wistfully and they clinked glasses.

*

The Queen's speech was actually quite moving, even though the Queen was as stoic as ever and completely dry-eyed. But it was her message about unity and humanity that resonated with Chloe, and yes, maybe it was the half-bottle of bubbles, but listening attentively, she felt a wave of overwhelming love for her fellow humans—especially the ones sitting with her in the front room.

At the sound of a knock at 3:27pm, Chloe jumped out of her chair, throwing, "I'll get it," over her shoulder. For the second time in a few days, she opened the door to the world's biggest film star. This time, however, it wasn't a giant shock.

"Hello," he said.

"Hello."

"Happy Christmas again." He smiled shyly and she waved him inside.

"Happy Christmas," she replied. *Wonderful*, she thought, *we've gone from casual and easy to completely frigging awkward and weird.*

"I brought this for the Capels." Archer retrieved a bottle of red wine from the carry bag slung over his shoulder.

"That's so lovely."

"Thank you again for inviting me to come with you. I was a little surprised to hear from you so soon after, well, you know." *He seems a little nervous*, thought Chloe.

"No, of course you should come with us. There's no question," she reassured.

A smile broke out across his face. "Actually, Chloe," he lowered his voice, "when we get back from theirs, I've something I want to ask you about. Something *else*, I mean. It's not the mess with the papp—"

"Hello, Alan love," said Susan, appearing behind Chloe.

"Hello again, Mrs Browning." He replied, giving her a kiss on the cheek. "And Happy Christmas. Again."

"Happy Christmas, love. Right, we're all set, I think. Just

come through here." Susan led them into the kitchen. "I've served up into some ovenproof dishes and I think Richard will be able to manage reheating them if need be." She wrapped up the dishes in tea towels and tucked them into a wide basket with a cane handle. "Hmm, Alan love, I think I'll need you to carry this."

"No problem at all."

Susan called out a goodbye to Max and the three of them embarked on their Christmas Samaritan journey—out the door, down the very short front path, along the road to the fifth house on the left, and up to the Capels's front door. The entire journey took less than a minute.

As Archer knocked on the door, all Chloe's worry about the Archer situation fell away, and she felt a rush of excitement. When she had proposed the Christmas swap back in July, all Chloe had wanted was a traditional English Christmas. She had no way of knowing then how much the hamlet of Penham would come to mean to her in just a few short days, or how much an English Christmas would feed her soul.

The door opened and a beaming Richard Capel welcomed them inside.

*

"I've got a crush," said Chloe. They were back inside the Browning's entry, just her and Archer, Susan having excused herself to get Christmas lunch on the table. Susan had invited Archer to stay, but he would be sitting down to lunch with his parents soon. Chloe thought again how odd it was to call it Christmas lunch when it was practically dinner time. It was almost dark outside.

"So, your crush? Is it on me?" Archer was playing; it was in the tug of a smile at the corners of his mouth. Perhaps he felt emboldened by their visit to the Capels, which had gone unbelievably well. Mrs Capel had been cognisant of their arrival and had clasped her hands together in almost childlike glee as they helped unpack the Christmas dinner.

"You? No, definitely not." Chloe could play too. "On the *Capels*. Like, a serious crush. As in, I want to have a love like—" She stopped herself; she'd given away too much.

"I know just what you mean." They shared a smile and there was a moment when Chloe wondered if he was going to kiss her. What *was* the protocol with the Brownings in the next room? And even more pressing, would a kiss resolve the multitude of questions that still hung between them? Chloe doubted that very much.

He didn't kiss her—Chloe was both relieved and disappointed—but instead, took her hands in his. "So, that thing I wanted to ask you about. I've just found out that I'm expected in London the day after tomorrow, for an interview with *Vanity Fair*. And I know I dropped a bombshell on you this morning, and I can't say I would blame you if you said no, but I thought that maybe you would like to come with me to London—tonight, actually. I'll be driving back after Christmas lunch. It would just be three nights. We'd be staying at the Four Seasons. And, of course, I'd be more than happy to get you your own suite. I don't mean to presume anything. So ..."

Chloe was torn. She'd been loving the Christmassy bubble of Penham, but the mess with the paparazzi aside, she suspected it would now feel empty without Archer. Then again, how would Lucy's parents feel about her disappearing off to London—and on *Christmas*?

"Um ..."

"Of course. This is probably all a bit much. It's just ... I'm mindful that you're not here for very long and I want to spend as much time with you as possible. But, with everything that's happened, I shouldn't have presu—"

"No, it's not that," she interrupted. "I mean, yeah, I'm still trying to wrap my brain around the paparazzi thing, but ..." She looked over her shoulder towards the kitchen.

"*Oh*, right," he said, lowering the volume of his voice further. "You're worried that it might seem rude."

"Yes, exactly. The Brownings have been so lovely, and they've really gone out of their way for me."

"Of course, I understand." He frowned.

"Chloe love, can I borrow you in the kitchen for a moment?" asked Susan. "Alan, pop in and say hello to Max, will you?"

The two thirty-somethings did as they were told and within moments, Chloe was on the receiving end of a conspiratorial whisper. "I hope you don't think I'm poking my nose in, but I couldn't help but overhear." If Susan said the word, she'd stay, no questions asked. "You should go with Alan."

"Really?"

"If it's what you want to do, then absolutely," came the whispered reply. *Oh, thank god!* "Alan—sorry, *Archer*—as I said, he's a good egg. And if you can sort out all this other

209

business, well, then ... go. Go and have a lovely time, and we'll be here when you return."

Chloe dropped her cool façade and bounced up and down on the spot. "Thank you. I do really like him."

"Yes." A simple reply, but it meant the world to her.

"But Chloe love, we're going to have to do something about a proper coat for you. I can't bear to think of you freezing half to death like you were yesterday. I think I have something that will do."

"Oh, I was fine. You don't need to—" Susan's raised eyebrows said otherwise. "Okay, you're right. Thank you!" She gave Susan a kiss on the cheek and went to tell Archer the good news.

Chapter 19

Jules

"Hi, Dad! Merry Christmas!"

"Hi, sweetheart. Same to you, although it's the twenty-sixth, there, huh?"

"Boxing Day, yes."

"The Canadians call it that too, although I've never met one who could explain why."

"Same here. As far as I can gather, it's a lot like the Friday after Thanksgiving—leftovers, watching Netflix, and lounging about in a food coma. It's also ninety-eight degrees today, so we're inside with the A/C on."

"I can't even fathom that. It's a balmy five degrees here today."

As much as she missed her family, especially her dad, Jules was glad to be where she was. "So, what's going on? The usual craziness?" she asked.

"You guessed it. I just finished cleaning up after breakfast." She could imagine the giant spread—cinnamon rolls, pancakes, bacon, and eggs. Her dad's Christmas Day

211

breakfasts were legendary. "I think we'll be opening presents soon."

Jules knew the scene by heart—the giant scraggly Christmas tree decorated in popcorn and paper chains, just like when they were kids, surrounded by a mountain of presents which would turn into a mountain of discarded wrapping paper over the course of an hour. She'd always been someone who enjoyed the giving part more than the receiving, waiting to see the delight on her family's faces as they unwrapped what she hoped were the perfect presents.

And not that she was ungrateful, but it was rare that she received something she wouldn't buy for herself if she wanted it. Her best present last year had been from her dad. He'd gifted her a chunk of air miles, enough for an international flight. Actually, his gift had "paid" for her flight to Australia, but it was the thought that counted most to Jules, that message of, "I see you, that you need to go and explore this world. Here, go and see some of it on me."

"Take photos for me, Dad?"

"For sure, sweetheart."

"Especially of the tree," she laughed. "How bad is it this year?" As much as her family Christmases felt claustrophobic at times, she cherished their tradition of finding the worst tree in the forest—one that no one else would want—then draping it in as many homemade decorations as possible. Chloe would have hated it, she realised, thinking of the department-store-ready tree that dominated the living room.

"We have hit optimal awfulness, an *extremely* poor

specimen. But I think it may have baffled Lucy. I'm guessing from her reaction that you didn't warn her."

Jules laughed, "Oh, no, poor Lucy! I totally forgot about that." The thought made a U-turn in her mind as she remembered that things weren't right with Lucy—totally her doing. Feeling the sting of remorse, she added, "Hey, Dad, so how is Lucy?"

"Oh, sweetheart, if we can't have you here, it's almost as good having Lucy. She's a doll."

Jules gulped down the lump in her throat.

"Is she there? Can I talk to her?"

"Sure. Hold on." She could tell her dad was on the move, because the screen blurred, and she had to look away so she didn't get motion sickness.

Her mom's face appeared on the screen. "Merry Christmas, honey."

"Oh, Mom, hi! Merry Christmas. You look beautiful."

Her mom laughed off the compliment as she always did. "So how was your Aussie Christmas?" In her mom's accent, it came out as "Oss-ee".

"Great! Really different from home, though. Ash put on this *awesome* Christmas lunch. You'll see when you check my Insta feed. We set this epic table and we all dressed up for a formal sit-down meal. We had ham, like at home, but everything else was a complete departure. We even had this massive platter of shrimp, or 'prawns', they say here. *So* good. Oh, and I baked my Christmas cookies. Total hit." Her mom grinned at her.

"That sounds fun, honey. And what about Chloe's friends? You're having a good time?"

"Yeah, I mean, Ash's been amazing, schlepping me about Melbourne. She's almost as hard core with her organising as Chloe is, but all the heavy lifting's over now, so hopefully she'll just chill out for the next few days. There's this whole thing with her ex that I won't go into, but he was here yesterday, and he's so sweet, and he's obviously still into her ... Anyway, I hope they figure it out.

"Oh, and we're going away for a couple of days," Jules added.

"You and Ash?"

"Yeah, and um, this guy, Matt. Actually, he's a winemaker and we're going to his vineyard." She was playing it down, hoping her budding crush on Matt wasn't too obvious, but her mom had *always* been able to tell when she was hiding something—like her *feelings*. "I miss you, Mom," she said spontaneously.

"We miss you too, honey. Did you want to say hello to your brother? He's right here."

"Oh yeah, sure, but actually ... I thought Dad was handing me over to Lucy."

Her mom looked off screen, her face instantly readable. Lucy was there, in the room, but didn't want to come to the phone.

Her best friend didn't want to talk to her.

Her mom made some lame excuse that didn't really register, then the phone was passed to Will. "Hey, Jules. Merry Christmas."

"And to you!" she said brightly as she faked a smile. The phone was on the move again and Jules waited, uneasy, for her brother's face to reappear.

"Hey," he said, his voice barely above a whisper. Jules saw that he was back in the kitchen and she tried to concentrate on the mundaneness of his surroundings, dreading what she knew was going to come out of his mouth. *Oh look, they got a new kettle. That must be for Lucy.*

"So, Jules, Lucy, man, she's ..." Yep. He'd gone straight to where she knew he would.

"She *is*, isn't she?" Her brother's grin nearly broke her heart. He was already in deep.

He ran his hand through his hair. "Yeah, look, it's really new, but I don't know, I feel something, something ... and uh, it's ..." He blew out a breath, the smile growing bigger if that was even possible. "It's, well, you know ...?"

Her brother was babbling, yet everything he was thinking and feeling was right there on the screen. Yep, she had totally screwed this up. She really needed to talk to Lucy and make things right.

*

"Are you sure you don't want to come?" Jules was packing her carry-on bag for the weekend at Matt's vineyard. He was due in the next half-hour to collect her.

"Nah, I'm good," replied Ash from the doorway. "Besides, you don't want me being a third wheel." Ash climbed on the bed and hugged one of the throw pillows.

Jules stopped in the middle of folding a T-shirt. "Had you ever intended on coming?" She fixed Ash with a look, but she seemed wholly absorbed in the tassels on the pillow. "Ash, hello?"

"Sprung," Ash grinned with a shrug, "You guys are cute together, you know."

"*Cute?*" Another shrug. Jules finished folding the T-shirt and tucked it into her carry-on.

"Chloe and I had a hunch that you guys might like each other."

"What, seriously? Chloe was in on this? And if you shrug one more time ..."

Ash's shoulders made it halfway to her ears and dropped. "Look, I'm not going to apologise. I mean, why would I? Matt's been single for a while, you've apparently been single for, well, for*ever* according to Chloe, and what's the harm in a little holiday fling?"

"Your argument is flawless," Jules teased. "Did Chloe really say I'd been single for forever?"

"Yeah. So, what does that mean? How long are we talking here?"

"Well, it depends. Are you asking about a relationship or sex?"

"Both, either—no, both."

"My last serious relationship was in my early twenties."

"Really?"

"Yeah."

"Why so long ago?"

"That was when my parents split up. Doesn't take a rocket scientist to connect the dots. I just saw what it did to the two of them, especially my dad. And yeah, they're friends now, like I said, but my dad was devastated back then. I know he thinks he hid that from me, but I was dialled into it."

"But it hasn't been that long since you had *sex*, right?"

"No, definitely not, but it's usually with guys I don't like all that much. Easier that way. Distant, you know?"

Ash stared at a tassel, flipping it between her fingers. Jules paused her packing. Was all this talk about relationships and sex even a good idea with Ash still hurting over Davo?

And what about her and Matt?

She'd been toying with the idea of a fling with the hot winemaker since her first day in Melbourne. But that was before she'd got to know him, before the beach and the feeling of his arms wrapped around her, before the lingering cheek kisses and the easy conversation. Before she saw those dimples. Before he was *Matt*.

Jules stared at her carry-on, now packed, then sat heavily on the end of the bed. "Is this a terrible idea?"

"Why, what do you mean?"

"Going to the vineyard. Just the two of us."

"No, it'll be fun."

"That's what I *mean*. I think Matt and I might be beyond 'fun'." She made the air quotes. "I know it's only been a few days, but I'd be kidding myself if I said it was just physical. He's ..." She stared at her hands in her lap.

"There's something there."

"Yeah. And I don't want to start something that's more than a fling. *Especially* 'cause this time next week, I won't even be here. That's not fair on Matt."

"But how fair is it not to see?" Jules's head popped up. "On you or Matt?" Ash leant forward and stared at her intently. "What if he's your *person*, you know?"

Jules did know, yes. She'd had that once—her person—and it had all imploded. She'd fudged the truth about her last relationship. He had cheated. She'd been devastated about her family breaking in two, and instead of being there for her, he'd fricking cheated.

The knot in her stomach twisted tighter.

"One of us has to be brave," Ash whispered.

Jules met her eyes. They were shining again, and Jules didn't need to ask why. She reached over and squeezed Ash's hand. Right here was the perfect example of what happened when you let fear rule your heart.

"Oh, to hell with it. I'm going!"

Ash sprung off the bed and clapped. Maybe living vicariously through her was as close as Ash wanted to get to love, Jules thought.

*

"He likes you."

Dexter, Matt's border collie, was covering Jules's face with dog kisses, then running between them and leaping into the air. Her throaty laugh quickly turned to squeals of delight. Had a dog ever been this excited to meet her?

"Dex, off!" Matt reached down and offered her a hand, then pulled her to her feet. Dexter did exactly as he was told and lay at Matt's feet panting from the excitement. "Sorry 'bout that."

"No, no I love it." She reached down and scratched under Dexter's chin. "You love it too, don't you, you beautiful boy?"

Dexter smiled at her and she laughed again. "See? We're already the best of friends."

Matt chuckled. "You've gotta know that he's not like this with everyone. One of our distribution guys, Wayne—well, Dex isn't a fan of his. Oh, hey, did you see that? Watch." They both watched Dexter's face and Matt said, "Wayne," again. Dexter stood and gave a sharp bark, and Matt threw his head back and laughed.

Jules grinned at the pair of them. "So, I guess you have to spell his name out now, huh?"

"I dunno, he's pretty clever."

"Who, Dexter or Wayne? Oops." She clamped a hand over her mouth right as Dexter barked again. "Sorry." She giggled through her fingers.

Matt petted his dog on the head. "Actually, he's bang on. I'm not much of a fan of W-A-Y-N-E either. C'mon, let me show you around."

He retrieved Jules's carry-on and his duffel bag from the car and led the way inside.

"Oh, my god, I love this!"

"It's home—a little rustic, but we like it, right Dex?" Matt set the bags down and Dexter responded to his question by curling up on a dog mat next to the couch.

The main room—a combined kitchen, living, and dining room—was light and airy with wooden floors, off-white walls and a high apex ceiling. A wall of windows looked out over gently rolling hills covered in neat rows of vines.

The modular couch invited lounging and a long, low, wooden coffee table offered a variety of activities—coffee-table books, a stack of novels, a chessboard, and a backgammon set.

The long wooden dining table looked like the perfect place to spend an evening with friends having dinner and playing board games, and the large kitchen had polished stone countertops and, not surprisingly, a built-in wine fridge.

And even though the room was spacious, it felt cosy, inviting. It was also super tidy.

"No, really, Matt, this place is awesome." She walked over to the windows and looked out at the vines. "And this view ... I bet you never get tired of this."

He stood beside her, draping an arm around her shoulders and, as though it were the most natural thing in the world, she leant against him and breathed in his scent—woodsy and masculine. His fingertips gently stroked her arm. "I'm really glad you're here," he said quietly.

Her breath caught in her throat. "Me too," she whispered. She felt his head rest against hers and steadied her breath, a defiant move against her racing heart.

She wasn't sure who moved first, or if perhaps they turned together, but his arm slid to her waist and she tipped her face to his as their mouths came together. His other hand found the nape of her neck, the touch of his fingers sending tingles down her spine as he pulled her closer. Their tongues flicked, tips touching, and she sank into the kiss.

Oh, yeah. This. Exactly this.

It was hard to know how much time passed, but eventually they broke apart. "Roawwrr." They looked down as Dex raised his paw to Matt's thigh.

220

They shared a look and grinned, then Matt bent over until he was face to face with Dexter, his hands ruffling Dexter's fur. "I know, I like her too, bud."

Oh, yeah, I'm a goner.

*

"That was delicious. You're a good cook." Jules put her cutlery down, then sat back against the wooden patio chair and regarded the beautiful vista of Matt's vineyard. Rows of vines, all pruned, rolled over the shallow hills as far as she could see, and the property was bordered with eucalyptus trees. When Matt had taken her out on the quad bike earlier for a tour, Jules had kept an eye out for koalas, but no luck; apparently, they were rare in this part of the country.

Still, she'd snapped dozens of photos of the property and had posted a selection on Instagram tagging them with #Aussielife, #Aussiewinery, #naturebreak, #vineyard, and #justbreathe. She'd also sent a message to the girls on their chat thread:

Down at Matt's place for the weekend. It's so beautiful here. I feel like I can breathe for the first time in forever. My heart has been stolen by … Dexter the dog! He's such a sweetheart. Matt is a sweetheart too—will fill you in when we talk. Horse riding tomorrow! J xx

She'd attached a couple of her photos, including one of Dexter looking out over the vineyard. Chloe had replied almost immediately:

*Knew you'd love Matt's place. And Dex. Give him a kiss
for me. Dex, not Matt. Haha. Have fun horse riding and
watch out for Matt. No repeat of Cabo! Love you. C* ☺

There hadn't been a reply from Lucy, but Jules told herself
that she was probably busy or asleep.

"Uh, I don't know that I'd call myself a *cook*," said Matt,
"but I know my way around the barbie, *and* I can throw
together a decent salad."

"You got that right." Jules reached over to the almost empty
bowl, plucked a cherry tomato from the salad and popped it
into her mouth. She groaned.

"That good, huh?" Matt teased. She nodded, closing her
eyes and savouring the sweet tang of the tomato and the
peppery olive oil—both from local producers, Matt had told
her.

Jules swallowed her bite. "Seriously, dinner was amazing.
We don't eat a lot of lamb where I'm from. And, seriously,
everything—I mean *everything*—tastes better here, you know?
More intense, *fresher*. Maybe that's just 'cause back home it's
winter and this time of year I tend to hibernate and live off
takeout pizza and pot noodles." Matt chuckled.

She stretched her arms above her head and inhaled deeply.
"I love being here." It was a rare moment for Jules, being
totally unguarded, and she could almost *feel* herself sloughing
off the layers of her staid existence. When she glanced back
at Matt, she saw him watching her intently, a smile playing
on his lips. "What?" she asked.

He reached across the corner of the table to capture her

hand in his. "I'm glad you like it here. It's not often we have guests." He must have seen that she didn't understand who he meant by "we" because he added, "Dexter and me." At the sound of his name, Dexter lifted his head and looked at his master, his ears pricked and his eyes alert. Jules patted the top of his head and he plopped back down reassuming his position on the ground next to her chair.

Matt ran his thumb over her knuckles, his gaze following the movement of his thumb—a simple gesture that sent more of those tingles down her spine. It had been years since a man's touch had affected her like that, and Jules luxuriated in the feeling.

Matt looked up at her. "I think it's good for us having you here—well, good for *me*. You seem to notice all these little details, things I usually take for granted, things I don't even *see* anymore."

Jules was in two minds, one right there with Matt, taking in everything he was saying, and the other wondering who it was that he was describing. It certainly didn't sound like her—or at least the Jules of late.

In an instant, a thousand memories flooded her mind at once.

Laughing at herself in a piazza in Italy, as she caught the scoop of gelato just before it hit the ground, then not knowing what to do with it—helpless with a hand full of gelato and her two best friends laughing along with her.

Racing Will to the bottom of a black diamond run and for the first time ever, beating her baby brother.

Singing loudly to Neil Diamond in the car with her mom,

Aunt Jackie, Briony, and Bridget and laughing so hard when they got to the "bah, bah, bah," part that she could barely breathe.

Playing backgammon with her dad up at the cabin when everyone else had gone snowshoeing and winning their best-of-three tournament, and her dad high fiving her, saying he was proud of her.

And a final thought, as she returned to the present …

Sitting on a patio in the middle of wine country in Victoria, Australia, with a thoughtful, sweet, and incredibly sexy man and his awesome dog.

Where the hell had *this* Jules been? The one who, like Matt said, appreciated the little things, who had a sense of adventure, who laughed easily, and didn't sweat the small stuff.

"I've been a little stuck lately." Matt's words pulled her back to their conversation and she scoured his face for the meaning of his simple words.

"How so?" she asked, not prodding, just hoping her gentle tone conveyed that his secrets were safe with her.

"Just …" He sighed, taking back his hand. He fiddled with his paper napkin, tearing off shreds and rolling them between his fingers. He shot her a look that was intense and raw. "I have a good life, I do, but sometimes I feel like an observer, you know. Like there's this guy Matt and he's got his life set up a particular way, and he makes wine, and he travels a bit—not as much as he used to—and he sees his friends—also not as much as he used to.

"And it's like, he's here," Matt held out his left hand, "and I'm over here." He held his right hand apart from his left.

"Like I'm an observer of my own life."

His frankness had Jules captivated, but it was how he expressed exactly what she'd been feeling that tipped her over the edge.

He got it.

He got *her*.

Matt shook his head. "Sorry, that was ..."

"*No*," she said, protesting his apology. "I love that you ..."

He spoke over her to finish his thought. "...A load of gobbledygook," and the word made her laugh.

"Wait, sorry," she said quickly. "I'm not laughing at you. I'm not, seriously. Just, 'gobbledygook'? What even *is* that?" She started laughing harder, her hand lifting to her mouth. When she met Matt's eyes, his were full of mirth and he joined in on the laughter, shaking his head at himself.

Jules laughed freely, long and hard, aware at some point that Matt's laughter had died down and he was just watching her, an enchanted spectator of her amusement. "Yeah, yeah ..." he said after a while. "Make fun of the Aussie."

When her laughter subsided, she reached for his hand. "No, you are perfect."

He started to brush off the compliment, but with Jules now knowing that Matt's default was self-deprecation, she half-raised a hand. "Stop," she said quietly. He stopped, his face suddenly a picture of seriousness. "You are. This place, you, Dexter, this is perfect for me. Right now. This is exactly where I am supposed to be."

He frowned slightly, as though he was analysing her words, then he stood, pulling her up with him, and slipped his other

225

arm around her waist. His eyes stared into hers, then he dipped his head to seize her mouth in a kiss. She tugged her hand free of his so she could reach her arms around his neck, her fingers caressing the soft curls at his nape.

His mouth was insistent, and when his tongue met hers, he tasted of wine and the gaminess of the lamb. His hand moved to the back of her head, cradling it as his lips pressed against hers, almost bruising them, a sweet kind of pain steeped in longing.

When the kiss broke, they were both breathing raspy breaths. "Do you want to go inside?" he asked, his voice hoarse.

"God, yes," she replied. He turned abruptly, clasping her hand in his and led her towards the sliding glass door.

Chapter 20

Lucy

After she and Chloe rang off, Lucy showered and dressed in her Christmas outfit of leggings and an oversized red jumper—even though people always said that redheads shouldn't wear red. She pulled her tresses into a messy bun on top of her head and slicked on some shimmery lip gloss, then forced a smile at herself in the mirror.

The smile dissolved. With her sore head and the situation with Jules, she felt about as festive as the discount bin at Sainsbury's on the day after Boxing Day—fifty per cent off some fake Christmas cheer, anyone?

"Come on you," she muttered to her reflection, "time to be Christmassy."

Downstairs, amid exclamations of "Merry Christmas" which she half-heartedly returned, Steph ushered her to a place at the breakfast bar in front of a steaming mug of tea. A glance at Will, who winked at her from across the room, confirmed that he'd made it for her. She mouthed "thank you" and gratefully sipped the tea as the ruckus of family festivities buzzed about her. Nate seemed to be in his element as he cooked up a Christmas breakfast feast, aided by Will and Steph—his "sous chefs" he called them.

When Nate slid a pair of pancakes onto a plate and set it before her, Lucy wondered if she could choke them down. She couldn't remember the last time she'd felt this awful. Bridget, who was seated on her left, passed her the butter dish and a large glass bottle of maple syrup. "Uncle Nate's pancakes are to die for," she said right before putting a loaded fork into her mouth.

Maybe a plate of buttery, sickly sweet pancakes was exactly what Lucy needed. She smeared on a pat of butter and drizzled on some syrup. "You'll need more than that," said Bridget. "Here." Bridget took the syrup bottle from her and poured until an enormous pool of syrup surrounded the pancakes.

"That's definitely enough," Lucy said, laughing as she took the bottle from Bridget, a momentary and a welcomed reprieve from her glum and queasy state. And Bridget was right—the pancakes were delicious. By the time they'd cleared up after breakfast and moved the festivities into the front room to exchange gifts, Lucy was feeling marginally better.

She'd brought some carefully chosen gifts for Jules's family that she hoped showed off some of the best of Britain, and handed them out in turn, watching to see if she'd hit the mark. The tartan scarf for Will that she'd bought while on a trip to Edinburgh with her parents, turned out to be perfect, its hues of blue bringing out the colour of his eyes, and she smiled shyly as he kissed her cheek in thanks.

She'd brought a bottle of Eden Mill gin for Nate. "Oh, that's gonna be great, sweetheart, thank you," he said, after reading the label. And for Steph and Joe, she'd sprung for a set of Jo Malone home fragrances. She knew it was a little generic, but *she* loved Jo Malone and every now and then, she'd treat herself to a candle or a bottle of home fragrance to cheer herself up. She'd had to douse the flat in fragrance after Val's cheesemaking experiment back in July, she remembered, chuckling to herself.

"This is for you, Lucy," said Will, "from all of us." Will placed a large gift box on her lap, which she opened to reveal a plush cloth bag. She lifted it from the box and gently pulled open the drawstring. She wouldn't typically get excited about a handbag, but as she slid the Coach bag from its wrapping, she couldn't help but coo in awe. Tan leather, a broad base narrowing elegantly to its double gold clasps, and two handles in perfect arches—simple, elegant, and oh so luxe.

"Thank you," she said breathlessly. She looked from Will to Nate to Steph, who she just knew had been the one to choose it for her.

"You're so welcome, honey," said Steph, patting her knee. The moment was lovely, but it was immediately swallowed up by the noise and bustle around her, and as a mountain of wrapping paper amassed and family members leapt from their seats to give thankful hugs, Lucy started to feel more and more miserable. She was still a little hungover, things weren't right between her and Jules, and now she had to distance herself from Will.

In that moment, Lucy just wanted to go home.

Somehow, she managed to keep it together, helping clear

away the detritus of present unwrapping and playing a lengthy game of Trivial Pursuit in which she came second to Briony, who was, it turned out, something of a trivia savant.

She even put on that ridiculous snowsuit so she could build a snowman in the front garden, like she'd promised herself. Bridget joined her, and they chatted companionably about their favourite novels while they rolled three large balls of snow and hoisted them into place. After putting the finishing touches on their "snowperson", as Bridget called it, Lucy pushed aside her sense of ill ease and smiled broadly for a photo.

But in the early afternoon, as Nate's phone was passed around and she could hear Jules's voice, Lucy realised with a jolt that she'd practically slept-walked through the day— *Christmas* Day—the white Christmas she'd been excited about for months. She'd also spent the morning steering clear of Will, not wanting to encourage him, or pursue whatever was budding between them—lovely, *lovely* Will, who'd done nothing wrong.

So, even though Lucy knew it would upset Jules that she didn't want to talk to her, she didn't care. What had started out as concern that something between her and Will could affect her friendship with Jules, had morphed into something else since their Christmas morning video call.

Lucy was furious with her BFF.

At times, she'd wondered if this day would ever come. Twenty-two years of friendship and the three of them had never really quarrelled—she didn't count the sisterly bickering that Jules and Chloe seemed to relish. What surprised Lucy most, however, was that it was *Jules* who had tipped the scales. Surely, if anyone was going to enrage her at some point, it would be Chloe, but Chloe had been the empathetic one.

As Will got up from the sofa and left the room to talk to Jules, Steph caught Lucy's eye. Lucy looked away quickly, suddenly riveted by the pilling of her jumper.

"Lucy, come with me," said Steph from behind her. It was practically a whisper—not a command as such, but a warm summoning. Lucy stood and followed Steph into a little room off the foyer, a study. Lucy had known it was there but had never been inside. Steph closed the door behind them, then sat on the office chair next to the desk, swinging it around to face the centre of the room, and Lucy curled up in the comfy armchair opposite.

"This is my little sanctuary when I need to get away from ... well, from all that." She waved her hand in the direction of the front room.

"It's nice. Quiet."

Steph smiled. "Nate got his kitchen. I got this. Anyway, that's not why I asked you to come in. Although, I should say, that you're welcome to escape here any time you like—to read, or ... whatever." Lucy looked out the narrow floor-to-ceiling window and marvelled at how the sunlight made the snow clinging to the trees twinkle like fairy lights. She breathed out a long, slow breath.

"Is everything okay?" Steph asked. Lucy's eyes met Steph's, then immediately filled with tears. She brushed the tears away briskly, annoyed at their appearance. "You must be missing home. Did you get to talk to your folks this morning?" Lucy nodded. "It can be tricky, huh, the adventure of a Christmas on the other side of the world, but missing home too?"

Steph snatched a handful of tissues from the box on the desk and handed them to Lucy. "There's something else though, isn't there?"

It was just the prompt to break the floodgates and it all tumbled out, Lucy managing to shove aside the thought that this was Will's *mother*. When she'd caught Steph up on everything that had happened, including how hurt she'd been to discover that Jules didn't think she was good enough for Will, Lucy expelled a huge breath and sat back against the chair, her fingers playing with the soggy tissues. "Sorry to put such a dampener on Christmas Day."

"Oh, honey, don't you worry about that." She gave Lucy a kind smile as Lucy dragged the wad of wet tissues under her nose. "Here," Steph handed her a fresh batch.

"Thanks."

"So, let's break this down." Those words and the way she said them were so like Jules—the engineer's mind at work, sifting through the problem, making order from chaos. While Chloe was the planner amongst them, when things invariably went wrong on their travels, it was typically Jules who found the solution, and she'd be just as calm and systematic as Steph was now.

"You and Will have something between you ..." Lucy felt the heat rise in her cheeks. It was easy enough to forget who she was talking to mid-rant, but now she was calmer, it was just embarrassing.

"Please don't be embarrassed." Oh, lord, that only made it

worse. "I see it—even in just a couple of days. He's quite taken with you, Lucy, and Jackie was right—" She must have seen the horror in Lucy's eyes and laughed. "No, no, not about the 'grandbabies' thing, sorry. About Will not bringing a girl home for Christmas for a long time. Actually, he hasn't brought a girl home, period. Not in years.

"Look, I won't go into details—he can tell you himself if he wants—but Will was in a serious relationship all through college and for several years after that. I'm pretty sure he thought he was going to marry her, but it ended badly—*very* badly."

Lucy was overcome with compassion for Will, sorry that he'd had to endure such a devastating breakup. "Do you think that's why Jules is cross with me, because she thinks *I'll* hurt Will?"

"It could be, honey, but what you said about Jules not thinking you're good enough for Will ... I'm certain that's not true. Jules loves you, Lucy, even if she did a poor job of showing it today."

"I suppose," Lucy replied, not wholly believing it.

"Hey, do you remember Peter, the guy Jules was dating around ten years ago?" Lucy nodded. Jules and Peter had been together for a couple of years when she caught him cheating with a co-worker. "So, you remember how it ended, then?" Another nod from Lucy. "Well, that was around the time I met Joe ... and when it became obvious that Joe and I were serious, well, I think for both my children—even though they were young adults—*that* was when they had to accept that Nate and I ... that our separation was final.

233

"And it isn't lost on me, Lucy, that both their relationships imploded not long after. Will took the divorce hardest, I think, and when he turned to Tiffany, she wasn't the support he needed. And Jules, well, you know what happened with her and Peter. Jules and Will became closer than ever after that. I'm just grateful that they had each other. The bond between them … it's special."

Lucy felt her empathy for Will shining onto Jules, her anger dampening. She knew that Jules was close to her brother, and that she'd steered clear of love and relationships ever since the breakup with Peter. But this additional insight into how devastated Jules had been about their parents' divorce—how devasted she *and* Will had been—made it a lot clearer why Jules would react so viscerally today. Not only was Jules incredibly protective of Will, on some level, she must have been worried about Lucy coming between them.

"Jules never really talked to us about any of this," said Lucy. "I mean, she may have confided in Chloe, but she kept a fairly close hand. Even when we were travelling together, she never brought it up."

"That sounds familiar. I tend to keep things inside too." Steph gave a little snort of self-derision and her mouth flattened into a tight smile.

"And then here *you* are, Lucy. Beautiful, kind, an open book … Well, no wonder Will has feelings for you. You are such a breath of fresh air. And let's just say that I haven't seen my son so lit up inside for a very long time." At that, Lucy's tears threatened to reappear.

"So, how about you set all this aside for now? I'm *sure* that you and Jules will be fine, and it would be terrible if this ruined Christmas for you." She paused, then added, "What do you think?"

What *did* she think? "Honestly, I have no idea what's happening with Will, except that, until this morning, it made me happy."

"Then just go with that. Live *this* day."

So, according to Steph, Lucy, who loved all things straight-forward, predictable, and fair, was going to have to take a leap of faith.

But Jules could be pretty stubborn, and if she really was worried that Lucy would come between her and her brother, then what would that mean for their friendship? Lucy would never be able to live with herself if she and Jules fell out over Will.

Steph was watching her expectantly. "I'll try," Lucy said. Steph's mouth pulled into a taut smile that didn't reach her eyes. Perhaps she was as dubious as Lucy was.

*

"This is brilliant!" Lucy exclaimed. It was hard to know where to look. The entire town of Breckenridge was like one giant ball of Christmassy wonder and being there amongst it all, Lucy's worries about Jules receded into the background.

Will laughed beside her. "I knew you'd love it," he said into her ear. The warmth of his breath sent a wave of shivers over her—the good kind.

Late that afternoon, Lucy, Will, and the cousins had been

kicked out of the cabin and sent into town. Steph had claimed it was to get "the kids" out of their hair while she and Jackie made Christmas dinner, but Lucy suspected she was nudging Lucy in Will's direction.

"Hey, you guys," called Bridget, "check this out!" She was standing next to a barricade surrounding a small patch of snow and a dozen snow sculptures, all Christmas themed.

"I've never seen anything quite like this," said Lucy. She studied the sculptures, taking in the intricacies of each design. "Unbelievable," she added to herself.

"Oh yeah?" Will leant in closer. "It's a competition. I swear, every year they get more impressive."

"How cool is that?" squealed Briony. "Look! Someone's made Will Ferrell's head, you know, from *Elf*."

"I *love* that movie. We're watching it tonight, right?" Bradley directed his question to the group.

"Duh. We watch it every year." Apparently, Bridget was less of a fan.

"What's your favourite, then? Christmas film, I mean?" Lucy asked her.

Bridget seemed to take the question seriously, as though she'd never been asked before.

"*Little Women*," she replied after a considerable pause. Lucy should have guessed, as it had featured heavily in their book discussion earlier, but Bradley groaned. Regardless, Bridget forged ahead. "The Winona Ryder one. Although, I do like the newer one, with Saoirse Ronan, but I think Christian Bale was a better Teddy." She'd clearly given this a lot of thought.

"It's not even a Christmas movie!" Bradley had, too, apparently.

"It *is*, Brad," Briony interjected.

"Nah-uh."

"Just because you don't like it. You think *Die Hard* is a Christmas movie!" Another point for Bridget.

"*Die Hard is* a Christmas movie!"

"Hey, guys?" Big Cousin Will waded into the fray. "They're all Christmas movies, okay. Any movie that takes place at Christmas, or has a Christmas scene, or even remotely mentions Christmas is a Christmas movie."

The three cousins gawped at him, then Lucy saw Briony's mouth twitch. As the eldest sister, she'd probably heard this exact argument between her siblings a hundred times.

Bradley's head dropped in defeat and Will rubbed it good-naturedly. "Two against one, hey bud?" Bradley nodded, a smile appearing. "Sometimes, it's just easier to let them have their way," Lucy heard him add quietly.

Lucy wasn't quite sure what to make of Will's advice to his young cousin and turned her attention back to the snow sculptures. "Which one's your favourite?" Why did his voice in her ear have such an effect on her?

"Are we talking films or sculptures, now?"

"Either."

"*The Holiday* for film, and that one for sculpture." She pointed to a giant gingerbread house.

"Good choice … on the sculpture anyway."

The cousins wandered around the snow sculpture display to the other side and Lucy could still hear their squabbling, but there was something in Will's voice that rooted her to the spot.

"So, you're not a fan of *The Holiday?*" It was no big deal if he wasn't, she told herself. It *was* the ultimate chick flick after all. Will puffed his cheeks and blew out a long slow breath. *What? What does that mean?* she wondered. They *were* just talking about a film, right? "Will?"

"Nah, it's nothing. Don't worry about it." He lifted his head, his eyes panning across the town square, but Lucy didn't want to let whatever it was lie.

"Will ..." She tugged gently at his hand and he finally looked at her. She could *see* the machinations of thoughts processing behind his eyes.

"I *do* like that movie, although don't tell Brad. We're already outnumbered, and he'll think I'm leaving him in Camp *Die Hard* all by himself." He smiled conspiratorially and Lucy felt the breath she'd been holding escape. She returned the smile.

"It's just that ..." *Uh-oh.* There was a caveat. "I don't know how to say this ..." Will lifted his gloved hand and rubbed at the back of his neck, then bit his lip.

"Seriously, Will, just say it."

"It's just ... I feel like a bit of a Miles, is all."

Lucy's brow furrowed in confusion. "Sorry, what? I'm not sure ..." What in the world did he mean?

"You know, Miles? The Jack Black character?"

"Yes, I know who Miles is, but I don't understand your meaning."

"Look, you're like, so beautiful, *and* you're British and super interesting. You're like Iris, and then there's me, the dorky but—*hopefully*—loveable American guy—the Miles. And I know that you're way out of my league, that you're older and more sophisticated, but ..."

He dropped his head and closed his eyes, and Lucy could *see* his embarrassment. She knew she should say *something*, but with so many thoughts whirling through her mind, where to start?

"Will, I ... I ..."

He was shaking his head now, clearly in self-derision. "I shouldn't have said anything. It's just that you've seemed really distant all day, and I've been trying to figure out what I did wrong."

"Will," she said firmly. "Look at me." He did, even though she could tell it was making him uncomfortable. "Do you think we could find somewhere to get a hot chocolate or something? To talk?"

He hesitated for a moment, then replied. "Sure." He called out to the cousins, who made their way back to them. "We're going to go grab a hot chocolate. Why don't we meet you back here in, say, an hour?" He looked at Lucy, as if to confirm the timing, and she nodded.

Lucy caught Briony's eye and Briony didn't miss a beat. "Come on you two, let's go watch the snowboarders." She pointed to a giant half-pipe where snowboarders were doing tricks for a large audience of "oohing" and "ahhing" spectators.

"But *I* want a hot chocolate ..." Lucy heard Bradley say as Briony herded him and Bridget away.

"Come on," said Will, taking her gloved hand in his. He led the way through the crowd to a bustling coffee shop on the edge of the square. The bell above the door tinkled as they entered, and the scent of coffee and cinnamon filled the air.

It was toasty warm inside the coffee shop and Lucy could already feel the prickle of sweat under the many layers it took to withstand the outside temperature. She pulled her pompom beanie off her head and slid her hands out of her gloves, and by the time Will had led her to a table in the corner, she had already unzipped her coat and was slipping it off her shoulders.

"You get used to doing that," Will said. At Lucy's confusion, he quickly added, "Stripping off every time you go inside. Oh, I didn't mean *strip* ..." He shook his head at himself, obviously embarrassed, then grinned at his own expense. "Why can't I say anything right today?"

Lucy grinned back, grateful for something funny to break the tension between them. "I knew what you meant."

"Uh, yeah, even so, I'm going up to the counter now before I embarrass myself further. What can I get you?"

Lucy looked at the hot chocolate in front of the woman at the next table. It was in a tall glass mug and looked exceptionally rich and delicious. It was even topped with whipped cream and shaved chocolate. That line from *When Harry Met Sally* popped into her head, "I'll have what she's having," but it was loaded with innuendo and she and Will were already dancing around what was happening between them.

Lucy pointed to the woman's hot chocolate surreptitiously. "One of those please," she said quietly.

"Be right back."

240

Lucy watched Will as he manoeuvred amongst the tables, glad to have a moment alone to sift through everything she was feeling. What *was* she going to say to him? "By the way, Will, your sister was properly ticked off about us kissing, and I think we should go back to being 'just friends'."

But if Lucy was completely honest with herself—and she'd been mulling this over ever since talking it through with Steph—she didn't want to be just friends with Will. He was the first man who she could really talk to *and* she fancied the pants off him.

If only it would come to that—Will with his pants off. Oh, Lucy, that's crass, she chided herself.

She watched as Will approached the counter and smiled at the teenaged boy taking his order. As he engaged in the simple transaction, her thoughts tumbled over each other.

He is so handsome. That smile, those eyes, those strong, capable hands. Much more of a Graham than a Miles. Although Miles truly is a lovely man. Just that I don't fancy him. But I definitely fancy Will. And he's lovely. He's like Miles and Graham all wrapped up in one.

So, Lucy was properly falling for Jules's brother, something that just might destroy her friendship with her best friend, and she had no idea what to do about it. She'd have to decide soon, however, because he was making his way back to the table with her hot chocolate and a smaller mug, which she presumed was coffee.

"Here you go," he said, placing the hot chocolate in front of her. He took his seat and wrapped his hands around his mug. "So ..." he said.

"So …" she replied. *Come on, Lucy. Be a grown-up.* "You were right about me seeming a little distant today, and I'm sorry."

"Was it me?"

"No."

"Are you sure? Did I do something wrong?"

She'd give anything to wipe that miserable look off his face. "No, Will, I promise. I just …" Lucy realised there was no way to say what she needed to say without throwing Jules into the muck. She took a sip of hot chocolate. *Goodness, that's delicious.* When she looked up a Will, he was watching her intently.

"I like you … rather a lot, as it turns out." His face split into a grin.

"You did say that last night, but I wasn't sure … you were, uh …"

"I was completely off my trolly."

"I haven't heard that expression before, but yes, you were." He smiled at her gently, which gave her the confidence to keep going.

"Well, as they say, '*in vino veritas*'. And those things I said— and I do remember—I meant them. You're quite extraordinary and I know you think of yourself as a Miles, and in a way you are, because he is so thoughtful and lovely, but you're also a Graham, truth be told, because I think you are absolutely gorgeous."

She dropped her gaze and took another sip of the delicious hot chocolate. Will was grinning at her when she summoned the nerve to look at him again and she involuntarily smiled back—until her stomach twisted at the thought of what she had to say next.

"But ..." His smiled faded and a crease took hold between his brows. "I let it slip when I spoke to Jules early this morning that I'd kissed you, and she didn't seem particularly pleased with me."

Will's head cocked to the side and his frown intensified. "Hold on, what? Jules ...? What did she say exactly?"

There was no way Lucy was going to repeat verbatim what Jules had said. "She just seemed shocked, that's all, and not in a good way. She made it quite clear that you and I being together ... well, she made me feel a bit rubbish, to be honest."

"Well, yeah. I mean, I'm feeling 'a bit rubbish' too, now that I know what's going on."

"Maybe she was just being protective." Lucy now found herself in the odd position of defending Jules to Will.

"I'm twenty-nine, Lucy. I have my own place, my own company. I don't need my older sister to step in and protect me. She's out of line. Oh, hey, *that's* why you didn't talk to her when she called."

"Yes."

"And then I went and gushed to her about you."

Lucy's eyes widened. "You did?"

"Yeah, I did. But I didn't know then that she'd given you a hard time. Do you want me to handle this?"

"Perhaps, but what if ..."

"What if what?"

"What if we ..."

"Lucy, *say* it."

"What if we fall for each other, I mean, properly, and it all goes pear-shaped and you get hurt again? I don't want to be the person who does that to you."

"Lucy, what are you talking about? What did Jules tell you?"

"It wasn't Jules; it was your mum." Lucy realised too late that she'd revealed far more than she should have.

"My mom? Geez, Lucy, who else have you been talking to about me?"

"No, I ... that's not how it was. Will ... Oh, I don't know how I've made such a mess of things."

He stood. "We should just go. Let's find the others." Before she knew what was happening, Will had zipped up his parka and was out the door, the tinkling of the bell sounding more ominous than welcoming. She quickly gathered her things, shoving her hands into her gloves and pulling on her beanie as she slipped on her coat and hurried after him.

"Will," she called to his back. He stopped but didn't turn around.

She ran past and stood in front of him, placing her hand on his chest. He seemed both hurt *and* frustrated and he wouldn't look at her. She dropped her hand, dismayed.

"Oh Will, I've completely messed things up and it was the last thing I wanted to do. Jules and your mum, they love you. And yes, Jules was a cow to me, but it's only out of love for you, I'm sure of it. And yes, I was cross with her—furious actually—but I think I understand her motivations now, even though I'm still not sure what to do about it. Anyway, that's why your mum sought me out, because she knew that something wasn't quite right, and all *she* said was that Jules was probably worried you'd get hurt like you did with your last serious girlfriend. That's *all*. She didn't want to say anything else, because it's your story to tell, if you want to—and I agreed, so I didn't press her. Your mum, I mean. Oh, bollocks, did any of that make sense?"

There was a long moment when Will didn't speak, his face creased into a frown. Then the frown lessened, and he met her eyes.

"Yes, Iris, that all made perfect sense."

A smile lifted the corners of Will's mouth, and he seemed about to say something else when they heard, "Hey, you guys! I've been looking for you."

They turned together and saw Briony jogging up to them. Lucy saw Will flick his wrist towards him and check the time. He'd said they would be an hour and it had been far less than that. When Briony reached them, Lucy realised there was panic in her eyes.

"It's Bradley," she said, out of breath. "This way." Lucy glanced quickly at Will, seeing the concern on his face, before they followed Briony into the crowd.

Chapter 21

Chloe

"So, I won't be too long, two or three hours at most," said Archer as he packed up his leather satchel with essentials. "There's the photo shoot first, then the interview, and they'll drop me back here afterwards."

"Cool," said Chloe, standing on her tiptoes to give Archer a kiss goodbye. He gave her a smack on the lips and wrapped his arms around her waist as hers went around his neck.

He leant back, his arms still encircling her. "I am so pleased you came with me to London, *and* that you refused my offer of your own suite." It was a polite way to refer to the fact that they'd not only shared a room, but a bed. Chloe's mouth quirked at the memory of everything they'd done in that bed.

"Now, if you get hungry, order what you like from room service. And there's a spa here, if you'd like to get a treatment, or something. Just charge it to the room. I should be back in time to take you to lunch before we go to Winter Wonderland. You're still keen on that, yes?" His inquisitive half-frown was incredibly sexy.

"Definitely. All things Christmassy, remember? And I'll be fine on my own. I'm going to take the longest, hottest, bubbliest bath in the history of the world and just chill out here 'til you get back."

"You're absolutely sure?"

"*Yes!* Now go, or you'll be late, and they'll write nasty things about how much of a diva you are."

He laughed and gave her another quick kiss. She was tempted to turn it into a much longer kiss, and maybe something more illicit, more of what had taken up most of last night, but she really didn't want him to be late. She waved him off from the door of the suite and shut it quietly behind him. "God, he's just so ..." she said aloud, followed by a guttural "grrr".

Basking in the first moments of solitude she'd had in what seemed like forever, she practically skipped to the bathroom where she turned on the water to fill the giant bath. "Who knew I'd come to think of hot water as a luxury," she murmured. While the tub was filling, she foraged around her toiletries bag for a sheet mask and some hair treatment.

She slid out of the fluffy bathrobe, hung it on a hook, then wet her hair in the shower with the handheld nozzle. In front of the mirror, she slathered on the thick, creamy hair treatment, then from the selection of Four Seasons bath salts, chose the cinnamon-scented one and sprinkled it liberally into the bath. It was nearly ready.

She tore open the foil of the face mask, unpeeled it, and pressed it onto her face. "If you could see me now, Archer ..." She giggled at her reflection, knowing that there was no way in the world he was ever going to see her looking like that.

The bath was three-quarters full, and she turned off the tap before stepping in carefully and stretching out along its length. The water came up right under her chin and, with a satisfied groan, she let her arms bob gently in the fragrant water as the water sluiced through her fingers. She closed her eyes, slipping into a luxurious doze.

"Who the hell are *you*?" shouted a brash American female voice.

Chloe's eyes flew open, her battle to sit upright in the deep and slippery tub causing a tsunami of bath water to cascade over the edge onto the floor. It took a moment for her to realise where the voice had come from and when she looked behind her at the bathroom door, she was more surprised than when she'd opened Cecily's front door to Archer.

Madison Strumpet was in her hotel room.

What the actual fuck?

In the few moments Chloe hesitated while she struggled to comprehend what was happening, Madison strode into the bathroom and stood tub-side glaring down at Chloe. "I said, who *are* you? Besides the skank he was kissing in those photos."

Ouch. It had been easy enough to forget about her likeness being splashed across the internet when it was just her and Archer, but Madison's words were like a slap. And not only was Chloe naked, her head was slathered in in goop and she was wearing a flaccid hockey mask. She may have felt amazing only moments before, but she knew she looked a sight. Madison, however, looked every bit of the million dollars she earned per movie, and just like the girlfriend of the world's biggest film star.

Still, Chloe was *the* Chloe Sims, event manager extraordinaire, recently bedded by Archer Tate, and not going to be intimidated by this interloping cow. Mega-bitch activated, Chloe peeled off the face mask, planted her feet firmly on the bottom of the bathtub and stood. She was pleased to discover that standing in the tub, she was slightly taller than Madison. She looked down at Archer's ex and, with as much authority as she could muster in her naked state, growled, "Hand me a towel."

Madison blinked twice and, mouth agape, looked about for a towel. She seemed on autopilot when she lifted a large, fluffy bath sheet from the railing and handed it to Chloe, averting her eyes from Chloe's nakedness.

"Now give me a moment," Chloe commanded.

Still seemingly dumbstruck, Madison acquiesced and, mumbling an apology, left the bathroom. Chloe's heart was thumping so fast, she took a steadying breath. Activating her mega-bitch mode always came with a jolt of adrenalin, and she'd need to calm down if she was going to handle this situation with any kind of composure.

She dried off and wrapped herself in the bathrobe, all the while trying to determine her next move. With a towel, she removed as much of the hair treatment as she could, then scooped her shoulder-length bob into a hair clip at the back of her head. She splashed water on her face to remove the sticky residue of the face mask and looked at herself in the mirror.

She would have preferred to be fully dressed and made up before dealing with Madison Bloody Strumpet, but she knew that would be pushing it. It was time to face the ex.

She pulled her shoulders back and lifted her chin, then walked through the bathroom door to the rest of the suite. Madison was seated on one end of the couch, looking like she'd been blindsided. She didn't seem to notice that Chloe had come into the room and started a little when Chloe spoke.

"You're Madison."

Madison drew in a sharp breath and lifted her eyes to Chloe's. Chloe stayed standing, wanting the keep the upper hand for as long as possible. "Yes. I am. And again, who are *you?*"

In event management, Chloe had handled her share of tyrants, micromanagers, whingers, whiners, and idiots—clients, vendors, and colleagues alike. She was also well-versed in "diva" and knew a bluff when she saw one. Madison was all bravado and no substance. It clearly wouldn't take much to make her crumble into a sobbing ball of misery, but Chloe hesitated.

As experienced as she was in an array of people-management situations, she'd never handled a petulant ex who seemed to be on the precipice of a breakdown. She was also not a cruel person and, really, her own position as Archer's love interest was also rather fragile. She had no idea where they were heading, if anywhere at all.

She was going to have to tread lightly to navigate these uncharted and muddy waters.

"I'm Chloe," she said simply. She sat on the armchair

opposite Madison, who seemed to have recovered from her stupor and glowered at her. "I'm here with Archer." Though true, she could tell the words had stung. It was in the quiver of Madison's lower lip—her very beautiful lip. *God, she's so pretty—even in this state*.

"Why?"

"I'm sorry. I don't know what you mean."

"Why did he bring you here?" Madison asked, her tone making it clear that she thought Chloe was dim.

"Well, you'll have to ask him that. But I am here with Archer, and *I'm* wondering what *you're* doing here. How did you even know where he was staying?"

Madison looked down at her hands, then raised her right forefinger to her teeth and nibbled on the cuticle. "I know someone in his publicity team," she mumbled.

Chloe shuddered, knowing that discretion was paramount in any kind of publicity role and that whoever had leaked to Madison would be looking for another job by the end of the day. "And I'm assuming you also know someone on the front desk too? This *is* the Four Seasons. They have famous people staying here all the time. Surely, they have stringent security measures in place."

Madison stopped nibbling her cuticle and shot her a look, and Chloe just *knew* she was about to be served. "Well, yes, *obviously*, but you see, they *do* know me here, because Archer and I have stayed here together many, *many* times." *Ouch. A point for Madison*.

"You weren't expecting *me*, though."

"Of course not. Why would they have given me a key card

to his room if they knew someone *else* would be here?" *Oh, game on Ms Strumpet.*

"Oh, so now you're implying that he *doesn't* know I'm here, that *I'm* the interloper. We checked in last night. *Together*." Madison's eyes darted to the unmade bed and she scowled. "I'm assuming there was a change of shift on reception since then," added Chloe. "But all that's irrelevant now. The important question isn't how but *why* are you here?"

Madison's chin lifted. "It was a mistake."

Well, that was completely vague. Thank you very much, Madison. Chloe was starting to tire of this ridiculous verbal match, and she sighed loudly. "*What* was a mistake?"

"Us breaking up, *obviously*." *Why does she think everything's so obvious?* Chloe puzzled, fuming.

"It was just a silly fight. We've had them before, and we've reconciled before. You wouldn't know this, and there's no way that you *could* know, but this dance is quite familiar for me and Archer."

Chloe vaguely recalled an assortment of tabloid headlines that supported Madison's assertion, but Cecily's comment about the breakup a few days before had made it seem final.

Confusion was not a feeling that sat well with Chloe. She was pragmatic and a planner. She was also unfailingly confident. But there was something about Madison's words, and even her presence—as though she was daring Chloe to challenge her assertion that this was nothing more than a lovers' tiff—that made Chloe doubt what was happening between her and Archer.

Scrutinising the relationship (for want of a better word)

from this fresh perspective, Chloe knew that it *was* more than just physical—at least for her—and it was certainly more than fangirling. That moment they'd shared at the fair with the Capels, that had changed their flirtation into something more substantial. She'd seen then, and many times since, what was in his heart. He was a good person—kind, intelligent, thoughtful. She didn't need Susan extolling his virtues to see all that.

She realised, as she sat in a luxurious suite in inner London, wearing only a fluffy bathrobe and under the scrutiny of Archer's ex-girlfriend, that she was falling for him. She was falling hard for Archer Tate, the man she'd been papped with. It certainly complicated things, but in a way, it also fuelled her. She was not walking away from this without telling Archer how she felt.

"You're welcome to stay until Archer gets back, but that won't be for a few hours. In the meantime, I'm going back to my bath. Stay or don't stay, I don't care. But it's clear that you and he need to talk." *If only for him to tell you it's truly over*, she thought.

Chloe stood and left the room, slipping off her robe once more and stepping into the now-tepid bath. She lifted the tap to draw more hot water and just as she reclined, she heard the door to the suite open then shut.

She let out a ragged sigh, releasing all the tension her body had been holding. Just the thought of losing Archer, even after this brief time together, made her feel nauseous. So much for a relaxing morning alone.

Chapter 22

Jules

"Are you sure about this?" Jules scrutinised Matt's face, which was creased with worry.

"Uh, yep." He was standing alongside a black and white mare that seemed to be getting antsier by the minute.

Jules, not wholly convinced, placed her left foot in the stirrup and effortlessly hoisted herself onto her ginger-coloured mare, settling into the leather saddle. "Because you don't look sure."

Matt glanced from her back to the horse, his frown intensifying.

"Matty, mate, you all good?" Matt's friend and owner of the stables, Jase, held the reins of Matt's horse, petting her gently along the length of her nose and shushing her in a low tone.

"We don't have to go, Matt, if you're worried," offered Jules. Her own horse, Gingernut, stamped a foot and nodded her head as though she agreed.

Matt scratched the back of his head, his hand colliding

with his riding helmet, tipping the brim over his eyes. He righted it. "Ah, bugger it. Jase, gimme a hand, mate?"

Jase laid a hand on horse's front flank and leant into her, and she stilled. "Good girl, Oreo. There's a good girl." Turning to Matt, he said, "Okay, just like what Jules did. Left foot into the stirrup, then throw your leg over."

Jase snorted at his own joke, one that went over Jules's head, but was clearly something lewd. *Aussies*, she thought, laughing to herself. Maybe it was some sort of slang for sex—which she and Matt had not had. Not *yet*, anyway. He'd been a total gentleman the night before, putting a pause on proceedings at the clothes-still-mostly-on stage of their make-out session.

Jules hoped to cure him of his gentlemanliness later that afternoon. It had been agony sharing a bed with someone she was so attracted to, and she'd woken several times in the night, hyper aware of him next to her.

After one false start, which left Matt hopping about with one foot in a stirrup and one still on the ground, Matt got himself onto Oreo. He blew out a relieved sigh. "It's a long way to the ground from up here," he said.

"Then don't bloody fall off," teased Jase.

There were three other guests in their party and with Matt finally atop his horse, it was time for the expedition to head out. Jase mounted his horse and took the lead, and one of his employees, Andie, brought up the rear.

Seven horses, and each one named after a cookie, apparently. All the names besides Oreo were unfamiliar to Jules—Gingernut, Kingston, Tim Tam, Monte, Tiny Teddy (who at fifteen hands was the tallest horse), and ANZAC. The horses, clearly well-practised in following the leader, formed a line unprompted as Jase led them into the bushland.

The motion of Gingernut beneath her, that steady familiar plod, calmed Jules in a way she hadn't experienced for a long time. She tried to recall the last time she'd gone horseback riding, something that had consumed much of her adolescence, but struggled to remember. "Too long," she said to herself. Even so, she felt right at home. *Just like riding a bike*. The thought made her smile.

The trail zigzagged between tall and unruly eucalyptus trees, their fragrance almost citrussy and Jules breathed in deep breaths of the clean Australian air. It was warm that day, but not too hot, and she'd heard Jase say they were lucky with the weather. Apparently, the next day would be "a scorcher" with the mercury pushing past a hundred and ten Fahrenheit—too hot for the horses—and they would have had to cancel the ride.

There were magpies somewhere close by; she could hear their warbling. She'd asked Matt about it when they'd had breakfast on his veranda that morning. It was a unique sound and she would forever associate it with Matt's place.

It's so beautiful here, Jules thought. It was a rugged kind of beauty that lifted her spirits—everything from the smell of the air, to the unfamiliar wildflowers growing in the scrub, to the sounds of the bushland. She ducked under a low branch and turned around to grin at Matt, who was right behind her. "You doing okay?" she asked.

"Sure, yep," he replied. It was hardly the reply of an

accomplished horseman but seeing how nervous Matt was about the ride made Jules appreciate the thoughtfulness of the gift even more.

Not long after, the party emerged into a grassy clearing and up ahead, Jules could see a single-storey red brick building surrounded by a split-rail fence. Jase led them to the fence, where they dismounted, removed their helmets, and tied up the horses. Jase and Andie walked the line of horses and checked the ties before Jase asked the group to follow him into the first winery of their three-winery tour.

Matt clasped her hand in his as they walked, and she felt a flush of warmth that had nothing to do with the eighty-degree day. "I'm guessing you've been here before?" she asked.

"For sure, heaps. Their pinot's nearly as good as mine." When she looked at him, he was grinning, those sexy dimples on show. She smiled back and he dipped his head to capture her mouth with a quick kiss. "Don't tell them I said that, though."

She haphazardly trailed her fingertips over her chest in opposite directions. "Cross my heart."

The tasting room was rustic yet beautiful, with a high timber ceiling that met in an apex about thirty feet above them. The polished wooden floorboards were made from some sort of redwood, and three heavy beams crossed the breadth of the room where the ceiling met the brick walls. The bar, also made of redwood, held up a single piece of timber, a slice from what was obviously a large tree, with natural edges and a gleaming finish.

Behind it stood a smiling woman of indeterminate age.

"Welcome to Red Ridge," she said as the group approached the bar. "This is our tasting menu, here." While Jase and Andie hung back, the rest of them stepped forward and started perusing the wine menu. "We've got seven wines on tasting today, and you're welcome to try them all, or you can skip to your favourites."

Jules was hardly a wine connoisseur, although she did enjoy a California pinot on occasion, and she was keen to increase her wine knowledge, especially with Matt now in the picture—whatever that would come to mean in the few days she had left in Australia. "What do you recommend, besides the pinot?" she asked Matt quietly.

"You should try all seven," he replied. She thought of Gingernut and even though it was an organised tour, and Jase and Andie seemed responsible, she wasn't keen on getting tipsy before getting back on her horse. Matt must have seen her consternation. "You can always taste and spit." He indicated a free-standing barrel next to the bar with a silver funnel in the centre.

She was dubious about spitting out wine in front of Matt. She knew it was perfectly acceptable, that serious wine tasters did it without a second thought, but she also thought it was gross.

"Um, I'll just taste two or three, on your recommendation."

He seemed to understand. "All right, then." He read through the tasting menu, then went back and pointed to an unoaked chardonnay and two pinots from different vintages. "Those should give you a good indication of what the region is known for."

"Thanks." He was watching her intently and Jules bit her lip. Oh yes, she was definitely going to seduce the hot Aussie winemaker when they got back to his place.

"Ahem," she heard from the other side of the bar. "Which one did you want to start with, love?" asked the woman.

"Oh, uh, the chardonnay, please," she replied, a little embarrassed that she'd been caught out crushing on Matt.

Matt grinned across the bar. "Make that two, please, Nina."

"Sure thing, Matty."

As Jules swirled the two glasses of pinot noir and held them aloft to compare their colour, Matt explained the characteristics of the different vintages. "See how this one is a brighter colour," he said, indicating the glass in her left hand. She nodded. "This is the younger of the two and as pinot ages, you'll see more of a rusty brick colour, like this one. So, the one in your left hand will be more fruit forward and this one will be more complex, earthier even. Try them."

She did, taking time to inhale the bouquet with her mouth slightly open, as Matt had shown her, then having a sip and letting the wine coat the width and breadth of her tongue. Only then did she swallow. "That one's delicious," she said after the younger wine.

"Now the other one." Matt watched her face as she repeated the ritual with the second pinot, almost as if he hoped to catch the nuances of the wine reflected onto her face.

"Hmm," she said after she swallowed. She went back to inhale the bouquet again and took a second sip. "It's almost like a completely different wine. I like it, though. It is earthier, like you said, but it also has a spiciness that the first one doesn't."

Matt's smile oozed with pride. "Precisely. That's the magic of it. As a winemaker, you use your best judgement to make decisions about each vintage—and there are so many factors that go into those decisions—and then you pretty much hope for the best. Sometimes it's lightning in a bottle, and other times ..." He shrugged.

"Why don't you have a tasting room?"

"It's next on the list."

"Really?"

"Definitely. Twoey and I have already got an architect booked to come see us in mid-Jan."

"*That's* exciting." She grinned at him.

"Yeah, it is. Slightly terrifying too, but it's the next logical step. I mean, I showed you yesterday where we do tastings from the shed, but that's only on request and it doesn't happen much. As I said, we already sell most of what we produce to local restaurants and shops. The tasting room, that's next level, you know?"

"Will you have to produce more wine then?"

"Yeah, it's a bit 'chicken and egg'. The timing can be tricky, and we reckon we'll have to buy in some grapes for the first couple of years, maybe launch a table-wine label. Anyway, this is all really boring."

"No, not at all. My brother, Will, he started this company that works with local distilleries—boutique ones—and they have similar kinds of decisions to make. When to expand their range, when to open tasting rooms, that sort of thing. I find it really interesting; there are so many moving parts."

"Yeah, yeah, exactly."

They were pulled from their conversation by Jase. "Okay everyone, if there was anything you liked, you can give Nina your orders, settle up, and we'll have someone come collect them. Your wine will be waiting for you at the stables when we get back."

Jules looked excitedly at Matt. "I definitely liked that first pinot, so I'll get some of that." She leant in close to him, "Although, it's not as good as yours," she whispered conspiratorially.

He grinned at her. "Told ya, but it is good to mix it up from time to time."

*

They were back on the trail, heading to winery number two, when Jules heard a call from the rear of the group—Andie. "Matt, keep calm, but there's a tiger snake just off the trail to the left there." Jules's head spun, and she caught sight of Matt's terrified expression, his eyes locking onto hers across the thirty feet between their horses. "Just keep calm," continued Andie, "and slowly lead Oreo off trail to the right. If she sees it, she'll shy."

Jules saw Matt nod sharply and pull gently on the right rein. Oreo resisted and flicked her head back; she must have caught sight of the snake. One moment she had all four hooves on the ground and a moment later, her front legs pawed the air and Jules watched, horrified, as Matt was flung off Oreo and into the scrub next to the trail.

"Matt!" Hers wasn't the only voice calling him, but everything and everyone else receded into the background. She swung a leg over Gingernut, both feet landing on the ground at the same time, then broke into a sprint to get to him.

Fortunately, Oreo had thrown him off on the right side of the trail, away from the snake. But when Jules arrived at his feet, he was grimacing and holding his right wrist. She knelt next to Matt. "Are you okay?" she asked breathlessly.

Jase appeared beside her. "Mate, how's your wrist. Show me." Matt winced as he let go of his wrist and Jase took hold of it gently, turning it slowly, seeming to look for signs of a break. Andie knelt next to them and opened a plastic first aid kit.

"It doesn't look broken, mate," said Jase, "but we'll get a splint on it just in case, okay."

Andie went to work on Matt's wrist, while Jules looked on helplessly. All she could do was hold his left hand, taking the brunt each time Matt squeezed it tightly in reaction to the pain.

"Ah, yeah, Jonno. We're gonna need you to come out in the Land Rover." Jase, on his mobile, looked around. "Uh, we're about a click north of Red Ridge. You know where Jackson's property backs onto the fire break. Yeah, that's right." Addressing Matt, he asked, "Hey, Matty, you reckon you can walk up to that gate with me? Jonno's gonna come get ya."

Matt nodded. "Yeah, that's doable."

"Can I go with Matt?" Jules asked, looking up at Jase.

"Yeah, course. Andie, when you're done there, can you take Gingernut, and I'll grab Oreo and follow you lot once Jonno's here."

"No worries," Andie replied. She secured the end of the bandage with a silver clip, then gathered up the cellophane wrappings and put them into the first aid kit, clipping it shut. "You should be fine Matty. I don't think there's a break, but you'll want to get it X-rayed, okay?"

"Thanks, Andie." She stood and packed the first aid kit into her saddle bag, then gathered Tim Tam's reins and led him over to Gingernut who was eating dried grass on the side of the trail. She took Gingernut's reins, the mare seeming reluctant to abandon her trailside snack. Back on her horse, Andie called over her shoulder. "See you back there." She gave Tim Tam a firm kick and led Gingernut to the front of the group. The others waved their grim goodbyes from their perches, and then it was just Jase, Jules, and Matt.

"I feel like a right idiot. Sorry, Jules. Not exactly how I thought the day would end up." Not for Jules either, but all she cared about was making sure Matt was okay.

"It's not your fault. It was just bad luck. That could have happened to any of us. *I've* certainly been thrown from a horse before."

"Really?"

"Yes, when I was eleven."

Matt started chuckling. "Great, so you're saying I have the horse-riding ability of an eleven-year-old?"

"Oh, hell no, I was *way* better at eleven than you are now. I was thrown when my horse shied right before a four-foot jump." She scrunched her nose at him and they shared a laugh at his expense.

"It's a good thing I like you."

"Yes," she said. "I'm starting to think it's a very good thing."

"He's here!" Jase called. He'd been standing about twenty feet away, perhaps to give them some privacy while they waited for Jonno. Would Jules ever get used to all the "Aussiefied" names? She doubted she would ever call Matt, "Matty".

"Let me help you," she said to Matt as she stood. She took his left hand in both of hers and pulled him to his feet. "Anything else hurt?"

"Just my pride."

Jules smiled, keeping hold of his hand as they walked to the Land Rover.

Chapter 23

Lucy

"**M**om is going to *kill* you, Bradley," hissed Bridget. "What? I'm fine. Nothing happened!"

"Your mom is *not* going to kill him, Bridget, because we are *not* telling her what happened."

"But—"

Will cut her off. "Bridget, no. Bradley's fine and that's all that matters. Your parents left me in charge, and if you think I'm getting told off by Aunt Jackie 'cause you tattled, think again."

Will's tone told every occupant of the car that what he'd said was final. Lucy found his take-charge attitude extremely attractive, but she also agreed. They could just as easily have been on their way to A&E as back to the family's cabin, but Bradley was unharmed, so everyone should keep quiet about it.

"We won't say anything, Will," assured Briony. "But what were you thinking, you doofus?" Lucy turned just in time to see Briony cuff her brother upside the head.

"Ow," he whined as Briony continued her rant. "You've

267

only been snowboarding for, like, *what*, two years? The guys who do those tricks, they're *professionals*, you idiot."

"*Okay, geez.* Forgive me for raising my hand! They *asked* for volunteers."

"They didn't mean sixteen-year-old novices, you dork." Bridget was clearly not ready to let things lie.

"*And* they had all the gear there. What was I supposed to do? *Not* put my hand up?"

"Yes!" his sisters responded in unison.

Lucy was fascinated by the interplay between the siblings. As her parents' sole child, the closest she had to siblings were Chloe and Jules. *Oh, dear*, she thought. *Does that mean Will is kind of like a brother to me?* She dismissed the thought immediately; the last thing she felt towards Will was sisterly love.

And she was sure that, right before they'd been alerted to Bradley's stupid decision to ride the half-pipe and try a snow-boarding trick he'd never done before, Will had been about to say how *he* felt about *her*.

They pulled up in front of the cabin and Will switched off the car's engine, unbuckled his seatbelt, and turned around in his seat, pinning each of his cousins with a look that said, "don't mess with me".

"Remember, we went, we saw ice sculptures—'Ooh, ahh, they were amazing'—we had hot chocolate and *watched* the snowboarders. That's it. Got it?"

"I didn't have hot chocolate," said Bradley. *The little blighter*, Lucy thought. *He's going to get a right bollocking if he's not careful.*

"Bradley, I swear to god, I love you, man, but I *will* end you," said Will.

Briony smirked at that, followed by Bridget, and Lucy couldn't help but join in. In moments, all the women in the car were sniggering while Will, shaking his head, blew out a breath of frustration, and Bradley conceded with raised hands and said, "Okay, okay I get it."

The cousins got out of the car and as Lucy opened her door, Will set a hand on her arm. "Lucy, wait for sec?" Two car doors slammed, and Lucy watched as the cousins made their way to the front door. When they were inside, he continued. "I just wanted to talk to you before we went back inside to the craziness."

Lucy gulped. Somehow, she knew that this conversation would be a turning point for her and Will. Either they'd keep their distance for the next few days, making polite conversation until it was time leave, or ...

Or, what?

Or this could be the very moment that brought them together.

"Do you happen to know what time it is in Melbourne?" The question caught her off guard. She'd been expecting something a little more romantic, more *heartfelt* than a lesson in time zones.

"Uh, well, this time of year Melbourne's eleven hours ahead of London and London is seven hours ahead of Colorado, so—" she glanced at the clock on the dash and did a quick calculation in her head "—it's 1:00pm in Melbourne."

"Okay."

"And you're asking because ..."

"I'm calling Jules."

"Oh, right." This conversation was not, in any way whatsoever, going how Lucy had imagined.

"She had no right to give you a hard time and I want to see what's up with her." His face bore the mark of frustration and perhaps a little anger. Lucy was used to mediating between Chloe and Jules, but this was new territory for her, and she couldn't help thinking that it was somehow her fault.

"Will? I don't really think it's ..." She frowned.

He turned towards her and he must have seen the concern on her face, because his expression softened. "Hey, it's okay, Lucy. Jules and I are close, and most of the time we get along, but this time, she's stepped over the line."

Lucy nodded, the weight of the situation resting heavily on her heart. She liked Will—she hadn't felt like this in a long time, if ever—but Jules was one of the most important people in her life. If being with Will would jeopardise her relationship with Jules, then she'd choose Jules, no questions asked.

"Hey," he said quietly. She caught the quick flick of his tongue to wet his lips as he leant towards her and their lips met.

His kiss was tentative at first, his full lips moving against hers softly, slowly. Another flick of his tongue, but this time she felt it against hers. She tilted her head as the kiss deepened, then pressed her hand to his chest, not to push him away, but to steady herself as the shivers rushed the length of her body.

Her fingers curled, encasing a handful of his coat as she leant back against the seat, pulling Will with her, the weight of him feeling both thrilling and familiar, like a perfect fit.

He broke the kiss, breathless, and looked at her from mere inches away. "Lucy ..." he said. "Oh, god, I want you so much ..." He pushed himself upright as he finished his thought, "... but not like this, not here."

Lucy's senses returned and for a fleeting second, she saw the scene inside the car as though she was standing outside it looking in. Will was right. No matter what they were feeling, they should absolutely not do anything more in the front seat of a four-wheel-drive parked in the driveway of the family's cabin.

She took a deep breath. "Quite right," she said, her hands lifting to her cheeks and feeling how warm they were. She must look like a beetroot.

"But Lucy?"

"Mmm-hmm." She glanced at him, still trying to catch her breath.

"I don't want to wait much longer."

"Oh, yes ... right. I see ..." For goodness' sake, why did she have to be so bloody *English* sometimes. She mentally slapped herself while Will chuckled at her with a mischievous look on his face.

"Ready to go in?" Will asked. "I don't want everyone to think we've been, uh ..." It seemed it was Will's turn to be embarrassed and a laugh burst out of Lucy. She pressed her lips together to stifle a snigger.

"Yeah, yeah," said Will, shaking his head and readjusting his trousers. "Come on, let's go." He shoved his gloves on roughly and Lucy slipped her hands into hers for the short walk up to the house. She knew *exactly* how cold it was out there.

When she climbed out of the car and met up with Will, he reached out for her hand and she didn't hesitate before taking it. Glove-to-glove was hardly the most romantic thing in the world, but it felt lovely regardless.

Inside, the cabin was alive with activity. There were some delicious smells and a lot of clatter coming from the kitchen, and male voices coming from the front room talked over a crooning Michael Bublé. Lucy could hear the cousins upstairs and a shower running. She sighed. A shower seemed like the perfect way to wash away the less enjoyable parts of the day—*Christmas* Day. Her white Christmas.

It had been far from perfect, but was she actually disappointed? She pulled off her gloves and touched her fingertips to her lips, remembering the feel of Will's lips against hers.

"Everything okay?" Of *course*, he'd seen her do that. He must have thought she was the type of woman who read romance novels and watched those silly Hallmark films. Well, she did watch those, but only at Christmastime.

"Yes, sorry, a little lost in thought."

"I could see that," he teased. He shrugged out of his coat and hung it on a hook by the door, while she unwrapped her scarf. "Here," he prompted, returning to her and unzipping her coat. He slid it down her shoulders, his gaze unwavering, and Lucy's breath caught. They were fully clothed, standing in a brightly lit foyer in a house full of people. How was this an erotically charged moment? Yet it was because it held the promise of what they both wanted.

Will glanced around then tilted up her chin with one finger and landed a peck on her lips. They were smiling at each other when Steph walked into the foyer from the kitchen wiping her hands on a tea towel. "Hi, you two. Have fun?"

Will dropped his hand and adopted a casual tone. "Oh, yeah, for sure." Lucy knew he wasn't fooling anyone, let alone his *mum*. "Uh, I've got a call to make," he said to excuse himself. He took the stairs two at a time and Lucy watched him go.

When she looked back at Steph, Will's mum wore a knowing smile. Lucy shook her head and smirked at her own expense, and Steph grinned at her—clearly no secrets in that house. "Come into the kitchen. We've got wine open and you can keep us company," said Steph as she headed back the way she'd come.

Lucy followed. "Us" was Steph and Jackie, and Lucy saw immediately that they needed more than company. The kitchen was a disaster area. "Oh, don't look like that," said Steph, laughing. "It may seem like chaos, but, really, we have everything under control."

"We do this every year," added Jackie, who was whisking an orange substance in a glass bowl, splashing it all over the counter.

Lucy, dubious about the "everything's under control" part, took a seat on one of the stools at the breakfast bar. "Here," said Steph as she poured Lucy a glass of red wine—a Californian zinfandel, she saw on the bottle.

"Oh, thank you." She eyed the glass; it was an overly-generous pour, like a pub pour back in the UK.

"A toast," said Steph. "To Lucy, who has been delightful." She leant across the counter and tapped her glass to Lucy's and Jackie lifted hers in a sort of toast. Lucy wondered how many bottles had been opened before she arrived, then took a sip of the wine. Sweetish and a little spicy, like Christmas.

She still hadn't shared her Christmas cake, she realised. She'd have to bring it down to have after dinner, but right then she was itching to get into that kitchen and help set things right. The food smelled delicious, but the mess! She spared a thought for poor Nate, whose kitchen was being abused, and even though she wasn't the hardcore neat freak that Chloe was, she couldn't stand it any longer.

"I'm helping!" she declared as she climbed off the stool.

"Oh, Lucy, honey, you don't need to help." Steph was stirring a pot of something on the stove. "We've done this menu a hundred times. We're fine."

Lucy ignored her. With all the confusion about Will and Jules, she needed to do *something* to feel like there was a modicum of order in her life. While Steph and Jackie continued cooking, she flitted about them, trying to stay out from underfoot as much as possible. She gathered used bowls, pans and, utensils and moved them to the sink for rinsing. She loaded the dishwasher and ran it, then found a cloth and some all-purpose spray under the sink and got to work on the counter tops.

The sisters were making more work for her as every moment passed, but she liked being able to help and in less than twenty minutes, it looked like a kitchen again, rather than a disaster zone. She returned to her perch on the stool and took a sip of her wine, satisfied with a job well done.

"Thank you, Lucy. It is actually better to work in a clean

kitchen, but I've never quite mastered the clean-as-you-go approach," said Steph.

"We get it from our mom," added Jackie. "She was an incredible home cook, but every time she made a meal, even a simple dinner on a Tuesday night, the kitchen looked like a bomb had gone off."

"Hey," Steph stopped and looked at her sister, an expression of realisation on her face. "How did I never of think of this before, but that's probably why I hate cleaning so much ... because *we* were the ones who had to clean up after her"—she looked at Lucy—"and I mean *every night*."

Jackie laughed. "Seriously, you're only just now figuring that out?"

"Yeah." Steph nodded slowly, then punctuated her thought with, "Hunh."

"I don't *love* cleaning per se," said Lucy, "but I do like when things are in their place, when there's a sense of order." Steph glanced up and smiled and Lucy, certain that was approval on Steph's face, beamed.

"I think the ham is ready to come out," said Jackie. Steph jumped into action and soon there was a giant glazed ham on the counter, glistening and golden.

"That looks incredible," said Lucy. Her family didn't ever have ham at Christmas. It was usually roast goose, maybe a turkey, one year a duck. Goose was Lucy's favourite.

"Wait 'til you taste Jackie's mustard sauce with it." Steph waggled her eyebrows and Lucy's stomach growled loudly, as though it was replying. She hadn't realised how hungry she was until that moment. She'd had Nate's pancakes at breakfast, but that was all she'd eaten the entire day. This was going to be a momentous meal.

She sipped her wine and watched as the sisters bustled about the kitchen, putting the finishing touches on Christmas dinner, working in a harmony that she admired and, she realised, longed for. One day, she'd have a home that she could share with a loved one, not just a flatmate, and they'd cook together like this.

I wonder if Will cooks. She smiled to herself and took another sip. *Loved one. Will …*

Her thoughts were about to take hold when Steph interrupted. "So, Lucy, hon, do you know who Will had to call?"

Wistful thoughts of Will and a possible future together vanished, and Lucy caught the slight edge of concern in Steph's voice. She couldn't lie. She was a terrible liar and Steph would know.

"Uh, he was calling Jules, actually." Steph nodded as though she'd suspected as much. "I told him it wasn't necessary, but—"

Steph cut her off, resting both hands on the counter. "I think it is, though, hon. Like I said, Will is a grown man and Jules needs to understand that. Sure, they're close, but she can't keep him all to herself. She needs to let him be with whoever he wants to be with, especially if that person is you."

Lucy blinked back unexpected tears.

Steph came around her side of the counter, took one of her hands, and looked at her lovingly. "*Especially* if that person is you," she said quietly. Lucy glanced at Jackie who winked at her and smiled.

Lucy smiled through her tears and bit her lip. "Thank you," she replied. Steph squeezed her hand.

"Now, there's one more thing. You're gonna need to be firm with my daughter too."

"What? Oh, no." Lucy shook her head vigorously.

"Lucy, listen to me. Jules can be headstrong and sometimes that's to the detriment of those around her. She shouldn't have attacked you like that and, even if you're not thinking it now, at some point, resentment will come into play."

Lucy looked inward and realised that resentment might already be in play. Why else would she deliberately ignore Jules's message on the group chat? Yet ... "But what if it damages our friendship?"

"Saying nothing will do worse damage." Steph let go of Lucy's hand and returned to dishing up.

A small sigh escaped. Steph was right, and not just about Jules. A niggling thought that wouldn't be shaken popped to the forefront of her mind. Lucy also need to sort things out with her manager, Angela. "Um, Steph?"

"Mmm-hmm," Steph replied, her attention fixed on the platter of roast potatoes she was dishing up.

"Do you think we could find some time to talk later?" Steph looked up and a flicker of concern crossed her face. "It's just that there's something happening at work that I need your help with."

"Of course, honey."

Lucy smiled. Everything was still leaning towards pear-shaped, but perhaps with Steph's help she would manage to sort it all out.

Chapter 24

Chloe

It was impossible to enjoy soaking in the bath after what had happened. The adrenalin crash had left Chloe feeling anything but mighty, and the water was too cold to save with a top-up. She gave up after a few minutes of bobbing about, got out, dried off, and went about the business of cleaning up the water on the floor.

She knew she was in a five-star hotel and all she needed to do was phone housekeeping, but the task would allow her to get out of her head and focus on something she could control.

But as she sopped up the last of the water and threw the sodden towels into the bathtub, she gave up on clearing her mind. Nothing was going to cut through her whirlwind of thoughts and the nauseating feeling they left in their wake.

She simply couldn't ignore that Archer's ex-girlfriend had shown up in his—rather, *their*—hotel room, or that she'd felt entitled to do that. *Or* that she'd seen Chloe naked!

She glanced at the clock on the bedside table. Archer had

been gone a little more than an hour. If Madison hadn't shown up, she would have been slathering herself in high-end toiletries and ordering room service by now.

She eyed the bed, surveying the wreckage. They'd managed to make quite a mess of those high-thread-count sheets and that fluffy doona; most of the bedding was trailing onto the floor. Ordinarily, she'd have tidied it up before housekeeping arrived, but a more pressing thought took hold.

What would it have looked like to Madison? she wondered.

"It would have looked like he'd made mad, passionate love to some other than her," Chloe said aloud. No wonder Madison had behaved like a bear with a thorn in its paw. She'd probably thought she would sneak into Archer's room first thing in the morning and climb into bed with him.

Chloe's stomach lurched. She didn't want anyone to crawl into Archer's bed ever again—except her.

"Well, bugger," she muttered to herself. She was completely smitten with the world's biggest film star.

Housekeeping called mid-morning to ask when it would be a good time to service the room. Chloe, who'd been biding her time by scrolling her social media accounts, welcomed the prompt to leave the room, and situated herself in the Rotunda Lounge downstairs where she nibbled on a £20 croissant.

It *was* excellent and so were the strawberry jam and butter she slathered onto it and the pot of breakfast tea, which she finished. And apparently, in a swanky hotel in inner London, it was not called *English* breakfast tea—that part was implied. In any case, it was perfect—strong with a heady scent and served with a small jug of Jersey's creamiest milk.

But even a delicious breakfast couldn't distract her from a series of vicious thoughts. *What if this is just a bit of fun for Archer? What if he's with me to make Madison jealous? What if I never see him again after this holiday?*

Eventually, it was time to go back to the room, which she did to find it in pristine condition with all the amenities replenished. She checked her appearance in the large mirror that ran the length of the two-sink vanity, then looked herself in the eye.

"Right, Chloe Sims. When he gets back, you are telling Archer how you feel. And if he doesn't feel the same way, you're getting on a bus straight back to Oxfordshire, and you will spend the next few days having a lovely time with Max and Susan before getting on that plane."

The pep talk did little to assuage the turmoil she was in, however, and she spent the rest of the time waiting for Archer reading a book she'd brought with her—well, staring at the same page over and over and not taking in any of it. Usually she dived right into a gory crime thriller, but that day, blood spatter was far less gruesome than what had occurred earlier.

She heard the key card in the lock just before lunch and looked up. Instead of Archer, in walked an enormous bunch of pink lilies, and her face involuntarily broke into a smile. Archer moved the flowers to the side and grinned at her. "Hello, lovely," he said, his face filled with affection.

Everything she'd rehearsed, the stoic, calm greeting, flew out of her head as she launched herself off the couch and threw her arms around his neck. He pulled her close with his free arm, laughing gleefully at her effusive hello. She breathed in his spicy scent mixed with the sweetness of the lilies.

"I missed you," she mumbled into his neck. When she lifted her face to his, he looked into her eyes for a moment before bending to press his mouth softly to hers.

"I missed you, too." He stepped back slightly, and she felt the loss of his touch intensely. "These are for you, as a thank you gift for being so patient." *If only he knew how much I deserve these*.

"Thank you," she said graciously. She was about to take the flowers from him when his expression changed, suddenly serious. "Chloe, something's happened. What is it?" That he could know that *just* by looking at her answered Chloe's most pressing question, the one that had played on repeat in her mind ever since Madison's intrusion.

He feels the same way.

"Well ... look, there's no easy way to tell you, so I'm just gonna say it. Madison let herself into the room and found me in the bath." In any other circumstance, the look on his face would have been comical. "Yes, *that*. That was pretty much my reaction too."

Archer seemed to gather his wits somewhat, placing the bouquet on a table near the door before making his way to the couch. He plopped down, a frown settling onto his handsome features. Chloe sat next to him and tucked her feet beneath her.

"But I don't ... why? And how was she even let in here? Oh, Chloe, I'm so, so sorry." He shook his head, obviously still in disbelief.

"It's not your fault. You don't need to apologise. *She* does, but not you."

Archer angled his body towards her, his expression changing from confusion to concern, his hand reaching to stroke her cheek. "Are you all right? She didn't *do* anything to you, did she?"

From the way he'd asked the question, it was clear that her encounter with Madison could have been far worse.

"Oh, no, nothing like that. Unless you count saying cruel things to me but, you know ... I'm a big girl and all that." Chloe smiled feebly.

"God, I'm so, so sorry. Here I am inviting you to London with me so I could spend proper time with you, and I've gone and put you in the firing line." He ran a hand through his dark hair and blew out an exasperated sigh.

"Archer, this isn't your fault. But I do think you need to talk to her."

"Oh, yes, I suppose so. Quite right. *And* the hotel. I can't *believe* they let her in here."

"Yes, well, she had her own key card, so someone on the front desk was a little lax in the security department. And she did say that a member of your publicity team alerted her that you were staying here."

"Bollocks! Bollocks, bollocks, bollocks!"

Chloe couldn't help the snicker that burst from her mouth. It was such a silly swear word, like something out of a Monty Python sketch.

"What?" His eyes, filled with mirth, met hers. "Are you disparaging my choice of profanity?" he asked with a mock-serious glare.

"Never."

"Like buggery, you weren't, Ms Sims." He gave her a look worthy of a pantomime. Chloe wouldn't have been surprised to suddenly hear a chorus of, "Look behind you, look behind you."

She sighed dramatically—two could play at this game—and returned the hard stare. "Mr Tate, may I remind you that I am from Australia where we say the F-word on TV and include words like 'bloody' and 'bugger' in award-winning ad campaigns. Yes, I know that those are the height of profanity here in the UK, but in *'Straya"*—she bunged on a broad Aussie accent—"they are regularly heard on the playground."

His mouth puckered in an obvious attempt not to smile. "Is that so?"

It was time for the big guns, the Ocker accent! "Yeah, mate, so drop the airs and graces and let's call a spade a spade. Your ex is deadset batty, mate. For realz."

He threw his head back and laughed, then, regarding her with an amused smile, conceded the win to her. "Good lord, that accent. Very Australian, well done you."

"You know, there some are people who, when they meet me, think I'm English—Americans mostly."

"Is that so?" He seemed dubious.

"*Yes.* Maybe it's because they think all Australians sound like the Crocodile Hunter."

"Crikey!"

"That was an appalling accent, by the way. I thought you we supposed to be a *good* actor."

"Oh, you're in trouble, you are." He stood and before she

284

knew what was happening, he had scooped her up in his arms and carried her to the bed, where he deposited her unceremoniously with a plop and climbed on top of her. She was giggling so hard she didn't have time to escape.

"Archer, stop, *stop!*" His legs straddled her hips and, hovering over her, he peppered kisses over her face and neck, before finally sitting back and regarding her with a grin.

"Do you really want me to stop?"

She shook her head and he dipped his to capture her mouth in a delicious kiss, then raised it just enough to meet her eyes. One finger trailed the features of her face and she watched as his gaze followed. "You have the most extraordinary eyes," he whispered. She lowered her lashes and smiled softly, flattered by his appreciative gaze. "And mouth and cheeks," he added, then nuzzled her ear and kissed it. "And ears ..." She giggled again, his breath tickling her.

He sat back, his smile revealing that he was both playing with those cheesy words and completely serious. "You know, we could skip Winter Wonderland and stay here, let me make love to you all day, show you *just* how much I adore you." he said.

Chloe's breath caught in her throat. He adored her! And no man had ever said they wanted to "make love" to her before. It was all achingly romantic, and she was almost swayed. Yet, she really did want to go to Winter Wonderland.

"Come back," she said, tugging on his shirt. He complied, nestling in next to her. She rolled onto her side to face him, her turn to take *him* in. As she revelled in the sculpted features of his face, she mentally pinched herself; he was just *so* beautiful. She kissed him, his lips moving against hers instantly as the tip of her tongue sought out his. The taste of him was incredible, almost sweet, and she found herself lost in the sensation of not just his mouth, but the feel of his body pressed against her, his hand splayed on the small of her back pulling her close to him and the scent of his spicy cologne making her heady.

Chloe had never wanted anyone more.

"How about this?" she murmured against his lips. "How about we mess up this perfectly made bed and *then* go to Winter Wonderland?"

He grinned at her from an inch away. "You really do love Christmas, don't you?"

Not as much as I love you.

The thought startled her so much, she nearly said it aloud. "Yes," she said instead, her lips resting against his. "It is my second favourite thing in the world."

"And the first?" His eyes were alive with mischief.

Chloe pulled him closer and answered the question with another kiss.

Chapter 25

Lucy

"Excellent meal, Steph, Jackie—thank you. Menfolk, we're on clean up," Nate declared. He stood and stretched his arms out with a grunt. When there was no movement around the table, he looked at Bob, Joe, Will, and Bradley in turn, his eyebrows raised.

There was a beat before every male at the table stood and started clearing plates and platters. Will winked at Lucy as he took her plate and she rewarded him with a smile. He was the cutest waiter she'd ever had. With that thought, she realised that she was more than a little tipsy and memories of that morning came flooding back. She reached for her water glass.

As she watched the bustling "menfolk", as Nate had called them, she tried to imagine her father on clean-up duty. She hiccupped a little laugh and clapped her hand over her mouth.

"So, Lucy," said Briony, picking up her wine glass and settling in next to Lucy, "you and Will, huh?" All eyes were on Lucy and hers flew to the doorway to the kitchen, where she heard the clatter of cleaning up and men's voices. She looked around the table. The twins, Steph and Jackie, sat opposite her and she was flanked by the cousins, Bridget staring at her wide-eyed and Briony clearly waiting for a response.

She was in the hot seat.

"Uh, yes, I suppose you could say that we're something of an item." Bridget giggled and Lucy felt ridiculous. Why was she talking like a character from *Downton Abbey*?

"Sorry, I shouldn't have laughed," said Bridget. "I think the two of you are sweet together." Bridget's cheeks flushed and Lucy felt that solidarity with her again.

Of all the women around the table, Lucy and Bridget were the most alike, and it would have been the same if Jules were there. As Lucy saw it, the women in Jules's family—Bridget excepted—would never know what it was like to be socially awkward or feel unattractive and gawky. With their lean figures, long glossy waves of flaxen hair, and extremely pretty faces, it was like they'd stepped out of a GAP ad, every one of them.

In contrast, she felt like the great pretender. Yes, she'd been told she was pretty, beautiful even, but she'd never really believed it. It certainly wasn't what she saw when she looked in the mirror. *She* saw a pale, freckled, and gangly woman with bright red hair, whose eyes were too large and too far apart, whose nose was unremarkable, and whose mouth was too wide. She had only ever been complimented by men when they wanted to sleep with her. She'd even let herself believe them a few times.

"I think you're good for Will," added Briony.

"Really? Why, what do you mean?"

"I haven't seen him this happy since Tif—"

Lucy caught the quick look Steph gave Briony as she cut her off. "Since a long time ago."

"Are you going to marry Will?" asked Bridget.

Lucy had timed her next sip of water poorly and spat most of it out onto the table, coughing and spluttering. She barely registered Briony chastising her sister with a sharp hiss of, "Bridget!"

Was she really supposed to answer Bridget's question? She hadn't been serious, surely? Lucy chanced a glance at her. Seeing that Bridget was now bright red, Lucy desperately wanted to save her from further humiliation.

"Oh, you were just teasing, right Bridget?" Bridget gawped at her in surprise, eventually catching on and nodding her response. "I mean, I've only just met Will. And this isn't one of those silly holiday movies—you know, boy meets girl, they both want the same Christmas tree, they argue over it, all cross with each other, then fall madly in love."

"No, instead it's your best friend's brother, and you're super into each other, and you're hands down the nicest woman he's ever shown interest in." Briony was definitely her mother's daughter. Lucy looked across the table at Jackie, who nodded in agreement.

Lucy was not used to this kind of honesty. In her family, they talked *around* things. No one ever came right out and said what they were thinking.

"We've probably grilled Lucy enough for one evening," said Steph. Lucy could have kissed her. "Girls, why don't you finish clearing the table?" Bridget popped right out of her seat as though a reprieve had been granted, but Briony took her time getting up, then joined her sister in gathering various pieces of dinnerware before retreating to the kitchen. "Hey, Jackie, Lucy's mom sent over that Christmas cake. How about putting on some coffee and cutting some slices?" It was hardly subtle, but Lucy was grateful that Steph was clearing the room on her behalf.

"Oh, sure. It's wrapped in aluminium foil, right Lucy? On the kitchen counter?"

"That's right. Thin slices would be good. It's extremely rich and boozy."

"No problem." She and Jackie shared a smile, then Jackie left the table.

When she was out of earshot, Lucy threw Steph a grateful look. "Thank you. That was a little, um ... intense."

"Yeah, tact doesn't exactly run in their family. How about we go into the living room?"

Lucy and Jackie settled on either end of one of the long leather sofas, the sounds from the kitchen becoming background noise. "We'll have a little time before the others join us. You said there was something you wanted to talk to me about?"

"Oh, yes!" Lucy had been so stuck on replaying the awkward conversation about Will that she'd all but forgotten about the matter of her manager, Angela. Mindful of the short time she'd have Steph to herself, she gave the digest version of how Angela seemed to be undermining her at every turn, and how a job that Lucy had enjoyed was becoming more and more demoralising.

"Hmm, and how long has Angela been with the company?"

"Close to eight months now. Although, in some ways it seems far longer."

"And how long was her predecessor there, your former boss?"

"Oh, that was Nigel. He was so lovely. He hired me, actually, and that was ... eleven years ago. I think he'd been with the firm thirty-odd years when he retired." Lucy had adored Nigel, learning so much from him, and appreciating his gentle and nurturing management style.

"So, Angela came in to replace someone who was at the firm for three decades?"

Steph was getting at something, although Lucy wasn't quite sure what it was. "Yes, that's right."

"I imagine that would have been somewhat challenging."

Oh, right. Now Lucy understood. Steph was helping her find a way to empathise with Angela. "Quite. I hadn't thought of it like that. Do you suppose that she may be trying to find her footing, to assert herself in some way?"

"Something like that. I'm not saying it's okay for her to walk all over you or undermine you, but it sounds like it could be coming from a place of insecurity. I've seen it before. In fact, I've been guilty of it myself."

"Really?"

"Mmm-hmm. Years ago, now, when I was promoted into my first managerial role, I thought I had to go in guns blazing, ready to defend my ground." She raised her eyebrows, a wry smile on her face.

"How did that go?"

291

"Terribly." Steph laughed quietly. "But I had a good mentor, and she taught me how to be firm and fair without coming across as a tyrant. It was probably the steepest learning curve of my career." That was saying a lot, as Steph was the CEO of a Fortune 500 company, one of only forty women to hold that position. "I also had a couple of key employees who knew how to manage up. You've heard of that, right?"

"Vaguely, but I'm not sure exactly what it means."

"It means that they helped coach me to be the kind of manager they needed me to be."

"So, that's what I should do?"

"Look, I'm only going on what you've told me, but I think it may be the right approach. Send her an email and set up a meeting. Tell her that you're excited for the New Year, especially everything you can learn from her. You could even ask her to be your mentor." Lucy scrunched up her nose and Steph smiled. "I know, it seems counterintuitive, but if she feels like she has something to offer you, she's going to be more inclined to listen to you and to stop undermining you. *You* make the first move; *you* set the tone for how you want things to be going forward."

Lucy bit her lip and stared into the blue and yellow flickering flames in the fireplace imagining Angela as her mentor. It *could* work. And, really, anything would be better than being miserable at work or having to look for a new job. She looked back at Steph. "I'll do it. I'll take your advice. And thank you—for your help, and for letting me have a whinge."

"Oh, no problem, honey. And, you know, once you get home

and you're working through all of this, if you want to talk some more, just get in touch. Okay?"

Lucy nodded, trying to quell the mild panic that arose. She didn't want to think about being back home without Will. As her stomach twisted itself in knots, Jules's family streamed through the doorway en masse, bringing with them loud and cheery conversations and after-dinner treats, including a plate piled high with her mum's Christmas cake. Not typically one to eat her feelings, Lucy practically lunged at the plate, taking the fattest slice and biting off a corner.

"I'm definitely getting me some of that," said Will. He handed her a paper napkin from the stack beside the plate and she took it sheepishly. How rude of her to help herself before anyone else had, *and* without a napkin or a plate. Will didn't seem to notice her poor manners and when he had his own slice, he sat next to her and draped his free arm around her shoulder.

A quick glance around told her that no one thought this was out of the ordinary, or if they did, they were doing a fabulous job of pretending. "You and my mom have a good talk?" he asked, his voice low and gravelly in her ear and sending those now-familiar shivers down her spine. She really wished they weren't sitting in a room full of people.

She nodded her reply to Will's question and shared a quick smile with him. "She's been wonderful, actually. Very helpful with the Angela situation."

"Oh, that's good. From what you've said, it's not sustainable the way it is."

"I think I have a viable solution. We'll see in any case. And what about you and Jules?" Lucy had been dying to ask, but Christmas dinner was hardly a good time to bring it up.

"Oh, sorry, Lucy. I should have said. I got her voicemail. I'll call her tomorrow." Lucy felt the sting of disappointment. How unsettling to think of going to sleep on Christmas night with things still tense between her and Jules. Hopefully, they'd sort it all out and soon, but her stomach tightened when she remembered what Steph had said about being firm with Jules. This was new ground—both for Lucy and for her friendship with Jules—and she wasn't sure if she could do that. What if it just drove a bigger wedge between them?

"Oh, my god," Will said, his mouth full of Christmas cake. He gave her an incredulous look. "It's even *better*," he said after he swallowed.

"Than the *one* bite you had in the car?" Lucy teased, happy for the distraction from her Jules dilemma.

"Mmm-hmm."

"It is quite magical, isn't it? Proper British Christmas cake, all spicy and delicious."

"You're spicy and delicious." She rolled her eyes and giggled. "Are you laughing at me?" he asked.

"Oh definitely. That line was terrible."

"That's fair, but in my defence, I am a little rusty."

"At flirting?" she asked, surprised.

"Hell yeah. Didn't you hear? I've practically been a monk for *years* now." Lucy could hardly imagine that Will had been "monkish". Single, yes, but celibate? Surely, he was joking. Well, if he wasn't, she was quite happy to be the person to break his bout of celibacy. She giggled to herself, becoming aware that someone was calling her name—Briony. She was dealing out Cards Against Humanity and did Lucy want to play? She glanced at Will who shrugged.

"Oh, yes, I'll play." She popped the last of her Christmas cake into her mouth, then picked up each white card as it landed on the table in front of her. "Um, Will, I have no idea who this person is." She stared at the card—"Vanna White". Who in the world was Vanna White when she was at home?

"Oh, we have an unwritten rule. If you don't know who someone is, or what something is, you can swap out the card. Here." He held out his hand and took the card. "Really, you don't know Vanna White?"

"Should I?"

"Wheel of Fortune?"

She stared at him blankly. "I think it's a bit like if we were playing the British version and you drew Rachel Riley."

"Who's Rachel Riley?"

"Exactly."

"Lucy's swapping out a card—Vanna White," he declared, placing Vanna on the bottom of the deck, and handing Lucy a card from the top.

She read it—"Steve Harvey".

"Oh, for Pete's sake," she said, exasperated. "Who in the world is Steve Harvey?" The was a beat of silence before an eruption of laughter. Lucy joined in, happy to laugh at her own expense. There were two more swaps before she finally drew a card with something on it that she knew of. It was a particularly disgusting card, but she was certain it would win her a round. Now she just needed to wait for the right black card to be played.

Two hours later, Bridget was declared the winner with seven black cards. Lucy remembered what Jules had said about her cousin, that Bridget wasn't as strait-laced as she seemed. Apparently not, especially considering that her winning card had involved a particularly graphic depiction of a sexual act that Lucy suspected was illegal in some countries. As Bridget raised her hand to claim the win, her cheeks had turned a lurid shade of pink.

Lucy leant back against the sofa, her eyes droopy. The Christmas cake had been eaten, they'd gone through two pots of coffee—she'd had tea—and between the large group, another three bottles of wine had been drunk. But, with her Christmas morning hangover still fresh enough in her mind, Lucy had declined the "incredible pinot from Oregon".

"I'm absolutely shattered," she said quietly to Will, as the others start to pack up around them.

"You should get some sleep. Big day tomorrow."

She threw him a frown. "How so?"

"Didn't anyone tell you?"

"Tell me what? Does your family have some sort of Boxing Day tradition?" Lucy wondered what it could possibly be and almost every thought seemed exhausting. Would it be awfully bad manners to sleep the day away?

"I'm not sure what Boxing Day is, but tomorrow, everyone clears out."

"Sorry, what?" She shook her cloudy head, still frowning.

"Bob, Jackie, and the cousins fly out tomorrow night, so

they're driving back to Denver in the morning, and Mom and Joe will be gone by lunchtime. Dad's staying a couple more days—there are a few maintenance jobs he wants to get done—but, as you've seen, he keeps to himself."

"Hang on, do you mean that tomorrow all this hullabaloo goes away, and we'll have some proper time together?"

"Exactly." Lucy's thoughts flew straight to her "snowed-in" fantasy, the one she'd been nurturing for several days now. "And I thought that once everyone's gone, we could take the snowmobile out and go snowshoeing."

Snowmobiling and snowshoeing? Outside? Away from the warmth of the cabin?

The fantasy crumbled. "Oh, right. That sounds lovely," she lied.

Chapter 26

Jules

Jules's ringtone surprised her, and it took a moment for it to register that it was her phone ringing. She saw her brother's name on the screen and suddenly remembered that she'd missed a call from him the day before when they were driving down to Matt's place. She smiled; a call with her brother was just what she needed to keep her from worrying about Matt.

"Hey, Will, sorry I missed your call yesterday. So, how is everyone? You guys having a good time?"

"Uh, yeah."

She could hear the hesitancy in his voice. "Hey, is everything okay?" A loud PA announcement intruded on the call and she pressed a finger against her free ear.

"Jules, where are you?"

"The emergency room," she replied, only realising how careless that was when Will practically shouted, "*What*?" into her ear. "I mean, I'm here with a friend. I'm fine. He's fine too, mostly. Sorry, I didn't mean to scare you."

"So, he's okay? *You're* okay?"

"Yeah, he's just getting an X-ray. He fell off a horse and it's probably just a sprain, but we're getting it checked out."

She heard her brother blow out a long sigh, picturing him clearly. He'd be rubbing the back of his neck and puffing out his cheeks in relief. She smiled, missing him like crazy. "So, what's up?" she prompted. He sighed again, but this one didn't sound like relief. "Will?"

"Actually, I'm really pissed at you, Jules."

Her stomach plummeted. She loved that she and Will were close enough to tell each other when they were pissed off, but she knew exactly what this was about. And she felt terrible that she hadn't made things right with Lucy yet. She'd put it off and now Will was calling her from half a world away.

"I know, I get it," she said, falling on her sibling sword.

"Well, what the hell, Jules?"

She shook her head even though she knew he couldn't see her. "I don't know ..."

"That's not good enough. You've made Lucy feel like crap. For no reason, and she basically avoided me most of Christmas Day."

Jules tried to swallow the lump in her throat. Will and Lucy were two of the most important people in her life, a select group she could count on one hand, and she had completely screwed this up. "Will, I—"

"She's *amazing*, Jules," he said, interjecting. "Amazing, and I ..." He trailed off and Jules took the opportunity to jump in. She had to try to make things right.

"I know. She is amazing. She's warm, she's kind, and *super* smart."

"Yeah, she is—all those things. And she's fun. And she gets along well with everyone."

"All true." Jules knew that letting Will rant at her was part of her penance for being such a crappy sister.

"So how is it that she's not good enough for me? 'Cause that's how you made her feel."

"I didn't ... she *is*, Will. Of course, she is, but—"

"Wait, do you think *I'm* not good enough for *her*?"

"No! That's not it." She stood, the need to pace intense. She'd let Will rant, but now she needed to set the record straight and explain how they'd come to this horrible situation. "Can I just ... can you listen? *Please?*"

"Fine."

"Hey, where are you? In the cabin, I mean?"

"I'm in my room. Don't worry, she can't hear me." Jules heard the curtains slide on their track and imagined him staring out the window at the wintry landscape, feeling a pang for home.

"Is it snowing?"

"What? Uh, no. No fresh snow since the twenty-fourth. You're stalling, Jules."

"I know. Look, I'm really sorry I screwed this up. It's no excuse, but when I was talking to Lucy and you came up, I was pretty tipsy, and it was late." Will was silent and she could sense his impatience. "Like I said, it's not an excuse, but it was a surprise and I reacted poorly. I know you probably don't want to hear this, but as soon as I heard that you and Lucy had kissed, all I could think of was Tiffany—" A short groan from Will made her pause.

"That was years ago, Jules."

"Yes, it was, and that's my point. It's been *years* since you dated anyone seriously. Your breakup with Tiffany, that was … It's like you've never really got over it. And then there's Lucy, who's one of my best friends, and she lives in *England* … and I guess all those thoughts tumbled together at once and I let my worry come out as judgement."

Another long sigh from Will. "I get it."

Jules pressed her lips together, her eyes tearing up. It was only three words, but she knew from Will's tone that he'd forgiven her. Now she just had to make things right with Lucy—dear, sweet Lucy.

"Look," said Will, "you're right about the breakup with Tiffany. It almost broke me, and I know you know that. I mean, you were there for most of it. But that's why you *shouldn't* be worried about me and Lucy. She's literally the first woman I've had strong feelings for in years. I haven't been single all this time because I'm afraid, Jules. It's because I haven't met anyone who mattered enough. Do you understand that?"

A thousand thoughts and worries slotted into place in an instant and she smiled. "Yeah, yeah, I do," she said. "Look, Will, whatever happens, I just want you to be happy, okay? *Both* of you."

"Thanks, Jules."

"And I promise I'll call Lucy." Matt appeared at the end of the hallway, his arm in a sling and an abashed smile on his face. He raised his good arm in a greeting. Jules's heartstrings abandoned the mess she'd created in Colorado and landed with a thud in the hallway of an emergency room in Australia.

"Will, I have to go. I love you. Tell Lucy I'll call her later." Without waiting for a reply, she pressed her thumb on the red button and rushed down the hall to Matt. She stopped a couple of feet away. "Hey."

"Hey."

"Is it broken?"

"Nah, just a sprain."

Relief flooded through her and she threw her arms around Matt's neck and hugged him, careful not to press against his sprained wrist. "It's all good, Jules. Just a silly fall, that's all," he said softly.

Jules leant back leaving her arms where they were. She felt the warmth and strength of Matt's hand against her back as her eyes roved over his face, taking in his chocolatey brown eyes, heavy arched brows, broad nose, stubbled chin, and full lips which curled up in a gentle smile. "I was worried," she whispered.

"And all the way here you were telling me there was nothing to worry about," he teased, his smile widening and those gorgeous dimples making an appearance.

"It was an *act*. A broken wrist takes a long time to heal and you're a winemaker and how are you supposed to make wine with a broken wrist? Let alone *drive* yourself anywhere... And what if ..." It was no wonder she was getting worked up. While she'd remained calm on the outside, she'd been replaying the awful scene in her mind since they'd got into the SUV with Jonno. What if he'd been bitten by that snake? Weren't all snakes in Australia deadly?

What if something had happened to him, something serious, and she'd lost him?

"Hey, hey, it's okay, I'm good." Jules dropped her head and rested it against his chest. She felt the soft caress of his thumb through her top and it sent a shot of warmth through her. All she wanted was to curl up in bed with him and ...

And what?

It wasn't just sex she wanted. She wanted to hold him and kiss him and just lie next to him, just *be* with him. *I've fallen for the hot Aussie winemaker*, she realised, surprising herself.

Matt brought her back to reality when he said he needed to sort out some stuff at the front desk. "Would you mind calling a taxi for us? Here, use my phone. I've got a number saved in my contacts." He unlocked his phone and handed it to her.

"Oh sure, or I can get us an Uber?"

"Uh, not sure we have many of those out this way." He winked. "You happy to wait here?"

"Yeah, sure." Matt jogged off towards the front desk and Jules had to stop herself from calling out to be careful. She was about to call for a cab when Matt's phone rang, startling her and nearly making her drop it. She recovered, pressed the green button, and raised the phone to her ear.

"Hello? This is Matt's phone."

"And who are you?" asked a woman's voice.

"Oh, I'm ... a friend—of Matt's. He's just ... He can't come to the phone right now. Can I take a message?"

"It's his mum. Wait a minute. You're not *Kirsten*, are you?" Jules had no idea who Kirsten was, but it was clear from her tone that Matt's mom did not like her.

"Uh, no, ma'am, this is Jules. I met Matt at Christmas. I'm a friend of Chloe's. Do you know Chloe?"

"Mmm." The response sounded like a growl and Jules just *knew* it was accompanied by a frown, even though she couldn't see the woman's face.

"Oh, look, Matt's here!" she exclaimed as she held out the phone. "It's your mom," she mouthed.

Matt's inquisitive expression morphed into one Jules couldn't read, and he took the phone from her and pressed it to his ear. "Hi, Mum, what's up?" It was obvious from the false cheer he affected that Matt wasn't about to reveal his whereabouts or what had happened.

His expression changed again, and Jules watched as he looked at the floor, his mouth flattening into a thin line and his brows meeting. "Yeah, no—" He'd clearly been cut off and although she couldn't make out most of the words, she did hear "Kirsten" a couple of times and from the tone of Matt's mom's voice, she was not pleased.

"Mum. *Mum*, we can talk about this another time ... Yeah, well, it's not why you called, so what's going on? Oh, right. Yeah, I can make that work, no worries. No, I'm happy to, Mum. Look, I'd better go. I'll call you later, okay? Yeah. Love you too. 'Kay. Bye."

He dropped the handset by his side and finally met Jules's eyes. "Sorry 'bout that."

"Is everything okay?"

"Yeah, she just needs me to take her to the doctor the week after next."

"Ah, I see." Was he really going to ignore the whole "Kirsten" thing?

"Do we still need to call a taxi?" he asked. Apparently, he was, yes.

"Yeah, your mom called before I had the chance."

"No worries." He scrolled through the phone one-handed and made the call. "Ten minutes," he said, adding a weak smile.

Jules nodded. *Say it*, she prompted herself. "So, who's Kirsten?"

"Oh, uh ..."

"*Annnd* ..." she drew the word out, "why did your mom freak out when she thought that *I* was Kirsten?"

Matt bit his lip, then reached for her hand. She let him take it. "How about when we get back to my place, we talk? 'Kay?"

"Okay." Jules's stomach tightened into a knot. This was it. This was where she learnt that Matt had an ex-wife, or possibly a current wife, and that for him, she'd just been a bit of fun. Ordinarily, she wouldn't have cared. This was how she liked her romantic liaisons—no promises, no feelings, *casual*.

But that was before the beach when he'd wrapped her up in that beach towel and held her, before those sexy cheek kisses at Christmas, before the honest conversations and sleeping next to him, before a dramatic fall from a horse, throwing him into the path of a deadly snake.

For years now, Jules had liked things casual, but that was before she fell for Matt.

Damn it. I really am a goner.

Chapter 27

Chloe

"This is amazing!" Chloe had to shout above the sounds of the carousel, its music box trills as loud as any club she'd ever been to.

She and Archer were riding side-by-side horses, his going up as hers went down and vice versa. She was getting dizzy, but that may have been the two cups of *Glühwein* they'd had before the ride.

Winter Wonderland was "going off" as the Aussies would say, with thousands of fair-goers milling about the stalls, and the carnival rides blinking garish coloured lights and blaring tinny renditions of famous pop songs from the 80s. Archer had won her a particularly tacky stuffed reindeer with his shooting skills, something he credited to his time playing a sharpshooter in a gritty American Gulf War drama. The reindeer was perched in front of Chloe on her carousel horse; she'd named it Dexter, like Matt's dog back home in Melbourne.

Eventually, the horses slowed, as did the carousel itself, and a booming voice asked them to exit on the left. Chloe wondered how there could *be* a "left" when they were on a giant circle, but she climbed off her horse and with Dexter under her arm, followed the others, including Archer.

Back on the thoroughfare, she noticed that the sun was nowhere to be seen and the milky light of twilight coloured the sky with a pale-yellow merging into a paler pink.

She stopped walking and grinned at Archer. "That was fun. I can't remember the last time I went on a merry-go-round." She earned a kiss for her enthusiasm and he slung an arm around her shoulder and pulled her close as they started walking again.

"Would you like to head back to the hotel now?" he asked, almost having to shout. Screams punctuated the air above them, and Chloe looked up to see a whirligig of a contraption, with people being flung from here to there in an instant. It looked like a blast.

Chloe tore her eyes away and looked up at Archer. Another ride, or more time alone with him? Maybe they could climb into that giant tub together? It was an easy answer. "Let's go back," she said.

"Oh, my god, are you Archer Tate?!"

The question came from a group of five young women, although Chloe would have been hard-pressed to identify which one had said it. They all looked at him expectantly, with varying degrees of "gobsmackedness".

"Uh, yes, hello." Archer nodded and smiled politely. Chloe watched, mesmerised, as he posed for photos, signed random pieces of paper, fielded inane questions, and let them fawn over him. He was so amenable that the entire encounter was wrapped up in a handful of minutes. It was another taste of what life was like with someone as famous as Archer. Although, this was far more pleasant than being ambushed by his ex or being photographed kissing.

"You are very gracious," she said when they were on their way again and out of earshot of the giggling gaggle.

"It's part of the job—be kind, say hello, take some pictures. I'd rather be like that than the brooding, surly film star."

"Sure, but I thought you didn't want to be recognised today." Before leaving the hotel, they had donned what Archer called "light disguises". They both wore baseball caps, the peaks pulled low, and Archer wore a pair of thick-rimmed prop glasses.

"True, but ..." He sighed, his shoulders raising in a shrug.

Chloe finished the thought. "A disguise only goes so far."

"Exactly. It will work on most people and, honestly, in London, you can hardly swing a dead cat without seeing someone famous, so a lot of people are blasé if they notice me. But, unless I want to spend hours in the makeup chair before I pop down to Tesco for milk, it's just part and parcel really."

"Mmm, I get it." Intellectually, she did, in any case. It was still a lot to comprehend, his level of fame and how it affected his everyday life, how it might affect *her* everyday life. But there was something else. "You know, all that aside ..." He glanced at her inquisitively. "I've worked with quite a few celebrities, and the way you were with those girls ... well, you're more gracious than most."

"Honestly—and I truly believe this—if it weren't for the

people who buy tickets to my films or my plays, I wouldn't *be* 'Archer Tate'. I wouldn't have this incredible career, so when I meet them, they deserve my kindness."

"You enjoy that aspect of your fame, then?" she asked, somewhat perplexed.

"Being mobbed in public?" She looked up to see that he was joking.

"Well, when you put it like that ..."

"I enjoy meeting people who like my work. Some fans, probably that group of girls, can be a little fixated on who they think Archer Tate is, as opposed to liking *me*, or my performances, but, as I said, it's part and parcel, isn't it?"

"I honestly wouldn't know."

He gave a grunt of a laugh. "Quite right, but what I mean is, I consider it a privilege to do what I love for a living, so the aspects of my job that I don't particularly enjoy—the intrusions on my privacy, especially—they are the price to pay. Sometimes, I wish I could do what Harry and Meghan did; although, their spotlight is far brighter than mine. I mean, I've only been noticed what, a handful of times since we got here? They couldn't even *come* here."

"Sorry, do you mean *Prince* Harry and his wife, Meghan?"

"The Duke and Duchess of Sussex, yes."

She narrowed her eyes. "So, do you *know* them, or just know *of* them?"

"Harry and I are quite good friends, actually. After I shot *Fallen Soldier*, I got involved in the Invictus Games Foundation—I'm a patron—and he and I hit it off. He's a brilliant bloke, great sense of humour, and Meghan is a truly gorgeous person. I felt terrible for them with everything they went through, all that scrutiny and mistreatment. Sadly, I haven't seen them in forever, not since they moved to America. Ironic, really, since much of my work's there."

Chloe, faced with another facet of Archer's surreal life, shook her head. She could barely wrap her brain around how much her life would change if she and Archer became a proper couple.

Just as they got to the exit of the fair, Archer asked, "Shall I telephone for the car?" Chloe, preoccupied, nodded her reply, her mind going a million miles an hour as she contemplated becoming besties with Meghan Markle. Jules and Lucy would understand, right?

She was called back to reality when Archer pocketed the phone, then grabbed both her hands and pulled her close. With her head tipped towards his, it struck her yet again how very tall he was. "Now, Ms Sims, what would you like to do for dinner?"

He released her hands as she wrapped her arms about his waist. His hands traced her back over the bulky borrowed coat she was wearing, coming to rest on her waist. "Can we just order room service?" He pulled her towards him and kissed her softly.

"Yes, lovely, we can absolutely order room service."

She beamed. "You know, I'm pretty sure that we'll both fit in the tub."

"Is that so?"

"It *is* so."

His phone must have vibrated because he took it out of

his pocket. "The car has arrived." He lifted his eyes and scanned the road outside the fair. "I think I see it. This way." Archer took her hand again and Chloe let herself be led through the milling crowd.

"You were right, Ms Sims, we do fit."

"I think you will find that I am often right." He chuckled, and Chloe felt the reverberation of his voice pulse against her bare back.

They were ensconced in the giant bathtub, Chloe cocooned between Archer's legs, his limbs encircling her. They had said very little since climbing into the bath, and Chloe was content to luxuriate in the feel of his body against hers, ignoring the niggling thought that out there in London somewhere was an ex with a grudge.

"What's this?" Two fingertips trailed over a small scar running along the back of her left wrist.

"Oh, that's what happens when you let your best friend talk you into going horse riding on holiday."

"You fell." It was statement rather than a question.

"I did. We were in Mexico—me, Jules, and Lucy on one of our May Ladies holidays—and Jules talked us into riding horses on the beach. For her, it's like riding a bike. For me and Lucy, not so much." His fingertips traced her arm and brushed the side of her breast. His soft lips found just the right spot behind her ear and she closed her eyes, breathing in deeply.

"So, what happened?" he murmured his mouth against her skin.

The memory replayed in her head in record time. She had been given the tallest horse, a behemoth of terrifying equineness, and when a quad bike rode by, her horse had shied, and she had landed with a plop on the wet sand. She'd flown home early from that holiday to have orthopaedic hand surgery. It had been a lengthy and painful recovery and Jules *still* apologised on occasion.

But Chloe had no intention of going into all of that now. "Like you said, I fell." His hands were cupping her breasts, stroking gently, while his mouth continued its magic caresses on her neck. She could hardly breathe with the anticipation of him.

"Archer ..." She turned to kiss him, their mouths meeting with the urgency. Water slopped over the side of the bath and somewhere in the recesses of her mind, Chloe thought of the clean-up—again.

When Archer groaned, Chloe thought it was with pleasure, but he pulled away from her. "What?" she asked, breathless.

"We ordered room service for seven-thirty. It's seven twenty-seven." He must have been eyeing the clock over her shoulder.

"Room service is never on time." She captured his lower lip between her teeth. "Oh." It occurred to her where they were. "The Four Seasons."

"Precisely."

"Bollocks, bollocks, bollocks, bollocks."

He laughed. "I told you it was a good swear word."

She shook her head and sniggered, then reluctantly climbed out of the tub. When she'd patted herself dry, she wrapped the fluffy bath sheet around her and, as if on cue, the suite's doorbell rang. "Shall I get that?" she asked.

"Would you mind?" Archer stood in the bath, the water sluicing from his lean frame, and she handed him a towel.

"I do not mind."

"Perhaps exchange that for a robe, though."

She dropped her chin and looked at the towel, which on her small frame looked as though she was wrapped in a blanket. "Sure," she said humouring him. Sliding into the robe, she let her eyes rove over Archer's glorious nakedness while he dried himself off.

The doorbell rang again, and Chloe pulled herself away from her handsome, naked lover. She rushed the length of the suite and flung open the door, first taking in the white-linen-clad trolley covered in silver cloches, then the uniformed porter who was wearing a somewhat mortified expression, and then the harried looking woman standing behind him.

"Oh, for fuck's sake," Chloe said.

"Is he here? I want to see him. Archer!" Madison craned her neck to see into the room. "Aren't you ever dressed?" she spat at Chloe.

Chloe, perplexed by this bizarre scene, had no time to form a response before feeling Archer's arm wrap protectively around her shoulder. She looked between him and Madison—both glowering—then clocked the porter's expression.

You couldn't write this shit, she thought before snapping into action.

"Right, could you bring that inside, please?" Chloe said to the porter. The poor man looked so relieved to have an instruction that he wasted no time before complying. Chloe squeezed Archer's hand on her shoulder, then stepped aside, making room for the trolley. The porter didn't unload it or even wait for a tip before he hastily retreated.

"Now," said Chloe to Madison, "*you*, go wait downstairs in the bar next to the lobby." Madison's eyes widened and Chloe could *feel* the outrage seeping from the other woman's pores. She started to say something, but Chloe cut her off. "Go." Then she slammed the door.

Only then did Chloe look at Archer, suddenly sheepish. He blinked a couple of times, scowled, and shook his head as if to dislodge some awful thought. "I've overstepped," she said simply, her stomach clenching as she waited for his face to settle into a single expression. This could be the end of whatever it was they were doing together.

"No."

A single, simple word, yet it meant everything and Chloe let her breath escape.

He stepped closer, taking both her hands in his. "No, you didn't overstep. You've no need to apologise. I do, however."

"Wha—"

"Please ..." His eyes dropped from hers to the floor and he scowled again. "I should have dealt with Madison before we left for the day, as *soon* as I found out she'd been here. I put you in the firing line this evening—again—simply to avoid an unpleasant task, and I am so very, very sorry."

Chloe pulled her hands free of Archer's and reached up to encircle his neck. "An unpleasant task? Really? You English truly are the masters of understatement."

He gave a wry laugh, finally meeting her eyes. "You're being too good to me, lightening the mood." She shook her head. "You *are*." He regarded her intensely for a moment. "You're incredible, do you know that?" Chloe shrugged in mock modesty, trying to lighten the mood again. "I mean it. You're authentic, you're brave—*so* brave. I don't think I've ever seen anyone speak to Madison like that. I certainly never did." Chloe bit her lip, false modesty replaced with its true version.

Archer sighed. "How about this? I'll get dressed and go and talk to Madison. I'll be firm and clear, something I obviously wasn't before, and then I'll take you somewhere for dinner, somewhere quiet where we won't be bothered. Can I do that? Can I make it up to you?"

She nodded. He leant down and kissed her softly, then rested his forehead against hers. "You are a wonder, Chloe Sims. Oh, my heart." With those last words, Chloe felt hers burst in her chest, flooding her with something she hadn't felt in, well, ever.

Was she falling in love?

*

Thirty-two minutes seemed to take an awfully long time to tick over, especially when you were waiting for your lover to tell his ex that it was finally, truly, and completely over.

Chloe could either fret and obsess and imagine the worst—a passionate Archer-Madison reunion in the lobby bar of a five-star hotel—or get dressed for dinner.

Her insides in upheaval, she dried off her damp hair, carefully applied a smoky eye and nude lip, slipped on her dark-wash skinny jeans and a low-cut black jumper that nipped in at her waist, and stepped into her ankle boots.

She looked incredible, but she felt like crap. How had she let herself develop such strong feelings for Archer? When had *that* happened? It wasn't that she was anti-love or anything. She hadn't had some excruciating breakup in her past to turn her sour on love and her parents were still (reasonably) happily married. She just hadn't prioritised it. She had a good job, even if she *was* starting to think about her next career move, she had her close friends, she had a *life*. She didn't *need* love.

But did she want it? And if she did, what would she need to give up to have it?

"Besides, who falls in love in less than a week?" she scoffed at herself.

It reminded her of those Christmassy romcoms that Lucy liked so much, where entire relationships unfolded in a matter of days. Truthfully, Chloe also liked *The Holiday*, but as sexy as Jude Law was, his character came as a package deal with two children *and* Natalie had to give up her mansion in Beverly Hills. Chloe had secretly crushed on Miles, Jack Black's character. He seemed like a lot of fun and he was so thoughtful and romantic.

Romance! Ah-hah! A clue. Chloe's thoughts rocketed back to the village Christmas Fair and the Capels. Every exchange she'd had with them, every time she'd thought of them since the day she and Archer had rescued Mrs Capel, she'd been practically obsessed with ...

With what?

She lost the trajectory of her thought and, stumped, poked about in the corners of her mind.

With love, Chloe, you twit. Despite the unkind tone of her inner voice, she agreed with it. She'd been obsessed with love—the Capels's love, for sure, but also her own. The love she felt for Archer, feeling protective of him, that she was completely herself when she was with him, that she had started imagining how their lives could fit together, that she felt loved *by* him.

When she heard the key card activate the door to the suite, she had one thought. *I'll know for sure when I see him.*

He opened the door and looked straight at her, his eyes swarming with emotions—relief, resolve, joy and, yes, there it was, love. *Well, that's my answer.* Chloe leapt up and threw her arms around his neck. He clasped her tightly to him and they held each other for what seemed like minutes. When she felt his arms ease, she stepped back a little and looked up at him.

A frown clouded his beautiful features. "I worried you," he said softly.

"No." She shook her head to reassure him, but her eyes welled up, betraying her innermost thoughts. Deep down, she must have worried that Archer would reconcile with Madison.

"I have. I'm so sorry, Chloe ..." Her tears turned into sobs as relief coursed through her and in a heartbeat, she was in his arms again, his hands cradling her gently as he made soothing sounds.

Eventually, her sobs subsided, and she pressed away from

him. Why on earth had she chosen to go with a smoky eye? She must look like a panda. Embarrassed, she dropped her head and wiped her tears with her hands. "Hey ..." His finger- tips found her chin and lifted it, but she didn't want to meet his eyes. He dipped his head to place a soft kiss on her lips, somehow not caring that she was a blubbering mess.

Chloe chewed on her bottom lip. Usually sure of the protocol for handling any disaster, she was at a loss in this one. "I must look a mess," she said with a half-laugh. Perhaps self-deprecation was the right way to go.

"Darling one, you do look upset, but if ever there was a woman who could pull off tears and smudged mascara, it's you."

Chloe pressed her hand to her mouth as a breathy laugh burst from her. When she looked at Archer, he was smiling at her with such warmth that it nearly set her off crying again.

Instead, she contained herself, and retrieved a tissue from her jeans pocket to wipe her face. *Always be prepared for any eventuality.* Her mentor's words echoed in her mind as she mopped up her tears. After a slow, steeling breath, Chloe asked the one question she knew she had to ask, hoping she'd been right about Archer's feelings for her. "So, how did it go?" her voice cracked on the last word and she clenched her jaw in annoyance at herself.

Archer reached for her free hand. "As well as can be expected. There were tears—hers—*and* some shouting—also hers, but I was crystal clear with her. I told her it was definitely over." Chloe let out the breath she hadn't realised she'd been holding. "She protested even *that*, however ..."

"Oh." Chloe's jaw clenched. This conversation was wreaking more havoc on her insides than the merry-go-round.

"*But* I assured her there was no chance of her and I reconciling, *ever*, because I have fallen in love with someone else."

Her eyes widened and her lips parted. It was not often that Chloe Sims was rendered speechless.

"I told her that I love *you*, which as I'm saying it now, means that I told someone else—an ex, of all people—before I even told you and, bollocks, I've cocked this up, haven't I? I'm so sorry."

A giggle erupted from Chloe. "You know, if we're going to be together, you're gonna have to stop all your over-the-top British apologising."

"I'm sor— Uh ..."

"Now," she snaked her arms up around his neck, "can you please go back to the part—"

"Where I say, 'I love you'?" She nodded. "I do. I love you, Chloe." Chloe blinked back tears. "It's mad and it's quick ..."

"It is," she interjected breathlessly. The change in his expression told her that he was unsure how *she* felt, and her heart cracked a little at his vulnerability. "But I love you too," she rushed to say. He broke into a grin and planted a hearty smack of a kiss onto her lips. "It was the floral rubber gloves, wasn't it?"

"I think it was you nearly dropping that plate of biscuits at the door and not letting me into my childhood home that did it for me," he teased. Her mouth dropped open to form an O in mock-indignation and she swatted him playfully. "You thought I hadn't noticed." Chloe pinned him with a hard stare and quietly growled.

Amusement danced across Archer's face, then his expression softened, and Chloe's breath caught. "I definitely noticed, Chloe. I've noticed everything about you since we met. You're a wonder to me." His eyes glossed with a sheen of tears.

"I love you," he said simply.

"I love you too," she replied.

They skipped dinner out, instead nibbling from the cold plates of room-service food. Chloe couldn't remember enjoying a meal more.

Chapter 28

Lucy

The next morning's eruption of activity reminded Lucy of the opening scene in *Home Alone*—the one where they've overslept and have to get two sets of parents and all those children to the airport in less than forty-five minutes. She tried to stay out of the way as seven family members packed up and got ready to depart the cabin, retreating to her room after breakfast to start working on her email to Angela.

There was so much commotion, especially from the cousins as they gathered their belongings and Christmas presents from various corners of the cabin, that Lucy barely registered that Will was gone for most of the morning. He'd returned by the time Steph called her downstairs to say goodbye to Jackie and her brood.

"I hope you don't mind," Bridget said to her quietly, "but I sent you a friend request on Facebook." The hopeful look on her face sent a wave of affection through Lucy, but before she could reply, Bridget added, "But you don't have to accept it or anything."

"Oh, I absolutely will." They shared a smile and Lucy saw the colour creep up Bridget's cheeks before she reached down to give her a hug. She wished that she'd had an older friend when she was Bridget's age, someone who saw the world through a similar lens, someone who understood what it was like to be introverted and awkward.

When the door closed behind Jackie, Bob and their three children, there was almost a collective sigh. "We'll be out of your hair soon, too," said Steph. Lucy wanted to protest that she was in no hurry for Steph and Joe to leave but worried it would come across as trite. Besides, it was only partially true.

She returned to her room and opened up her laptop to read over her draft email to Angela. There was a gentle knock on the doorframe and when Lucy looked up, Will was filling most of it. His hair was messy as though he'd just pulled his beanie off. It made him look especially handsome, she thought.

"Hey," he said, "can I come in?"

"Of course." She closed the laptop and made room for him on the bed, clearing away a notepad and pen and smoothing the duvet.

"What ya working on?" he asked, indicating her laptop.

"I'm taking an excruciatingly long time to write a very brief email to my manager, Angela."

"Ah, yes, the whole 'Mark Twain' thing."

"I'm not sure I follow."

"There's this famous quote from Mark Twain about that. I think it's, 'I apologise for the length of this letter; I didn't have time to write a short one'. Something like that anyway."

"That sounds spot on."

"I could take a look, if you like?"

"Oh, absolutely." Lucy opened up her laptop and spun it around so Will could read her draft. It wouldn't take him long as she hadn't got very far. Still, she wasn't sure if it was a good sign when he bit his bottom lip.

"It's not bad. I think this part may be laying it on a bit thick, though." He pointed to a line about how much she admired Angela. She'd gone back and forth on that part.

"Hmm. I thought as much."

"I mean, it could be okay. *Do* you admire her?"

Lucy giggled. "No, not especially. But as your mum pointed out, quite rightly, I *could* learn from her. Maybe I'll grow to admire her."

"It could come across as disingenuous, though, especially as she must know how you feel about her."

"How so?"

"Lucy, you have to know that your face is an open book." Lucy's eyes widened, horrified that she'd somehow conveyed her disdain for Angela without saying a word. "See? Right there, just like that." Her hands flew to her mouth, as though to stop it, even though she hadn't said anything. Will reached for one hand, prying it away from her face and lacing his fingers through hers.

"Hey, it's okay. Even if she knows how you feel about her—actually, *especially* if she knows—you can use it to your advantage. I think my mom was right. She sounds insecure, like she's still trying to find her place in the firm. You reaching out like this gives her a chance to redeem herself. I think she'll respect the hell out of you for it."

"Really?"

He didn't answer right away and regarded her intensely. "You have no idea, do you?" he said.

"I don't know. Possibly. What do you mean?" It was as though her question had proven him right and he seemed amused. Even so, Lucy sensed that he wasn't belittling her or being cruel.

"What I mean," he said, leaning over to place a soft kiss on her lips, "is that you have no idea how formidable you can be."

"Formidable" was hardly a word Lucy would use to describe herself. She'd spent most of her life feeling timid, often terrified of upsetting the apple cart. Still, it was clear that Will saw something different in her, and she wanted to know why. "How so?"

"You are clearly smart, and I'm guessing from everything we've talked about that you are awesome at your job." Well, that part was true. She gave him a tentative nod, reluctant to come across as conceited. "And you're a genuinely good person. You're not the kind of person who would treat others badly to get ahead." Also true—Lucy wouldn't dream of doing that to someone. It was one of the reasons she disliked Angela so much. She acknowledged Will's point with a small shrug.

"*And* you're super-hot." Well, that was just silly. Even if it were true, how would that make her formidable? She shook her head as if to shake all the pieces of Will's argument into place.

"Hey." She met Will's eyes, confused. "I mean it. You add up your intelligence, your good heart, and your looks, and you could intimidate the hell out of someone, especially if they're insecure." Lucy believed Will meant what he was saying, and she swapped out her frown for a shy smile. "I mean, you gotta know that it took some serious courage on my part to kiss you, even though it was obvious that you wanted me to."

She tutted and swatted him gently on the chest. "You are so full of yourself, Will Reinhardt."

He grinned. "Yup," he replied, laughing. His laughter trailed off as his eyes dropped to her mouth. "Hey, come 'ere," he said softly before kissing her again.

There was an, "Ahem," from the doorway and they leapt apart. Steph looked at them apologetically. "Sorry. I didn't mean to interrupt, but Joe and I are heading out."

"Oh, right." Lucy jumped up so quickly that the top of her head caught Will under his chin, the collision causing both to emit a loud "ow".

"Oh, my god, are you two okay?" Steph rushed into the room, looking from one to the other in concern.

Lucy started to giggle as she rubbed her forehead. "I'm so sorry, Will. Are you all right?" He touched a finger to the end of his tongue, which was bleeding. Lucy stopped laughing. "Oh, I'm so clumsy," she chastised herself.

"It's all good." He stood, towering over both Steph and Lucy. "I'll help Joe load up the car," he said before jogging out of the room. Lucy could hear his footfalls on the staircase.

"You're okay?" asked Steph.

"Just embarrassed." Steph waved her comment away. "Anyway, it doesn't matter," Lucy said, even though she was still cross with herself. Why was she always so ungainly? "I've been working on my email to Angela, like you said. I showed Will, and he thinks I'm close to a draft worth sending."

"Oh, that's great, honey."

"I wanted to thank you. For, well, everything, really. You've been wonderful and I've had the best time."

Steph took both Lucy's hands in hers. "We've so loved having you here. I'm kind of sad we're leaving so soon. I wish we'd had more time together, just you and me, but Joe's back at work tomorrow. You'll have to come see us again, and soon."

"I absolutely will," said Lucy, the words popping out of her mouth before she could unpack the magnitude of what they might mean.

"Enjoy the rest of the rest your stay," said Steph. She pulled Lucy into a tight hug and when Steph released her, she could only smile, not trusting her voice.

"Hey, babe?" Joe's voice called from downstairs.

"Come on. Come wave us off. Coming, hon!"

Minutes later, it was just Will and Lucy alone in the giant cabin, Nate having driven into Breckenridge to go to the hardware shop.

"How's your chin *and* your tongue?" Lucy asked, giving Will her complete attention.

He waved off her concern, a playful smile on his face. "I'll live."

Lucy reached up and ran her fingertips along the edge of his jawline, then traced his lips. They parted slightly and she could hear his intake of breath. "Will ..." They were all alone.

She rose on tiptoes, her hands finding Will's chest to steady herself, then snaking up around his neck and nestling in his hair. He seemed mesmerised, his playful smile evaporating as his eyes rivetted to hers. She was gentle with her kiss at first, not wanting to hurt him, but in moments, his soft lips responded, and their mouths joined with a fervour that echoed her sole thought. *We're all alone.* His tongue touched to hers and tasted faintly metallic. His arms encircled her, one hand flat against the small of her back, the other cupping her head, pulling her into the kiss.

It was impossible to know how much time passed and Lucy would have very happily retired to any of the rooms—upstairs or down—to take advantage of their solitude, but Will broke the kiss, panting slightly, and pressed his forehead to hers.

Had she done something wrong? Lucy stiffened, still caught in Will's embrace, but unsure what to do next. What was the right thing to do after a kiss like that? From the recesses of her mind came a realisation. She had no idea how to answer that, because she'd never *had* a kiss like that before. No, she realised with some disdain, she'd got to the age of thirty-three without having any kind of true passion in her life. No wonder Will was backing away. Clearly, he was overwhelmed by how needy she was.

"Lucy, god, I want you so much ..." *Or not!* "But ... we've got that snowmobiling and snowshoeing thing." Was he serious? He wanted to forgo making love to her to go bloody snowshoeing?

She pulled out of the embrace and smoothed down her hair. "Oh, quite right." Will looked crestfallen, but how was she supposed to act? She'd thought that her sexy fantasy was about to come to fruition. Instead, she would be donning the giant eggplant snowsuit, possibly the least attractive article of clothing ever invented, and going out into the snow. The snow that she had travelled across the world to see. She bit her lip, cross with herself for being so petulant. There was definitely an unease between them now.

"Well …" Will shook his head, a bit like a cartoon character trying to set his mind right. "As soon as we're ready, we'll head out." He gave her a smile that didn't reach his eyes and Lucy instantly decided to enjoy every ounce of their snowy excursion. It was obviously important to him.

She reached out and squeezed Will's hand. "I'll go and get ready." She ran up the stairs without waiting for him to reply.

*

There was no way Lucy could have known just how perfect Will's plans would be. After she'd bundled herself up in that wretched snowsuit and all the other cold-weather accoutrements, she'd met him outside where he stood next to a giant red and black snowmobile. She realised that she'd only ever seen one in films. It looked a little terrifying, as though a motorcycle had eaten a tractor.

Her open book of a face must have revealed her terror, because Will laughed. "It's completely safe, I promise. And I've been riding one of these since I was twelve."

"All right. I believe you."

He climbed on and patted the seat behind him, and she clambered aboard the motorised beast.

"Here." He handed her a hefty black helmet, before lowering his own onto his head and fastening the strap. Lucy fumbled with her helmet and had to take her gloves off to secure it. "Okay?" Will asked swivelling to get a look at her. His eyes dipped to the fastener as though to check it and he smiled before lowering his face shield. She lowered hers, just as he started the engine. "Hold on to my waist," Will called out above the engine. She did. "Ready?" he called. She didn't know if he'd be able to hear her, so she squeezed his waist tightly and then they were off.

It was thrilling to fly along the narrow trails, a plume of snow following them, the rev of the engine beneath them, and Lucy laughed gleefully almost nonstop as they rode deep into the woods. It was the most fun she'd ever had outside—even better than skiing.

Will was a good driver, too, and despite the proximity of the trees to the trail, she never felt scared, trusting him completely. As they rounded bends, she leant when Will did, all the while clasping his waist tightly. When he came to a stop, she was breathless from laughing and a little disappointed.

He turned off the engine and flipped up the visor on his helmet. Lucy reluctantly let go of him and climbed off the snowmobile to make it easier for Will to do the same. "Was that *you* laughing the whole time?" he teased. She nodded, her head still ensconced in the helmet. She flipped up her own visor. "Yes," she replied, still catching her breath, "it was just brilliant." They grinned at each other.

"Awesome. That means, you won't dread the return journey then."

"Hardly."

"So, are you ready for the next part of our excursion?" He pulled off his helmet and placed it right side up on the seat of the snowmobile, and Lucy did the same with hers. Will had strapped the snowshoes to the side of the snowmobile with bungee cords which he released with a snap. He helped her put on her snowshoes and while he was outfitting himself, she walked about trying them out. They were less cumbersome than flippers, although she did have to walk with her feet further apart than normal. It certainly wasn't the most elegant way to get about.

"Ready?" he asked, as he slung a backpack over his shoulder. Lucy nodded and Will took off down a small trail she hadn't yet noticed. She followed closely, loving how still and silent the forest was around them, the only sound the light crunching of their snowshoes against the snow.

"How deep is it here?" she asked after a few minutes, her voice low and quiet in reverence of their surroundings.

"The snow?" Will asked, turning back towards her.

"Yes."

He stopped walking and looked around. He regarded the nearest tree, looking up at the trunk, then glanced at the other trees next to the trail. "Hmm, best guess is about four or five feet." Lucy's eyes widened in disbelief. Even when it did snow in Oxfordshire—or London for that matter—it usually melted before it could accumulate. In London, a few inches would be considered heavy snow fall. Five feet was mostly unheard of in England, except maybe in the north after a particularly bad storm.

Will grinned at her. "That's why the snowshoes. Otherwise, we'd just sink into the snow." The thought gave her the willies and she shivered. "Come on, it's not far to where we're going."

"Oh, I thought we were just going for a walk."

"No, I have a destination in mind." He raised his eyebrows at her a couple of times and started off down the trail again. Lucy stuck close to him, intrigued and abandoning her grim thoughts about suffocating in a snow drift.

There was a burst of movement in the periphery of her vision, and she swivelled in that direction. There between the trees was a doe, standing stock still and watching them. "Will," Lucy whispered. The sound of her voice carried, and Will stopped then followed the line of her gaze. "She's gorgeous."

"She is," he agreed. The doe's head flicked to the left and in a flash, she was off, running deeper into the forest. Lucy beamed at Will and he returned her smile. "Come on," he said softly, and she started following him again.

They walked on and about ten minutes later, emerged into a clearing. In the middle sat a compact cabin, with windows either side of a wooden door, each glowing with light from within. Lucy looked at Will questioningly, but he just smiled, revealing nothing. They climbed six steps onto a tiny porch, and Will undid his snowshoes, so Lucy did the same, having to take off her gloves to manage the fiddly task. When she stood, he was smiling down at her. "Ready?"

She nodded, then he unlatched the door and pushed it open. "Oh, Will …" It was all she could manage to say before she stepped inside.

Chapter 29

Jules

The cab ride to Matt's was long and costly, but Matt didn't bat an eye when the fare came to ninety dollars. He just handed over two fifties and told the driver to keep the change. Maybe they'd given him some serious drugs at the hospital, and he was too high to care. Jules couldn't remember ever paying that much for a cab ride and the Denver airport was nearly half a state away from Boulder.

Still, she was probably only fixating on the cost because it was far better than fixating on their situation.

She had tried to distract herself during the ride, her eyes scouring one tree after another in search of the elusive koalas. Matt had told her how lucky they were on the peninsula, escaping the unprecedented bushfires that had ravaged the country the summer before. She couldn't even imagine all that beautiful land, scarred and blackened.

Koala hunting was not enough to keep her worries at bay, however. As she and Matt sat in silence, she mulled over question after question—none of which she could answer. Eventually, she landed on just one, a question that gnawed away at her as the cab wound its way along deserted tree-lined roads.

What was she doing hanging out in rural Australia with a guy she barely knew?

She'd come for Christmas, to hang out, to get some beach time and sunshine—not to get caught up with a guy who may or may not already be "caught up" with someone else. *Who the hell is this Kirsten, anyway?*

Jules needed her girls. Maybe she'd try to call Chloe later. Or Lucy, if she'd even come to the phone. God, she'd created a mess. She wasn't usually the one in the thick of drama; that was more Chloe's department.

When she stepped out of the cab and onto Matt's gravel driveway, she could hear Dexter's excited yaps at their arrival and her inner turmoil receded into the background. Dexter made a beeline for them as soon a Matt unlatched the gate, darting excitedly between them, clearly overjoyed that his pack was back together. He sniffed at Matt's bandage and gave it a lick, then looked up at his master. Matt reassured him with a vigorous rubbing of his head and ears. Jules was next, receiving a paw on her leg, a plea for more petting. She laughed freely, kneeling to comply.

Jules had forgotten how much she missed having a dog around. She'd grown up with dogs—a Labrador that Will, aged five, had (for some reason) been allowed to name Dorito, then a kelpie named Bash. Bash had been a crazy dog who barked at practically anything and earned his name by bashing his paws against the front door when the doorbell rang. His behaviour got so bad that they couldn't turn on the washing machine unless he was in the backyard—kind of hard when there was five feet of snow on the ground. Laundry days during winter were fun—*not*.

Jules had missed the little guy when he died of old age, though. They'd never got another dog, and then Jules had left for college, followed by Will.

As she fawned over Dexter, Jules realised that there was something special about how she felt around dogs—that distinctive doggy smell, the wet nose landing in her lap while she had her morning coffee, the feeling of a furry being leaning against her leg, the bright intelligent eyes looking at her as though she was the most important person in the world. Well, with Dexter, the second-most important.

Maybe she was falling for Dexter rather than Matt.

She stole a look at Matt. He was watching her, his eyes alive with warmth, affection even. *For me, or for Dexter?*

"He's definitely taken by you," Matt said.

Jules laughed self-deprecatingly. "It's easy to win over a dog. Just give them lots of kisses and love. Isn't that right, Dex?" she added, baby-talking as she ruffled the dog's fur. Dexter yapped in obvious agreement and she grinned.

"I don't know about that," said Matt. "I wasn't kidding when I told you he's selective about making new friends. He's smitten." Jules pressed her lips together anticipating his next words. "That makes two of us." She'd been right, but there was no use in getting her hopes up. Those were just words and she had no idea how she felt about their situation. The only thing she was certain of at that moment, was she liked his dog. A lot.

*

"Comfy?" Matt asked as they swung gently in an oversized hammock.

"*So* comfy," Jules replied. She nestled into the crook of Matt's arm, her head resting on his shoulder. He drew his fingers gently back and forth across her upper back and she could occasionally feel the brush of his bandage against her skin.

The motion—both the hammock and Matt's hand—helped soothe her frazzled nerves. It was his explanation to give and she knew she shouldn't rush him, yet she felt seconds away from blurting out, "Who the hell is Kirsten?" She bit the inside of her mouth to stop the words.

Matt sighed and Jules tried to read its tone. Then he sighed again, sparking annoyance. "Just say it," she snapped, instantly regretting it. "Sorry," she mumbled.

"Hey." He reached under her chin and tipped her head towards him. She wasn't comfortable contorted like that, so she tried to readjust her position, sending the hammock into a jarring lurch to one side.

"Whoa," they both said together. Matt placed a steadying hand on the ground, righting the hammock.

Jules bit her lip, trying without luck to supress a giggle. "Oops, sorry."

He shook his head at her, grinning. "I've never had another

person in here with me. It's a little more precarious than I thought it would be. You should be getting danger pay." It was enough to break the tension she'd felt building since they'd left the hospital and she laughed along with him. She made a small adjustment in her position, slowly this time, so she could see his face.

"So ..." she said, bravely wandering into unknown emotional territory. It seemed to be just the gentle nudge that Matt needed.

"So ..." He sighed again, catching himself when Jules gave an exasperated, "Argh."

"Sorry! No more sighs, I promise. Right. Kirsten. I should probably start at the beginning." Jules watched his face closely, seeing a dozen emotions cross it and, without him saying it, Jules knew that Matt had loved Kirsten. And she did not like how that realisation made her feel.

"You know how I told you about my trip to America?"

"The wine sabbatical," she replied.

"Exactly. Well, when I got to Oregon, I met someone."

"Kirsten."

"Uh, no. It was Monica, Kirsten's best friend." Jules's brow creased. *Womaniser, much?* She thought. Maybe she'd got Matt completely wrong. Maybe he wasn't one of the good guys.

As if he could read her mind, Matt back-pedalled. "Hang on, I'm not telling it right. Monica and I were just friends. I worked with her brother and her dad at the family's vineyard." Jules felt the knot in her stomach uncoil a little. "She reminded me a lot of Chloe, actually. Maybe that's why we became such good mates. Anyway, we kept in touch and after I'd been back in Australia for a few months, she messaged me to say that her best friend was coming over to do some travelling and asked if I'd show her around. And I did, and, uh ... we got together."

"With Kirsten? You hooked up?"

"Yeah, something like that. She was supposed to be travelling around the country—Adelaide, Perth, then across to Brizzie, down to Sydney, and then back here, but she didn't do any of that."

"She just stayed in Melbourne?"

"Well, here, mostly."

"Ahhh." Jules didn't want to think of another woman in Matt's house—*or* his bed. She asked the next question, dreading his answer but knowing she needed to hear it. "And you fell in love with her?"

"I did ... or I thought so at the time."

"Right, okay. So, what happened?"

"Well, when it was time for her to go home, she asked me to go with her." He paused.

Why was she having to drag this story out of him? Every other time they'd talked, his stories had practically poured out, *filled* with details. This was excruciating. "And did you? Go?" Jules tried to temper the annoyance in her voice.

"No. But I thought about it. As in, *seriously* thought about it. I even told everyone I was going—my family, Chloe, Ash, Davo, the girls, everyone."

He glanced at her, the pain etched onto his handsome features and Jules felt awash with guilt. He wasn't spilling the story like it was a funny anecdote because this was hard for him, reliving it, retelling it—and to *her*.

He closed his eyes for a moment then looked away. "My mum was devastated. We've always been really close, and it had been hard enough for her when I'd moved overseas for a few months. This time, I'd be going indefinitely, and I think it was too much for her. We had this massive fight. It still makes me sick to think about some of the things I said to her."

Jules knew that feeling. She'd unleashed her own fury on her mom around the time she had married Joe. Jules knew that buried deep, even now, she still held that kernel of resentment towards her mom, blaming Steph for leaving her dad. It rose its head sometimes, but she regretted the things she'd said that night. That was the thing about saying stuff out loud; you can't un-ring a bell. Maybe that was why she kept her rawest emotions locked away, so she could get through life reasonably unscathed, not getting too invested, not hurting anyone.

Except Lucy. Her heart ached for her best friend and she promised herself she'd call Lucy before the end of the day.

When Jules abandoned her thoughts to give Matt her full attention, it was obvious that he was lost in his own. "Hey," she said in a whisper. She touched his chin with her fingertips, running them along his late-afternoon whiskers.

Matt looked at her and she saw the sheen of tears in his eyes, then surprisingly felt her own well up. "I was such a shit to her, Jules. She didn't deserve that."

"No, probably not. But is that why you didn't move to the States? The fight? Wait, *did* you move there?"

"No, I didn't go. I came back here after the fight with Mum and ended up having it out with Kirsten."

"Well, that sucks. Two massive fights in a row."

"You have no idea. I haven't even got to worst part yet," he said, his tone ominous. "Turned out that Kirsten wasn't who I thought she was. Well, hang on, she wasn't like a spy or a crim or anything like that. But she *was* pregnant."

"Oh." Jules's stomach plummeted. So, this was it, Matt's big reveal—he was a *father*.

"Oh no, no! The baby wasn't mine. Sorry, babe, I should have led with that. Sorry." He blew out a breath and amid the tumult of her emotions, Jules latched on to the joy of Matt calling her "babe".

"No, see, she'd arrived in Australia knowing she was expecting. No plan, just running away from her life. She hadn't told the father—didn't even give the guy a chance, 'cause they'd broken up by the time she found out. And, so, when she met me, she saw a way out—a nice guy who could give her a good life. She wasn't even going to tell me. She was just gonna let me think the baby was mine ..."

"Oh, Matt. What the *hell?*"

"Yeah, that's what I thought too."

"But how did you find out?"

"Well, after I told her about the fight with Mum, she got the guilts and came clean."

"*Ohhh*, right, so, when your mom heard my voice on the phone ..."

"She must have heard the accent and thought the worst, yeah."

"Well, no wonder! *I* would. God, Matt, I cannot believe that happened to you." She tried to imagine how someone

342

could be so deceitful, then remembered that Ash had mentioned Matt going through a hard time a while back—talk about an understatement.

"I heard through Monica that Kirsten told the baby's father when she got back to the States. They're not together, but they are co-parenting, so at least there's that."

"And you made things right with your mom?"

"Yeah, 'course. I mean, that's what mothers do, isn't it? Take us at our worst and love us anyway?"

"Mmm," she murmured, her thoughts returning to her mom. She'd have to schedule some time for them to hang out when she got home. *Home*. She'd be there in a few days.

Soon she'd be saying goodbye to Matt and Ash, *and* Dexter. Maybe she'd get a chance to see the others again, maybe not. And with their flight schedules, she'd be missing Chloe by a day, which left her feeling empty—all of it did. But as much as she missed her mom, and her dad and Will, she wasn't ready to leave yet. She'd fallen a little in love with Australia. She may have been falling a little in love with the hot Aussie winemaker too.

Only, now he was far more than that. He was *Matt*, the man with warm, gentle eyes, who was quick to laugh—often at his own expense—a loyal and loving friend, affectionate, thoughtful ... And yes, smoking hot. He looked just as good fresh out of the shower as he did in a suit or in faded, dusty jeans and a checked shirt.

How was she going to say goodbye to him in just a few days?

Jules inhaled deeply, taking in the tangy citrusy smell of

the eucalypts. It reminded her of lemon grass or verbena, and she found it energising. A loud cackle erupted above them, startling her and almost upsetting the hammock again.

"You all right there?" she felt Matt's gentle laughter against her, but the sound of it was drowned out by the cackle turning into a loud cry, "Ack-ack-ack-ack".

"I'm okay, but what in the hell *is* that?"

"Kookaburra." He pointed and she followed the line of his finger. In a nearby tree there was a large-headed white bird with dark brown wings, its beak open as it emitted its distinctive call. Another kookaburra joined it, swooping in a long, low arc from another tree and perching next to its friend, then adding to the avian chorus.

"I've got to see this," said Jules. She climbed out of the hammock as carefully as she could, leaving Matt in it swinging wildly. "Come on," she added, stretching her hand out towards him. Matt steadied himself with his good hand, before swinging his legs to the ground and following her as she wandered slowly towards the tree with the kookaburras. She craned her neck and from her new vantage point under the tree, she could see that their brown wings were tipped with an iridescent blue.

"They're *beautiful*! Loud, but beautiful." She laughed as both kookaburras stopped their cackling, cocked their heads, and seemed to peer down at her. Her mouth wide with a grin, she watched them as they watched her with their large eyes. The birdlife in Australia certainly had a lot of personality. She'd thought the magpies were awesome, but the kookaburras were next level.

She felt Matt's arms slip around her waist, and careful of his bandage, she pressed her hands to his and sank into him. "I like having you here," he said, his voice soft in her ear.

She breathed out a long, slow breath. "I like being here." There was no guile, no hesitation in her words, just the truth of knowing that Matt was going to be far more important to her than just a fling and the surprise of not being afraid of that.

But how would they reconcile living so far from each other? It was a prickly, tangled mess of circumstance, especially as both were so close to their families, *and* after hearing Matt's horrible story about dodging the Kirsten bullet.

But those were worries for another time. All Jules wanted to do right then was soak up their moment together in that beautiful vineyard.

Chapter 30

Lucy

Inside the cabin, there was a fire burning in the fireplace; although Lucy could see that it would need stoking soon. Several lamps lit the one-room cabin with a warm glow, and even though the furniture was sparse, it was homey and welcoming. There was a tiny kitchenette along one wall, with a mini fridge tucked under the counter, and a corner of the cabin was walled off—the bathroom, she presumed. There was a sofa that faced the fireplace, a low table in front and next to it, a small dining table and two chairs.

The table was set simply but thoughtfully, with plates, cutlery, two wine glasses, and plain white cloth napkins. While Lucy took in all these details, Will rushed about striking match after match to light the pillar candles dotted about the room.

When the last one was lit, he stood still and looked at her. "Do you like it?" She could see him gulp down his uncertainty and she crossed the room in a heartbeat.

"I love it," she said, reassuring him with a grin.

He blew out a breath, and she sensed his relief. How could he have doubted that the most romantic thing anyone had ever done for her would hit the mark? She looked about the cabin again, taking in as many details as she could, and noticing a bottle of whisky on the table in front of the sofa. "Is that one of yours?" she asked.

"If you mean, did one of my clients make it, then yes."

"Mmm."

"Do you *like* whisky?"

"Um, sometimes. I mean, there are so many different sorts, aren't there?"

"Well, this one's a favourite of mine. Have a seat and I'll pour you some." Lucy peeled off her outer layers and Will did the same before retrieving two tumblers from the cupboard and joining Lucy on the sofa. He cracked the seal of the bottle and poured two generous glugs of whisky, then handed a glass to Lucy.

"So, what shall we drink to?" she said, relegating the task of the toast to Will.

He seemed to think on it longer than she would have expected, then lifted his glass and looked her in the eye. "To snowstorms and traffic jams." He clinked his glass against hers and winked before taking a sip.

Lucy was momentarily rattled. It was almost as though Will knew all about her "snowed-in" fantasy. There was no way he could have, but this was all a bit uncanny...

She lifted her glass to her lips, breathing in the spicy sweetness of the aroma of the whisky, then took a sip. It tingled on her lips slightly. "Oh my, that's dangerous, that is."

Will frowned. "Too strong?"

"Oh no, dangerous because it's delicious—possibly too *drinkable*." He chuckled. "But Will, this place ... was this why you weren't about this morning? You were here?"

He cocked his head. "Guilty."

"But how ... how do you do *all of this* in one day?"

"Oh, no, the cabin's always like this. I mean, it's kept up. It's a hunting cabin that we share with some of the other families in the area. I just made sure we'd have it to ourselves, then came early and dropped off the food, cleaned it up a bit, lit the fire."

"Oh, right." Had she really thought that he'd lugged *everything* there, as though there was some sort of dogsled division of U-Haul specifically for outfitting isolated cabins in the woods? She giggled at herself for being so silly, foregoing her usual self-flagellation.

"What?"

"Nothing. It's lovely. Very thoughtful."

He bit his lip and stared down at the tumbler that he was turning in his large hands. *He's nervous.* The thought did incredible things to Lucy's insides because in her mind, that could only mean one thing. He'd brought her there to seduce her! *Oh, happy day!*

Lucy took another sip of her whisky, feeling it warm her through. "Will," she said in her best sultry voice. He looked up at her and she met his eyes with an unwavering stare. "Here." She took his glass and placed it on the table, adding hers next to it. Will watched her, his lusty expression telling her that she had guessed correctly. He released his bottom lip and his tongue flicked to wet it. Lucy turned to face him, her hand reaching for his chest. He captured it in his and pressed it to him.

Just when she thought she couldn't bear being apart from him any longer, he pulled her onto him in one swift movement, burying a hand in her hair. Her face close to his, she took in the flushed colour of his cheeks, the fullness of his lips, and the dreamy expression in his eyes, then felt the firm touch of his other hand on her hip.

This was it—this was the fantasy!

Her phone pinged from her coat pocket, yanking Lucy's focus away from Will. It was an email notification. Worse, it was a *work* email notification. *Angela!* Angela had replied to her email. It *had* to be that. No one else would be emailing her during the holidays. There was no need, as they were all on holiday too. But what appalling timing!

"Do you want to check that?" She glanced at Will and it was clear that their sexy spell was well and truly broken. *Bollocks.* She sighed, then tried to push herself up, one hand landing on Will's groin. She realised almost right away, but not before she'd put half her body weight on that hand. Will groaned and, likely on impulse, jerked his knees in to protect himself, catching Lucy in the back of the head.

She tumbled off the sofa onto the floor with a thud, her hand flying to the back of her head to nurse the emerging lump. Both had, "I'm sorry," on replay as they each tried to soothe the other, and soon they were doubled over in fits of laughter, Lucy gasping for air as she fanned her face with her free hand.

"Well," said Will when he had enough breath to speak, "it is certainly never dull being with you."

"Nor you," she countered. "How is it that we seem unable to be in the same place at the same time without smacking each other about?"

"To be fair, this is only the second time that's happened."

She winced as she dragged herself back onto the sofa. Will was stretched out along its length and she perched on the edge next to him, lifting her hand to smooth his hair. "Are you *really* all right?"

He closed his eyes and took a deep breath. "I will be. I just ... I just need a minute."

"Mmm, quite. Whisky?" she asked brightly. His body started to shake with laughter, which set her off again. Still giggling, she handed him his glass and he scooched up to a seated position. She took her own glass in hand and raised it. "I'd like to propose another toast," she said in mock-seriousness. "To my sore head and your sore bollocks." She purposefully tapped the edge of her glass against Will's then downed the rest of her whisky in one go.

"Ahh," she said, wiping the corners of her mouth with a fingertip. She glanced at Will who looked gobsmacked. "Bottoms up," she said, like some maniacal Mary Poppins.

A slow smile spread over Will's face as he regarded her. "You're pretty fantastic, you know."

"Oh, I do know, yes." Lucy quite liked this version of herself—confident, daring, *hilarious*. She watched as Will tipped his head back and finished his whisky. "Another?"

"I'm good for now."

"Still need a moment?" she eyed his crotch.

"Yes," he said, shooing her away with a grin. "I need a minute."

"Right, then I shall check my email!" She leapt up, crossing the room to where her coat hung by the door, and retrieved her phone. As Lucy had guessed, the email was a reply from Angela, and it didn't take long to read. She'd barely written two lines.

> *Lucy,*
> *Let's meet first thing on your return. I'd like to discuss your*
> *future at the firm.*
> *Regards,*
> *Angela*

"Oh, double bollocks."

"What? Let me see it."

Far less ebullient, Lucy walked back to the sofa and sat next to Will. She handed him the phone and watched him frown slightly as he it read through twice.

"It's not necessarily bad. It could be, 'hey, you're a rising star and it was great to hear from you. I'm promoting you!' Or something like that."

Lucy, dubious, looked at Will. "*Or* it was, 'Your email was completely out of line. Clear out your desk and off you go to Jobcentre Plus'." Lucy held out her hand for the phone and Will laid it in her palm. She read the email again and frowned. Her mouth pursed in concentration and before she could talk herself out of it, she tapped out a reply.

Dear Angela,
Thank you for your prompt reply. I look forward to
discussing my future at the firm, as I am keen to continue
developing professionally and agree that I am ready for
the next challenge under your stewardship. I've CC'd Trevor
on this email, as I am sure he will be pleased to hear of
this next chapter in our division.
Happy New Year!
Best,
Lucy

She sent the email and blew out a satisfied sigh. Will leant over and read it. "Who's Trevor?"

"*Her* manager, the VP of Finance," she replied simply as she stared off into the fireplace. "The fire!" she declared, jumping up from the sofa. Lucy used the fire iron beside the fireplace to move the coals around, then added two more logs. She stood watching the logs catch, mesmerised by the flames.

"That was awesome," said Will behind her.

"What, stoking a fire? I should hope so. Three years of Brownies, four years of Guides, and a father who insisted I learn how to look after a fire properly."

Will chuckled and she turned. "Well, yes, you did lay those logs with a precision I haven't seen before, but I meant the email."

"Oh, right. You don't think I'm going to get a right bollocking for it? She could have me sacked for insolence, you know."

"Firstly, there is no *way* she can fire you after that email.

Copying her boss in like that was genius. It comes across as genuine, so if she was legit talking about a promotion, you seemed sincerely into that, and if she was going to fire you, well, checkmate. She's got nowhere to go. She'd come off as spiteful, maybe even delusional." He got up from the sofa and wrapped his arms around her waist. "You, Lucy Browning, are incredible," he said softly.

"Really?" All her bravado, the Dutch courage from the whisky—*or should that be Scotch courage?* she wondered—dissipated and she felt like herself again, trembling under the weight of what she'd just done. What if she lost her job?

"Hey ..." Will must have read the consternation on her face. "You have nothing to worry about. If you want, we could call my mom. She'll tell you the same thing, believe me. You played that perfectly and your job is safe. Okay?"

Lucy nodded absentmindedly as she sifted through everything she was feeling. So much had happened in just a few short days. She'd thought she was coming to a winter wonderland to experience a proper white Christmas, but she'd been hauled into family mini-dramas, there'd been the dilemma with Angela, and she was currently not on speaking terms with one of her best friends.

And then there was Will—gorgeous, lovely Will, who had come here early to set all this up, who was looking at her as though he believed she could do anything.

And he was right, she realised.

She *could* do anything. She'd just stood up to her bully of a manager. She'd survived the Christmas madness of a large . family—happily, she realised, as she thought of Jackie's brood.

She'd even skied down a giant mountain! Granted, it was on the easy slopes, but she had done it. Her! Lucy Browning, from Penham, Oxfordshire had accomplished more in a few days than she could ever have imagined.

And, surely, things would right themselves with Jules. Perhaps not that day, but eventually—at least she hoped so. That left just one more thing for Lucy to be brave about. She thought back to how terribly wrong her last seduction attempt had gone, but try, try again, right?

"Will?"

"Yes." He smiled, encouragingly.

"Is there a bed in this cabin?"

His eyes widened. "Uh, yes, the couch ... it's a pull-out. I, uh, I changed the sheets this morning, so it's, uh ..." It seemed that it was Will's turn to be embarrassed.

"I do think I know, yes. That was very, well, *prepared* of you."

He shook his head and grinned, "Yeah, yeah."

"No really, it was thoughtful." She stood on her tiptoes and cupped his face with her hands, regarding it closely. Goodness, he was handsome, like the icing on a particularly scrummy cake. "You know something? I quite adore you, Will Reinhardt."

His eyebrows lifted, and his lips curled into a slight smile. "And I adore you, Lucy Browning. Adore, want ..." His lips were brushing her neck as he whispered that last word, and the tiny puff of breath she felt as he hit the "t" sent a jolt of lust right through her.

Her "snowed-in" fantasy would pale in comparison to reality.

Chapter 31

Jules

Jules perched on the edge of a wooden bench on Matt's veranda while he was inside prepping dinner. They were barbecuing again—salmon this time—and he'd insisted on doing everything himself so she could make her call, even though he was still bandaged up.

She was nervous, and no wonder. She'd managed to hurt two of the people she loved the most. With Will, even when her was telling her off, Jules knew it would be okay between them. It always was. But what if she'd screwed things up with Lucy for good? Well, if she had, she wouldn't know for sure unless she tapped the "call" button on her phone.

Six rings and she was about to hang up when Lucy's sleepy face appeared on the screen, grainy from the lack of light on her end. "Hello?" Lucy yawned and shook her head quickly, as though to wake herself.

"Hey, Luce." God, she'd missed Lucy. Why had she let their rift go on so long?

Lucy blinked at her several times. "Jules, hello," she said in

357

a quiet voice. "What time is it?" Jules wracked her brain trying to calculate the time difference and came up short. It didn't matter anyway, as she'd obviously woken Lucy up.

"It must be late there, I'm so sorry. I can call another time."

"No, wait!" Lucy whispered. Lucy looked off screen, a small frown on her face. "Um, Jules ..." She looked back at the screen. "I may as well come clean. I'm not *alone*, if you get my drift."

Blergh! It really *was* a bad time to call. Jules had a firm and very quick talk to herself—*It's weird, but it's fine and you love them both*—and ploughed ahead. "Oh, right. So, do you want to move into another room?" Practical solutions, that's what Jules was good at.

"Oh, it's just that we're at the cabin. The hunting cabin, I mean. There is no other room." Jules did her best to hide her surprise; her best friend and her brother were *literally* shacked up. "Unless you think I should go outside," added Lucy. Jules scrutinised her friend's face and saw the smile tugging at the corner of Lucy's mouth. She was kidding.

Jules loved Lucy even more for the lifeline—joking with her instead of telling her off, which she was completely entitled to do.

"Look, if Will hasn't woken up yet, he probably won't. That guy could sleep through anything. It's one of the things I hate about him." Lucy sniggered and the two friends shared a smile. "Look, Lucy—"

"I know what you're going to say, and you don't have to say it."

"I do. I do have to, Lucy. I was a total asshole to you, and you didn't deserve that. I'm *so* sorry."

Lucy pressed her lips together and nodded. Jules saw in that small gesture that she *had* hurt Lucy with her harsh words on Christmas Day. How was an apology over FaceTime ever going to be enough? "Luce, please forgive me."

"I forgive you."

"Really? I mean, you can tell me off if you want to. Will did." Lucy's eyes widened, then narrowed as her brows furrowed and Jules could see her chewing on her thoughts.

"All right, then. You were hurtful."

"Yes."

"You acted like I wasn't good enough for Will." Jules nodded, the tightening in her throat preventing her from speaking. "You made me feel small, Jules," Lucy whispered.

Anguish tore through Jules's heart. "Oh, Lucy, I'm so, *so* sorry. You *are* good enough for Will, of *course* you are. And you are not small. You're one of the best people I've ever known. I wish I could take back everything I said, but please know that it wasn't about you. It was my own fucked-up way of seeing the world and not because of you, okay?"

Lucy was crying now, tears streaming down her face, and Jules's heart lurched. "I wish more than anything that I was there to apologise in person—well, I mean, not right *now*, in the cabin with you and Will, but ..."

"Hah!" exclaimed Lucy. *Was that laughter or crying?* Wondered Jules. Lucy ran her fingertips under each eye and, as her whole body started to shake, Jules watched anxiously. "Oh, my god," said Lucy, her face erupting into a broad smile. "Can you *imagine*?" She laughed again, shaking her head and Jules blew out a long sigh of relief.

Lucy had forgiven her.

"Are we good, Luce?" asked Jules, *just* to be sure.

Lucy's laughter subsided. "We're good, Jules." Lucy blew out her own sigh. "So, tell me all about Australia. Where are you right now?"

"At Matt's ... Chloe's friend. He's ..." Jules wasn't quite ready to articulate what Matt was to her. "It's beautiful here, Luce. Look." She swivelled the camera on her phone and panned slowly across Matt's property, then turned the camera back on her.

"Oh, that *is* lovely. It's definitely going on the list. Given all our holidays together, it's hard to believe that we've never gone to *Australia*."

"Right? Maybe because Chloe always wants to go somewhere new."

"Speaking of which, I talked to my mum this morning and apparently Chloe went off to London for a few days with Alan—I mean, Archer."

"Really? So, they're a *thing*?"

"Possibly. Do you think we should call her? I'd love to hear all about it." Lucy giggled excitedly, raising her eyebrows. Her laugh was infectious and Jules found herself grinning, relieved that they were back to being besties again.

"Well, what time is it there?"

Lucy's eyes flicked to the bottom of her screen. "It's 8:00am."

"Let's do it." Jules tapped on her phone to bring up Chloe's profile and connect her to the call. Two rings and Chloe's face appeared, her eyes wide and her mouth grinning.

"What's up, bee-arrrches?"

Lucy tutted in mock outrage and Jules grinned back at her. Chloe appeared to be bopping to unheard music, her shoulders working a groove. "Hey, Chlo, you look like you're in a particularly good mood," said Jules. "What's goin' on?"

"Well, ladies, I suppose the big news is that I'm in *lurve*."

If either Lucy or Jules had been drinking something, it would have been a spit-take moment. "Sorry, what?" Lucy smiled. "You are in love?"

"Yep."

"With Archer Tate?" asked Jules to clarify.

"Uh-huh." Chloe was still chair dancing, her head bobbling along to a rhythm the others couldn't hear.

"And, uh, is he *also* in love?" tendered Lucy. Jules silently gave Lucy props for asking. It was one thing to have a celebrity crush and call it love, but was Chloe talking about actually *being in love*?

"Yeah, of course." Chloe stopped her chair dancing. "Ohhh, did you girls think I was just crushing on some poor unsuspecting famous actor?" she asked.

"Well, no, not exactly," said Lucy.

Jules figured she might as well come clean and raised her hand. "Yeah, I did."

"Hah! Well, no, it's *way* weirder than that." She filled them in on their jaunt to London, including her two run-ins with Madison and the exchange of "I love yous".

Lucy and Jules hung on every word, and when Chloe wrapped up her update with, "So, yeah, it's pretty frigging cool, right?" They both burst out laughing.

"It's incredible, Chloe!" said Lucy, her enthusiastic voice at full volume.

"Yes, totally. That's amazing, Chlo." Added Jules.

There was a murmur from Lucy's end of the call. She looked off screen and, eyes wide and lips pressed together, looked back at Chloe and Jules. "Um, someone wants to say hello."

Her screen blurred and a sleepy looking Will replaced Lucy. "Hey, Jules. Hi Chloe."

"*William*, hellooo there," said Chloe, her voice loaded with inuendo. Jules could tell from her expression that she was chanting, "Go, Lucy," in her head. Jules wasn't quite *that* onboard with the "Lucy and Will" thing, but she smiled at her brother.

"Hey, Will. How's it going?"

Will turned to his left and grinned. "It's going great, actually." Okay, that was enough. Jules didn't want any details of her brother's sex life, especially now that it included Lucy. He must have caught her expression. "Hey, since we're up, I'm going to, uh ... go make tea or something. Here." He handed the phone back to Lucy and Jules saw lights come on in the cabin and heard a kettle starting to boil.

Lucy looked off camera, then back at her and Chloe. She flashed a huge grin, her shoulders lifting in a silent "Squee!"

"Lucy, you are adorable," said Chloe.

As Lucy and Chloe chatted about Penham, Jules watched her friends closely. She had loved these women as sisters for as long as she could remember, and she missed them immensely. They were as important to her as her parents, as Will, as ...

Did Matt belong on that list? Perhaps ...

"Hey, guys?" she said, interrupting Chloe's lengthy account of all the delicious food she'd been eating. Two pairs of eyes looked at her expectantly. "Sorry, no big announcement, or anything, just ... I miss you guys like crazy."

"Yeah, me too," said Chloe.

"Me three," added Lucy.

"So, next time we travel, it's together, right?"

"For sure."

"Absolutely!" declared Lucy.

Chapter 32

Chloe

"I've been ruminating," Archer said, his hands at ten and two on the steering wheel of his vintage MG.

"About?"

"Well, lots of things, actually, but this one in particular is related to the film."

"*Ohhh*, the Capels's love story. I *love* the Capels's love story." Chloe had once made fun of the giddy lovestruck fools who loved everyone and everything. Now she was one of them. She thought back over the conversation with the girls that morning and giggled quietly to herself. She was surprised they hadn't asked if she'd been body-snatched. *Who are you and what have you done with our friend?*

"Yes, I know you do," replied Archer as he lifted the hand at ten o'clock to capture hers and bring it to his lips.

She threw him a coy look over one shoulder, then turned to watch the passing scenery outside her passenger window. She was amazed that only minutes after turning off the M25, one of the largest ring roads in the world, encircling one of the largest cities in the world, they were already surrounded by pastoral scenes, with mist settling into valleys and flocks of grazing sheep oblivious to the wet weather.

"So, you've been ruminating," she prodded.

"I'm thinking of a dual narrative, perhaps one of the characters as an older person, having just lost the other and coming to terms with that loss ..." Chloe sucked in a sharp breath. "What's wrong?" he asked, glancing across at her. "You don't like that approach?"

"No, it's not that. I think it would be a great way to tell the story. I'm guessing the other timeline is them meeting and falling in love?"

"Right, exactly, but going back to you ... Why that reaction to the modern timeline?"

"It's just ... it breaks my heart to think of them like that and, very soon, that could be one of them. Imagine if Mrs Capel is the one left behind, especially with her dementia; she'll be beside herself. She won't understand why he's not there for her, and then she'll just stop remembering him at all, and ..."

Chloe was letting herself get far more worked up than she'd anticipated and sniffled softly. Archer's hand rested on her leg and gave it a gentle squeeze.

"You're absolutely right. It is heart-breaking to think about and I hope this doesn't come across as callous, but for her sake, I hope she goes first."

"Mmm," Chloe murmured. The thought of Mr Capel losing his beloved wife was almost as dreadful as the alternative and Chloe realised that her lovestruck state was wending its way towards melancholy.

"Sorry, I didn't bring this up so we would get mired down in the sadness of what's to come. I want to honour them, to tell the story of an extraordinary love and an extraordinary woman. Actually, I was thinking Cate would be brilliant for the role of Eloise. She could play her from forty onwards and maybe Jen for the younger version."

"Sorry, do you mean Cate as in *Blanchett* and Jen as in ..."

"Jen Lawrence, yes." Again, Chloe was reminded that Archer's world was vastly different from her own. *How will our lives dovetail now that we're in love?* She wondered, not for the first time. "They look enough alike and they're both brilliant, of course." Archer's observation about the two Oscar-winning actresses pulled Chloe from her thoughts.

"Oh, for sure," she responded, as though it was just a normal everyday conversation. "Have you thought of who would play Mr Capel? You'd play him, right?"

"Actually, I was thinking I might like to direct this one."

Chloe regarded him across the interior of the compact car. "Wow, yes, I could see that. You would be amazing, Archer. You'd be great."

"Really?" Archer flicked another glance towards her and in that second, she saw his self-doubt, his humility. His eyes returned to the road. "I've never directed before ... well, not since plays at drama school. I mean, I've wanted to for a long time. I've never been that actor who goes straight to his trailer as soon as they call 'cut'.

"I'm the annoying one who sticks around and wants to talk about shot set-ups, the one who watches the dailies meticulously—and not to swoon over my own performance, nothing like that—but to see how the director is playing out their vision, how what they say to us, the actors, gets translated by the DOP, the production designer, the lighting designer ... everyone. I'm fascinated by all of it."

Chloe grinned, her wonder at him growing by the moment. "I love how passionate you are about all this."

His mouth pulled into a shy smile. "Thank you, my love. Now I just need to convince someone to let me write and direct my own film and find the perfect actor for Richard Capel. Tom perhaps ..." he mused.

Chloe had no idea which Tom he meant, but she was still pondering the idea of Archer writing and directing. She had no doubt he'd be brilliant, and surely some film executive somewhere would leap at the idea. He was Archer Frigging Tate, for crying out loud.

"Oh, and there is something else ... about the film, I mean," Archer said, his tone laced with mystery.

"What's that?"

"Have you ever thought of producing?"

Chloe's eyes widened. "A film?"

He laughed. "Yes, a film."

"Uh, no. I can honestly say that the thought has never crossed my mind. I wouldn't even know where to start."

"Well, *I* think you'd be smashing at it, with all your experience in event management and PR. And you did say you were thinking about a career shift. This could be a wonderful segue into something new. I mean, producing is ultimately about logistics and building relationships—both of which I think you'd excel at—particularly with how quickly you got my mother on side. She is a bit of a tough nut, I'll admit." *Understatement of the century,* thought Chloe.

"But you should hardly take my word for it. I was thinking," he continued excitedly, "that I could connect you with a good friend of mine, Fiona. She's a producer and she can tell you everything you need to know—share her insights, that sort of thing. So, what do you say? Will you talk to Fi?" It had all tumbled out so quickly that Chloe was momentarily speechless.

"Uh, yeah, of course, that sounds amazing. Thank you."

Being part of a film production! There was no way Chloe could ever have imagined how things would turn out when she'd planned a quiet Christmas in a tiny town in England. She snorted a little laugh at the thought, leant her head against the headrest and imagined herself on a film set, clipboard in hand and ... *producing*—whatever that entailed.

Chloe's contemplation was interrupted by the sound of Archer's phone ringing. He gave a voice command to answer it and put it on speakerphone.

"Hello."

"Archer, thank god I've caught you. Are you free? Do you have a moment?" asked a *very* posh English accent.

"George! Absolutely. We're just on the M40, heading back to Penham. I'm with Chloe and you're on speakerphone, so behave." He glanced at Chloe. "George is my publicity manager," he told her. She nodded.

"Right, well, I'll keep this brief—and I want you to know that I'm on top of it. I'm already penning a press release as we speak—"

"George, what's going on?"

"Well, if you're asking, then I take it you haven't been on Twitter in the past couple of hours?"

Chloe and Archer shared a look across the car and Chloe reached for her handbag to retrieve her phone. "Uh, no, we haven't. Why?" Archer replied.

Chloe's stomach clenched into a tight little knot as she navigated to Twitter and typed "Archer Tate" into the search field. She gasped, just as George responded. "It's Madison, Archer. She's gone on a bit of a tweeting rampage."

"How bad is it?" asked Archer.

"Bad," replied George and Chloe at the same time. Chloe could hardly tear her eyes away from the feed. Accusations and vile, spiteful, nasty words, many of them about "that skank". About *her*. Chloe felt the bile rising and swallowed repeatedly to keep from vomiting.

"As I said, I'm penning the press release now and as soon as you get to your parents' house, read over it, so we can get it out as soon as possible."

Chloe tore her gaze away from her phone and looked at Archer. His jaw was tense, and she'd only seen him scowl that intensely on film. "Will do. Thank you, George. Oh, and you took care of that other matter, I expect?" Chloe figured that the "other matter" was sacking the person on the publicity team who had leaked to Madison where Archer was.

"Of course. I sorted that out yesterday and I assure you, that will not happen again. Anyway, I shall wait to hear from you. And Chloe?" Chloe realised with a start that George was addressing her.

"Uh, yeah?"

"I'm so very sorry about all of this *and* to be meeting you, so to speak, under such terrible circumstances."

"Oh, right. Yeah, no worries."

"We'll get it sorted, all right?"

"Uh-huh."

"Archer, I'll speak to you later. Bye."

The call ended and Archer reached across to take her hand again. He lifted it to his mouth and gave it a soft kiss that Chloe barely registered.

This was real. This was her life now. Being in love with the world's biggest film star came at a price—a massively huge and ugly price. As she took a long, steadying breath to quell the nausea, Chloe stared out the window at those poor wet sheep.

If only the girls were here.

*

"Right, can I get you some tea? Sherry? I think Max has some whisky somewhere." Susan peered at Chloe, worry etched onto her usually smooth features.

"Well, I do, love, but it's not even noon yet," replied Max.

"Oh, right, of course."

"Um, tea, please," Chloe said. Archer had dropped her off, depositing her carry-on and handbag in the Browning's entry, and giving Max and Susan a digest version of what had occurred. He'd left with a promise to return as soon as he could and a smile that didn't reach his eyes.

Chloe, who had watched the exchange like some sort of out-of-body experience, was now bundled up on the couch under one of Susan's mother's crocheted blankets, as though she was seven years old and off from school with a cold.

Susan disappeared from the front room, presumably to make the requested tea and Max, who sat across from her in his favourite chair, cleared his throat far more than was normal and glanced across at her intermittently over the top of his book. Chloe suspected that he wished he were anywhere else and felt terrible that she'd brought so much drama into the Browning's home.

"That skank Australian snuck into his hotel room and stole my boyfriend!" The words played over in Chloe's mind like a 1940s newsreel, as she stared into the flickering flames of the fireplace. Skank-y, Chloe thought. It was supposed to be an adjective. "That skanky Australian ..." Somehow, focusing on Madison's poor grammar was easier than delving into the implications of the predicament.

George had said he'd written a press release, but what on earth would it say? She'd written press releases—dozens of them—but never once had she needed to refute the skanki-ness of one of her clients.

Archer Tate would like to say that Ms Madison Strumpet is gravely mistaken. Ms Chloe Sims is not a skank. She is, however, the love of Mr Tate's life and, as well as enjoying a rigorous and highly satisfying physical relationship with Ms Sims, Mr Tate finds her to be delightful company, extremely funny and capable, and very, very pretty. She is

372

also highly respected by Mr Tate's rather formidable mother, who reportedly was impressed by Ms Sims's efforts as a last-minute addition to the planning committee for the Penham Christmas Fair.

Chloe imagined George reading it out at a press conference with her and Archer behind him, both wearing enormous dark sunglasses and waiting to take questions. It was a ludicrous image and a giggle bubbled up and took hold. When Susan arrived with a tray of tea and biscuits—milk chocolate Hobnobs—she found Chloe giggling quietly to herself.

Susan eyed Chloe with a mix of concern and confusion. "Are you all right, Chloe love?" She placed the tray on the coffee table and poured Chloe a large mug of tea, adding a generous dollop of milk.

Chloe stopped laughing and took the proffered tea. "Thank you and I guess so. It's just all so ridiculous, don't you think?"

Susan's eyebrows knitted together, and she pursed her lips. "Mmm." She didn't seem wholly convinced of the ridiculousness of the situation and busied herself with pouring tea for her and Max. Chloe, riding the pendulum of emotion back towards dismay, reached for a biscuit and nearly upset her tea. Susan's eyes widened and flew to the crocheted blanket, but Chloe recovered without spilling. "Sorry," she said sheepishly.

Susan shook her head, "No need, Chloe love. But I'll just leave these here, shall I?" She placed the plate of biscuits on the end table next to Chloe. Max harrumphed—he probably wanted one—but Chloe could foresee comfort eating through the lot. She took a bite. Delicious.

Susan sat in her chair, closest to the fire, and retrieved a folded newspaper and pencil from the table next to her to resume her crossword. Like Max, she peered across at Chloe from time to time, but Chloe barely registered the curious looks. She just snuggled further under the blanket, systematically eating her Hobnob and sipping her tea, all while staring into the fire. She was just starting on her second biscuit when Susan piped up.

"So, Chloe love, what more can you tell us about what's going on? You and Alan seem—"

"I've just thought of something I need to do upstairs," said Max, standing abruptly. He was out of the room almost before he finished the sentence.

"Not one for gossip, my Max," said Susan, taking a sip of tea. Max's departure was enough to break Chloe from her reverie and she sighed. She could continue to wolf down biscuits and wallow in her thoughts—most of them unpleasant—or she could talk it out with Susan, who'd already proven to be a wise and willing confidant.

"Well, you see ..." Chloe brushed some biscuit crumbs from the corner of her mouth and licked her lips. "Archer and I ... well, we've fallen in love." Susan's head dropped to the side and one hand pressed to her chest. It was a gesture Chloe had seen Lucy make dozens of times—her coping mechanism when she was on the verge of an anxiety attack—but Susan seemed anything but anxious. On the contrary, she appeared to be quite taken by the romance of it all.

It was just the impetus Chloe needed to get out of her head and without going into too much detail, she explained what had transpired over the past few days, concluding with, "And now I'm of two minds. When it's just me and Archer, it's lovely and perfect, but to everyone else, he's 'Archer Tate'. Well, not to you, or the other people in the village. *You* know who he really is. I suppose, in a weird way, the man I love is Alan." She stared down at the dregs of her now-cold tea, then leant forward to place the mug on the coffee table.

She looked up at Susan who was watching her intently. "But after today ... how do I make a life with him? How's that even going to work?"

Susan was about to answer her when there was a knock at the front door. "I expect that will be Alan, love. Shall I see him in? I can make myself scarce."

"Thank you, yes," Chloe replied quietly. She burrowed further under the blanket while she strained to hear the brief exchange in the entry. A moment later, Archer appeared in the doorway, his face stern.

As soon as she saw him, Chloe's heart swelled and her breath caught in her throat. *One* mind. She was of one mind and no matter what, all she wanted was to be with him.

If that was what *he* wanted, that is. His expression was impossible to read. Was he still steaming about Madison, or ...

"May I come in?" he asked. Chloe's stomach lurched at the formality of the question. He'd come to end things with her, she just knew it. *Oh god.* Was it only that morning that she'd been riding high, spouting all about love to her best friends?

She felt the bile rising again, then cleared her throat, sat up tall, and flicked the blanket aside. If he *was* breaking up with her, she didn't want to be wrapped up in a pale pink blankie. She lifted her chin, game face on. "Uh, sure, yes. Have a seat." She indicated Susan's chair, but before she could comprehend what was happening, Archer was on the couch beside her.

"So ..." he began cryptically, his face softening slightly. Chloe had no idea what to read into that either. They hadn't been together long enough for her to know his repertoire of tells.

"So," she mirrored tentatively.

"I've read George's press release. It's good—succinct, clear, and *far* more respectful towards Madison that I would have been. He has refuted the accusations outright, and ..." Archer took a deep breath. "If you agree, then the final sentence will state that you and I are in a committed relationship."

If I agree?

He looked at her, his eyes full of hope, and swallowed as though he was nervous. So, he wasn't there to end things. "Oh," gasped Chloe, tears springing to her eyes. A raspy, shuddering breath took hold and she placed a hand to her chest, just like Lucy would.

"Chloe?" Archer was studying her, his eyes still hopeful. "Are you all right?" She nodded, grinning through her tears that spilled onto her cheeks. "What's ... I'm not sure I follow?" He shook his head slightly, as though confused.

Chloe caught her breath. "It's just ... the expression on your face when you arrived ... I ... I thought you wanted to end things."

"What? Why?"

"But you don't ..."

"No, no of course not. But I was worried that you ... that given some time to think things through, this would all be too much for you, that *you* wouldn't want *me*. That's why ... I was terrified coming here." He looked down at his hands that were wringing in his lap.

"Hey." Chloe placed her small hands over his to still them. "Archer, look at me." He looked up, his eyes now a stormy steel blue, and Chloe touched her palm to his cheek. His eyes closed for a second, then he took her hand in both of his and pressed it to his lips.

Their eyes met again. "We're both quite stupid, aren't we?" she asked.

He grinned, then shook his head as another look of confusion passed across his face. "Wait, how so?"

"Well, we've told each other, 'I love you' and here we are, one day in, experiencing a minor blip, and we're already doubting how the other feels. Like I said, stupid."

He sniggered softly and nodded in acquiescence. "It is rather, though I am not quite sure I'd call this a minor blip." They exchanged wry smiles. "Are you sure?" he asked softly, suddenly serious again.

"About you, yes?"

"I mean ... about, well, everything else."

"To be honest, I'd been going back and forth since we got the call from George." He nodded and dropped his eyes. "But then as soon as I saw you, just now, I knew. I love you, and if that means there are blips from time to time, then ... well, then we face them together. Okay?"

He looked up. "God, you're just ..." He stopped his own thought by leaning in and kissing her hard on the mouth. When he pulled back, he gazed at her intently. "I am the luckiest man on earth."

"Damned straight, and don't you forget it."

"How could I? Especially with you to constantly remind me." She scrunched her nose at him and they grinned. "There is just one more thing." She looked at him curiously. "How can I ever make this up to you, all this palaver. Please tell me there's something I can do, something special."

Chloe's eyes narrowed and her lips curled into a smile. "Actually, there is something. It's kind of a big ask though."

"Anything," he replied, and she knew he meant it.

"Well, I have an idea. It's about New Year's ..."

Chapter 33

"Will! *Will!* A car's pulled up."

Lucy ran down the staircase to the foyer and, not stopping to put on her coat, shot out the front door, down the steps, and onto the driveway of the Colorado cabin.

She bounced on her toes as the large, black four-wheel-drive pulled to a stop. Will appeared beside her, slinging an arm around her shoulders. Car doors opened and within moments, there were squeals of delight, hugs, and handshakes.

Lucy wrapped her arms around her best friends, and they enveloped her in a three-way hug. "I can't believe you're here," she said, her voice muffled against Jules's shoulder. When they broke from their hug, Chloe stepped away to talk to Will and Jules stood rooted to the spot, staring at her intently.

"Are we good, Luce? I mean, *really?*"

Lucy grabbed Jules's hand and squeezed tightly. "We're good, Jules, I promise."

Jules hugged her tightly and Lucy heard a sigh, then a whispered, "I'm so glad, Luce. I've missed you," against her ear.

"Hey, I'm Will." Lucy looked over Jules's shoulder to see Will shaking hands with Matt, then Alan. *Archer*, she reminded herself. As she and Jules stepped back from their hug, Archer strode over and scooped her up into another one. "Hello, Lucy. Wonderful to see you." It was the greeting of a dear friend, even though they hadn't seen each other in years, and Lucy was both surprised and touched that he regarded her that way.

"Hello, Al—*Archer*, sorry." She shook her head at herself and he waved off her apology.

"Honestly, it's fine. They're both me. Besides, Chloe tells me that we English apologise far too much."

"Oh, she does, does she?" Lucy asked, smiling. She glanced at Chloe who was chatting to Will, then caught Matt's eye. He was unloading the car and seemed to be hanging back, perhaps a little shier than the others. "Excuse me for a moment? I want to meet Matt." From everything Jules and Chloe had told her about him, Lucy just knew she'd adore him.

"Absolutely. I should help him with the cases, too. And we should get you inside. You forgot your coat." Lucy suddenly realised how cold she was.

"Oh, yes, quite right." She wrapped her arms around herself as she bustled past Jules, Will, and Chloe, who were chatting animatedly.

"Hello, you're Matt."

"I am, and you're Lucy." He smiled warmly as he placed a case on the ground, then pecked her on the cheek. "Great to meet you." *Oh, he's lovely.*

"Do you need a hand? I can take one of the smaller cases."

"How about you go inside before you freeze to death, and I'll help with the bags?" Will said from behind her.

"Yes, Lucy, come inside!" said Jules, wrapping an arm around Lucy's waist.

"Oh, thank god," said Chloe, who was stamping her feet and rubbing her hands together. "I didn't think there could be any place colder on the planet than Penham, England."

"Come on, you two." Jules shepherded her friends into the cabin and before Lucy knew it, she, Jules, and Chloe were standing in front of the fireplace defrosting.

Lucy looked from one of her best friends to the other. "I still can't believe you're here, even though you're *right* here."

"It's totally surreal, but that pretty much sums up my entire Christmas," said Chloe. She held her hands out in front of her and Lucy could see that the tips of her fingers had a blueish tinge.

"Chloe, here." Lucy took Chloe's hands in hers and rubbed the fingertips gently.

"Guys, I know I said I wanted a traditional Christmas, and it's been ah-mazing—well, most of it, anyway—but seriously, how the hell do you *live* in such cold weather year in, year out?"

Jules laughed. "By sucking it up, or booking vacations to somewhere sunny so you have something to look forward to, or—"

"Moving to Australia?" Chloe said, looking past Lucy at Jules. Lucy dropped Chloe's hands and spun on her heels to catch Jules giving Chloe a pointed look.

"You're moving? To Australia?" Lucy asked incredulously.

*

"Shhh, *Will*," Jules whispered, looking behind them. She could hear the others in the foyer and Will's voice telling Matt and Archer to follow him upstairs. Hopefully, he hadn't heard. She looked back at Lucy. "I've decided I'm moving to Australia," she said, her voice low.

"For Matt." Lucy posed it as a fact, rather than a question, and Jules thought it was an odd assumption.

"For *me*, Lucy."

"I don't ..." Lucy looked perplexed.

"This is about me shaking things up. You know that I've been stuck in place for some time now, and ... I sorta fell in love with the place."

"And Matt?" Wow, Lucy was really attached to the "Matt" thing.

"He factors into all this, for sure, but this is something I'm doing for me. And it won't be right away. I've got to get a job and my work visa. They've got these skilled migrant visas in Australia and programmers are in demand, so that shouldn't be a problem. There's a lot to do, a lot to *think* about."

"But Matt *knows*, right?"

"Yeah, for sure. We've talked it through. And when I move there, we'll date, like normal people," she smiled. "Look, the guys will be back down soon, and—"

"I know." Lucy nodded. "You need to be the one to tell Will."

"Thanks, Luce. That part is gonna suck. Will, my dad, my mom ... telling them *and* leaving them." She blew out a breath. No matter how hard it was going to be, she knew to her core this was the right decision for her. Her time in Australia had felt like a homecoming of sorts, like that was where she needed to be, at least for the foreseeable future.

Lucy took her hand and squeezed it tightly, pulling her from her thoughts. "Jules, no matter what, they love you and they want you to be happy, right?" She nodded. "And look at the three of us. We love each other and miss each other, but we still get together every year, and when we do, it's wonderful. And you'll have Chloe there. I'm practically mad with jealousy that you'll be—"

Lucy must have caught the look Jules threw Chloe because she stopped talking. "What? There's something else, isn't there?"

"Hey, so all the bags are in all the rooms." Will entered the living room, his announcement catching Jules by surprise.

"Later, okay?" she whispered to Lucy. Lucy nodded in reply, her large brown eyes alive with curiosity.

"Jules, you and Matt are at the end of the hall on the right, and I put Archer and Chloe in Mom and Joe's room. Come on in guys, make yourselves at home."

Look at my baby brother being the host with the most. Jules beamed at him proudly. "Thanks for taking care of all that, Will."

"Hey, no problem. So, I'll get some drinks going. We've got beer, wine, Coke, water ...?" Leaving the question hanging, his eyes landed on Lucy and he winked at her. Lucy's face was, as always, an open book, and Jules saw just how smitten Lucy was with her brother.

Maybe *that* was why all the questions about Matt—Lucy was projecting. Holy crap, was Lucy considering moving to the States for Will? She *definitely* needed some alone time with her best friends.

"Actually, I could murder a cup of tea," said Archer, interrupting Jules's thoughts.

"Oh, definitely," added Chloe.

"I'll sort it," offered Lucy.

Matt asked Will for a Coke and Jules added a request for water. "Sparkling, with—"

"With ice and lemon. Yep, got it," replied Will as he left the room.

"Hey, Luce, do you have any of your mum's Christmas cake left?" asked Chloe. "I'd kill for some of that."

"*Maybe.* Come and check the pantry." Lucy and Chloe followed Will, Chloe swinging past Archer for a quick kiss.

"Actually, I'll join you. Too much sitting," said Archer as he stood and stretched his arms above his head. He gave a hearty "ahh" of a sigh and jogged after the others.

Matt crossed the room to Jules, wrapping his arms around her waist and she regarded him affectionately. He'd shared his home with her, and now she got to do the same. She could never have known how much her life would change because of her Christmas swap with the girls, and she was about to shake it up even more.

She knew it would be difficult moving away from her family, especially her dad and Will, and, down deep, there was some fear that she hadn't yet unpacked. But mostly, she was excited about her unknown future. And a lot of that had to do with the hot Aussie winemaker.

"There're about a million and one thoughts going on in there, I can tell," he said, his eyes boring into hers. With how intensely he was looking at her, she wouldn't have been surprised if he could read every one of them. "You good?" he asked.

"I'm good."

"It's still weird, though, right?"

Jules tried to comprehend his meaning and came up empty. "What's that?"

"Archer Tate. I mean, I can actually see us becoming friends, 'cause he's, like, this normal, chilled guy, which is ... *weird*, right?"

"He is super chilled ... *and* normal. And he seems like a good match for Chloe." She lowered her voice, "But, yeah, it's weird for me too. I mean, oh, my *god*! He flew us here first class, like, *total strangers*."

Matt chuckled softly. "Yeah, that was really nice of him, but it just adds to how bizarre this is."

"Oh, for sure. I have *never* slept that well on a plane. I'm probably ruined for life."

"And *I've* never come out of long-haul travel feeling this good. And it was, what, nearly forty hours door-to-door?" Jules could tell he was calculating their travel time from Melbourne to Doha to London, then on to Denver. They'd met up with Archer and Chloe at Heathrow when they changed flights for the Denver leg.

"That would have *sucked* flying coach," said Jules.

"It's the only reason I agreed to travel first class. I mean, I've never met the guy and he's spending that kind of money on me?" Matt had mentioned this before they'd left Melbourne, and twice on the journey.

"I know, but Chloe assured me he didn't bat an eye. And after everything that happened ... he *wanted* to do it, to make it up to her." Matt pressed his lips together. "We won't make a habit of it, okay? We'll pay our way from now on. It was just the best way to get us all here so quickly."

"Yeah, yeah, you're right. It's all good."

"And I'm guessing that hanging out here, we'll get to know him, and it will stop being weird and we'll be all cool with it, you know. Like, 'Oh, Archer? Yeah, he's, like, one of our best friends.'" She giggled. "We're dorks."

"Hey, speak for yourself." She stuck her tongue out at him and his brows lifted. "That's a bit rude."

She bit her top lip, then released it. "Sorry."

He grabbed her butt. "You *will* be."

"Get a room, you two," teased Chloe from the doorway. She was followed by the others, Will bringing up the rear bearing a tray.

Jules retaliated by sticking her tongue out at Chloe, and Chloe reprimanded her with, "Rude!"

"Told ya," Matt said to her quietly, the timbre of his voice sending the now-familiar "Matt tingles" down her spine. She wondered how rude Chloe would think it was if she and Matt disappeared for an hour—*or* two.

"I'm gonna take you guys snowmobiling," Will said to Matt as he handed over a Coke. "If you're up for it?"

"Right now?"

"In a little while."

"Yeah, sure, sounds good," Matt replied with a smile.

"Do you know how to ride a snowmobile?" asked Jules, panicked. She eyed the pressure bandage around Matt's left wrist. "And what about that?"

"Oh, yeah," said Chloe, "Sorry about that, Matt. I should have warned you ahead of time that Jules has a history of horse-riding accidents."

"That's not fair. Cabo wasn't my fault, and neither was this. There was a *snake*." Jules felt bad enough that Matt had gone horseback riding even though it had scared him—and for *her*, to make her Christmas special.

"Hey, it's all good. The wrist is nearly a hundred per cent, and to answer *your* question," he turned back to Jules. "No to the snowmobiling, but I've got the quad bike, remember, *and* my motorbike license."

"He'll be fine," added Will. Neither of their assurances did anything to ease Jules's concerns. Will could be pretty hardcore when he went snowmobiling, He was way too much of a daredevil for her liking.

*

"You've ridden before, right?" Chloe asked Archer. She was perched on the couch next to him, her legs tucked underneath her, a mug of tea in one hand and a piece of Christmas cake in the other—her idea of bliss.

"It's been a while—I had to ride one in *A Forgotten Promise*—but I suspect it's a bit like riding a bike."

"See?" Will asked the room. "We're all set."

"You did your own stunts in that?" asked Matt.

"Some of them, but only the ones that wouldn't kill me if I cocked them up," Archer replied, grinning.

"I've seen that movie, like, four times," said Matt.

"That's four more than me," announced Chloe. She took a bite of cake and when everyone except Archer eyed her incredulously, she spoke with her mouth full. "What?" A quick glance at Archer revealed an amused expression. She swallowed. "My friends seem aghast, Archer. Maybe when you go snowmobiling, I should get started on watching your back catalogue," she deadpanned.

At that, he threw back his head and laughed heartily. Then he drew her close and gave her a smack of a kiss. "And that, Ms Sims, is one of the many reasons I love you. You will never allow me to wallow in my own importance."

Chloe shrugged, threw a somewhat smug look at her besties, and went back to her cake. Archer stood. "Right! Snowsuits, I presume?"

"Yeah, whatever you'd wear skiing or snowboarding. Matt, I've something you can wear, if you need it."

"All good, mate. Brought my own." Chloe caught the surprised look on Jules's face. Matt clearly did too. "So much you don't know yet," he said to Jules. He gave her a gentle kiss on the cheek before leaving with the other guys to get ready. Chloe watched Jules watching him go, a dreamy expression on her face.

She loved seeing two of her closest friends together—Jules, the anti-love poster child, and lovely Matt, who deserved far better than that lying cow of a woman, Kirsten. It wasn't that she and Ash had conspired as much as hoped that Jules and Matt would like each other. *And they did and they are in love and yay, yay, yay.*

"You okay, there, Chlo?" asked Jules, eyeing her suspiciously.

388

"Yep." She blinked deliberately and fluttered her eyelashes—her I'm-so-innocent look.

Jules plonked down on the couch next to her. "What?"

"Nothing. Just that you guys are sweet together. It's nice."

Jules rolled her eyes. "Yeah, yeah, it's still early days yet. We're a long way from 'I love you', just so we're clear."

"Why do you have to do that?"

"Do what?"

"Pretend it's all just ..." She waved her hand in the air and looked to Lucy for backup. *A little help, here, Luce*, she pleaded with her eyes.

"I think what Chloe's saying is that we're happy for you." *Not quite, Lucy.*

"Good, 'cause I'm happy for me too," replied Jules.

"So why play it down?" demanded Chloe.

"I'm not!" Jules hissed, "Geez." Jules glanced furtively at the doorway.

"*Sorry*," Chloe whispered. "Look, the guys are going out. Maybe we should wait 'til they've gone to talk properly."

Jules groaned out a sigh. "Why do we have to talk everything to death?"

"Hey, that's not fair. I don't do that. And besides, I still haven't told Lucy *my* news yet."

"Oooh, that's right," said Lucy, her anticipation obvious.

Will stuck his head around the doorway. "Hey, we're heading out. Wanna come see us off?"

"I'm not going outside," said Chloe. Her hands were only just starting to return to their normal colour. "Will a goodbye from the door do?"

Will grinned at her. "Sure." He jerked his head. "Come on."

They sent the guys off on their outing—Will mentioned they'd only be gone a couple of hours—as though they were about to climb Everest or something. *They're only going outside to play in the snow!* Chloe thought.

*

The door had been closed approximately three seconds before Lucy blurted out. "Right, Chloe, your news—now." She marched off towards the living room and when she turned to see that Jules and Chloe were both standing still and staring at her, seemingly dumbstruck, she added, "Well, come on!"

Lucy perched on one end of the sofa and watched the doorway expectantly. It didn't take long before her best friends joined her, their expressions still bearing the stamp of surprise.

"So, Luce, *this* is new," said Jules.

Lucy lifted her chin. "I'm being more assertive and asking for what I want." Her bravado slipped a little and she nibbled on a thumb nail.

"I like it," declared Chloe. "It looks good on you." Chloe's eyes narrowed. "You don't believe that, do you?"

"Is it that obvious?"

"Don't worry, it's only because I know you so well. And, hey, you can practise on us." Chloe looked at Jules, as if for agreement.

"Oh, yeah, whenever we're being massive pains in the ass, feel free to rein us in."

"You mean like when you bicker all the time?"

Chloe and Jules shared a guilty look and burst out laughing. "Yeah, like that, Luce," said Jules through her laughter. "Does it drive you crazy?" she added, her eyebrows waggling.

"You have no idea. Anyway, enough about all that. *Chloe*, what is going on with you—other than being madly in love and already surviving your first scandal."

"Are we calling it a scandal?" Chloe asked. "I don't know if that's the right word."

"Yeah, more like a shitstorm," offered Jules. Chloe nodded her agreement, but Lucy threw Jules a look. "What? What would you call having your name dragged through the mud on social media?"

There was a moment of silence. "A scandal," Jules and Chloe said in unison. They laughed and Lucy tutted.

"Sorry, Luce, you were right," Jules conceded.

"Yes, I know. Now can we please get back to Chloe's news?"

"Right, my news. So, just before we got the call about Madison and the Twitter *scandal*, Archer and I were talking about the film—you know, the Capels's story—and he asked if I'd ever thought about producing, and of course, I'm like, 'Uh, no, it has never even crossed my mind.' Anyway, he told me he has this producer friend, Fi, who I should talk to, so he set up a call for us. Actually, I ended up speaking to her in the departure lounge at Heathrow.

"And oh, my god, she is ah-mazing. We talked about my professional experience, and she had all these questions about my skillset and my goals and then she told me all about what *she* does. *And* she said that if Archer's film does get the go ahead, she'll be producing it and she'll take me on, sort of like an apprenticeship."

Lucy pressed her hands together and clapped them lightly. "Oh, Chloe! That's amazing. I'm so proud of you."

Chloe beamed. "I *know!* It's ... I have no words. It's beyond my wildest imagination, and if I think about how I met Archer ... I mean, seriously, this is all like something out of a movie."

"*Especially* the part with the scandal," offered Lucy.

"Uh, yeah, right."

Lucy scrutinised Chloe's face. Was she just *pretending* to be fine with everything? "Chloe, are you sure you're all right?"

"Yeah. Why, what do you mean?"

"Well, it's just that only a couple of days ago, your face and your name were splattered all over the internet."

"Well, yeah, that was awful—still is in some ways. I mean, the dust has barely settled. And, sure, if I think about it too much, then it can be a little overwhelming. But I love him, so ..." She shrugged.

"I just wish we'd been there for you," said Lucy.

"I know you do. And that's exactly why we're all here. I needed my girls. I *need* my girls."

"Me too," said Jules. "I still can't decide if us swapping Christmases was the best idea we've ever had or the worst."

"How so?" asked Lucy.

"Well, it's just that so much happened—for each of us—but we weren't there to share it. And that thing with you and me, Luce ... Maybe that wouldn't have happened if we'd all been together."

"Hmm, maybe." They were quiet for a moment and Lucy

guessed that the others were contemplating "what ifs" the same way she was. What if she'd stayed in England and had Christmas with Chloe? Then she and Will would never have got together. She shuddered at the thought.

"Sorry," said Jules. "I didn't mean to be a Debbie Downer. Chloe's got more news, by the way," she prompted.

"Oh, right. I almost forgot!" exclaimed Chloe and Lucy perked up with anticipation. "So, after New Year's, Archer is flying to LA to meet with the studios—that's how they say it—'meet with the studios'—love it!" she sing-songed. "Anyway, all going to plan, they'll start shooting mid-year and ..." she paused for effect. "*I* will be based in London for the duration." She gaped at Lucy, her mouth and eyes wide with excitement.

"You're moving to London? You're moving to London!" Lucy leapt off the sofa and jumped up and down, clapping her hands.

Chloe grinned up at her. "Well, a bit like with Jules, there are a lot of things that have to fall into place, but that's the tentative plan."

Lucy sighed happily and plopped back down onto the sofa. Then she had a thought. "But what if the film falls through? I mean, it probably won't because it's Archer, but he *is* a first-time director, and what if they say no?"

"Well, we've talked about that, of course, and even if it does fall through, we'll still want to be together. And at this stage, it seems like London makes the most sense."

The sob erupted from Lucy without warning. "Hey, Luce?" she heard Jules ask. "Are those happy tears?" She nodded, then shook her head, and tried to stop the sobs. Yes, of course, she was happy for Chloe *and* that one of her best friends would be living in London. But all this talk of plans—Jules moving to Australia, Chloe in love with Archer and making a life with him—only shone a light on the fact that she and Will hadn't discussed *any*.

And it would be New Year's in a couple of days and then she'd have to go home to England. The thought turned her stomach upside down and the sobs started up again. She was only vaguely aware that Chloe was now perched on the end of the sofa and Jules had drawn close to her other side. They both petted her and made soothing sounds, but what was she going to do?

This was what it felt like every time she travelled with her two best friends, and it got closer and closer to the end of their holiday—only a thousand times worse. And she knew it was too early to know what her feelings for Will even *were*, or what they could become, but at the bare minimum, she adored him—*and* fancied the pants off him.

Actually, she adored fancying his pants *right* off him. She choked out a laugh at her own terrible joke, but it did the trick. The sobs started to subside and she was left ragged and raw, still with a dilemma, but at least with her sense of humour intact.

"Is this about Will?" Chloe asked.

Lucy nodded, taking in gulps of air to help her calm down, her hand pressed to her chest.

"You have to talk to him, Luce," Jules said in a gentle but firm voice.

"I know," Lucy wailed, swinging back towards misery.

"Hey, I know my brother and he's super into you, I can tell. Just talk to him, okay?"

"I will, I promise."

"And don't you *dare* move to Colorado and leave me in London by myself. I *need* you, Lucy, and don't forget, it's all about *me* now, 'cause my boyfriend's super famous, and I'm very likely to turn into a diva."

"*Turn*? *Turn* into a diva?" Jules teased.

"Oh, ha ha!"

Jules threw up her hands. "Hey, if the Louboutins fit!"

Lucy had lost count of the times she'd sat between her two friends as they bantered, but she loved them more in that moment for making her smile through her tears than she ever had.

Chapter 34

The May Ladies

"Did I tell you that you look gorgeous tonight?" Will asked, one hand grazing the small of Lucy's back. "*Extra* gorgeous, I mean. You're always gorgeous," he added quickly.

Lucy giggled and shook her head. "You don't have to do that, you know."

"Do what? Admire you?" She felt a hand lift her hair then the brush of his lips against her neck. She revelled in the feeling, abandoning the task of rinsing dishes and leaning into him.

"No," she said softly. "I mean reassure me. I *am* aware that you fancy me, you know."

"Oh, I more than fancy you, Lucy." He nuzzled her neck and Lucy seriously considered leaving the washing up and slipping upstairs before the countdown to the New Year. She still couldn't believe that she, Lucy Browning, had turned into quite the lusty nymph.

And all it had taken was half a lifetime of dating boring, practically asexual men, then meeting a vibrant, scrummy man, who emboldened her and made her laugh. The last time, she'd laughed so hard that she'd snorted, which had set them both off again. Her stomach muscles had ached for hours.

But she had volunteered them for the washing up for a reason, and it was far more important than disappearing for a quickie. "*Will* ..."

"Mmm?"

She turned her head. "Come on, let's get this done."

He groaned, then started loading plates and cutlery into the dishwasher while she filled the sink with hot water and dish soap. She donned rubber gloves and, elbows deep in suds, she finally broached the subject she had been putting off since the day the others arrived.

"Uh, Will?" He joined her at the sink, taking a clean pot from her and drying it. Lucy took a steeling breath—at least they were side by side and she didn't have to look him in the eye. This was already hard enough. "I just wanted to talk to you about ..." *Breathe*, she told herself. "What will happen now."

She felt him tense beside her for a moment, then take the next clean pot from her. "You mean, with us."

It wasn't a question and Lucy tried to read the tone of his voice. Focusing on the scrubbing of some particularly stubborn baked-on grease, she swallowed the lump in her throat and proceeded. "Yes, exactly. I mean, I'm off to England the day after tomorrow, as you know, and I wondered if ... well, I'd like to continue with us ... That is, if you want to."

He stopped drying the pot, his hands coming to rest on the countertop.

"Do, you ... want to?" she asked. This was even more difficult than sending those emails to Angela. She stared into the sudsy water with bated breath.

"Lucy. Hey, Luce, look at me." *This is it—be brave.* She lifted her gaze to his, hopeful, terrified.

"Look, neither of us could ever have known how this Christmas would turn out. I mean, Jules came back from Australia early—with a *boyfriend*. Archer Tate just cooked me dinner, and now he's sitting in my living room." He grinned down at her and, without thinking, she reciprocated. "But the biggest surprise—the *best* surprise—is you, Lucy. And, yes, I think we should continue with us. I've never done long distance before, but we've gotta see, right?"

It was the perfect response, and it left her speechless. "Lucy?"

"Yes, yes, absolutely right. We have to see. So, long distance it is!"

"Awesome," he said, leaning in to seal their plan with a kiss. "So, is this why we're cleaning up the kitchen, just the two of us?"

She blew out a sigh, then resumed the washing up. "Yes, sorry about that. It's just been hard to get you alone since the others arrived, *and* I've been putting it off ..." She tilted her head and shrugged.

"Hey, it's all good. And you weren't the only one putting it off, you know. So, thank you."

She looked up. "For what?"

"For being brave enough to ask me about it." He leant over and kissed her forehead.

Brave. Until recently, she would never have called herself that. But perhaps the Lucy that other people knew—that Will knew—was closer to the *real* Lucy.

Lucy Browning—brave, formidable, beautiful, and a lusty nymph to boot.

She giggled to herself and handed the last of the clean pots to Will.

*

Chloe leant back against the soft leather of the couch, her feet tucked under her and Archer's hand resting on her thigh. Would she even make it to midnight, she wondered. She'd hit a wall and it could have been anything from jet lag to the highs and lows of the week's events catching up with her. Maybe it was a mix. Still, she wouldn't want to be anywhere else right now.

She'd spoken to Ash earlier, just after the clock struck midnight in Melbourne, eager to see her friend's face and to wish her a happy New Year. Ash and her team were running an event for the City of Melbourne—live music, food trucks, fireworks, the lot—but she'd been able to sneak away for a few minutes.

Even though it was a quick call, Ash had spilled her own news. She and Davo were going on a date to talk everything through and see where they were at. Chloe hoped that one way or the other, Ash would get some sort of resolution. She loved Davo, but it hadn't been a clean break, leaving Ash not only missing him but hopeful that they'd get back together. Chloe didn't know if she'd be returning home to a reconciled couple or a miserable bestie, but either way, she'd be there for Ash—at least for the immediate future.

Her heart tugged at the thought of no longer living with Ash, but Chloe promised herself she'd make the most of the time leading up to her move to London. Besides, Jules would be making *her* big move soon. That would ease the sting a little, knowing that they had each other as Jules settled into her new life in Melbourne.

New life ...

Chloe had always loved seeing in the New Year—all that promise, a clean slate. But if she'd been told a year ago what would be on her horizon this coming year, she would have written it off as nonsense. She'd been happy in her life before meeting Archer, or so she'd thought. She'd been *content*, she realised now, which was not a bad thing, but she'd been playing it safe, never doing anything that terrified her, or thrilled her, or that left her breathless.

Jules had been frank about *her* rut, but Chloe now realised that she'd been living in her own. Well, not anymore ...

Archer leant in close. "I'll give you a whole pound for those thoughts," he said quietly.

"You don't have to pay me one penny." They shared a smile. "I was just thinking how excited I am about everything that's coming up." She lifted a hand to her mouth, stifling a yawn.

"You're hiding it very well," he teased.

"I've hit a wall," she confessed.

"Are you going to make it? To the New Year?" he asked, his eyes alive with amusement.

Chloe glanced at the clock on the mantle above the fireplace. "I think I can make it another twelve minutes."

"Well done, you. Taking one for the team."

"Wait, isn't that a baseball expression?" she asked, a crease forming between her brows.

"It is indeed. *Left Field*, remember? That film I did with Ron Howard about ten years ago."

She looked at him blankly. "I really do need to get stuck into your back catalogue."

He shook his head at her. "No, you absolutely do not. But if you do, at least let me tell you which ones to avoid."

"So, you've made some crappy films, then?"

"Some absolute stonkers, yes." He paused. "Do you know that I love you?"

"I do. And I love you right back," she replied. "You know, other than the girls and my family, I've never said that to anyone before."

"I did not know that, but that makes it all the more special." He leant over and softly pressed his lips to hers. "I *have* said it before, but I know now that I didn't mean it."

"But you absolutely do now," Chloe replied, cheekily.

"Oh, I absolutely do now, Ms Sims." He leant in for another kiss.

*

"It's a big year coming up," said Jules.

"It is," Matt agreed, a small smile curling his lips.

She peered up at him, one hand draped over his shoulder as she toyed with the curls at the nape of his neck. God, he was handsome. She thought back to the first time she'd seen him, when she was checking out his ass in those jeans. He looked really good in jeans. He looked good out of them too.

The hot Aussie winemaker. Matt. Her Matt. Matty. Maybe she *would* call him that.

She looked down at her glass—empty. "I'm a tiny bit tipsy," she realised aloud.

"I can see that." The smile widened.

"I'm also a *tiny* bit afraid." She'd been sitting on this for a couple of days, her little secret. She hadn't even told the girls. Maybe it was being back home that had unlocked her fears about moving to Australia.

"Well, that's understandable. You're about to make a massive change. It's a big deal."

Jules wasn't sure what she was expecting from Matt, maybe a stock standard reassurance. "You've got this," or something along those lines. His candour surprised her—in a good way. "You're honest," she said, matter-of-factly.

"To a fault."

"I like that. I *need* that."

"Good. 'Cause, there's no point in me blowing smoke up your ass and pretending that it's going to be all fun and games. It won't be. Well, it *will* be—some of the time." He smiled at her warmly. "But other times, it'll be hard. You're gonna miss your family, you'll be settling into a new job, a new city. It's bound to get overwhelming at times. But, hey, you've got me—and Ash, and Callie, and Thea."

"And Dexter."

"Aww, man, that dog *loves* you."

She grinned, already missing Dexter's cute little face. She hoped he was enjoying his time with his aunties, Callie and Thea, being a beach dog for the week. "Seriously, though, thank you for that. It does help, you being direct with me. I mean, I'm still *terrified*, but—"

"Hang on, you've gone from 'a tiny bit afraid' to 'terrified' …" He sucked his breath in through his teeth. "I thought I was helping." She could tell he was kidding.

"No, you *are*. I promise. Just hearing it all laid out like that, it demystifies it, you know? And you're right. It will be a mix of good and bad—mostly good, I hope. But I just have one follow-up question."

"Shoot."

"This, uh, 'smoke up the ass' thing … that's not, like, some weird kind of Australian hazing ritual, is it?" Matt's body shook with laughter, a deep rumbling sound that Jules had come to love. "I mean, it sounds sorta whacky, so I just wanna know ahead of time what I'm getting myself into."

He sighed loudly. "Are you done?"

She nodded, a grin splitting her face and feeling a little more than pleased with herself.

"Well, if you're sure, then we need to crack open the bubbly, 'cause there's only a few minutes 'til midnight."

"Oh, crap!" Jules jolted with surprise. "Guys! Will, Lucy!" she shouted. "It's nearly time!"

"Geez, Jules, chill," whined Chloe from the couch.

"I've got the fizz!" called out Lucy. She entered the living room with the bottle held high, followed by Will who carried six flutes—three in each hand. "Here, Matt, you're the expert," said Lucy, handing over the bottle.

Matt got to work on the foil, while Lucy took the glasses from Will and placed them on the coffee table. Matt removed the cage from the cork, then cracked the bottle with a whisper, just as the DJ on the radio announced in his silky voice that there was one minute to go.

"Oh, my god!" Jules was practically dancing with excitement and, as Matt poured each glass, she handed them out.

"I just wanna say something before the countdown," Jules said hurriedly. "Archer, Chlo, come on, you two, stand up." Archer leapt up and held out a hand to Chloe, who tutted good-naturedly as she peeled herself off the couch.

"I'll make it quick, I promise," said Jules. "I just want to say that I love you girls like sisters, my fellow May Ladies, and I'm *so* happy that we're all here together." Lucy gave her a broad smile and an "aw" and Chloe pursed her lips to blow a kiss across the room. "Archer, thank you *so much* for making this happen. Will, Lucy, you were amazing getting the place ready for us.

"And Matt ..." Jules turned to look up at him, feeling his hand tighten on her waist. "Thank you. Thank you for coming all this way with me—*for* me." She grinned, surprised by the tears in her eyes, and Matt dipped his head to land a quick kiss.

"Ten, nine, eight ..." Jules shared an excited look with Lucy, then Chloe, as they all joined in on the countdown. "Seven, six, five, four, three, two, one!"

The six voices rang out, "Hap-py New Year!" as their flutes came together to toast the New Year and all the promise it held.

THE END

Acknowledgements

It's hard to believe I am writing the acknowledgements for my fourth book, but here I am. I have dedicated this book to my parents—my mum, Lee, my dad, Ray, and my step-mum, Gail. I am extremely fortunate to have parents who not only love me, but champion me and inspire me. They have also instilled in me the importance of family—including the family members we choose—as well as having a sense of adventure and following your dreams.

Family is a prominent theme in this book and as I write these acknowledgements amid the second round of COVID-19 lockdowns here in Melbourne, 'family' has become more important to me now than ever. And for me, a person who has lived on three continents, that word encompasses all the people I love, all the people who inspire me, lift me up, confide in me, and ease my path. Thank you, family—wherever you are. Stay safe and we will meet again someday soon.

As always, I am grateful to my two partners-in-writing, my editor, Hannah Todd, and my agent, Lina Langlee. It is wonderful having you in my corner and you are both gifted collaborators. Hannah, thank you for being my champion at

One More Chapter and HarperCollins, and for your excellent feedback, which always elevates my writing. I continue to grow as an author under your guidance. Lina, I greatly appreciate your advocacy, your astute guidance, and your ongoing support of my writing career. Ever onwards and upwards—together.

Thank you to my fellow authors for supporting, championing, and inspiring me, particularly my fellow Renegades, Nina, Andie, and Fiona. Our daily catchups sustain me; they are chocolate for my soul. Thank you to Lucy Coleman (Linn B. Halton) whose quote appears on the cover of this book. I hope that one day I will be as prolific and as accomplished as you. Your books are the stuff of dreams. Thank you to all my fellow romance authors who forge and shape this genre, and to the book lovers, bloggers, and reviewers whose passion for romantic fiction lifts us all, especially my friends at UKRomChat, The Reading Corner Book Lounge, and Chick Lit and Prosecco. Thank you to the volunteers at the Romance Novelists Association and Romance Writers of Australia for your tireless efforts to sustain and elevate romantic fiction. And thank you to my fellow Aussie authors at the Australian Writer's Centre and #AusWrites.

Lastly, dear reader, thank *you*. Thank you for traveling across three continents with me and enjoying some Christmassy goodness. Christmas is my favourite holiday, and over my lifetime, I've spent it in the US, the UK, and Australia—each Christmas special for its distinct traditions and the loved ones I've shared it with.

Happy Christmas and stay safe.

~ Sandy Barker